"AMERICAN BOYS
may rightly take its place alongside *All Quiet on the Western Front, The Naked and the Dead,* and *From Here to Eternity.*"

San Francisco Chronicle

"An awfully good novel...Really impressive."

St. Louis Post-Dispatch

"A stunning novel—brutally appalling"

Philadelphia Inquirer

"A literary achievement...Smith has earned a place in the ranks of American war novelists."

Los Angeles Times

STEVEN PHILLIP SMITH served in 1966 with the 1st Cavalry Division in Vietnam, where he was awarded the Air Medal and the Army Commendation Medal for Valor.

Other Avon Books by
Steven Phillip Smith

THE LONG RIDERS
AN OFFICER AND A GENTLEMAN

AMERICAN BOYS

Steven Phillip Smith

AVON
PUBLISHERS OF BARD, CAMELOT, DISCUS AND FLARE BOOKS

AVON BOOKS
A division of
The Hearst Corporation
1790 Broadway
New York, New York 10019

Published by arrangement with the author
Library of Congress Catalog Card Number: 74-16619
ISBN: 0-380-67934-5

First Avon Printing, March 1984

Printed in the U. S. A.

WFH 10 9 8 7 6 5 4 3 2 1

For Binny

Author's Note

I WOULD like to thank all those people who have read and criticized and offered encouragement throughout the writing of *American Boys*. I would especially like to thank Richard Lillard for his sound and patient suggestions as he helped me get the novel off the ground, Gary Lepper for his enthusiasm and for his commentary on earlier drafts, Jay Neugeboren for the close readings he gave the major draft, Louise Goldhaber—she knows what for, Bob Warde for his overall suggestions and a painstaking critique of the final draft, and my wife, Wendy, for her continuous support and for her hardheaded editing when I needed it most.

I wish that Harvey Swados were alive to see this book in print. As my teacher at the University of Massachusetts he gave me many hours of sane advice and, at the end of my time there, helped me put together what I think was a solid first draft of this novel. I hope these pages bear out his faith in me.

S. P. S.

1

THOMAS SLAGEL had just wriggled between two riflemen on the thin vinyl seat when the helicopter jerked off the ground. It rose six feet, floated ten yards to the left, turned a hundred and eighty degrees, dipped its nose, and sped upward, away from the brown grass of the helipad. He locked a magazine into his M-16, put the stock between his boots, and squeezed the barrel, watching the cords of muscle stand out on his tanned hairy forearms.

The four lift ships that carried the rifle platoon flew almost in T formation. One in front, two abreast behind it, and one in the rear. A chopper from the gunnery platoon flew on each side of the formation, one close to the treetops and the other about two hundred feet above. Slagel rode in the quarterback ship.

They flew east for fifteen minutes, then circled above a narrow open space in the jungle. One gunnery ship rose, the other descended until they were abreast of the lift ships, then all six birds started down together.

He tried to look ahead, but the door gunner blocked his view. He picked up his rifle, pulled back the bolt, and released it, chambering a round. Orange tracers streaked out of the gunnery ship's side guns; rockets smoked out of the pods sounding like sudden gusts of wind. The door gunner opened up. Slagel turned his head away as the ejected casings bounced off his pot. He flipped the selector switch on his rifle from safe to semiautomatic.

As the ship hovered into a thin cloud of smoke and touched its skids to the ground, he leaped out, took two steps forward, lay on his stomach, and squeezed off eighteen rounds into the bushes. This is what we're here for, he thought, me and Padgett and Chambers and Morgan; anything to escape the boredom in Fulda. The departing helicopters rippled the dewy grass, making it sparkle in the sunlight and driving tiny balls of moisture up the thin blades. The smell of gunpowder and burning phosphorus hung pleasantly in the air. He rammed a fresh magazine into his rifle.

"Move 'em out!" the platoon sergeant bellowed.

The platoon leader strode into the bushes, followed by the radio operator, platoon sergeant, and first squad leader. Slagel watched the tall grass divide and flop back as his team leader's boots kicked through it.

"Come on, big Tom," Irwin said, prodding him with his rifle.

Slagel moved into the wet bushes, Irwin and the rest of the squad following him. They stopped after about a hundred yards. Captain Webber, the platoon leader, was on the radio, but the lead gunnery ship hovering above them drowned his voice. The lift birds were far in the distance now, heading back to the field base.

The recon battalion was probably the most interesting unit he could have been assigned to. Supposedly few were like it in the entire Army. Besides the Headquarters Company there were four combat companies. D Company did ground reconnaissance on jeeps mounted with machine guns and with foot soldiers. They also had a heavy-weapons platoon of mortars and recoilless rifles. C Company—his own—and A and B were helicopter companies. Besides support personnel, each had a scout platoon that flew in small bubble helicopters, a gunnery platoon in armed Hueys, and a rifle platoon that was lifted out every day in the slick Hueys and did ground recon while being guided and protected by the gunships. Much better than the boring armored cavalry regiment with its clumsy tanks patrolling the East-West German border. Here he was right in the middle of things.

He squatted, squeezing the tightened muscles in his thigh. Only three weeks in the field and his legs were as solid as when he'd played ball. After thirteen months of sitting on his ass as a supply clerk in Fulda, Germany, he'd thought he'd never get in shape again. Especially after all the beer. But the heat had sweated off excess pounds, and the long climbs up the mountains every day had made his legs like hard rubber. Perfect halfback: six feet, one eighty-five. He swiveled and threw his forearm playfully into Irwin. "I'm getting ready for some action."

"You have to wait for your mustache to grow out."

"Another two weeks and it'll look like a pussy." He stroked the stubble of his upper lip while Irwin twirled the wispy blond handlebar that looked silly on his baby face.

"You better watch it then."

"Don't worry." His short mustache was a dead giveaway that he was a new guy and a cherry too as far as combat was concerned. But no one teased him, probably because of his size. After Irwin, who was from Ohio and had seen him on TV, had told the others about his gridiron feats, they looked up to him as if he'd been in combat for a year. Maybe they were right. To get into combat all you had to do was get drafted. Or volunteer like him and his three buddies. As the platoon started up the mountain, he looked back at the second squad, but Padgett's head was down, his arm up to push away branches.

He faced front as a wet branch slapped his cheek. Screw it. So far he hadn't regretted volunteering. He'd gotten back in shape, he wasn't bored to death with a shitty job, and, best of all, his ass was out of fucking Fulda. Might get shot in five minutes, but at least it wouldn't be in the Fulda Gap. Most dingdong place he'd ever been. Just thinking about it made him bend deeper toward the musty mountain ground, push his legs up harder.

He liked being in the first squad. Kept you on top of whatever happened and close to the platoon leader and the NCO's. They were all beginning to like him. Not just because he'd played football, but because he humped hard and kept his weapon clean. During the past week they'd even put him in charge of two small patrols. He didn't like the wet much, but the monsoon was technically over, and although it still showered every other day, that would be finished after the first of the year. The sun had been out every day for the past two weeks, already beating Fulda's yearly record.

Webber's hand went up at eleven, signaling the platoon to stop. Slagel moved up beside his team leader.

"Watch it!" A black arm slammed into his gut and pointed to the ground. The punji stakes looked like tiny javelins sticking diagonally out of the earth.

"Damn! Must be a hundred." He bent down and yanked out a stake.

"Careful. They dip 'em in shit or poison."

He pressed his thumb softly against the point. Not that sharp, but walking into one could make a nasty hole in your leg.

Webber got on the radio, then gathered the squad leaders at the front of the platoon. He detailed the third squad to clear a path through the stakes while everyone else sat down with his C rations. Some fresh footprints were found to the side, and the stakes had been recently cut.

"They might be close," Webber said to the platoon sergeant. "Let's keep on our toes this afternoon."

Slagel's heart started pounding, and he nudged Irwin. Irwin shrugged casually, but his fork of turkey loaf wavered on the way to his mouth.

No wonder the prints were fresh. The Cong had to know what they were doing. The platoon had been reconning the mountains northeast of Ban Me Thuot for nearly a month, so methodically that any idiot could figure it out. Every day they'd climb one of several ribs that ran down from the spine of the mountain range, move along the spine, then come down another rib. If the VC were there, all they had to do was move over another rib every day, sit tight, or maybe set up some booby traps. Five of the little devils could keep the platoon bottled up for a month.

To hell with it. He wasn't worried. Platoon Sergeant

Austin knew what he was doing. Two Bronze Stars and one Silver from Korea, and he was supposed to have killed more Chinese than he could remember. Captain Webber was okay too. He'd been a sergeant before going to OCS, so he wasn't a phony gentleman. And he walked point every day, which proved he wasn't chickenshit.

The gunships flew in low over the spine, a hundred yards above the platoon, splattering machine-gun fire and rockets into the thick bushes and trees. They made two runs, then headed back to the field base as a new team replaced them. The lead ship established radio contact with Webber, and the platoon humped up the mountainside.

They stopped for five minutes at the top, then proceeded cautiously north along the spine. Easier going than on the morning climb, but the tension made his heart beat faster.

In an hour they stopped again. A trail led off from the spine, disappearing into the underbrush twenty feet away. Its surface was slick with mud and showed no footprints.

"Blue, this is Four-one,"crackled over the radio. "What's up down there?"

"Four-one, this is Blue," Webber said. "We found another trail on the west side. Want to check it out?"

"Roger, Blue."

The gunship made several quick dives over the trail.

"Blue, this is Four-one. We can't see anything except what looks like a broken-down hooch. Too old for anyone to use."

"Roger, Four-one. I'll send down a patrol. Why don't you throw a few rounds in there."

"Roger, Blue."

"Slagel, come here," Webber said.

"Yes, sir." His voice drowned in the machine bark. He squatted beside the platoon leader.

"I want you to pick someone from your fire team and recon that trail. Two to three hundred meters. Looks like it should run parallel to this one once you get down a few meters. Three quick shots if you get in trouble. You're in charge."

"Yes, sir!" He got Irwin and they started down the trail. He felt weird leading him because of his combat experience. But Irwin was only a PFC, and he'd been promoted to Spec-4 just prior to leaving Fulda. Again because of football, because his new CO, some ROTC turkey from Ohio State, had seen him play. Enough thinking about that. He had a trail to recon.

The trail didn't go the way Webber thought. Once in the bushes it did turn north briefly, then went west for twenty meters before snaking around to the south. What the hell? The platoon would at least be above him this way. The trail turned to the west again and after fifty meters split into three narrow paths. He heard the gunships crisscrossing above him, but couldn't see a thing.

Irwin walked a few meters down one of the new paths, then came back shaking his head. "Nothing down there, Tom."

"Shit!" Slagel glanced over his shoulder, then faced front. Suddenly his ear filled with whining and the right side of his head caught fire. He spun around and dived behind a tree. "I'm hit! I'm hit!" It sounded like eighty guns were firing at him, then everything went silent. He ran the fingers of his right hand across his temple; they came down tinged with blood.

Irwin crawled up beside him. "You okay?"

"I don't know."

"Looks like just a graze."

The firing started again and he slid his M-16 around the tree and let a magazine go on automatic. He tried to stand, but more bullets slammed into the tree. He dived back down and fired three clips, hurled two frags and one white phosphorus grenade as far as he could. His face buried in a small bush, he listened to the ferocious beating of his heart.

"What do you think?" Irwin whispered.

"What do *you* think? You've been in more of this than me."

"I don't know."

"Then here's one I learned in the movies." He hung his steel pot on the barrel of his rifle and moved it in front of the tree. Nothing. He wiggled it. Still nothing. "Screw it, Irwin. I'm going up there."

"You want me to come?"

"Cover me." He put his pot back on and crawled slowly, following the phosphorus smell. He froze when he heard the moaning.

After a moment he began to crawl again. One of them must be gone. He parted some tall grass and stared into a black head of hair. He couldn't move until he realized the man was dead. Somewhere to his right the moaning started again. He stood up with his rifle in the assault position, bayonet fixed, and stepped into a tiny clearing roofed by tall trees. When he kicked the dead man over, his stomach fell out on the ground. He turned to the moaning Vietcong. His black pajamas were torn, his leg shredded. One hand covered his chest where blood oozed through his fingers. His other hand was raised.

Slagel raised the stock of his M-16 to his shoulder, setting the site on the VC's face. He aimed for a moment, then lowered the rifle. He breathed out violently and shook his head. You didn't kill prisoners, even though they were half dead. He slung his weapon over his shoulder, then picked up the thirty-caliber rifle next to the dead man, popped out the magazine, and pulled back the bolt, ejecting the chambered round. He slung the weapon beside his own.

The wounded man weighed less than a hundred pounds. Trying to shut out the moaning, he hung the VC over his other shoulder. He crossed his arms over the bleeding legs, revolted by the sticky crust on the black pajamas. When he got back to Irwin, the front of his fatigues was soaked with blood. "They only had one weapon between them." He set the man down and threw the thirty caliber to Irwin.

"That's all they carry. One carries the rifle, one carries the rice. They trade off. Jesus! Is he all right?"

"I guess he'll live. The other one's dead."

"Good going. You all right?"

"Yeah. Let's get out of here." He shouldered the man

again and toiled up the path. After fifty meters they met the entire third squad. Breathing heavily, he stopped, staring at them.

"What's happening?" the squad leader asked.

He told him.

"What'd you bring that one out for?"

"He's still alive."

"He ain't got long. You want to finish him off right now, we won't say nothin'."

"That's all right."

"You want some help carrying him?"

"I can do it." He grinned at the squad leader and moved away. His ears rang and his head throbbed, but he wanted to carry the prisoner all the way. Sweat stung his temple. His strength faded as he lugged the wounded body, and he nearly puked thinking of the dead man's stomach. When he finally staggered up to where the platoon waited, he dropped the VC and collapsed on the ground, feeling more tired than after the late-summer preseason running drills.

"Good work, Slagel," Captain Webber said. He and the medic spread the man on the trail.

"There's a dead one back there, sir."

"Good, good." Webber drifted away and began talking on the radio.

Cam, the little interpreter, bent over the prisoner, shouting questions at him in a high, whiney voice. The prisoner said nothing. Cam shook him, asked more unanswered questions, then finally slapped him. The medic shooed Cam away.

Slagel wondered if Cam really hated the prisoner or if it was an act. No way to tell. The interpreters were often gone at night, and half the guys thought they did double duty for the VC. How could you know whether or not the South Vietnamese were friendly? They all wore black pajamas; they all looked alike.

The hell with it. He wasn't here to worry about who was who. He didn't care about knowing the Vietnamese or learning their customs. Fulda had cured him of thinking that foreigners were any different from Americans. He'd thought they would be, but it hadn't taken more than a few weeks for him to realize that the Germans were just as money hungry, just as concerned about the latest fashions and cars as the people he'd left back home. The Vietnamese might dress differently or go to a different church, but show them a taste of the long green and they'd get just like everybody else.

Platoon Sergeant Austin squatted in front of him. "Good going, Slagel. Head looks all right." Austin glanced over his shoulder, then back. "You didn't have to bring that one out."

"He might have some info." Exhausted, he lay back and stared at the sky.

"He tried to kill you. You could've zapped him. No one would care. You did all right, though. Keep it up."

The platoon got in line as a helicopter hovered above them, lowering a litter by rope. Slagel stood up and pushed his dirty blond hair forward so the medic could swab his head and plaster gauze on the wound. As the platoon trudged down the hill, the men behind him laughed as they jiggled the litter, bouncing the morphined and bandaged prisoner.

Both his squad leader and team leader had told him he should have killed the man. He was unconscious—no way the interpreter could get anything out of him—and it was a pain in the ass to haul him out of the jungle. What the hell was going on? One man was dead but no one cared about that. Or that he'd been wounded. His head felt as if it might fall off.

"Oh, shit!" The voice came from behind, followed by mingled laughter and moaning. The prisoner lay on the ground, the litter bearers barely able to keep straight faces. "Jesus, Slagel," one of them said. "Why didn't you give this fool the max?"

He opened his mouth, then shrugged and stumbled on down the hill. No use explaining; he was still learning the ropes. But combat was serious business—for men—and you didn't horse around with wounded people. You saved your fun for boozing and whoring. Jesus, he didn't even know if he'd killed the other guy. Maybe the gunships had. Or Irwin. Or all of them together. No time to think about it.

The unconscious man's groans had ceased by the time they reached the landing zone. The platoon stopped in the tall grass at the edge of the clearing as Webber got on the radio.

"Four-five, this is Blue, over."

"This is Four-five, Blue."

"Four-five, why don't you send one of the gunships down to pick up the litter, over."

"On the way."

"Forget it, Captain Webber," the medic said. "He's gone."

Slagel turned as the captain walked back to the litter. The man lay still, his lips pulled back like a snarling dog's. Webber got on the radio and told the gunship to stay up.

"Okay," Austin said, his thumb out to the side, "dump him in the bushes."

Back at the aid station he was given a pill that took away his headache and calmed his queasy stomach. Webber came by to congratulate him once again, and a few minutes later Major Quinn, the company commander, brought him a beer. The major talked to him as though he were a seasoned vet and told him he'd make sergeant as soon as he was eligible.

A medic brought him a tray of chow and another beer. He gobbled the food, then took the beer back to the tent he shared with Irwin. Sitting on the three-foot wall of sandbags, sipping from the can, he suddenly realized that he'd be getting a Purple Heart. The first of them to get anything so far. Well, he had been brave, just as he'd figured. Maybe they'd even put him in for a medal.

He leaned back and grinned as Chambers and Padgett approached his tent. Hadn't even been four weeks since they'd landed in Saigon, sweating about the war. Padgett, a Negro, was nearly Slagel's height, but a good twenty pounds lighter and quick as a bug. Chambers' head cleared Padgett's shoulder by only a couple of inches, but his short chunky body was strong as a tank. He had restrained Slagel from several brawls in Fulda.

"*Was ist los*, Mr. Purple Heart?" Padgett said, extending his hand, palm up.

"Just coolin' it." He slapped the palm. "How you doing, Orville?"

"Okay," Chambers said, his big square face serious as always. "Everything okay with you?"

"I'm sneakin' by." He glanced at the front of his fatigues. The dried blood really made him look like a trooper. "Some shit, huh?"

"Scared me when I heard that firing," Chambers said. "Seems too early to start this stuff."

He shrugged it off. "Guess this is the way it's going to be. Can't figure why everyone had the ass at me for not killing the prisoner."

"Remember what Austin said when we got here?" Padgett asked.

"Sure do." When they'd been assigned to the platoon, Austin had given them a speech on the spirit of the rifleman. You weren't a true one until you could look a man in the face, kill him, and feel nothing.

"Morgan's gonna shit when he sees that casualty report come in," Padgett said. "Probably call the Red Cross."

Slagel had forgotten that the report would go through S-1. "Might make him a little happier he ain't out here." Morgan, the fourth volunteer from Fulda, had wanted to come to the field too, but had been made a clerk in the battalion headquarters. It was the only way Slagel could arrange for them all to be in the same unit. The night they'd arrived at division base camp he'd gone immediately to the sergeant who made unit assignments and bribed him with a fifth of Wild Turkey to keep the four of them together. The sergeant had sent them to the recon battalion, but he had to assign someone as a clerk. Slagel had picked Morgan because of all of them he was the least ready to take the field. He was bigger and stronger than a lot of the riflemen, and smarter too, but he'd got his smarts in college and didn't have the savvy needed in the field. You never knew when he'd get a hair up his ass and do something weird. Not that Slagel wouldn't like to have him here, but if one of them had to stay behind, it might as well be Morgan.

"Will they give you time off?" Chambers asked.

"No one said anything. I'm ready to go out again."

"I'd try to get a few days if I were you."

"We're going back in a week anyway. I'll rest up then." He wasn't going to ask out if no one offered it.

They talked for a few minutes more, than he grabbed a change of fatigues and headed over to the rude shower at the corner of the platoon. The other soldiers heaped congratulations on him, slapping his back, even yelling to him as he scrubbed his hairy body in the cool water. Just like the jocks after he'd made a good run. Others told him that he'd learn not to worry so much about the prisoners. Maybe they were right; his worrying sure hadn't meant very much.

Back at his tent he slid into the sleeping bag, wallowing in the warmth and softness and fatigue. He *had* nearly killed the prisoner, but he'd been excited and afraid. You had to keep cool in combat, not get so crazy that you did things without thinking. That would be hard for him, because once he got going it was hard to stop.

At Fort Dix they'd had a bayonet course that you went over sometime near the end of infantry school. It was like an eighteen-hole golf course that you ran around as fast as you could, stopping at various spots to demonstrate your ability with the bayonet against old tires, sticks, trees, and straw-filled dummies. He'd run it twice one hot September afternoon, and the second time he got so carried away that he nearly went nuts. Running to get the best time in his company, he huffed like a maniac, plunged the bayonet into tires, parried and butt-stroked stakes to the ground, ripped at the dummies until he'd torn all the straw out of them. At the second-to-the-last stop he had butt-stroked a tree so hard that the stock of his M-14 training rifle smashed to splinters. When he finished the course, he had no idea where he was, and two sergeants had to hold him back from charging around again. The sweat in his eyes had nearly made him blind.

The time he'd gone sixty-seven yards for a touchdown against Illinois had been the same. Just an off-tackle slant he figured for three or four yards. But the hole was wide, the linebacker slipped, and he was suddenly in the secondary dodging tacklers and trying to line up behind blockers. The adrenalin hit him, and he did some fantastic broken-field running until a last block set him free on about the thirty-yard line. He'd streaked into the end zone as the roar went up from the crowd, and by the time he got back to the bench he hardly knew where—or who—he was. He understood how you could get so excited that you'd run the wrong way.

He rolled over in his sleeping bag, the air mattress hissing and giving beneath him, and folded his hands under his cheek. Being in combat sure wasn't Ohio State football. At least here he was doing something, even though he didn't know what. Football had gone down the tubes after his big run. He'd been a sophomore, a starting halfback because of his own hard work and an injury to another player.

After his long run they wrote about him in the papers, and great things were predicted for his next two years. He'd soaked up the praise for a week, then it began to make him sick—stupid interviews by the suck-ass sportswriters, then an invitation to speak at a high school athletic banquet. The old washed-up beer bellies from the nowhere small town hovered around him as though he were some kind of god, squeezing his muscles and telling about their great moments in high school games twenty years ago. Then he had to pose for pictures with the best player on the high school team, besides talking up college ball.

College ball wasn't shit. That's what really got to him. In

high school you played a couple of hours a day for three months for fun. In college you performed a full-time job—watching films, lifting weights, and hanging around the locker room talking about plays and the pros and next week's game. And you had to log your hours as an animal too. Drinking, falling down stairs, beating your head against the wall (that had been his most persistent trick), and sometimes going down to the hillbilly bars on High Street with the other jocks to kick ass on the stupid farmers.

He played well right up to the end of the season, even making a touchdown in the last game on national TV. The games and practice were okay, but you could have the rest of it. When he found out his father hadn't even watched the last game, he felt ready to quit for good.

For a month after, he stayed wild. Drunk and fighting every night, sometimes with the hillbillies, and other times he and a teammate would go to the basement lavatory of the zoology building to beat up the queers who met there late at night. He'd make the rounds of the sorority houses at least three times a week. Soon his behavior got him barred from several houses, from one for going head first through the door of a girl's room. The bitches usually went apeshit for two-bit football heroics, but they didn't like it when you showed them the big money. Even the guys in the fraternity looked at him funny. Everybody had some cheap-assed line you couldn't cross over.

He met Susie Rosen before Christmas, and she got him to see Dr. Bowen (he wondered how *they* were doing now), and by the time April rolled around he was able to talk himself into quitting.

It was the hardest thing he'd ever done in his life, not because he loved the game, but because the coaches made it so difficult. When he didn't show up for spring practice, they really put on the screws. Calling every day, offering this, threatening that, trying to make him feel like the ungrateful child. The coaches' psychology ended up working against them. At the point when he was about to break and report to practice, he got the handle on their game. The same lowdown crap his father always pulled, making him feel bad for all his sacrifices. With Dr. Bowen's and Susie's help he realized that the coaches had never sacrificed anything for him. He was just a good piece of meat that could work for them. Their final ploy was to tell him that he might as well play because he was just a piece of meat anyway. He had never felt so proud and happy as when he told them that he was more, and believed it.

Shit on it, anyway. The coaches had new meat, and maybe Susie Rosen and Dr. Bowen did too. He liked being a soldier better than being a halfback, and since he'd have to soldier tomorrow, he might as well get some sleep now.

In the morning he felt weak, but breakfast brought back his strength. When he woke up in the aid station, the last thing he remembered was strapping on his pistol belt. He swung his legs over the edge of the cot and stood up. "Whoo!"

The battalion surgeon jumped at the field table where he was making notes. "Up already, Slagel?"

"Yes, sir. What happened?"

"You fainted. How do you feel?"

"Good." Despite grogginess, his legs were steady.

"Strong enough to fly into the base for a rest?"

"Yes, sir!"

"Get out to the flight line, then. Mr. Booth is flying a scout ship back in half an hour. Have a merry Xmas."

He knew it was getting close, but he hadn't realized that today was Christmas Eve. A day like any other. You were supposed to feel sad being a lonely soldier overseas at Christmas. It wasn't so bad. He and Morgan could be in town this afternoon getting drunk and laid. Better than listening to his mother's three sisters and their pencil-necked husbands go on all day about nothing. If he'd stayed in football, maybe he'd be in a play-off game right now. He laughed as he thought about last Christmas in Fulda.

Drinking Tovarisch cherry vodka in the boiler room behind the latrine. Breaking the windows in the middle of winter.

Beside him in the chopper, Warrant Officer Booth dug an elbow into his side. "Laughing about all that pussy you're gonna get tomorrow?"

"Yes, sir. You be down there too?"

"You bet. I nailed some broad in that seat you're sitting in once."

"Sure you did." The OH-13 bubble helicopter was barely big enough for them and their gear.

"I ain't bullshittin'. Little farm gal when we were on maneuvers in Carolina. I was parked in a field. She got in, I pulled a camouflage cover over the bubble, and she sat on me right in that seat. Almost rammed the cyclic stick up her ass." Booth elbowed him again, then twirled his dark-brown handlebar. "Let's get on the highway and have some fun."

The helicopter peeled off to the right and headed east, twenty feet above the ground. Slagel leaned back and to the side, hanging his face into the wind. The mountains had given way to small hills, and in the distance the square rice paddies glistened green and brown.

"You don't mind a little detour, do you?"

"I'm in no hurry, sir. This low-level flying is nice."

"It'll get lower."

They passed over small clusters of brown hooches where old women and children waved at them. Old men and women watched them warily from the paddies where they worked. They headed east for about twenty minutes until a black ribbon of road appeared in the distance.

"Watch this." The helicopter dropped to six feet above the ground, aimed straight at a man working his rice paddy. He ducked to avoid the skid and fell face first into the shimmering brown water.

"Damn, sir, that was close."

"Ain't nothin'! I seen Wolf knock a coolie hat off one of them fuckers. At least I dipped him in shit where he belongs."

"What highway's this?"

"Nineteen. Runs from Qui Nhon to Pleiku. We got about five miles to go to base. Ought to meet something fun." Booth took the helicopter down to five feet. "What'd I tell you? Look at that sorry-assed bus. Time for a little chickie run. You ain't scared, are you?"

"No, sir."

The chopper dropped two more feet, and Booth's lips tightened. The faded yellow bus was about a quarter mile down the road, its top piled so high with furniture and other junk that it looked like a double-decker. People's heads hung out the windows.

"Can you clear it, sir?"

"Don't need to. They always chicken out. Hang on, though, in case I have to pull it up. Come on, little gooks! Let's see if your insides are the same color as your outside."

The peasants walking along the road leaped across the ditch and into the rice paddies when they saw the chopper coming. Slagel grabbed the bars on the side of the seat and squeezed. He hoped Booth wasn't too crazy. He squinted to see the driver's face as the bus got closer, but the sun reflected off the windshield as if the glass were a mirror. He closed his eyes when they were about fifty feet apart. His stomach dropped suddenly as the chopper rose.

"Eeeee*haw!*" Booth yelled. "Look back there, Slagel."

The bus lay on its side, furniture showered all over the rice paddy and ditch where it had landed. As the chopper went around a curve, people began crawling out of the windows.

"You don't play, do you, sir?"

"Shit!" Booth twirled his mustache. "I don't do nothin' but play."

2

WILLARD MORGAN looked up from his desk in the S-1 tent as a chopper floated down the base-camp helipad. The canvas wall blocked his view, and he turned back to his typewriter, cranked out the last citation, pulled the carbon paper, clipped the quintuplicate forms together, and stacked them neatly on the edge of the gray metal desk. He stood up behind the wooden counter that faced the tent entrance and flipped through the five recommendations for awards. Nearly perfect. Only two mistakes.

Ten minutes later Major Stubbs, the battalion executive officer, hustled into the tent, a coconut in one hand and a plastic bag of pistachio nuts in the other. Short, dark, and stocky, he was the only man in the battalion who wore his mustache thin and perfectly trimmed.

"Afternoon, sir."

"Good afternoon, Morgan. How would you like to go to town?"

"Sounds great, sir." He hadn't seen it yet. "I finished the citations."

"Good. Bring them back." Stubbs disappeared behind the bamboo partition, and Morgan followed him through the adjutant's office into the back of the tent. He placed the citations next to the coconut on Stubbs' antique Oriental writing table. A chest carved with small dancing figures lay on the floor against the back flap of the tent. On its top sat knives, two painted bowls, and a folded flag of North Vietnam.

"Morgan, you really do good work." Stubbs scanned the papers, then dropped them next to a hand-painted Oriental plate covered with crackers and cheese. "Want a little snack?"

He reached under the desk and pulled out another plate, piled with fruitcake and covered by Saran Wrap.

"No thanks, sir. I just had chow."

"Let's hit the road, then."

Outside, between the S-1 tent and the metal conex boxes of the S-2 and S-3 complex, sat five piles of goodies sent to the battalion from the VFW, American Legion, and other patriotic well-wishers. Books, food, candy, and magazines.

"Isn't this Christmas wonderful, Morgan?"

"Yes, sir." He fired up the jeep. Christmas passed the time. For the past week he'd been receiving letters and packages from his parents in L.A. and from a couple of old girlfriends. Even his former roommates in Berkeley had sent him a shoebox full of hard, black-bottomed chocolate-chip cookies. Bundles of unaddressed notes had come from Southern college girls, and anyone who wanted had some Georgia peach—usually a lifer officer's daughter—as a pen pal.

Stubbs was in ecstasy. Sitting in his office, he nibbled continually on tiny morsels of fine cheese or munched little cakes off his hand-painted plates. The officers' club was completed up on the hill behind A Company, overlooking the eastern side of the perimeter, and Stubbs and Colonel Billings were hosting a grand opening that night. The division commanding general would attend. Stubbs had been very busy arranging the party and inviting the appropriate brass. The division engineers and the battalion self-help team had planned wooden mess halls with concrete floors to be built after New Year's. Stubbs had written a form letter glorifying the battalion and the opening of its messes, and Morgan had to type copies on special stationery to the governors of each state and territory. It included a request for state or territorial flags to adorn the headquarters mess hall and give a sense of state pride to the men. Neither he nor Stubbs had known the capital of the Virgin Islands, and Stubbs had quipped that it might be St. Petersburg.

Morgan eased the jeep down the hill, past C and B and Headquarters companies, to where battalion road intersected the division perimeter road. Half a mile away Titty Mountain rose on the western perimeter, shielding the giant helipad that sprawled at its base. White parachutes that carried illumination flares hung in the greenery on the mountainside, the only reminder of last night's attack, in which four Americans and a squad of VC had been killed. The popping flares had awakened Morgan at midnight, and he'd stood on the road in his drawers watching as the helicopters poured machine-gun bullets and rockets into the mountainside, and as Puff the Magic Dragon, an old DC-3 fitted with Gatling guns, saturated the area with four thousand rounds a minute. Just like the Fourth of July. The VC had ignited a fuel bladder on the mountaintop, and the fire burned brightly for an hour, making the mountain look like a volcano.

They passed unit after unit on the muddy division road—infantry brigades, air-assault battalions, engineers, a medical company, the twenty-five tents of division personnel, transportation, and petroleum companies. "Really something else, sir."

"Yes, it is." Stubbs nodded seriously. "Nothing but jungle when we got here. Look at it now. Tents up all over, clubs, largest helipad in the world, even a radio station. The whole division's worked hard. We've only got ten percent of the men in Vietnam, yet we've taken twenty-five percent of the casualties. We've changed the war, Morgan. Put Charlie on the run." Stubbs sighed and looked off into the distance.

Morgan's interest in the division's complexity gave way to irritation with Stubbs. As though he did a thing besides politick and kiss his superiors' asses. His only concern with the war was to acquire more loot—the rifle platoon had brought him half the antiques in his office. He hadn't been to the field once since Morgan had arrived.

Guilt gnawed at him as he thought of his own worthlessness. Pushing paper again—same as in Fulda—after making all the fuss to get himself sent over here. He didn't mind it either—that really bothered him. He'd been pissed at Slagel when the assignments were made, but even then he'd felt relieved. After seeing the coffins at the Saigon airport, then getting his orders changed from the First Infantry Division to Air Assault because they'd lost four hundred men—who wouldn't be scared? He'd been tired too, from the drunken last month in Germany and the week of sleepless partying in New York and Berkeley before coming here. His first night in S-1, after reading through the daily bulletin that listed the names of all four hundred dead, he'd finally admitted to himself how glad he was not to be in the field, how good it was to be safe.

It had been the same in Fulda, with Padgett and Slagel too. The cold October morning of their arrival had nullified all desire to go to a rifle company in one of the outlying squadrons, and when the personnel sergeant had asked for clerks, all three of them jumped up. The choice had probably been wise. Clerking was stupid, but it passed the time, and the rifle companies did nothing but pull details anyway.

But here you couldn't help feeling like shit. Being the only lower-grade enlisted man in S-1, he didn't get harassed so much, and he pulled no KP or guard. So he worked hard—seven to seven, seven days a week (the next afternoon would be his first time off)—so did the riflemen and gunners and jeep drivers. No one did them any favors. It wasn't right not to be suffering in the middle of a war. He could always fight if he wanted to. But after hearing about Slagel's wound yesterday and after the attack last night, he had no intention of going to the field.

The tents ended, and a field of tall green grass, half a mile long, opened up between them and the gate of the division base camp. At the perimeter long lines of Vietnamese peasants, supervised by GI's, laid row after row of barbed-wire fortifications for the camp. He knew from the lecture he'd received upon arrival that the men got fifty cents a day, the women forty.

They drove out of the camp and turned left onto Highway

19. Shacks and shanties built from discarded Army rubbish lined the road, GI's crowding into them to buy washbasins, chairs, dressers, and brightly colored trinkets and dolls. "Looks like you've at least got some women over here, sir."

Stubbs looked to the side and nodded. "We've given these people a lot to do. Like people everywhere, some are industrious, some turn to easier ways of making money."

"What did they do before division came over?"

"Just farming, I suppose. They get more money from our business than they've ever seen. I just hope it doesn't get out of control. You have to be careful with underdeveloped countries."

They drove on in silence for another mile, Morgan perking up as he watched the Vietnamese skip along under their pole-suspended loads or sit listlessly behind the counters of their shops. He hoped he'd get to town more often after the first of the year.

"Turn in that dirt road up there, Morgan, then take a right into the laundry."

There were three mud and straw huts, two running parallel and connecting perpendicularly at the ends of the third. A canopy of corrugated aluminum covered what would have been the front yard. As he parked the jeep, three young boys ran out laughing from beneath the canopy. They poked him and Stubbs and pointed at them. An old man with a deeply lined face bent impassively over an ironing table. A fire beneath bricks heated his iron; he gulped water from a 7-Up bottle and spit it on the clothes before pressing. A younger man busily carried bundles of laundry into one of the huts. He saw Stubbs and quickly broke into a smile. "Major Stubb, one minute. I get laundry." Stubbs nodded once, scowling so that his thick black eyebrows made a continuous line across his forehead.

Morgan sat on a bench near the ironing table as a little girl emerged from the hut. Neatly combed black hair hung down to her shoulders. She had a lighter complexion than the boys, and her eyes were more round. She was shy and very pretty. He pointed to her and to his own name tag and asked one of the boys her name.

"Lang, Mor-gan," one of them said, then spoke to the girl in Vietnamese and laughed. Her name almost sounded like "Lung," the *g* held as though one were singing.

He called to her twice. She came closer and peered around the man who was ironing. After a few moments she walked back inside the brown hut. Stubbs refused to pay the entire price of his laundry since one pair of fatigue pants was missing.

They got back on the dirt road again, went up the length of a city block, and turned right into the main part of town. Stubbs cautioned him against taking large loads of laundry to the Vietnamese. "They haven't become responsible enough yet. Take small loads. Less chance of them losing it."

The street they turned on resembled a wild West show. Drunk soldiers staggered in the mud, arms around each other, pushing girls and swilling from brown bottles. Two of them walking near the jeep straightened up in feigned seriousness, saluted Stubbs, then burst into guffaws as the jeep cruised past them. Bars painted in blue and pink pastels lined the street, covered in front with thick wire mesh. A continuous din of shouts, curses, screams, and overturning furniture filled the air, accompanied by static and blaring music from portable radios. Morgan pictured opium dens and throat-slitting in the alleys and small muddy walkways that led off to the sides. "Town's something else, sir."

Stubbs sat erect in the jeep, eyes forward, blinking rapidly. "There've been some casualties with grenades down here. Soldiers just quit carrying guns to town a week ago. Too many of them were shooting each other."

A quarter mile down the pandemonium faded as they curved around a marketplace into the quiet north end of town. A pagodalike roof covered at least two dozen little stands where very old and very young Vietnamese traded fish, rice, bananas, coconuts, bean sprouts, and other vegetables. At one table a young girl sold dolls and trinkets as souvenirs, but otherwise the marketplace seemed untouched. Old dogs on leashes were tied to the supporting poles. Morgan felt a sudden flood of inspiration as he watched. The first thing he'd seen that looked truly Vietnamese, something with an ancient tradition that the war could not change.

Stubbs dickered in a trinket shop for fifteen minutes, wangling two ceramic Buddhas and three bronze medallions for a thousand piasters. They cruised out through the squalid back end of town and returned to the base.

He pulled into the parking place beside S-1. "Thanks a lot, sir. Good to see the town."

Stubbs nodded. "Morgan, it's going to be raining pretty hard tonight. I'd like you to bring the jeep up to the officers' club at seven. Park it so the lights shine on the door and about twenty yards of the ground in front. We don't have a walkway yet, and it would be very embarrassing if the CG slipped in the mud."

"Yes, sir. Seven o'clock." He got out of the jeep.

"Come in the office, Morgan. I've got a special job for you."

"Yes, sir."

Stubbs opened his attaché case and pulled out a thick piece of expensive-looking stationery and a small stickpin with the regimental crest on it. "I want you to send this to Lady Bird at the White House. It's a little note about the opening of our club and about the fine job our boys are doing."

He wanted to tell Stubbs to run it up his ass. He typed the note perfectly, left it on the major's desk, and went down to the mess tent for coffee.

He met Slagel walking up the road. "Tom, what the hell are you doing here?"

"They sent me in for a rest. Said I could stay till after Christmas. Let's go to town."

"I heard what happened. Are you okay?"

"Don't I look it? Just a little crease." He took off his hat to show the bandage.

"Damn, you were lucky."

"You bet your sweet ass."

"How's Orville and LaMont?" He suddenly missed them all, wanted to have them together again, drinking and talking as they had done so many nights in Fulda.

"Okay. We're all in different squads. Neither one of them had contact yet. Chambers lost about fifteen pounds. He'll be slim as me before long." Slagel patted his flat belly, feinted, then punched him lightly in the stomach. "State'd had me this year, they'd be in the roses. Morg, baby, let's you and me go to town this afternoon. I'm overdue."

"I can't. I get tomorrow afternoon off. Let's go then."

"It's a date. I'm going to shower and get pretty. I'll see you tonight."

By seven the road going up to the club was so muddy that the jeep barely made it. He backed off to the side, beaming the lights on the mud by the front door. At the back he reported to Stubbs.

"Glad you're here, Morgan. You'll direct the jeeps to parking places when they come up. Anywhere along the south side of the road will be fine. Just leave the lights on until the CG leaves." He gave him two cans of beer and shoved him out the door.

He'd known Stubbs was an asshole, but now he really made him sick. Sucking ass and not giving a shit for the troops. Other engines groaned on the road, and he jumped into the slime. He directed the five jeeps into parking places, then saluted as the brass hustled past him. None of them returned the gesture, hurrying for their booze as if he didn't exist; the CG, with two stars, his deputy with one, and the three infantry brigade commanders, all full colonels. Each had his aide and sergeant major with him. He slid back in the jeep, shaking off water, and wiped the fat drops off his glasses.

"Look at that shithook," he said to the rain when Stubbs and the colonel came to the door to greet the arrivals. Stubbs was six inches shorter than the colonel, and Morgan swelled with hatred as he watched him nod and smile and salute and shake hands. In the light Stubbs' eyes seemed to wink with hunger and greed. What a petty, conniving son of a bitch. The door to the club closed, and he hurriedly drank his second beer. Thoroughly soaked, he drove back down the hill at midnight.

The next afternoon he stopped at the laundry with Slagel to give Lang some candy before going to the bars. Her father brought beers while he and Slagel sat under the canopy. Lang came out of the hut, and he called to her. "Come here, Lang. I've got something for you."

"She doesn't want what you got," Slagel said.

He took three candy canes, some gum, and Life Savers from his pocket and waved them at her. "Come here, Lang. Good chop-chop."

She came closer and he gathered her in his arms and set her on his lap. "Merry Christmas, Lang." He undid the cellophane on one candy cane, and she licked it a couple of times. She smiled at him, and he hugged her, putting his cheek next to hers.

"Okay, Will, let's hat up," Slagel said. "You played Santa Claus real well."

He stood up and set Lang on the ground. He put the treats into her hand, and after waving at him, she went back into the hut. "Bye, Lang," he called after her. "Bye, Papa-san."

"Good-bye, Mor-gan," Papa-san said, bowing to him.

At the corner of the main street a great commotion arose behind them. A dump truck from the engineers barreled up the road, its horn honking furiously. At least fifty Vietnamese children ran behind the truck, screaming and holding out their arms. From the back of the truck a soldier in fatigues with a long white beard and a red-and-white stocking cap hurled candy into the street as fast as he could, yelling "Merry Christmas" over and over. The truck wheeled around the corner as he and Slagel stepped back to avoid the onslaught of children. It continued down the main street, brightly wrapped candy flying into the mud and onto the porches of the bars. Whores rushed out and joined the children, on their knees for whatever they could get. Soldiers leaned against the walls, laughing and giving Santa the finger as he rolled by. One soldier grabbed a young girl as she ran after the truck. "Ho, ho, ho, little girl," he said. "Come sit on Santa's face."

Morgan and Slagel went into a bar while things died down. In ten minutes two women came in. One sat in Slagel's lap and said, "You boom-boom, GI?"

Slagel nodded. "That's what I'm here for."

"Fi' hundred p."

Slagel raised four fingers. The girl rose and they disappeared into the back.

"You boom-boom too?" The other girl ran her finger over Morgan's bristly, half-grown red mustache. She was short and a little fat; her hair barely touched her shoulders.

"Four hundred p?" He grinned.

"Okay, GI. Four hundred."

They went in the back and the girl took off her black pajama bottoms and her white blouse. Her belly hung out over a scanty bush of pubic hair. He ran his hand up and down her thigh, then patted her stomach. She patted it too. "Me have baby-san, fi' months."

"I see." He took off his shirt and pulled his pants down. The guys at the base had told him to keep his boots on in case of a VC attack. She lay like a board, he came quickly, and they were back out in the bar in fifteen minutes. Slagel sat in a chair, drinking another beer.

"How was it, Morg?"

"Shee-it. You?"

"Same."

"First pregnant girl I ever diddled."

"That's an important first," Slagel said. "Let's go." He turned to the girl he'd been with and gave her the finger. "So long, pig."

"You number ten, GI."

"You number fuckin' ten," Slagel said.

By seven thirty that night at least thirty men had gathered around the Enlisted Men's Club door. Others streamed in for the free drinks to be given away at eight. Through the new screens, Morgan saw three bartenders in T-shirts lining up bottles on the bar. The crowd grew and pressed toward the door, soldiers yelling for the club to open. Chairs were piled in the doorway to keep people out. Someone jabbed him in the back with a canteen cup. "Excuse me, there, partner," the man behind him said, then beat the cup against the wall. The crowd pressed forward again, and a soldier in front fell into the chairs and landed on the floor. Others tried to bolt in, but the manager drove them back. The pushing continued, and he was jabbed twice more. Slagel jumped up and down, shoving the man in front of him.

The chairs were pulled out of the doorway and the crowd surged forward. Morgan was blocked from the bar, and he fell back into the room. He got up and looked toward the door. Heads bobbed up and down, and in the semidarkness outside the screens he saw an endless row of hungry faces, eager with the desperation of deprived children. Slagel thrust a paper cup of whiskey into his hand. He swilled it in one gulp, then watched Slagel's back wriggling into the mob at the bar. Again he turned to the screens. The whiskey nearly made him vomit, and he gasped. Too pathetic. He had to get out. Slagel again held whiskey in front of him. "I've got to get out of here."

"I'm stayin'." Slagel put his head down and plunged toward the bar.

Morgan fought his way through the door. Someone bumped his cup, and the brown fluid ran over his hand and down his sleeve. He ran a few steps from the club, then stopped and breathed in the cool evening air. Insane. The whole business was insane.

Only about thirty soldiers sat on the knoll above the club, watching a western that flickered on a bed sheet stretched between two trees. Morgan sat on an empty rocket pod, huddling over a cigarette and feeling terribly alone. From a tent across the path came curses and unintelligible shouts. The entry flaps suddenly parted, revealing two fat sergeants in their underwear, brawling beneath a dim naked light bulb. They spilled across the path, tumbled in the dirt, and rolled up next to Morgan.

"You gimme them new fatigues, you sack of crap," the mess sergeant said to his adversary from supply.

"You don't get nothin' till you quit robbing my belly in the chow line."

"I've given you extra rations plenty of times." Mess pushed supply away, sat up, and turned to Morgan. "Hey, it's the new S-1 clerk. You tell him. I give out plenty of chow."

"Sure thing, Sarge." Morgan stared into the sergeant's gray-stubbled face, then tipped back over the rocket pod in a fit of laughter. What the hell was wrong with him? He was a soldier, far from home on Christmas night.

He got up after five minutes and walked back by the S-4 tent, from where he could see both the club and the movie. He leaned against a tree and slid down until his ass touched the ground. "Three tears in the bucket," he yelled. "They don't flow, mother fuck it!" He grabbed a canteen cup from a shaving table and broke for the club. He kept it hidden from the bartender, and after pouring eights shots of rum from paper cups into it, he asked innocently for a Coke. He made his way back to where Slagel sat, nodded to him, poured the Coke into the rum, and drank it down in less than ten minutes.

3

"You you. You buy you."

LaMont Padgett looked up from the magazine he was emptying into an ammo can.

"You buy, number one." The small boy in torn gray pajamas flashed a yellow grin at him across the rusty concertina wire of the field-base perimeter. He held a basket up to his chin, full of Coke and beer bottles, a few bananas and coconuts.

"Deedee. Get away." Padgett went back to thumbing out the bullets, listening to them plunk into the olive-drab can.

"You you." The bottles rattled in the shaking basket.

He set the magazine down and rose off the wall of sandbags that protected his and Collins' tent. Stretching, he walked the ten yards to the wire.

"*Beaucoup* beer," the boy said.

He winced, thinking of the warm Vietnamese panther piss he'd drunk downtown two days ago. "Nix."

"Cola?"

He gave a pink scrip dollar bill for a Coke and a short, speckled banana and went back to the sandbags. The boy moved up the wire, shouting and shaking the basket.

Eleven light-brown hooches stood among the banana and coconut trees in the hamlet beyond the wire. If the VC attacked, they'd sure as shit come from there. Only ten yards from the perimeter, and his squad's tents would be the first they'd hit. The platoon had set up in a square in the southwest corner of the battalion's area.

He filled his magazines with clean rounds and stuffed fifteen of them into the pouches on his pistol belt. He clicked the last one into his M-16, then checked the rifle again for dirt. Clean. After sliding an old fatigue leg over it, he laid the gun on his sleeping bag.

"Second squad, y'all get over here," Staff Sergeant Baird yelled from Sergeant Austin's tent. "Platoon sergeant's briefing."

As the troops shuffled over to the light-green umbrella tent the little sergeant stepped out from between the flaps, gripping a clipboard in his right hand. "Listen up, men. First thing is rules in the field base. You will wear steel pot, pistol belt, and carry your weapon at all times. You will eat with your pot on and your weapon by your side. You will wear your pot when you take a shit. Any man caught without his pot and weapon in the area will get an Article Fifteen. Same goes for not sleeping under mosquito nets and not taking malaria pills. There'll be one guard for every hundred feet of perimeter, and we'll pull three men per night. If we take any fire from the hamlet, we destroy it. Grenades, machine guns, the works.

"Both gunnery and scouts did recon yesterday, and they took fire almost every time. We'll be doing search-and-destroy missions in these mountains here and over by Happy Valley. Charlie's got a lot of storage hooches and personnel up here, so you're gonna have to be ready. I want team leaders checking weapons every night, and I don't want no one holding ammo more than three days. That shit gets dirty, it'll jam the M-16 every time. You don't use it up out there, trade it in back here.

"You new guys who wasn't with us on the border may think this is a lot of shit, but you got some surprises coming. December was easy, but here you're gonna have to be awake every minute. Absolutely no talking on missions. No smoking unless me or Blue gives the word. Any man not field-stripping cigarettes deals with me personally.

"About firing: Anything that moves, we kill. And if you hear some rustling in the bushes, you better fire or your ass gonna be out. You wait on Charlie and he'll have your balls. We go out after chow in the morning. I want to see all squad leaders in my tent. That's all, men. Let's get our gear squared away. I want every weapon cleaned tonight, and I want every swingin' dick to get clean ammo."

Padgett walked back to his tent while the rest of the platoon went to the ammo point behind the mess tent. At least he was that much ahead of the game. He washed the banana down with Coke, thinking about going to bed, listening to the palm fronds swish above the hamlet.

It was a relief to be back in the field again, even though they might get in the shit this time. Fuck that too. Base camp had been a drag. Four days in, brush-cutting detail twice, guard last night. One day in town, bad booze, and the two shots of cock had been like dead folks. New Year's Eve, when they needed a little taste, club ran out at nine. Had to sit there sober listening to Slagel tell war stories and Morgan go on about the chumps in the base. But not as bad as the old Fulda Gap. At least you could buy you some pussy over here without going sixty clicks for it.

Base camp could make you soft; that's what you had to watch out for. The tenseness needed in the field goes away because you don't have to worry about anything. Austin's speech had got him going a little, but he still felt listless and sleepy. First mission in the morning ought to bring it back. Can't miss once you get in that chopper with all your stuff on. He decided to get to sleep before Collins came back talkin' trash about how he be so much tougher than the white boys. Jittybug ain't shit.

He was in the restaurant in Newark where he and the fat cat would go after the art shows or movies in New York. But he was solo this trip and getting up from the back dining room, ready to get hat. A door with a small window was closed between the dining room and place where the counter and cash register stood. He peeped through the window and saw him sitting on a couch by the cash register, wearing this cross between military dress rags and a heat uniform. He hipped himself to mother-fuck this chump, slipped on his shades, and says to himself to walk up there cool as ice, pay the tab, and split. All of a sudden he's got these white boxing gloves on his hands and feet, and as soon as he touches the door, his arms and legs go all spaghetti, and boom! he's laid up on the floor. Then he's together, struttin' right past the dude. But he doesn't catch his legs out in front of him. He trips, hits the floor, his shades fall off, and he's looking right up into fat daddy's ugly mug. And the cat's right into his number: "Well, LaMont Padgett. Your eyes have grown so dishonest I can barely stand to look at you. You bastard. You son of a bitch. You motherfucker!"

LaMont's on his feet and shoves this at him: "Me? Me dishonest? You low-lifed fat cat. You led me on for two years, talkin' all that shit about beauty and God and Jesus, tellin' me how cool my painting was when all you wanted was to get your pudgy little hand around my joint. You faggot. You goddamn black nigger-ass faggot!"

Meanwhile, the counter behind them had vanished, and this red-brick fireplace yawned there instead. The dude had walked over to it while LaMont was yelling at him, and grabbed a big poker. He got that black poker held above his head and that silly military hat, more hate in his face than LaMont had ever seen, ready to bash his brains in. LaMont just folds his hands on top of his hat and waits for it.

As always, he woke up with his hands over his head, waiting to get hit. At least he ain't been yelling. Still black outside. Pissing into an inverted rocket pod, he listened to the cooks clanging pots in the mess tent. Wouldn't be long now.

For ten days the platoon humped the short range of coastal mountains south of the river from Bong Son. No action. Everyone was tight because gunnery and scouts took fire every day, but so far no one had messed with the rifles. Sometimes he almost wanted something to happen, just to see if he'd pull his punch this time. He wouldn't; you couldn't in combat. Whole lot different from gambling in the street. There you just got knocked on your ass or cut a little. Here it was for good.

These mountains were nice, though. Sometimes made him forget what he was here for, especially when they were on the spine, looking down at the sea and being cooled by the breeze. Reminded him of the deep blue Mediterranean from last May. He'd be sorry when they moved west to Happy Valley.

He slept long hours because he didn't feel much like talking. Slagel was busy swapping war stories with the NCO's and kids. Like he can't wait to get in some combat. Chambers' new tent partner was a stone Mississippi Cracker, so it wasn't that easy to go over there. And the jittybugs were steady talkin' shit. It wasn't bad, though, sleeping, writing Jerrie almost every night.

In the morning he'd just squatted down beside Chambers with a mess kit of powdered eggs and a roll when Austin ran into the area with all his gear on. "Blue platoon, saddle up on the double and get out to the flight line. Forget about the chow."

"Mother fuck a lot of flight lines too." He dumped his chow in the garbage can and ran back to his tent.

"Come on," Staff Sergeant Baird said. "Special Forces camp broke radio contact early this morning. They can't raise anyone out there. We're going to check it out."

They flew southwest for twenty minutes, then started down over a deserted hamlet. A quarter mile south the lift ships circled the camp counterclockwise while the gunnery ships made low passes. From his seat in the right door he couldn't see the camp. Only the dense jungle around it. Take machetes to get through that shit.

The gunships made a run along the tree line fifty yards in front of the camp, then the lift ships went down. The platoon dashed into the foliage and, after lying still for five minutes, regrouped at the edge of the jungle. Still no sign of life. A man hung from the flagpole in the center of the camp. Captain Webber came over from the radio and squatted in front of the men. "Looks like a massacre, but it may be a trap. Gunships couldn't spot anybody but the captain on the flagpole. He's dead. Sergeant Austin, I'll take the second and fourth squads up there. First and third each fan out and take a side. If they open up, give them everything you've got. Shoot over our heads, and we'll try to get back. Let's go. Don't touch anything till you check it for booby traps."

As they moved slowly toward the gate, the man on the flagpole came into focus. A captain, all right. The sun reflected off the silver bars that had been driven into his forehead. Naked. His groin area completely black. Nothing hanging. Black spots speckled his legs and stomach, and his cheeks were bloated as though he had the mumps. Padgett's stomach turned over, and his palms began to sweat.

The six aluminum huts in the camp were each surrounded by sandbags except for the small entrances. In the biggest hut four men lay dead in sleeping bags covered with patches of dried blood. Three more slumped over a card table in a different hut. The radioman was on the floor of the commo shack, and they found another soldier in the supply hut, his face black and his gray hands gripping like claws at the wire tightened around his neck. The squad came out of the last hut and stood near the flagpole, where a black circle covered the sand beneath the hanging man. Webber yelled to Austin to bring up the rest of the platoon.

"Damn!" Baird said. "They really wiped them out, sir."

"Didn't they?" Webber said. He looked utterly confused. "Regional forces gone. Not a goddamn person here."

"Probably in cahoots with Charlie."

"Charlie didn't do this," Webber said. "Montagnards did. Captain must've fucked some Montagnard woman. Jesus! Who can climb? Someone's got to get this guy down. Anyone?"

"I can climb," Collins said.

"Carry him down if you can; otherwise, let him drop."

"I'll let Four-three know what's happening," Austin said.

"See if they can get some medevacs out here for these guys. How you doing, Collins?"

"Got him, sir." Collins had cut the rope and was inching down the pole, the captain under one arm.

"Dunlap, get over here," Webber yelled to the medic.

Collins set the corpse down gently and moved away. Dunlap bent over the captain's body and felt his head. Suddenly he groaned, jumped back, and puked.

"What's the matter?" Webber asked.

Dunlap turned around, his face pale and the sweat beneath his eyes glistening under the magnification of his thick glasses. "Sir, his balls and dick. They're in his mouth."

"Jesus Christ! Someone get a blanket and cover him."

Padgett couldn't stop himself from watching. The man's face was dark blue from strangulation. His lips were black, and between his white teeth his mouth looked like a cave that had been sealed off with dirt. He wondered how long they took to kill him, and his body shook as his mind made pictures of the torture.

"Come here, Padg," Hanshaw said.

He stepped back a few feet to the small group of splibs.

"I hope that shot of cock was worth it to him," one of them said.

"Had to be some fine pussy."

"Tell you what, though," Hanshaw said, grinning. "That's something you won't see a whole lot of in Alabama." He stuck his hand out and it was instantly slapped by three others.

Death was gray; that's how he'd have to paint it. He dropped his cigarette butt in a beer can and lay back on his sleeping bag, going over the image of the mumpy, deballed captain for the hundredth time since morning. He hadn't figured on seeing anything like that, hadn't even thought much that there would be things here to be painted. Now he imagined himself in a New York gallery, the walls dripping with the things he'd seen. Maybe the fat cat would be there to watch. In the darkness of his tent he went back to the day they'd arrived in Saigon. Stepping off the plane, they'd been greeted by an eighteen-wheel tractor-trailer pulling a load of coffins to a waiting transport plane. Perfect geometry on the outside. Inside, with X-ray eyes, he could see the formless lumps of gray death. Swabbed clean or covered with scabs? How to do it. Would he even be able?

He'd drawn some when he was little, like most kids probably, and had always dug pictures with lots of color and big books about birds and animals. But he never did much with it in junior high and forgot it completely in tenth grade, when he was boxing all the time. In eleventh he took art all the way through, the fat cat teaching him. More and more he stayed after class splashing the colors on paper and canvas and making some pretty things too. The fat cat began to dig it and one day asked him did he want to go to New York for a show. Said that seeing others would help him.

That was on a Friday, and he hated to give up the party that night, but he said okay. He dug that chubby dude. The show was fine, but when they got back to Newark, they went to this restaurant and rapped. The man really wanted to hear about him, seemed to understand the scene, and even gave him advice on how to get along. Now this plump daddy was *ugly* and big and fat. He had a round face with fat sweaty creases on his forehead, and the back of his neck hung over his shirt collar like a little jelly roll. Just moving out of the seat in the restaurant would get him huffin' and puffin' like an old steam engine. But it didn't bug LaMont, because he could talk to this cat like he couldn't talk to anyone. He told him everything. Even though a big part of his thing was endurance, he wasn't an Uncle Tom, because his rap was just that kicking white ass didn't make any sense, and that even though a man was getting hurt, he had to keep on pushing without hurting anyone else.

It took LaMont awhile to dig that, but he finally quit fighting. Hung up the gloves and just did art with his fat daddy. All that energy he'd spent on being pissed off at people went on the canvas and in his sketchbooks. And instead of spending his time at the gym, he went to at least an exhibit a week, sometimes two or three.

His mother was a little bothered about him going out with this older, unmarried man—she met him a couple of times and said something about him wasn't right—but he never saw anything wrong with it. Sometimes, like when LaMont did a good painting or they had a special talk, the cat might pat him on the back or give him a little hug, but it wasn't any different from what the coaches did after he'd won a bout or had a good workout.

In the spring of twelfth grade he got a scholarship to art school in Newark, mainly because of his teacher's help. When the thing came through, the cat was so happy that he gave him a little peck on the cheek. LaMont didn't dig it, but the pink light never flashed in his head. The fat cat asked him later if he thought it was faggoty what he did, but LaMont said no. The dude didn't have any family of his own and was really tickled when he could do something for someone else. Whatever friendship the lonely cat had was important to him. LaMont forgot about it soon enough, anyway. He just went on working like crazy, trying to build up his portfolio and get some new ideas going so that when art school started, he could keep up with everyone else.

All this time they were going out together the dude was giving him these fine art books, and rapping to him about what a hip dude Jesus was, and telling him what was right and wrong and all that. The fat cat didn't go to church, but he believed, and he got LaMont believing too. They'd go through whole numbers with Fra Angelico or Giotto, with the fat cat pointing out all this delicate religion and devotion in the paintings and frescoes, telling him about believing in the Lord, and how you have to live every day like it was your last. LaMont dug on that for a while until he started meeting up with these crazy cats in art school and going into some new forms. He got high a couple times and went into a pretty far-out bag, and all these grotesque shapes started slithering out on the canvas. He showed them to the fat cat, but he wasn't coming on it. Like they about had this falling out over him getting on the weed, and when he quit digging Jesus' shit, the dude got real disappointed, and they didn't see each other so much anymore. LaMont still liked Fra Angelico and Giotto as much as always, but they were painters more than preachers—and men before either one—something the fat daddy never could get hip to.

One night he fell in with some guys from school, and they were smokin' and sippin' when all of a sudden the fat cat's name come up. All the other dudes was poking each other and grinning like they all know who he is, then they start puttin' down this rap about him being a queen. LaMont defended him, figuring that since he knew him best, he could hip the other cats to him. None of them had really known him that well, but they'd all heard stuff from other clowns. By the end of the night he had them pretty well convinced that the fat cat wasn't a punk and that he was just lonely and needing some love.

He was fairly high by the time he got home, stumbling across the front lawn to the door, and boom! the chubby papa's short pulls up at the curb. He got in and they started talking and he finally told him that him and the other dudes had been discussing him that night, and that when he gets completely sober he wants to ask him some questions. The fat cat said okay, then leaned over and kissed him. LaMont didn't do anything, and then the dude really went into a number. He just tucked that fat hand of his under LaMont's nuts, and there were too many colors exploding in his head for him to say or do anything. Next thing he knew the clown took LaMont's hand and put it on his pants, and his joint was hard as a frozen hot dog. About twenty gallons of paint had gone off in his head by this time, but he was still sitting there. He finally squeaked out something about having to get some sleep, and he'd see him next week, and he got out of the short and watched him drive away.

By the time these gray and gold streams come running over from the east, he was still standing on the curb gazing out at nothing, watching the paint dry on his brain. He partied that night, though. Got so high that even the jittybugs he was with thought he was crazy, then he got him the blackest hole he could find and cut that bitch till her pussy hurt.

Later in the week he went to see the fat cat to tell his faggoty ass that they were through, but when he saw him, he couldn't say a thing. The dude came on with this soulful rap about how glad he was to see him, then he asked if LaMont wanted to talk about that shit, and he said no. Fat cat say, "I don't seem to have a part in anything anymore," and LaMont said, "That's the way the jelly rolls," and split.

He quit painting after that. Gave it up for fighting except times when he'd get high and maybe draw on a napkin or something. But mostly he let it go, and if he did start thinking about it, he'd just turn it into hate for that fat cat.

After New Year's of sixty-five, a couple months after him and Morgan and Slagel had got to Fulda, he really started down a slide, getting sorrier and sorrier. He quit shining his boots, wore dirty fatigues, and was lying around doing nothing more and more. They went to Paris for three days in February, and when he walked into the modern art museum, boom! frontal assault of color and memory, and even that night while he was offing some whore on St. Denis, he kept seeing these strange shapes and crazy colors in his head.

When they got back to Fulda, he tried to make some charcoal drawings of his friends, but it wouldn't come so he quit before he really got started. When April came around, he got a thumping in his head saying two more years in this dump. Then they decided to go to Italy for two weeks, and just thinking about that helped a little, and they worked off some fat at the gym, and by the first of May they were with the guineas, and it was like someone took the lid off and let the sun grow in his eyes.

The hammer he got hung on was cool too—for real—and she didn't come on with any phony shit about how she was ready to die for the Cause, and she wasn't just thinking there was a big thrill waiting for her in catching some black dick. As far as the Cause went, she was in his corner, but she wasn't about to get killed for anything unless it made a difference. She'd done some teaching down in the barefoot country one summer and got hassled by the Crackers, and she said she'd probably go back again. Because she wanted to get people reading and writing, but figured if the Crackers wanted to kill her, she'd split, because dying that way don't do nobody a bit of good.

It wasn't like they had a deep romance. They dug each other, but both of them knew that there wasn't that much sense in getting real involved, because she'd be going back to the world, and he'd be stuck in the Army another two years. But she said that wasn't any reason why they shouldn't enjoy each other while they could. And he was saying to himself, "I'm hip, I'm hip. Now just spread those legs." And they got into that pretty heavy too, and he was thinking that was all he needed when she hit him with this rap about painting and laughed and called him chickenshit, and before he knew it he'd bought some stuff and was painting her naked white ass up in this field one day.

She was a kind of heavy-legged gal, so after he painted her once like she was she asked him would he paint her again only make her legs a little slimmer. He looked at her funny and she said it was no big thing, but that's the one part of her body she doesn't especially like, and since he made her feel all right maybe he could paint her all right too. So he did it. He slimmed the legs down and when it was done it didn't look like her, and then she takes a look at it. She stood there with that bright afternoon sun making those peeps greener and greener, and then she smiled and the sun danced all gold through her saliva, and then she laughed and said she liked herself better like she was and smeared paint all over the canvas. Then she pulled him down and they started rolling in the grass like four-year-olds till all of a sudden they were all grown up and when he looked at her while she was tearing up his back she was sporting this smile like he'd never seen before, and he closed his eyes and while he was bustin' nut these gold and green vats of paint were washing his brain like nothing ever did before.

After he and the fat cat had fell out he used to have the dream off and on, and it always made him hate the dude for days. He had the dream again that night, but it was different afterward this time. Like he woke up not hating the fat cat as usual. This mellow riff was blowing in his head and got him to thinking that the plump chump didn't have a whole lot to do with what he was, and maybe it hurt him what he did as much as it hurt LaMont. Because if he hadn't been born with the flaked mug and the bad thyroid, he might have found a hammer that would've kept him from turning into a punk. It didn't excuse what had happened, but as he got hip to the whys and wherefores of the thing, he began to forgive that roly-poly dude.

Every day in Florence he saw more and painted more, and all that nasty hate softened up like putty or clay or something a person can shape and understand. For a few seconds he even fell out of himself and clean into the fat cat's shit. For a few seconds he could feel the weight of loneliness the dude must live with all the time, and since then, even though he hated him sometimes, he really did feel no-bullshit sorry for him.

So he painted a whole lot in Florence. Not that he didn't party and sip a little pluck too, but when they finally left, he had a whole stack of things he'd done or started. He was still a little rusty, but he knew the stuff might be good someday. Fulda froze it. He painted with glue. All that easy flow gummed up, and the brush would hardly move. He got mad in a hurry, hating the fat cat again. Then one day he was down in the park, trying to paint some flowers and getting nowhere, when some Kraut came up to him dribbling out some "*Entschuldigen Sie?*" and he said, "Get your mother-fuckin' knockwurst ass outa here," and the Kraut said it again, and bip! he fired on the clown. Just his luck to have two MP's driving by at the time. All this shit stormed up in him as they approached, and he fired on one, but the other got around behind him with a billy and bipped him up side the head, and he came to in the dispensary.

The first pig was pushing for a court-martial to get him in the stockade, but his commander gave him two weeks' extra duty and a bust. He and the other cats had been rapping about going to the Nam, and while he was out picking up rocks on the parade field his first night of extra duty, the feeling for going came on real strong. He started feeling shucked out of something down the line, like life's holding out all these promises just so the bitch can snatch them back when you get hip to them. And then he knew that if he stayed in Fulda another two years, he'd have to gamble with himself too hard to stay out of the iron house or the funny farm. So he started throwing rocks around the field pretending to hit the Cong, and then said mother fuck it, why not sign up, because it's better to be throwing rocks than putting them in a goddamn sack. And it wasn't that he felt anything bad for the Cong, but he couldn't take anything out on anyone but himself in Fulda, and fuck it if he was going to eat himself up that way.

He hadn't even brought a sketch pad to Vietnam. Well, it wasn't like he had all this time to draw, anyway. He'd just have to stay alert, not let his head get moldy like it always did in Fulda. If shit kept happening like it did today, he shouldn't have much trouble with that.

He squirted insect repellent on a leech that sucked his right forearm. It recoiled and fell to the ground. He squirted another off his calf. Ceniceros had got one on his balls three days ago and he couldn't get it off. Almost went crazy before the chopper came and got him. You had to leave your trousers unbloused for ventilation, making it easy for the leeches to get on your legs. They grouped in squads and attacked.

Happy Valley would be a nice place to come fishing. The valley walls were steep and high and rugged, and the stream that cut the floor wound through large orange and gray rocks and short stretches of sandy shore, occasionally leveling out solid and still before the ripples and eddies of the white water parts. Great place to lay up cooling beers in the stream.

They'd moved over to Happy Valley after another three days in the coastal mountains, and in two weeks the platoon had killed ten North Vietnamese regulars in small groups of two or three. He hadn't gotten any himself, but almost got hit once. One brigade of three infantry battalions had killed close to three hundred so far, and since the Bong Son operation had begun, the division had recorded more than five hundred confirmed kills. Slagel had killed four in Happy Valley, and was now notching his rifle butt. Padgett could hardly rap with him anymore. Cat was popping the diet pills the medic gave him, and his face looked ready to explode from nervousness. Eyes dilated and blinking, lickin' his dry lips all the time. Enjoying the killing too.

Sometimes the missions seemed stupid, even if they killed

a thousand or ten thousand. Mornings, as the platoon flew out, he could count close to a hundred long green jungly fingers leading down the mountain from the spine, and each ravine between them could hide two regiments. The Air Force was all the time bombing out landing zones on the spine with napalm, and while it gave the choppers a place to set down, it made no dent in the acres and acres of cover. Just made the mountains ugly.

The orange and gray rocks rose solidly about a hundred yards to their right front as they went up the mountain finger. Another jagged row fell away perpendicularly, paralleling the squad's movement. Behind the bigger, nearly boxlike rocks three tan hooches were barely visible through the trees. The platoon stopped, and word was passed that the others should stay put. Captain Webber came back and moved the fourth squad to where they could see the caves in the rocks, and the grenadiers were to fire two rounds each at the caves and hooches.

Chambers squatted by him as the grenadiers moved up, putting his hand on his shoulder. "How you making it, LaMont?"

"All right, Orville. This heat's something else." Although prettier than the coastal mountains, Happy Valley didn't get the breeze.

"We'll be out of here in a couple hours. Little warmer than Germany."

"Ain't that right?"

The grenadiers fired. One was a direct hit on a hooch, and the other hit the big rock a foot above the cave. Machine-gun fire started out of the cave immediately.

"Get down!" He pushed Chambers to the side, then rolled four feet the other way, coming up beside Collins. The first squad hadn't got twenty feet away from them.

"In the cave," Collins said.

Padgett leaned on his elbow and placed eighteen shots into the opening. The machine gun didn't quit. Someone tugged his pants leg. He turned around. Sergeant Reese, his team leader, lay beside him, his face twisted with pain. "They're in those rocks on the side," Reese said. "Got me in the leg."

"Medic!" Padgett screamed. He fired a magazine into the jagged rocks. Returning bullets flashed back at him. "Sergeant Baird, they're firing from the side too. Get a couple of grenadiers back here."

"Caldwell!" Baird yelled. "Get your squad on these rocks! Get them grenadiers back here."

"Medic!"

The machine-gun fire still came from the cave. Ennis crawled back and slithered in between Padgett and Reese. "Franklin's hit," he said. "Couple others too. Medic'll be back in a minute."

"Fire through those trees," Reese said. "It's too far to throw."

Ennis had an automatic chunker that fired three grenades in rapid succession. One hit a tree, and the other two exploded in the rocks. One man jumped up and started running. Padgett fired, and the man went down. He looked up toward the big rocks as he stuffed in another clip. Captain Webber, Slagel, and Irwin crawled toward the cave. Ennis fired three more grenades.

"Get them two there," Collins said.

Padgett and Collins fired at two more men trying to move in the rocks and dropped them. He loaded another clip, glancing momentarily at Slagel and Irwin, who'd moved ahead of Webber and were crawling around the far side of the big rock.

Dunlap, the medic, scrambled back to the second squad and began to bandage Sergeant Reese's leg. "You okay, Sarge? This ain't nothing. You'll be good as gold in a couple weeks."

"How's it up there, Dunlap?"

"Okay, Sarge. Franklin got it pretty bad. Couple guys in third squad too. There you go. That'll be all right for now."

The fire from the jagged rocks eased up. Padgett's ears rang, and he kept shooting. Ennis fired the last of his grenades and crawled up near the first squad to get Franklin's. Slagel stood right around the corner from the little lip that formed the edge of the cave. The machine gun kept firing. Slagel took one step down on the lip, swung around, and hurled a grenade into the mouth, then jumped back.

Padgett turned as the grenade exploded. A man charged through the trees toward him, no more than forty yards away. He emptied the clip into the man's chest. He faltered, smiled, and kept coming. He gripped a bayonet, but had no gun. He fired another eighteen rounds at the red and khaki shirt, but the man kept coming and smiling. He was thirty feet away when Padgett tossed a grenade in front of him and ducked down behind a tree stump. The explosion was muffled. He looked up. The man lay face down, his back completely gone from the bullets spinning through his body. He was nearly severed at the waist, so that his legs, flopped at an angle beneath the torso, seemed to be running away from his body.

Padgett turned away. Slagel stood on the lip of the cave, firing his M-16 into the dark hole. Everyone else had stopped firing.

"Okay, Slagel," Webber yelled. "That's enough." Slagel fired another burst, then went into the cave. He reappeared, carrying two machine guns, and threw them down so the first squad could get them. He went in twice more and dragged out four dead North Vietnamese soldiers and dropped them down by the guns.

"Ain't nothin' else in here but some rice."

"Okay, come on down," Webber said.

"Good work, Slagel!" Austin yelled. The first squad cheered as Slagel came down from the cave.

Captain Webber walked back to the second and fourth squads. "We're going to check out those rocks. When we get within fifty feet, I want everyone to chuck a grenade in there. Then move up. Wounded stay here."

They took no fire on the way up, and the grenades they

threw exploded like a seven-hundred-and-fifty-pound bomb. In the rocks they found twenty-nine dead North Vietnamese soldiers, most of them badly cut by shrapnel. They took their weapons and ammunition and rejoined the platoon. Two medevac helicopters hovered above them while Franklin, Sergeant Reese, Lovelace and Nelson from the third squad, and Verducci from the fourth were lifted out. Franklin was dead, Lovelace and Verducci both had bad leg wounds, and Nelson was shot through the stomach and seemed to be paralyzed.

4

ORVILLE CHAMBERS sat down on the sandbags in front of his tent at the field base and lit a cigar. Taking off his fatigue jacket, he winced at the sour stench. He'd shower tomorrow. The last two days had been long enough.

The hooches in the hamlet formed themselves blackly against the dark-gray sky, candles flickering and people shuffling back and forth behind small windows. Behind him, across the square of tents, the first squad celebrated yesterday's battle. Thirty-four confirmed kills to one killed, nine wounded. If you kept it in your head like field goals and free throws, cheering probably came easier.

He hadn't known Franklin very well, but the grenadier had been there, in the chow line, in the shithouse, on guard, and now he wouldn't be there anymore. There'd be someone else. Just as there'd be another thirty-four North Vietnamese, including the two or three he'd killed.

"Admiring the architecture of those hooches, Orville?" Slagel handed him a beer. "Why don't you join the party?"

"Don't feel too festive. I hear Webber's putting you in for the Bronze Star."

"You think that's bullshit?"

"I didn't say that. You couldn't have got me up where you were. You deserve it. They killed Franklin. Someone had to stop them."

"Too bad about Franklin. Nelson too. He looked all fucked up. I tell you, Orville, I'd rather be killed than maimed. If I ever get messed up like that, I'm just gonna blow my brains out. Wouldn't you?"

"Hard to say what I'd do. Who's taking Sergeant Reese's slot?"

Slagel brightened. "Maybe they'll give me some sergeant stripes. I could lead a team easy. If they gave me Irwin to fill in Franklin's spot. He's good, even though he's a kid. Lotta heart. He'll keep pushing when the stronger guys are worn out. You'd like him. Come on and have a few with us. I can get all I want. Major Quinn'll probably be over later."

"I'll stay here. I'm beat."

"Okay. See you tomorrow."

He turned and watched Slagel walk away. The swivel-hipped halfback from Ohio State. Slagel had forgotten to ask him how he liked killing.

The soldiers in the first squad cheered as Slagel returned and sang "For He's a Jolly Good Fellow."

Chambers turned away and watched the hamlet again. Since they'd come back from a short mission that morning, he'd been lying around drinking Cokes, trying to read his architecture books, and dozing. He couldn't concentrate on the reading. His memories of the buildings blurred, and figures danced through his head in grotesque combinations—hideous gargoyles overhanging delicate Florentine chapels, austerely frescoed ceilings flooded with baroque drapery and rippling skin. He hadn't felt this nervous in years. Even when Elaine called and said her husband was going to shoot him, he hadn't panicked. Just went to sleep. Joined the Army the next day. So what's the big deal now? Maybe because yesterday was the first real firefight. Takes a day or two for it to sink in. The bullets whining by like angry bees. His head two feet this way, two feet that way, could have been it.

The battle had been bad, but the images he couldn't shake were from the Special Forces camp two weeks ago. And the way the platoon acted afterward. They'd been sober as hell for two or three hours. The voices quieted, and everyone moved more cautiously. But things got right back to normal. The endless chatter about pussy and kicking Charlie's ass started up again, and by afternoon it was as though nothing had happened. It reminded him of an accident he'd seen riding a bus from Fort Leonard Wood to Minnesota after basic training. The traffic slowed as they passed the spot where a bloody man hung out of a mangled car, and another man, his face covered with blood, lay on the pavement beside his wrecked pickup. The traffic moved away more slowly than it had arrived and continued at slow speeds for three or four miles. Then people sped up, and within two more miles everyone was traveling as they had before.

He thought about Dennis Pond busting rock in Leavenworth. Skinny little Pond, who'd first called his attention to the German buildings as they leaned over the ship's railing at Bremerhaven more than a year ago. Pond had been sent to another squadron in their regiment and Chambers never heard of him again until he read the story in the *Overseas Weekly* six months later. Pond had confessed to being a virgin and was ridden mercilessly by the other soldiers in the barracks. Rumor had it that a couple of guys had forced him to blow them. One day at lunch he'd stopped an officer's wife outside the PX, pulled a knife on her, ripped open her blouse, and began stroking her breasts and leering at her with a glassy-eyed, crazy stare. A lieutenant had tackled him from the rear, and after a general court-martial Pond was sentenced to five years in Leavenworth.

Hunger for women. It made guys crazy. Probably more from talking about it than from any need. How could the captain do it? He must have known about the Montagnards. He might have even done it on a bet. The lays were so bad that it wouldn't hurt to keep away for a year or at least wait for a safer time. His whore back in town had only put a bad smell in his head. Jacking off was just as good.

As the sky blackened totally, he thought more about Fulda, about what a fool he'd been to leave. He'd volunteered to be with his friends and so he wouldn't have to watch the slow rot. He hardly talked to Slagel anymore, Morgan was at the base, and with Padgett he'd never felt the easy closeness he had with the others. He'd never known any colored people before joining the Army and had never really thought about them except as athletes or entertainers or people having trouble going to school in the South. Although knowing Padgett had made him feel more, there was just too much of LaMont he couldn't understand.

No slow rot in Vietnam. Bang! and it was over. Or something snapped and you ended up crazy after a month. The weird thing was that he'd been more scared his second night in Fulda than in yesterday's firefight. He'd arrived on a Sunday, slept one night in the transient billets, then moved to Headquarters Troop the next day. He spent that cold, gray December afternoon at the PX and drawing his gear. That evening he stayed in the barracks alone, getting squared away. He went to bed at ten and woke up when the parade started at eleven thirty. First a couple of ordinary drunks, then a few loud stumblebums, then Morgan yelling at the top of his lungs about how fucked everything was while Padgett held him up and egged him on. Shipley had come out of the cooks' room, his drawers soaked with piss, and reeled up and down the hall spewing disjointed fragments about unit pride and clean mess halls.

The storm windows were like double doors between adjoining hotel rooms. A drunk swung one open and vomited against the second window. Slagel walked down the hall beating on wall lockers while hillbillies broke into off-tune country songs. The laughter and screaming reached a hysterical din when a soldier known as the ostrich reeled to his bunk, threw his dustcover over his face, and furiously jacked off.

Some belligerent screaming started up by the stairwell, followed by a loud crashing. He got up to look and found another drunk crumpled and twitching in a pool of vomit at the bottom of the stairs, his head bleeding. Downstairs in the latrine one of the lifer sergeants was passed out on a commode while a group of young soldiers jeered and threw buckets of cold water on him. Two weeks later, when Chambers was charge-of-quarters runner on Saturday night, the same sergeant stumbled into the orderly room at six Sunday morning. As he told stories to another sergeant, a short pellet of shit rolled out of his pants leg, off his shoe, and onto the floor.

Later his first night, after lights out, he heard water splattering against a wall locker down the hall.

"Pop, what are you doin'?" someone yelled.

"Pissin'."

"Get your sorry ass to the latrine!"

"It's closed," Pop said dreamily. The water kept on splashing.

He hadn't fallen asleep until close to reveille that morning. Lying awake, listening to the moanings and gurglings, the curses bellowed from bad dreams, he felt as though he'd been cast in a horror movie that would run for two and a half years. Some nights were worse—people died—others better, but the pattern remained the same for the eleven months until he left.

So strange how his own life had changed for the better in Fulda. He was lucky enough to be assigned as a jeep driver (he'd been trained as a tanker at Fort Knox), a job that gave him privacy and extra time to read. But the place was so dead, and spiritual death lurked all around him. Yet his twelve-year slumber had been interrupted, first by his talks with Morgan, Padgett, and Slagel, then by traveling whenever possible and reading night after night in the small library next to the service club. The friendships had been what he'd prized most, but for a while, after the others began talking about Vietnam, he'd been prepared to sacrifice them to stay in Fulda. Dennis Pond's going nuts changed all that. Feeling he would lose everything if his friends left without him, he volunteered. Now he wondered if he might not lose his friends even while he was with them.

He crept carefully into the tent so as not to wake Todd or knock the candle over. He kept his book on European architecture wrapped in plastic, but it still had the funk on it. The Vietnamese funk was mainly musty and moldy, but whenever it hit him, it smelled like whores and outhouses too. A scorpion crawled over the edge of one of the ammo boxes, and he smashed it with the book. He wiped the smear on his fatigues, blew out the candle, and tucked the mosquito net underneath his sleeping bag.

In the next two weeks he killed two more North Vietnamese in small firefights and got three little hunks of shrapnel in his ass from a North Vietnamese grenade. The pieces were pulled out and he went back to duty. He didn't feel that bad about the killing. If there had been an alternative, he would have taken it. But he had to protect himself. The trouble with being in the rifle platoon was that you had no alternatives. Why not get out? If he stayed in, he'd end up crazy or dead.

Two men besides the cooks worked full time in the mess hall. He found out that they had been in the rifles, but weren't able to go back after the big battle on the Cambodian border. They'd lost their nerve and had been made permanent KP's. In the next two days he uncovered other jobs for those who wouldn't hump anymore. You could pull details back at the base—burn shit, haul garbage, fill sandbags. Or you could become a door gunner in the gunnery platoon or a spotter in the scouts. He couldn't be a KP or a permanent detail man. Too degrading. Always being ordered around to do a bunch of crummy jobs would make you as crazy as a rifleman. He'd try to get a gunner's job. Webber was going on R&R in two days, and the operation would be over by the time he got back, then the whole company would be in base camp for a week. He'd talk to Webber between operations, and hopefully the captain would let him go.

Thinking about transferring as they descended the last ridge of the day, he nearly fell over Todd, who had stooped to tie his boot. Todd motioned him down and whispered, "In the bush. You go around the back."

He backed up two steps, whirled, and ran into the bushes at the side of the path. Todd came around the other side and two men leaped up with their hands in the air. "Sergeant Caldwell!" Todd yelled. The squad leader stopped the platoon, then came back to the bush.

Todd bent down and picked up the thirty-caliber rifle from the ground. He started to frisk the man. "Better search the other one, Orville."

His heart beat furiously, and he didn't know what to do. He felt around the man's waist, chest, and down his legs. Nothing but bones. His black pajamas were crusty, and his skin felt like dried scales. A cowlick stuck up from the back of his head, the hair recently cut. He watched his captors with more fatigue than curiosity on his dirty face. A long black sack of rice hung from his neck, resting on his chest.

The other prisoner, built more strongly than the first, looked at the ground, shaking and sniffling. Probably had malaria. Caldwell had them fold their hands on top of their heads. "They'll march down to the clearing in front of you two," he said. "If they make a move, kill 'em. Fuckin' interpreter was here today, we might get some info."

The lift ships came into view as the platoon got to the clearing. Chambers crouched by a bush with his prisoner, wondering how the hell anyone could live like that. He stared at the Vietcong, embarrassed by a rush of admiration, and looked away. The sky was a nearly crystalline blue, dotted with large white cumulus clouds. As he studied the puffs, he lost the distinct outline where they broke with the sky, and the edges seemed to blur, making it impossible to tell where cloud ended and sky began. The lift ships glided in, noses pulled up and tail booms angled toward the ground like horses being reigned in from a gallop.

"Let's get on!" Caldwell bawled, and the platoon broke from the sides of the clearing and climbed aboard the choppers.

Captain Davis took over the rifle platoon when Webber went to Bangkok. A pilot from the gunnery platoon, he was also an infantry officer. By taking the platoon for five days he could earn his Combat Infantryman's Badge, then go back to flying. Davis had an eager, clean, college boy's face and always did the smart thing. ROTC in college, flight training because it was good for your future—always something to fall back on. He probably organized picnics and surprise parties and kept a budget and had lots of life insurance.

They were fired on the first day out with Davis, and the captain chased through the bushes until he captured the lone enemy. Slagel got his leg knicked by a bullet, but was out for only a day. The platoon stayed in on the fourth day under Davis. At four in the afternoon Austin had them saddle up. "No sweat, men. S-2 thinks they may be building up in the mountains west of the valley, so all we got to do is capture one prisoner, then come back out."

They had been on the ground less than a minute when Chambers spotted a khaki uniform behind a tree right near the edge of the landing zone. He walked out of the squad formation and gestured at the North Vietnamese with his rifle. "Get Cam back here," Staff Sergeant Caldwell yelled. The interpreter came back with Davis and the radio operator. Cam looked absurd—the little head beneath the big steel pot. He and the prisoner jabbered in Vietnamese for a minute.

"He say we surrounded by NVA regiment," Cam said. "He say we surrender, or it all over."

"Shit," Davis said. "What do you think, Sergeant Austin?"

"Hell, sir, we got our prisoner. Let's deedee."

"We're out here now, so we might as well stay awhile." Davis grabbed the radio mike. "Six, this is Blue, over."

"'Roger, Blue."

"Six, we're going due west from the Lima Zulu, over."

"Roger, Blue. Any sign of Charlie down there? Over."

"Negative at this time, Six. Out."

"Roger out."

"We'll keep the prisoner up front, Chambers. I'll let Six know you captured it when we get in."

"Yes, sir." He scowled at Davis, then fell in with the fourth squad. "Sorry bastard didn't even tell Six we had a prisoner," he said to Todd. "Must think this is a hike or something."

"He'll get over it," Todd said. "Take it easy, Orville."

"If he'd told Six we had the prisoner, Six would've had us come out. It's creepy. Prisoner says we're surrounded."

"I reckon he won't keep us out too long. Be dark in a little bit."

A hundred yards west of the landing zone they entered a clearing of soft grass that was overgrown by jungle and couldn't be seen from the air. It reminded him of the pool hid away in the woods back of his father's small farm in Minnesota. He watched Captain Davis, Platoon Sergeant Austin, and Staff Sergeant White go down before he realized what was happening. Then Sergeant Better, Flaherty, and Cam hit the ground. They were in another ambush, front and side, and it sounded like two hundred guns were firing at them. He lay on his face, his right arm burning, and he could feel the blood. He fired two clips into the foliage on his side, then looked up front. Irwin and Arguello fired grenades straight ahead. Slagel lay behind Flaherty, talking on the radio. Dunlap was slumped over Captain Davis.

"I'm going up there," Chambers said. "Those guys are in shit." As he ran into the clearing, blood and leather spattered into his face, and it felt as though a warm snake had raced between his big and second toe. He fell into Slagel.

"They're all dead," Slagel said. "Lift ships are coming back to the LZ. Let's get out of here." Slagel fired two clips to the front, then strapped the radio on his back. The second squad and part of the third were still in the clearing, and at least four of them were dead. "Let's get back to the LZ!" Slagel yelled.

He and Slagel began crawling. The prisoner was right. Also dead, but he had told the truth. Bullets hit the ground all around them. Chambers threw three white phosphorus grenades behind him to set up a smoke screen. "Throw your WP's!" he yelled. "There's no medic, and we've got to get back to the LZ. Leave the dead." What was he doing talking that way? He wasn't in command. But who the hell was?

As soon as the soldiers hit the tree line, they broke into a dead run for the LZ. He and Slagel stopped. Padgett and Irwin had stayed behind and were firing at the other side of the clearing. Todd and Billy Myles, Franklin's replacement, covered the retreat by keeping the side of the ambush pinned down.

"Blue, this is Six," came over the radio.

Slagel grabbed the mike. "Six, this is Slagel. I'm gonna throw some red smoke, and you get some gunnery fire twenty meters west of it and forty meters north. See if you can get some air strikes. Gooks all over. Out." Slagel hung up the mike, stood up, and threw two red smoke grenades into the clearing.

"Look out, Tom!" Padgett yelled. He jumped, pushed Slagel down, and dropped three charging North Vietnamese. "Mother fuck it!" He fell to the ground.

"LaMont, what's wrong?" Slagel said.

"My side, man."

"Can you move?"

"Yeah."

"I'll help you back to the LZ." Slagel put Padgett's arm around his shoulder.

Chambers stepped in front of them and fired three clips across the clearing. He threw two more white phosphorus grenades. The helicopters began firing from above.

"Orville," Todd yelled, "let's git 'fore them choppers hit us."

"Go," he said. They all ran into the LZ as the lift ships hovered down. Slagel and Irwin got on the first squad's ship. As it pulled pitch, Chambers realized that they were the only two who got on. The fire started from the side of the LZ, as intense as at the clearing. The first ship wobbled up into the air and flew away. He ran around to the fourth squad's chopper. There were six men, counting himself, all wounded. They fired into the trees around the LZ as the second squad's ship, carrying Padgett and four other men, got off.

The third squad seemed remarkably intact, its helicopter full. He fired his second-to-last magazine, then boarded his ship. The third bird rose about fifty feet, then jerked sharply, tilted to the side, and fell back toward the ground. Two men fell out before the bird crashed into the earth and exploded.

The fourth started up. He emptied his last clip into the ground, then looked into the front of the ship. Lieutenant Shepard slumped in his seat while Bates, the crew chief, pulled at his harness. The Plexiglas windshield looked like a jigsaw puzzle. Chambers stood up, trying to help Bates with Shepard. The helicopter shook violently. Warrant Officer Christiansen turned to him and Bates. Blood ran out of his mouth, and his flight helmet had been split by a bullet. It looked as though he'd turned to tell them he was going to die.

Bates jumped into Shepard's seat and grabbed the sticks, steadying the ship. Christiansen was out, and Chambers had to pull his hands off the controls. Bates looked at him, face white, and shook his head.

Chambers put on Christiansen's flight helmet and tried to call the field base. The radio was dead. Bates did a good job; they were out of the danger zone. Now he just had to land the thing. They barely cleared the hill near the west end of the field base, then Bates started pushing the collective stick down and pulling back on the cyclic. He got down to about twenty feet, tried to steady it, but the ship kept rocking. Finally he just pushed the collective to the floor.

The chopper bounced once before settling on its skids, and Chambers let go of Christiansen's dead hands and kissed Bates on the top of the head.

5

SLAGEL RETURNED to his tent from the squad leaders' meeting, drop-kicked his helmet into the back, and threw his pistol belt and rifle on the sleeping bag. Three days into a new operation and he was already sick of it. He unbuttoned his fatigue jacket, sat on the sandbags, and rubbed the hairy skin of his belly. Irwin walked up with a stack of letters in one hand, his helmet, full of beer cans, in the other. "Any mail for me?" He rumpled Irwin's hair.

"Beer's for you. How was the meeting?"

"Same old shit." He knew what they'd be saying every night for the next month. Battalion was reconning the mountains from Kontum to Dak To, and every day they'd go a little farther and the flights would last a little longer and maybe they'd be ambushed but most days they'd find nothing.

He had nothing in common with the new squad leaders—all staff-sergeant lifers—and he knew they resented him because he was young and wasn't a lifer and didn't give a shit. They were probably jealous too, knowing he'd been put in for two valor medals. At least he didn't have to sleep in the same tent with them. He wished the new staff sergeant would show up so he wouldn't have the responsibility for the squad. Tomorrow they'd move west across the valley to the mountains that eventually ran into Cambodia. G-2 had reports of communist buildups in the general area; they had reports of communist buildups everywhere. He could let his squad know in the morning. To hell with the new guys, anyway.

C Company had taken sixty-one casualties in Happy Valley, counting pilots and a few guys in the gunnery platoon. Thirty-four killed, twenty-seven wounded, twelve of those bad enough to be sent out of country. He was the only one in the platoon who hadn't been hit.

When the company had gone back to the base camp the next day, he'd gotten drunk and slept for thirty-six hours. For the rest of the week he'd felt like a zombie, going to the hospital to see Irwin, Padgett, and Chambers, talking with Morgan, going to town twice and getting the clap. He was wiped out. Slept twelve hours a night, napped during the day, and just couldn't get any edge on himself.

The replacements had come in at the end of the week, and he'd been glad to help train them. He could get psyched up on the morning flights, but at night, after two or three beers, he was ready for sleep again. He'd been promoted to sergeant after another week, Padgett rejoined the platoon, and they left for Kontum the next day. His new stripes raised his spirits; so did having Irwin and Padgett back. He'd been glad to start a new operation.

Chambers had been the only drag. He'd sat in his hospital bed looking ready to explode. He quit the rifle platoon, told Webber he could court-martial him if he wanted, but he wasn't going out again. Webber transferred him to gunnery, and for the last few days before they went to the field he'd been training as a door gunner. At night he was quiet and sullen, keeping to himself or smoking dope while the others talked.

So the operation was turning into a bust. He'd thought that being a squad leader would be fun. Being a platoon guide at Fort Dix, both in basic and infantry school, had been pretty good, especially in basic when Morgan and Padgett were platoon guides too. They'd all gone to training leadership school for two weeks after basic, but Morgan and

Padgett quit. Those two played the jackass all through infantry school, but he'd been interested in the weapons and the field problems and tactics, and he loved to test his endurance on the marches. The guys were scummier than they'd been in basic, but he beat the shit out of the first one that messed with him, and after that everything was cool.

During last week's training, the replacements had shown some heart, and they'd given him respect on the rifle range and at the rappelling tower. But once they got in the field everything changed. He hadn't felt scared as he'd imagined, but he could sense it in the others, and it made him mad. The spirit of the old squad couldn't be recaptured. He knew it would take time to build, but a lot of the new guys he plain didn't like. They were even physically different from the old guys—smaller, with baby fat on their faces. He wasn't going to make friends with any of them.

Captain Webber was all fucked up. He'd taken the responsibility for Davis' foolishness and acted like a baby, apologizing to everyone all the time. He lacked spirit too and feared for the platoon. The first two nights of the operation Webber had had Slagel down to his tent, telling him how uncertain he was. That wasn't right. He should talk with Major Quinn. A good coach didn't tell his team that they were going to lose.

The whole business was just like fucking football. Right when it started to get good, it turned sour. What he'd really liked about playing at State was the worldliness it gave him. For a kid off the farm sports was a great opportunity to meet different people, to travel, and to build confidence too. The women had helped with that, falling all over him most of the time. What irked him was that the attention wasn't for himself, but for his cleats or his jockstrap or his picture in the paper. And once you realized *that*, the whole thing got boring and all crapped up. He was beginning to think that combat was as big a crock as tossing the pigskin around.

The lack of enthusiasm during the next week made him feel as though the platoon was walking through chest-high mud. Even the helicopters seemed sluggish. The men in his squad trudged along, barely awake, and he couldn't say a thing. Webber was like a ghost. Platoon Sergeant Trapp, the hulking fatty, acted half dead. The jungle itself loomed silent and heavy, offering no sign of the enemy. The sound of their endless, tired walk sickened him, as did the continual popping of rotor blades above the jungle canopy.

On the tenth day out he nearly told everyone where to go. As he walked up and down the squad, checking each man, he fixed on their physical defects. Half the fuckers wore glasses. Soft and pasty, their faces had sprouted ugly little sweat pimples. They probably had shit stains in their underwear. They were so pathetic that once he laughed out loud, but mostly he fumed, almost hoping for an ambush so he could watch the babies panic and squeal as they were blown away.

Climbing up the ridge that morning had been rough. After eating their C rations and starting down another ridge, they discovered three storage hooches in a small ravine. Webber led the first squad down to search them. A little bit of rice in each one—about half a ton altogether—and no documents.

"Okay, Tom," Webber said. "You and your new men blow them up."

"Roger, sir. First squad, everyone take one WP and one frag grenade. Pick a hooch and toss the frag in first, and after it explodes, throw the Willie Peter on top of it. Duck after you throw them, and don't hit any trees two feet in front of you. Get to it. We ain't got all day." He stood behind them to watch. The phosphorus grenades spit fire and smoke, and as the straw began to crackle with flames, the squad started out of the ravine. When no one was looking, he lobbed another WP onto the far fire. The squad hit the dirt when it went off, and he burst into a guffaw.

Webber turned and shook his head.

"Just keeping them on their toes, sir. You greenhorns got to watch out for secondary explosions."

In another hour they were two-thirds of the way down the

ridge, plodding dully as before. No one appreciated his throwing the grenade. The old squad would've got a good laugh out of it. Even Webber would have, a month ago. Bunch of draggy-assed fools he was stuck with now. He could always make believe. That's how he'd gotten through the dull times in Germany. Pretend that the situation demanded the utmost concentration. Guard duty had always been bad in Fulda, especially in winter. Walking around the motor pool or on the road at the airfield where the wind blew like crazy. Blizzards and drizzles all the time. The only way he'd made it was to imagine leading a squad through some horrible situation. Walking across Manchuria or Siberia, where every man was about to crack physically and mentally. But he stayed strong, his frostbitten toes wrapped in rags, digging in the snow for frozen roots to eat.

Suddenly the entire platoon stopped. He dropped to one knee. The crashing in the jungle down from the ridge nearly drowned the noise from the helicopters circling above. Webber grabbed the radio mike. "Four-one, this is Blue, over."

"Roger, Blue."

"Four-one, we got something a hundred meters north of our position. Can you see anything?"

The sound of the helicopter increased as it made two low passes on the treetops, then diminished as the chopper rose again.

"Blue, this is Four-one. We can't see anything on the deck. Trees are too thick. We can barely see you, over."

"Roger, Four-one. I'm going to throw smoke, and I'd like some fire a hundred to three hundred meters north of it. Then I'll send a squad in there."

"Roger, Blue. Fire on the way."

Webber threw a smoke grenade into the jungle. "Everybody get down so those gunships don't blow your heads off." He squatted and leaned against a tree. "Slagel, you want to take your squad in there?"

"Yes, sir. What do you think it is? Sounded like a whole bunch of them trying to deedee out of here."

"I don't want you going more than four hundred meters. And watch for booby traps, punji stakes, and tunnels. It might be a decoy."

"Don't worry." He grinned at Webber, then stuck his fingers in his ears as the machine guns clattered overhead. Rockets roared in the jungle. The tension in the air woke everyone. What they needed was a little taste of action to get the lard out of their heads. The chase ship made its run, then both choppers went over again.

"Four-one, this is Blue," Webber said when the guns quit firing.

"Roger, Blue."

"I'm sending a squad in now."

"Roger, Blue. We'll keep them covered. Out."

The acrid smell of burning phosphorus permeated the jungle, and thin wisps of smoke hung on the leaves as though they were emissions from the plants. Both Webber and Trapp had stayed behind. He'd have to take care of the dirty work himself. He couldn't rely on Webber anymore. He moved the squad quickly over a hundred yards, then stopped them and listened. Nothing. Another hundred yards and again nothing. The freshly broken branches told him that they were on the track, but the thick ground cover showed no footprints.

Fifty yards more and he spotted blood glistening on the dark-green, shiny leaves. The gunships had been on target. Blood all over the place. Four or five of them might be hit, or maybe a couple were dead and being dragged out by their comrades. He stepped over a small tree that had been sheared off by a rocket and stopped the squad again to listen. Something rustled faintly, then crashed in a clump of bushes fifty yards in front of them. He gestured for the squad to fan out, then moved them forward slowly. A soft swishing rose from the bushes, then nothing but the sound of the creeping squad.

It must be some kind of trap. He'd make the first plunge, before they had a chance to open fire. He didn't give a shit, anyway, and it would be good for the others to see him in action, unafraid. Ten feet in front of the bushes he halted the squad behind the cover of some trees.

"What do you think, Tom?" Irwin whispered.

"Don't know. I'm going to jump in that bush and open fire. You hold the squad down till you know what's happening. If they get me, blast hell out of them, and don't try to get me back. Pass the word."

"Okay, man. Be careful."

"No sweat." He put an extra clip of bullets in his left hand so he could reload quickly. He flipped the selector switch from semi to automatic, then started forward. What the fuck did it matter? The gooks in the bushes were going to know that Tom Slagel had been there. He heard heavy breathing behind the dense green cover, then he thought it must be himself. His leg muscles tensed as he prepared to lunge forward, then he heard the breath again. It stopped for an instant, filling the air with an electric silence, then a deafening trumpet roar tore through the jungle. He fired into the bushes, reloaded, leaped, and fired again.

The elephant lay on its side, trunk curled inward toward its gaping, flappy-lipped mouth. The slate-colored, blood-streaked side heaved violently, shoving gurglings and groanings into the heavy jungle air. A fucking elephant. What could he say? He looked toward the squad; happily, he couldn't see them. The elephant gasped and the legs stiffened on the top side of its body. The side itself expanded, the skin tightening like rotten gray rubber. It exhaled in a high-pitched gurgle. The legs collapsed, the side fell in, and the entire mammoth body lay still.

"Slagel, you all right?" Irwin yelled.

"I'm okay," he said quietly.

"Tom, you all right? Answer if you hear me."

"I'm all fucking right!"

"We're coming up."

He turned and stepped out of the bushes and met them a few feet beyond.

"What was it?" Irwin asked.

"Just an animal."

"An animal? What kind?"

"See for yourself." Let the kids get a kick out of it. He moved away and leaned against a tree. When they laughed, he nearly exploded. What the fuck did they know? It could have been an ambush and gotten all their cherry asses killed.

Irwin came out of the bushes shaking his head. "Damn, Tom, that must've scared you."

"Shit! What are those fuckers doing in there?"

"A couple of them are cutting the tusks off."

He strode into the bushes where Brady and Lynch tore at the skin around one tusk with their bayonets. "Okay, let's go. You clowns want to look at elephants, you can go to the zoo back in the world. Let's move out."

Brady looked up at him through his glasses. "C'mon, Sarge. It'll just take a second."

"Brady, you want me to carry you out of here? This is a war, not no fucking souvenir hunt. Now move your ass out!"

"Jesus Christ!" Brady threw his bayonet into the elephant's side.

Slagel leaped on the elephant, facing the fat private. "If you want to throw something, why don't you throw me? You want to try that?"

"I guess not," Brady said.

"No, I guess not. Now sheathe that bayonet and haul your tubby little ass back up that hill."

He kept hearing them laugh as they moved up to the ridge, and he walked faster and faster, hoping to wear them out. But the muffled whispering and sniggering persisted, spreading out through the whole platoon after the squad joined them. Even in the helicopter every sound seemed directed at him, and he stared straight out the door, not wanting to look at anyone.

Back at the field base both Webber and Major Quinn commended him for running down the elephant. The enemy was known to use them as movers of supplies, so perhaps they'd been slowed down a little. Webber and Quinn laughed as he walked away.

After chow he took his beer out beyond the helipad on the

west end of the perimeter, near one of the small ammunition dumps. He had to get calmed down. If he stayed in the platoon area, someone was going to get his shit busted up. The anger stormed in his blood, and he knew it would go on for days unless he talked himself out of it.

Nothing you ever did was enough; that's what really pissed him off. The harder you tried, the more fucked over you got. Who'd have been brave enough to do what he did today? Still they all laughed him down. Same in football when he finally got up the balls to quit; the coaches just mocked him, told him he didn't have the brains to make it any other way. Maybe his IQ wasn't the highest in the territory, but at least he'd tried to study and learn, until Susie and old Dr. Bowen had laughed him out of that in their way.

And his fucking father too. Old man never could get ahead with his potatoes and small dairy farm in New Jersey, but he'd always been proud of his strength as a man, always urged his son to be strong because that was the only thing you could rely on. Their only contact had come in the form of strength contests, his father always winning, always belittling his weakness. Until Tom turned sixteen and beat his father arm wrestling in the barn one spring afternoon. His father couldn't believe it and kept trying again and getting beat. Slagel lifted heavier bags of potatoes too, then had to hold his father back from an all-out brawl. Slagel thought his father would be proud of his strength, but the old man only laughed at him, told him it meant nothing, and that for all his strength the kid would always be too stupid to run the farm.

His father had cared little for football, and as he got better, his father cared less. The bastard had never given him credit for anything, but this was too much. After the nationally televised last game of the season, in which he'd made a touchdown and three other good runs, he'd called home. He listened to his mother's praise, then his father bellowed that he'd gotten dead drunk before the game, passed out, and didn't see a play. Furthermore, he didn't give a shit. Slagel told his father that he hoped he'd die, then tore the pay phone off the wall.

The next spring, after things got good with Susie and Dr. Bowen, he'd made up with his father. His parents were going to drive out after exams, meet Susie, and take him home for the summer. It would have been perfect if Susie and the doctor hadn't fucked him over in the middle of finals. He was so crazy and ashamed that his main feeling had been relief when his mother's sister called to tell him that his parents had been killed in an auto accident coming across Pennsylvania on their way to pick him up. He caught a plane to Newark and never went back to Columbus again.

He threw his beer can from where he sat, and it bounced on the hard earth and tinkled against the concertina wire of the perimeter.

"You better pick that can up, soldier."

He raised his middle finger and held it behind his head.

"The great white hunter's got damn insubordinate."

He raised his other middle finger, stood, and turned around. "Okay, I don't need you guys on my ass too."

"What you doin' out here?" Padgett asked. "We've been looking all over for you."

"I'm staying away from that fucking platoon so I don't hurt anyone."

"You sound serious," Chambers said.

"I am."

"Hey, man, what's the matter?"

"Come on, LaMont, you heard them out there today, laughing their sorry asses off."

"They weren't laughing at you. I was laughing my damn self."

"What for? I didn't see anything funny about it."

"The elephant, man. The elephant was funny, you weren't."

"Shit." He knew that everyone thought he was stupid.

"Seriously, Tom," Chambers said. "No one's laughing at you. I heard a couple of them were mad because you wouldn't let them take the tusks, but most of them think you were damn brave to go in there."

"That's what they're talkin' back in the platoon," Padgett said. "Most of them are just happy Charlie wasn't there."

"I wish Charlie had been there to wake those clowns up. That platoon's sorry now, LaMont."

"You got to give them some time, man. We were sorry at first too."

"Something about these new guys isn't right."

"Tell you one thing," Padgett said. "We been in almost two years and I'll bet none of these dudes been in over six months. They was probably all drafted too, and none of them asked to come over here like me and three other fools I know."

"Right," Chambers said. "Probably a lot of them came right from home."

"I'm hip to that," Padgett said. "Didn't have no year in no Fulda to get their heads all nasty."

"Okay, okay. But the spirit's down, and that doesn't help in combat. Even Webber's lost his balls."

"He's probably still shook from what happened while he was gone," Chambers said. "It must have screwed him up."

"It screwed us all up, but if you can't cut it, you get out. I don't hold it against you, Orville. It'd be worse if you stayed and didn't do things right." Maybe Chambers was the only one of them with any sense. He sure as hell wasn't a coward, but if he thought something was stupid, he quit doing it. Slagel had given some thought to getting out—being a door gunner could be interesting—but besides his experience with the platoon, he just plain liked the infantry.

"Webber has been half-steppin'," Padgett said. "But what can you do?"

"You guys could probably get out."

"Shit," Slagel said. "Platoon would fall apart if we did. I wouldn't feel right about it, anyway. That might sound crazy, but I can't help it. If that had been Charlie today and I hadn't been there, the whole squad would've probably screwed up.

I'm not such great shakes, but those are some sorry troops. Shit on it, anyway." He pulled out some joints and they all smoked before going back to the company area.

When he got to the tent, Irwin was lying on top of his sleeping bag, writing a letter.

"Hey, Tom, where you been?"

"Out on the perimeter, feeling shitty about today." He slid into the tent and leaned on his elbow, propping up his head and facing Irwin.

"That elephant really got to you, huh?"

"Too much, I guess. I'm sorry I've been acting funny. This whole operation's brought me down. I talked to Chambers and Padgett tonight, and I think I'm snapping out of it."

"I thought you'd been acting a little weird, but I didn't want to bother you about it."

"It's okay, buddy. Those new guys were bugging me, but I guess they're pretty young. I'll have been in two years before long."

"It's changed a lot back in the world since you came in."

"You ain't said shit! I used to read magazines in Germany all the time—*Life, Look, Time*—and they made me think the world was going crazy. Then I got back to my hometown in Jersey and it was the same old dead little place. I figured things hadn't changed that much until we stayed three days in Berkeley with Morgan's friends before leaving. Shee-it! I'd have felt more at home in South America. And I've been around. A couple of them even offered to hide me out so I wouldn't have to come here. I had a good time, but I was happy when I got on the plane to this puke hole."

"I was glad to leave too. I just wanted to get away from everything. Service is good for that."

"That's most affirmative." When he'd come back to Jersey after his parents' death, he'd tried to make a go of it with the farm. His father's ghost plagued his dreams, laughing at him and telling him he couldn't do it. What a fucking drag. Harvesting that fall, planting the next spring, harvesting and planting again, all the time milking the cows and shoveling their shit and worrying about Puerto Ricans lousing up their jobs. Besides, he had to get his sister through high school and her nursing program at Trenton State.

After the third harvest he stayed drunk for a week, then straightened out the books and sold the whole mess. By the time he was done with taxes, giving his sister her share and setting her up in an apartment, he had five grand left to blow. And he blew it too. Florida, Mardi Gras, Mexico, California. Some nice broads and some good times, but the money went fast. He was nearly broke when he got back to his aunt's in Trenton, and after lying around there for a week, he sold his car and paid his visit to the friendly recruiter. Was promised Europe and got it. Oh, yeah! Part of Europe he never cared to see again. He couldn't remember any place he'd been that he really wanted to go back to.

6

MORGAN LEFT S-1 at five, trotting down the road to his tent. He couldn't believe that he'd finally leveled the mountain of paperwork that had been on his desk since C Company's big battle. Division casualty section had balled up the records, and he'd spent three days checking his book against theirs, then making sure awards and decorations had all the information so everyone would receive his Purple Heart. Then came the award citations. C Company's clerk had gone to the field as a door gunner, and his replacement could barely type. Morgan had ended up doing all the citations, some of them three times when the recommending officers changed their minds. He'd had to do four aircraft-accident reports, each requiring about twenty complex forms, plus the usual round of correspondence, officer-efficiency reports, and filing the endless regulations and directives and circulars from Department of the Army, MAAG, MACV, USARV, USARPAC, and from division itself. He was going to buy stock in a paper company when he got out of the service.

"Overhead, ten-shun!" He walked through the flaps of his tent, the losers' tent, where they'd stuck him because there'd been no room for him anywhere else. PFC Alexander and Sergeant Winston faced each other from two cots at the end of the tent, beer in their hands, a quart of Imperial on the dirt between them.

"Go ahead on and get you a taste, Morgan," Alexander said. "I see you eyein' the jug."

"I could use it."

"Get you a beer to chase it with."

He dug in the huge gray metal cooler next to Alexander's cot, found a beer, and sat down. He gasped on the whiskey, then cooled his throat with Budweiser.

"Shit's out of sight," Winston said, tucking a green towel beneath the collar of his fatigue jacket. His black face gleamed with sweat. Morgan didn't know his story, only that he'd been a squad leader in D Company and had gone "combat happy" in Ia Drang Valley. That could mean anything from turning chicken to killing forty prisoners.

Alexander, formerly a squad leader in B Company, had murdered a prisoner in Ia Drang and had been busted to corporal. After his helicopter crashed, he couldn't face getting on another one and had threatened to murder his platoon sergeant if he made him. He'd been busted to PFC and now drove for Major Stubbs. He made no secret of his fear.

The other seven men in the tent were quiet and secretive, and all had formerly been in combat and now did menial tasks around the battalion. Morgan was the tent joke as he worked more hours per week than the other nine men combined.

He loved Overhead. Every night friends of Winston and Alexander came down, and by the time Morgan finished work, the tent was wild with music and drunkenness and shit-talking. It had taken a few weeks for the others to accept him, but now he joined in, swilling liquor and running down the S-1 follies for the day.

He and Alexander went over to the new wooden mess hall. Stubbs had received thirty-two flags, which hung around the walls. A partition in the back shielded the officers' mess. The division had no refrigerators yet, and the support command wouldn't send them fresh meat. They'd had beef stew every night for the last two months except for one day when the cooks had slaughtered some chickens from the town and another when they'd killed a water buffalo and made leathery steaks. He looked at the stew as it slopped into his mess kit, then at Alexander, then motioned to the side door. They walked out and dumped the stew in the garbage, went down to the club, and had three bags of potato chips and two beers each for dinner.

Walking back to S-1, he could see Captain Greene, the adjutant, busily flipping through papers on the counter. The serious look on his long face meant nothing but trouble.

"Glad you're back, Morgan." Greene pulled nervously at his bristly black handlebar. "We've got a lot of work to do, starting right now."

"I just finished a lot of work, sir. I thought I was due for some slack time."

"Sorry about that, Morgan. The colonel was just here, and we're having an awards ceremony in a week. We've got to get all these awards separated by companies. Sorting the Air Medals alone will take two days. It'll be a combination memorial service for the dead, then the CG'll pin on the medals. Should be very impressive."

"So what do we have to do now?"

"Break down the medals by companies, then alphabetically by rank. We'll keep three-by-five cards on each person, especially for the Air Medals. Some people will get as many as ten, with more coming after that. I know you've been working hard, Morgan, but we've got to get this done. Once battalion's gone to the field again, you'll get plenty of time off."

"You're the boss, sir." He tried to get mad, but couldn't. Greene took it all so seriously, believed in it so much, that it would be like getting mad at a Jehovah's Witness. He wasn't at all like Stubbs; he didn't suck ass, wasn't a politicker, he worked hard and believed in the Army—and in all its rules and regulations. Stubbs signed anything you put in front of him; Greene read it all, slowing down the efficiency of the office. Morgan felt sorry for him. He'd been passed over for major once—pretty bad for a West Pointer—probably because he followed the rules instead of licking butt. Greene, pilot and infantry officer, really wanted to get out in the field and fight, but his duties were more important than his desires, so he seldom complained.

The next week's work was relentless. Sorting the awards seemed endless, and as soon as they'd get caught up, in would come another batch from division. With reading and typing so much on valor and heroism, Morgan couldn't help but fantasize. Would he stand on the skids, firing his machine gun over the pylons like Webster and McCutcheon in C Company? Charge the enemy in caves like Slagel? Face down attacking NVA's like Padgett and Chambers?

He recalled the accolades for bravery they'd all received when leaving Fulda for the war. Now his friends were getting Purple Hearts for wounds, Bronze Stars for valor, Air Medals for combat assault hours flown. As usual, he pushed the paper, typing things perfectly. Sometimes, in Overhead at night, he eyed the pistol belt and rifle and steel pot gathering dust beside his cot. Maybe he would get in the shit someday.

He had felt so useless at the hospital after the Happy Valley battle. Sitting there with the wounded, listening to Slagel talk with them, he didn't know what to say, when to be serious, when light. He wanted to join in the talk, be a part of it, but it would have been like a bench warmer hugging a regular who'd made a game-winning play. Whenever he'd tried to grin, his lips had felt like dried spaghetti.

By nine the last night they were nearly finished when Greene called for a break. "Morgan, why don't you get us some beer."

"My pleasure, sir. I'll even buy." It felt good to be finished. They'd worked methodically, and Greene had pitched in more than any other officer would have. Stubbs hadn't done a thing. They had a small pile of posthumous awards to be sent with letters to next of kin, another pile for the wounded in hospitals out of country, and a third stack for those at the ceremony. The citations for the valor medals were to be read aloud, but the Air Medals and Purple Hearts were just on sets of orders. Every wound got a Heart, from a cut on the finger to losing both legs.

Slagel was leaning on the counter when he got back. "What's happening, Morg? Guess whose chest is light?"

"Hope you didn't get the clap again."

"Lot of guys in C Company got it."

"Soldiers all over division have it," Greene said. "It's getting out of hand. They'll probably put town off limits before too long."

"It's some filthy puke hole now," Slagel said. "Old whores smell like they been dipped in shit. Morg, you ain't been there for a long time, huh?"

"Nope. They better not close it before I get down again. My chest is so heavy my ass is getting small. Maybe we can get you another Purple Heart for the clap."

"Shit. So they're having the big ceremony. What's Davis getting?"

"A Bronze," Greene said.

Slagel snorted. "Maybe I ought to protest, Morgan, like your buddies back there in Berkeley."

"Why not?" It seemed like a good idea.

"Okay," Greene said. "The guy's dead, after all."

"So's a lot of others, sir," Slagel said. "But I guess since they were enlisted they didn't get no medals, did they?"

"Morgan, time to go back to work," Greene said. "We'll see you later, Slagel."

"Yes, sir!" Slagel snapped to attention. "Later, Morg." He disappeared into the darkness, then guffawed from over by the officers' tent.

Greene left for the colonel's hooch to discuss the ceremony with him and the chaplain. He came back as Morgan finished sorting the last of the awards.

"All set to go, sir."

"Good. I've got a few more things for you to do, Morgan. Some tonight, some in the morning. I'm afraid you'll have to get up at five thirty."

"But the ceremony's not until eight."

"I know, Morgan. Just cool down. You'll have to make a couple of runs in the jeep, and then it'll take some time to get set up."

"What do I have to get?" He slapped the counter in frustration.

"Seven steel pots with clean camouflage covers for the memorial ceremony. One for each five dead men. You can take Major Stubbs' writing table to the parade field for the helmets. We'll need the guidons from each company, then the medals, plus one copy of all orders and all citations. We'll give the men their certificates and boxes for the medals after the ceremony. Also, you'll pick up a microphone and two speakers at S-4. You might want to do some of it tonight, but I want everything set up by seven fifteen so we can make sure it's right."

"Jesus Christ! Okay, sir. I'll be back later."

Driving down the battalion road to S-4, he wanted to floor the jeep and drive it through a tent or an orderly room. They never laid off. Always some last shitty detail. Screw it. He'd get a drink before he did anything more.

Alexander and Sergeant Winston sat on their cots by the

cooler. A half gallon of Boord's gin stood on the dirt floor, flanked by two canteen cups of ice water. "Hey, Morg," Alexander said. "You just in time for some gin and ice water."

"Lay it on me before I go crazy."

"Drink gin 'cause it ain't no sin," Sergeant Winston said.

"How do you like that, Morgan?" Alexander asked.

He gasped, put his hand on his chest, and shook his head. "Good shit." He drank from the bottle again, then took two long swallows of ice water.

"They driving you over the edge?"

"You ain't said shit, Alex. They act like this ceremony was the most important thing since D Day."

"They got any awards for Overhead? Any tent drink all this liquor ought to get something."

"Overhead get the Purple Shaft with horseshit cluster," Winston said. He lay down and wiped his face with the towel. "Overhead like a sore dick, Morgan. You can't beat it."

"Most defecatingly, Sarge."

He took their steel pots and his own and left. He picked up four more at S-4, along with microphone and speakers, and left the whole mess in his jeep at S-1.

Before going to bed, he drank another half pint plus two beers, and when the charge of quarters woke him at five thirty, he could barely navigate. He stumbled through the darkness to the water trailer behind the mess hall and hung his head beneath the spigot while the cold water hit it and trickled off in the dirt. He smoked a cigarette on the way to S-1, and soon his anger had him awake.

He turned on the light in the front of the tent, rattled the ashtray on the counter, then coughed, until he heard Greene turn over and groan in his sleeping bag behind the bamboo partition. The captain walked into the front as he revved up the jeep. "Morning, sir!" he shouted.

"Are you coming back for the table, Morgan?"

"Yes, sir. And for the guidons and the rest of that stuff. Jeep won't hold it all." He backed out of the parking space, then eased over to the battalion road and turned left up the hill. The jeep bounced and creaked in the ruts and on the rocks. He wheeled around the NCO Club, past A Company's mess hall, shifting into four-wheel drive where the road steepened by A Company's officers' hooches. He stopped the jeep and put it in first gear so it would whine while he drove through the area. He shifted back to second and two-wheel drive when the ground leveled off by the officers' club. A small road, barely wide enough for the jeep, ran between the club and an embankment, and he nearly hit the wooden wall as he moved on to the clearing behind the club. The last time he'd been up here was on a brush-cutting detail six weeks ago, when they'd cleared the area for a small parade field. He parked the jeep, dropped the load on the south side of the clearing, then headed back for the other things.

The sky was graying when he arrived with the second load, and from the back of the club he could look east over the seventy-five yards of clearing to where it ended in a tangle of bushes and small trees. A hundred yards beyond that the first line of bunkers began—one every fifty yards in a belt around the division base. The guards standing by them looked like small statues. Concertina wire coiled in front of the bunkers, then more barbed wire stretched tautly six inches above the ground, then the minefield, the white lookout towers studded with floodlights, and more wire complexes in lines and circles and rectangles. A good fifty yards separated the first bunkers from the tree line outside the last wire fortification, and any invader ran a good chance of being blown to bits by the claymores.

He took the five guidons out of the jeep and threw them like spears over to the south side of the clearing. Two of them ricocheted off steel pots; the other three stuck in the ground. Getting Stubbs' table in the jeep had been bad enough, but now it was jammed and wouldn't come out. He tried to ease it, but no luck. Then he pushed hard, quitting when the wood began to give. He felt suddenly weak, and his breath came fast. "Shit!" He kicked the tire of the jeep. He walked around to the other side and discovered the slim leg pinned between the seat and the metal wall. He pried it loose and carried the table over to the helmets and set it down, cursing Stubbs and Greene.

He placed the seven steel pots on the teakwood surface. One for each five dead men. Except one was for only four dead men. Too bad another one hadn't been zapped so they'd have an even thirty-five. He took one of the speakers fifteen feet to the east of the table, and as he carried the second to the other side, he tripped on the cord and fell, bruising his knee on the gray metal rim. "Cocksucker!" he yelled. Tears rushed to his eyes and he whimpered childishly for a few seconds. He hated the dead soldiers, the brave ones, all the sorry fuckers that had anything to do with this. Viciously he stuck the guidons in the ground by the table. He worked as hard as anyone, and what did he get for it? Shit. More work. After placing the microphone on the table, he pulled the three cords up by the club where they'd be hooked to extensions. He got in the jeep, then climbed out again and sat on a tree stump on the north side of the clearing.

All the movement and the banging metal had kept him from hearing the quiet. So strange, with no sounds coming from objects made by human beings. He bent forward, squinting, trying to hear better. Nothing but his breathing and an occasional spurt of fire from his cigarette. He rubbed his feet in the grass, then stopped and listened. Dead silence. He leaned back and exhaled smoke straight into the air. It dispersed and faded out of sight. A cloud drifted to the west, then he felt the rotation of the earth, and it seemed as if he were turning down a big hill. The earth turned down farther, revealing a dazzling crescent of the sun that grew slowly, igniting metal and thousands of droplets of moisture all around. His insides warmed slowly, dissolving the brittle petty meanness of last night and this morning.

Across two miles of lush vegetation beyond the perimeter the sun glinted off aluminum roofs in the town. Fucked-up starving people living like animals. And here he was hating a soft job, even thinking now and then about going into combat. Complaining about being a clerk—about being safe and doing no direct harm—was stupid and childish. As stupid and childish as admiring and envying the heroes and the wounded. No, he was too smart for that, too smart to let Greene and Stubbs and the Army drive him to desperation. He could last another eight months as a clerk. He'd lasted nearly two years in uniform already.

He did the rest of his jobs before the ceremony cheerfully, and once it started, he climbed a small knoll on the north side of the clearing to watch. What a sorry, shabby spectacle. Some of the old-timers in C Company were visibly shaken as the chaplain read the names of the dead. A feeling of awe returned as Chambers, Padgett, and Slagel received their awards, and he turned away from them and looked at the group of soldiers as a whole. Dirty, wrinkled fatigues, hollow faces, standing there getting primed with another shot of bullshit before going into the slaughter again. If you gave a man a medal, you didn't have to say that he had died or been wounded for absolutely nothing.

Captain Greene came over to him as the men began marching down the hill. "Get your ass down to S-1, Morgan, so you can give out the medal boxes and certificates."

"Yes, sir." He looked steadily and serenely at Greene. The captain wouldn't ruffle him anymore.

The men had to stand aside as he drove the jeep down the road. A few observed loudly that only clerks got to ride in jeeps, but it didn't bother him.

Down at S-1 he gave Chambers, Padgett, and Slagel their boxes and certificates, and they agreed to meet that night. The other soldiers filed in, and as he passed out the boxes, he decided not to get drunk anymore. A hard decision, especially in Overhead, but those guys knew how booze could ruin you, so they'd probably leave him alone. He'd stay at S-1 nights, reading and exercising. He was getting pretty weak. Maybe he'd quit smoking too, although that might be going too far.

The last man left, and he leaned on the counter, lost in a reverie about his future ascetic life. Suddenly Greene strode through the entrance and banged his hands flat on the counter. "Let's go, Morgan. Get up on the hill and bring that stuff down. You don't have time to stand around."

"Okay, sir. I was just handing out the boxes."

"No one's here now!" Greene snapped. "Get moving."

"Yes, sir." He'd never seen Greene so ticked. Jealous of the medals? Screw it. Greene could deal with his own problems.

When he brought the table into the tent, Major Stubbs looked up from a chair, his cheeks bulging with crackers and cheese. "Oh, thank you, Morgan," he mumbled. "Just bring it back here. Beautiful ceremony. You people certainly did a good job planning it."

"Thank you, sir." He turned to leave, disgusted that Stubbs had received a Bronze Star for Meritorious Service.

"Oh, Morgan, I want you to run an errand for me. The box my medal came in is a little messed up inside. Looks like water stains or something. We don't have any more here, so I want you to take it to division and get it exchanged. Anytime today is okay."

"Yes, sir. I'll do it right now." And fuck them all, too. They'd be lucky if he came back. He walked out of the tent. His head pounded, and he felt as if he might cry out with rage.

At Overhead he found Alexander opening a bottle of vodka. "Little taste, Morgan?" He handed him the bottle.

"Thanks. Fucking Stubbs. I'd like to kill him." He took two swallows.

"You and a hundred others."

"Christ, he can piss you off. Give me a beer, Alex. I've got to go to division for that sack of shit." He drank greedily, finishing in two minutes, then left for a fresh box.

Greene kept on him the rest of the afternoon, having him

run silly errands, sweep and dust the office. Any of it could have been done another day. He drank four beers in Overhead before dinner, and between five thirty and seven he had trouble keeping quiet. When Greene finally let him go, the beer had worn off, leaving him tired and depressed. After more whiskey at Overhead, he joined the others in the club.

"You're not looking too good," Chambers said. "What's the matter?"

"Same old shit. Bastards won't leave me alone."

"You got it tough," Slagel said.

"Talk your shit! You don't know what it's like up there."

"I don't know what it's like, he says." Slagel grinned at the others.

"Well, you don't. Fuck it. I'm getting some beer."

He brought five cans back to the table. "Look, Slagel, you saw what it was like last night. How would you like that shit twelve hours a day?"

"Okay, okay. I know it's bad, but so is everything else. We gotta go back to the field tomorrow."

"I don't see any of you getting out either. Chambers may switch jobs, but he's still in it."

"I can't type either," Chambers said.

"You could burn shit or work in the mess hall."

"You know I couldn't do that."

"It makes you crazy, right? Just like this clerking is making me crazy. Combat probably doesn't make you that nuts."

"Lighten up, Morg," Padgett said. "This is our last night together for a while. No need to be talking all this shit."

He drank an entire can without taking it from his lips, then slammed it on the thin metal table top. None of the others looked at him. "Well, pardon my motherfucking ass! I'm sorry I upset your delicate constitutions before you go blow away a bunch of people and get shit hung all over your chests for it. Maybe I'll go drink by myself so I won't bother you war heroes." He walked away from the table, stopped at the bar for three more beers, then pushed through the plastic strips in the doorway and stepped into the night. They could come and get him if they wanted.

He walked up on the little knoll by the S-4 tent and drank one beer, watching the doorway of the club. No one came out after him. He felt only the pounding in his head and the burning in his chest. He sat and leaned against a tree and drank the other cans. He wouldn't go back to the club to get any more. Screw them. He rocked on his behind, tapping the back of his head against the tree. He hit it harder two times, then increased the force until his vision blurred. He stopped to take off his hat and sobbed helplessly. Then he put his head firmly against the tree and rubbed it back and forth against the gnarled bark. When the warm moisture glided down his neck, he stopped, leaned forward, and rubbed his eyes and let the small hot streams run down his back.

He awoke in blackness, chilled, humming generators the only sound. He stopped on his way back to Overhead, peered into the orderly room, and the clock read a little after three.

Crossing battalion road, he looked up and the stars met him, twinkling laughter. He spat and lit a cigarette, then walked toward S-1. A two-stooled shithouse with an aluminum roof and bamboo walls stood forlornly on the hill on the right side of the road. Plastic strips hung in the doorway as in the enlisted men's club. He dropped his fatigues and drawers, sat down, and watched the empty road and the red and black ember of his cigarette. He played with himself slowly until he got hard, then speeded up until he could feel it coming. He squeezed his prick until it felt as if it would explode, then throbbed out sperm into a crumpled piece of toilet paper in his other hand.

Multirhythmed snores filled the air in Overhead, and he crawled into his sleeping bag and fell asleep. When he went out in the morning, the last of C Company's vehicles was bouncing down the road on its way to the flight line.

7

IT TOOK Padgett four days before he quit being pissed at Morgan. A couple of times he'd even wanted to go back to base and kick Morgan's ass up and down the battalion road a few times. Fool should be grateful he didn't have to be out in all this crap instead of being jealous about the medals or whatever the hell he was.

He leaned back on the chopper seat and hiked his collar up around his neck to fight off the cold morning wind. He'd eased up on thinking about Morgan last night. The dude did have it rough. Padgett wouldn't trade jobs with him, even if he could. None of them would, really. Things were just different now. They'd all been in the shit, Morgan hadn't, and there wasn't no way the four of them could sit around and bullshit about it. And Slagel and Chambers and him had to think about getting killed all the time—something Morgan couldn't imagine. The awards ceremony had brought that back for all of them—how close they'd been in Happy Valley—and they weren't in the mood for Morgan's complaining.

The lift ships started down and the gunnery choppers opened up. Padgett tensed in his seat, thinking that maybe he'd write Morgan one of these nights and explain. He didn't want them to grow so far apart.

He leaped into the tall grass, dropped to one knee, and added a magazine to the clatter of machine guns, grenades, automatic rifles, and popping rotor blades. Crawling into the bushes, he stuffed another magazine into his rifle. He waited, wondering why the choppers hadn't taken off yet. The firing stopped and the engines seemed to be running slower, shutting down.

As the engine whine decreased, the yelling got louder. The LZ looked clear, but his squad's ship blocked his view of the third's.

"Hold tight," Baird said. "Keep the goddamn area covered. I'm gonna find out what's happening." Staff Sergeant Baird disappeared behind the second squad's chopper.

The moans came louder with curses, screams for the medic. The first squad pulled back to one edge of the clearing, the fourth to another. Baird returned to the squad's position. "First team, over to the east side for cover. Third squad's all fucked up."

Padgett moved across the clearing with his team. Midway between the third squad's ship and the eastern side of the LZ, ten men sprawled on the ground. At least four were dead, others holding their arms, legs, stomachs. Moaning and crying. Most of them new guys, hadn't been in the platoon a month.

"Keep movin', second squad," Platoon Sergeant Trapp said.

"What's happening?" Collins extended the bipods on his machine gun at the edge of the LZ.

"It ain't VC," Padgett said. "Don't worry." He looked back over his shoulder. "Maybe a mine. I don't know."

Suddenly one of the wounded new guys jumped up. Tears glistened among drops of blood on his face, and his left hand covered his right bicep. "Fuck you, Sergeant!" he bellowed. "I knew this'd happen. 'Carry the grenades loose,' you said, you green piece of shit." He started walking toward the corpses where Webber was on the radio. "Fuck you, you dead turd, you motherfucking dead piece of shit! It's just too bad you're not the only one." He bent over and spit on Staff Sergeant Crowley's bloody body.

"At ease, Hodge," Trapp said. "It's no one's fault."

"It's his fucking fault and I'm glad he's dead!" Hodge spit on Crowley again.

"Okay," Trapp said. He tried to put his arm around Hodge.

"Don't touch me!" Hodge jumped back. "Don't none of you cocksuckin' lifers lay a hand on me!" Hodge backed up, then bent down to pick up his rifle.

Fat Trapp tackled him, pinning him to the ground.

"Fuck all of you!" Hodge screamed. His body stiffened beneath Trapp's bulk, then relaxed as he burst into great moaning sobs.

"Damn!" Collins said. "Someone must've dropped a grenade."

"Had to be more'n one." Padgett couldn't figure it. The low whine of the chopper engines started up, and the blades turned slowly as men from the first and fourth squads helped load the bodies on. The walking wounded went to different ships, two of them holding Hodge. All new guys. Padgett hardly knew any of them, knew only a couple of their names. They'd been with the platoon at Kontum, and now here around Cheo Reo for four days, but he hadn't gotten to know any of them.

He was surprised that they had to stay out humping. So was everyone else. No one was up for it anymore, and the whole platoon dragged ass. By the time they finished their C rations at noon, the word was out on what had happened. Crowley had everyone in the third squad carry his grenades with the pins pretty loose, so he could throw them faster. Mercado carried one of the platoon's two claymores strapped on his back. One of his grenades had probably shaken loose, dropping between his back and the claymore before exploding. Nearly cut him in half.

So now there'd be another batch of new guys. He was really beginning to feel like a vet. Only three other dudes had been in the platoon longer than him and Slagel.

In three days they had a new third squad, Padgett leading one of its fire teams. The squad was all soul, which had advantages, although sometimes jittybug jive sure was a bunch of shit. But so far they let him alone when he needed it, and didn't none of them look too big to handle.

He worried a bit at first, but after the operation was ten

days old, he knew they wouldn't find any Cong. You could feel it. Wherever they were wasn't here. Probably gone back up to Kontum or over to Bong Son. Regroup, resupply, and wait. None of the gunships or scouts had been fired on yet, and the rifles hadn't found one fresh footprint or any sign of recent life. The rice in the decaying storage hooches was rotten and full of rat shit. Only tracks on the dirt floors were rat claws.

The jittybugs were all so tense and ready that they might start killing each other if they didn't find any Cong. When they weren't talking about icing Charlie, they were rapping about pussy or some new dance back in the world. He wrote Jerrie only every week now, and he sure as hell didn't think about no dancing.

The walking became automatic. No matter how tough it got, it didn't hurt. If the jungle grew too dense, you hacked it away with machetes; if a funky leech got on your arm or leg, you squirted it off with repellent; if you heard a noise, you were on your knee with your rifle ready to fire, and all the things you were supposed to do were right there in your head.

Slagel had quieted down for a few days after the awards ceremony—like it really got to him—but he'd started popping the diet pills again and was nervous as a squirrel with wanting some action. Sometimes he and Padgett had a beer at night, but they didn't talk too much. Padgett didn't feel like a whole lot of talking any damn way. He went to sleep at eight every night and actually felt relaxed while the platoon humped all day. He tried to get his mind going on the jungle, how he'd paint it once he got his ass back to the world. If he thought about it a whole lot, it'd be there when he was ready. Sometimes he made little cartoons with sticks in the brown dirt, but the outline wasn't much compared with the colors he'd use or with the immensity of the shapes. Just a way to kill some time.

They'd been out two weeks when the new guys captured a monkey. Dumb-looking, with a dough belly and big nose and the face of a half-wit, right down to the grin when someone offered it some chow. It was big, though, and Padgett had to laugh at himself for feeling scared. He didn't want no monkey biting him with the rabies. He stayed at his tent that night and was nearly asleep on his bag when someone kicked his foot.

"Wake up, sweet papa," Slagel said. The reefer smell came faintly into the tent, then the dark-orange ember of the joint bobbed in front of his face.

"What's *los*, cool breeze?" He sat up, dragged on the joint, lay back down.

"Big war council tonight. Squad leaders need some more action."

"They could go in town, probably get some." He stuck his head out the tent as Slagel set some beer cans next to the sandbags.

"No shit. They got a new theory. Charlie's afraid of us. Won't make contact with our division anymore because we've kicked their ass so bad."

"Shee-it. Charlie just ain't gonna waste himself playing hero."

"They might be right, though. We haven't had any contact since Happy Valley."

"We go back to Happy Valley, our sweet ass be in contact again." The cool beer washed over the rottenness in his mouth.

"Fuck it, right?"

"Right. When you get the new squad leader?"

"Pretty soon, I hope. The new guys are a little better, but I'm still sick of it. Looks like your dudes are getting with it."

Padgett had been ignoring the shrieks and cackles coming from up the row of tents. Sounded like the news guys were playing with the monkey in the small banana grove at the edge of the platoon's area. Flashlight beams kept bouncing off the trees where something was being nailed up. Black faces glistened with sweat and grinned in the erratic light. "What they doin'?"

"I think they're going to kill the monkey. Let's go see."

"Why not?"

Thomas finished nailing the elastic cord to one of the trees as they walked up. "Hey, Padg, you just in time." Thomas grabbed the thick cord from the other tree, knotted the two together, then pulled back and let the cord snap forward. "Ready. Gimme that punji and get the bananas ready."

Padgett took the reefer from Slagel and sucked as the bamboo was handed to Thomas. The piece was a good two inches in diameter and about a foot and a half long, its back end notched to fit the sling. Six punji stakes were tied around the front end, points forward. "What the fuck you gonna do?" He looked at Thomas with disgust. Yellow nigger from South Philly always talking about how bad he was.

"You watch, brother. Come on, get him out there." Thomas fit the bamboo into the sling and pulled back until the cord was taut.

Flashlight beams played across the clearing in front of the trees, catching the monkey slobbering and grinning over a banana. Kelly and Adams began to lure it forward with more bananas.

"Come on, monk."

"Come on, walrus face."

"Get him closer," Thomas said. "I can't hold this thing forever."

Kelly had a rope around the monkey's neck. He moved back beside Thomas, pulling the monkey forward while Adams gave it more bananas.

"Two more feet," Thomas said. "Get him up straight."

The monkey moved forward, then sat down. Adams held a banana above his head. The flashlights came up and fixed the idiotic face in their white beams. The monkey took the banana, grinning gratefully like the fucked-up kid on the block who finally gets to play with the big boys.

Adams retreated and Thomas let the bamboo go. The banana went flying as the monkey squealed and fell back. The flashlights showed blood running out its mouth.

"Good shot," Slagel said.

Padgett stepped forward and kicked Thomas in the ass, spilling him forward.

"What you doin'?"

"Get up, motherfucker!"

Thomas backed up on his hands and heels. "What's the matter, brother?"

"I ain't your goddamn brother. Get up!"

Thomas got to his feet and Padgett knocked him down. He rolled back and pulled up around a tree. "I ain't afraid of you, man. Just let me get my shirt off."

Padgett dropped his fists and grinned. "Sure thing, breeze. I wouldn't want to have no unfair advantage."

Thomas stepped from behind the tree, unbuttoning his fatigue coat. As he pulled it halfway down his arms, Padgett shot forward, caught him with a left jab and a right cross, knocking him flat on his ass. Thomas didn't move for half a minute, then raised his head and shook it.

"What part of South Philly you say you from, chump? Ain't no one I ever warred with down there stupid enough to fall for that. Now why don't you get your ass to sleep, and don't be takin' your coat off before Charlie shoots you, dig?" He spun on his heel and walked away.

"What are you all bent out of shape about?" Slagel asked.

"I don't know, man. Jittybugs just give me a case of the gross ass sometimes. Maybe you ought to go ahead on back to your tent." He guzzled from his beer can. "Man, why the fuck did we get ourselves into this shit?"

He woke up from the dream with his hands over his head, waiting for the fat faggot to bash it in. Like fucking clockwork. Every damn time he thought about why, he'd have that dream. He'd had it in Germany the night after they'd signed the 1049's to go, and that's when the bullshit started falling into place. Because up until then he'd gone along with Morgan's theory of experience, that war was part of your education and that you couldn't understand things until you'd been through them. He'd said solid to that because he felt like he wanted to go, and not for love of country.

But after the dream in Germany he had to check himself, because he'd had plenty of that kind of experience back in the world. And then the violence sign glared red and purple neon in his head, and Vietnam was no longer some bad change he had to go through to fill up empty spaces. He was flat digging the idea of getting a gun in his mitts and layin' a few motherfuckers out.

Because that's the way it was with the boxing gloves. When he was little, his older brother would put on the gloves and lay dudes out right and left. LaMont put them on when he was eight, and the first chump he hit started bleeding at the mouth. It hurt him to see it, and when he tried again, he pulled his punch and ended up getting his ass beat. So he hung them up and went back to his picture books and less harmful sports. No one gave him shit because of his brother, and life went along fine until after seventh grade when his family moved to Orange, and boom! he was the only splib in the junior high school. Some people shied away, others made jokes, but he'd figured on that, so hipped himself that he'd have to outdo all those whites.

And he did. Made the all-city junior high team in basketball and picked up some blue ribbons running track. But that was to be expected of any nigger. They sho 'nough could run. Shoot hoops too. But someone slipped up because this nigger ran out of ninth grade as valedictorian. Most white folks would at least allow that a nigger with brains was different from the rest of them, but one guy in his class didn't even pen that message and came up to him after the ceremony, after he'd delivered his speech from the podium, and blew him a strong riff: "Some niggers sure do think they're hot shit." LaMont had all these clean white papers in one hand and they were crumpled in a second and his punch wasn't pulled and that dude was layin' on the cement bleeding like a slaughtered hog. He left the papers lying on him, threw his cap and gown on top of him, and began to run and cry and cuss.

After a bit he held up and had a good laugh. Like he dug bustin' into that dude's shit. It was a weight off his black back. But he started running again in a minute. Right to his brother. Not for protection either—for lessons.

And he got good, real good. No more being polite to white folks. By the time tenth grade started he was ready and known to fire on anyone who lipped him or ran his eyes over him the wrong way. And he got clean too. Fine threads and a pair of 'gator shoes. He got beat a couple of times, but at the end of tenth grade he started Golden Gloves.

The next year he got right up to the semifinals, and it wasn't any gray dudes beat his rusty brown ass neither. They'd moved again, back into a neighborhood with some of their own folks. Some of the cats on the block were fuckin' up gang warrin' and tippling and smokin' shit and snorting dust, but he was too busy at the gym for any of that. He still ran some holes and partied hard on the weekends—because he was a pretty dancer too—but he wasn't about to start carrying a piece or hunting white boys at night with a pack of wolves.

He wouldn't be any valedictorian this time, but school still went okay. He quit shooting hoops and running, because all he wanted to do was box. Then he got involved with the fat cat and hung up his gloves for good. Didn't fight all through twelfth grade or through most of his first year of art school. The spring term was nearly over when the fat cat made his move for LaMont's tool, and he barely finished the semester. His gloves stayed hung up because the fighting he did wasn't in a ring. His black ass was in the street after that. Like he couldn't get enough wine and shit, and he couldn't get enough fighting either. He had to suck up that grape and beat on dudes until the picture he was getting of the fat cat in a police uniform was washed out and beat out of his brain. He went on that way for about a year until one night he took half a Pepsi bottle to some dude's cheek, then just stood there watching his blood run out till someone else came at him with a tire iron. Then he split to his crib, and that's the first night he had the dream.

After that he started going with Jerrie. He wasn't the most faithful guy in the world, but he needed something regular, something he could go to when times got rough. Because by then he'd pretty much given up the painting. He wasn't doing much more than boozing and smokin' shit and poppin' all them young hammers' pussies. It was like a slide. Like every time he got with the jittybugs and listened to them jivin' about how bad they were, he'd start feeling all these things sliding out of him. Then he'd get mad at them and at himself and at everything else, and they'd meet up with some dudes who wanted to gamble, and then he'd be kicking ass. He hardly ever got beat, but sometimes he'd start dreaming in the middle of a fight—like it was far away and he was only watching—then someone would rap his ass back to reality real quick. One night the nab broke in on one of their fights, and he had this big board with razors stuck in the end of it, and bip! he hit Johnny Law right in the neck. Gashed him deep. The pudgy white chump looked like he was down for the big count, and LaMont was paperdollin' for the pad like fifty motherfuckers.

Next day he picked up the Newark paper and read that the nab's in the hospital and not expected to live and that they're holding a couple of the jittybugs. He was sweating those jive asses would talk. He had an uncle in Trenton, split down there and told him what happened, and uncle said he should sign up with Sam in a hurry. The jittybugs never did talk, but he promised three years in the meanwhile, so one morning about six he crawled on the muddy car on the Trenton to Newark milk train, sat down next to Slagel, and by the time they got to Princeton Junction they were talking together when this old splib leads half-drunk Morgan on the train and plops him down beside them, and in a week the three of them were platoon guides together at Fort Dix.

So he knew it was more than wanting experience that

made him volunteer, because he'd had that in the world. But when his tingling tippy toes were telling him how much he'd like to ice someone with the big gun, he knew something was wrong, because both times he'd had that feeling before, something had happened to set it off.

He couldn't blame it on the Army, at least not right away. Because Fort Dix had been fun. They'd had their ration of shit, but if you had any life in you, you couldn't help diggin' some of the screwy dudes and sergeants. And they went to New York or Newark or Atlantic City every weekend, and Morgan had a thing with Slagel's sister, and Slagel had a thing with LaMont's cousin, and he could get Jerrie to meet him anytime, anyplace. Even when they got to Fulda things weren't too bad at first. Exploring downtown like a bunch of kids, drinking wire caps and cognac, and rappin' to the Kraut hammers. But it got old in a hurry because the hammers didn't listen, and pretty soon there was nothing left to explore. The juices started going sour, and they spent more and more time making calendars, counting days, and watching the clock. Working as a clerk in the reenlistment office didn't help any. Just sitting there day after day, watching the wooden faces of these lost cats who ought to be passed out in a Lautrec café coming in and signing up, and he swam in this smell of paper rot.

And then a splib and a gray go to it outside the post gate on New Year's Eve, and in the morning that gray dude's froze to the pavement with a knife in his belly, and then the tension wire starts buzzing. He and Morgan went to chow together every morning, and sometimes they'd sit with Morgan's buddies from the aviation company and sometimes with the rusty cats he'd met up with. Scene one was him getting up to the milk machine and some splib cat's there asking him what's he trying to do, change his color? Scene two is Morgan getting up there and some gray dude saying to him, "That's quite a tribe you're sitting with this morning." They always got a few laughs about it back in the cubicle they shared. He knew it had its serious side, and he figured he was as hip to the Cause as anyone, but when someone starts telling him who his friends gonna be, he had to say mother fuck that cat, because he was a man before he was anything else.

And no whites gave him trouble either. Morgan told him how some of them in personnel said what a loudmouth nigger he was, but most of them were weasel-assed motherfuckers who'd never say anything to your face, and Morgan said a lot of it was just because LaMont had scored the highest in the regiment on all the dip shit Army tests. He was good-looking besides and could dance or fight better than anyone around. Morgan laughed about it one day and told him, "Man, you don't know what it does to those lily-white egos when a black's got more going than they do."

He'd gotten good and nasty again after coming back to Fulda from Florence, and maybe he'd figured being over here would take care of that once and for all. He didn't know why the thing with the monkey pissed him off so much. He didn't mind people being mean—that was life, and you had to expect it. But coming on friendly first, luring someone into a trap, was going too damn far. Maybe he should forget it. Or just remember it as something to paint.

The platoon moved along the spine about a mile, then headed down a ridge on the western slope of the mountain. They were halfway to the landing zone when the shouts started, followed by a burst of machine-gun fire and two automatic rifles. He crouched and waited. In a few minutes the platoon moved forward again, stopping after twenty yards. One man in black pajamas and no shoes lay on his face on the side of the ridge. Dead. Ten feet in front of him Slagel and Irwin stood over another dude, who moaned like an old wino on the edge of DT's.

Trapp walked over from where Captain Webber was talking on the radio. "Second and fourth squads follow me. First squad watches the prisoner, third covers."

The third squad fanned out around the prisoner, Padgett taking up position right beside him. He bled like crazy from the stomach, and blood soaked through his hands where they covered his balls. One of his legs had been close to shot off three-fourths of the way up his thigh. Slagel hovered over him, his rifle at the man's head. The medic must have gone down with the other squads.

"He ain't gonna make it on no stretcher," Irwin said.

Slagel nodded. "We ought to put the poor bastard out of his misery."

"Who's gonna do it?"

"Brady, get out your forty-five," Slagel said.

"I don't know, Sarge." Brady's voice quavered. "Better wait till Webber gets off the radio."

"What's it matter?"

What the fuck was Slagel doing? Padgett turned away and watched Webber at the radio.

"Slagel," Webber yelled, "any weapons on those two?"

"We didn't see none, sir."

"Okay."

"Come on, Brady," Slagel whispered. "One in the head'll do it. Otherwise we gotta carry the fucker out of here."

"I don't know. Better wait."

"Give me the forty-five, then." Slagel held out his hand. "I'll do it."

Brady looked scared, but somehow forced a smile. "I just cleaned it this morning. Don't want to get it dirty."

"Shit!" Irwin said.

The prisoner moaned louder. He rolled his head from side to side with his eyes closed.

"Shut the fuck up!" Slagel yelled. "I'm sick of your whining." He glanced nervously over his shoulder toward the radio.

Padgett turned away again. The leaves of the bush in front of him were gray-green, like on the olive trees in Florence. He jumped at the short burst of fire and turned as Captain

Webber ran over from the radio. Webber grabbed Slagel's shoulder and spun him around. "What the hell did you do that for?"

The prisoner was on his face, the back of his head red ooze.

"He tried to run," Slagel said.

"With that leg?"

"He made a move toward me and reached in his pants. He might have had a grenade."

"We searched him!"

"We might have missed something."

"Christ, Slagel, he didn't even have a weapon."

"He went for me. I had to do it."

"Okay, Slagel. Okay!" Webber went back to the radio. "Four-three, this is Blue, over."

"Roger, Blue, this is Four-three. What's going on down there, over," crackled back on the radio.

"Prisoner tried to escape. One of my men killed him. We're coming out, over."

"Roger, Blue. We'll radio in two confirmed kills. Lift birds are on the way. Out."

"Out."

That night Padgett got tired of listening to the jittybugs talk about how rough Slagel was. He walked out of the tent area, up to the helipad where Chambers sat in the door of his chopper, puffing a cigar.

"What's happening, LaMont?"

"Ain't nothin' to it. How you doin'?

"All right. Pull up some dirt."

Padgett squatted on the ground. "Our boy did it again."

"What happened?"

"He iced the dude."

"Did he try to run?"

"Shee-it!"

"Tom just blew him away?"

"I wasn't watching. But that cat wasn't about to move."

Chambers shook his head. "I wonder what he's thinking."

"Guess he's gettin' into this shit. Seems to dig it too."

"He's always had a temper. Remember when he took that guy apart in Fulda? Those pills probably don't do him any good either."

"Maybe." Old Tom had been like a crazy man when he'd fired on the fat Kraut during *Fasching*. Hadn't even been that drunk, but mad out of his head. Might've killed the guy if three of them hadn't pulled him off. "He was talking it up back at the platoon. Those kids think he's something." Slagel had been sitting in front of his tent, his back to Padgett, his arms gesturing up and down as he boasted to Irwin and four other young troops.

"I heard Blue wasn't going for it too much, though," Chambers said.

"He was a little hot, but what could he do? Trapp dug it. He was over there slapping him on the back awhile ago. Guess the lifers think he's got the rifleman's spirit. What you gonna do? I guess I'll go clean my weapon, get ready for tomorrow. Long way from Fulda, ain't it?"

"Ain't it?" Chambers squeezed his beer can, then dropped it on the floor of his ship. "I was thinking about Italy today. Those were two good weeks."

"Let's forget it. We liable to go AWOL."

"Been thinking of painting at all?"

"Shee-it! Been reading a lot of architecture books?"

"Little."

"Later."

8

"MORE AMMO! More ammo!" McGutcheon hollered. Chambers shook the crew chief's foot until he sat up. "What's happening?"

"It's five thirty. We've got first light."

McCutcheon jumped out of the ship, plopped down in the doorway, and laced up his jungle boots. Grease and oil stained his freckled face; his right cheek looked zippered from where it had been resting on the sleeping bag. "I like first light, Orville. Good chance to catch Charlie with one eye open. I like last light too because sometimes you can catch him on the move."

As if he didn't know McCutcheon loved first- and last-light recon after flying with him for five weeks. He himself didn't mind either one because they took place at the quietest times of day. But you nearly always had to fire.

When they took off, McCutcheon sat in the left door like a studious panda. Was each flight a momentous event that called for private prayer? The war must have had some religious meaning for him. He'd been put in for a Bronze Star after the big battle on the border and for a Distinguished Flying Cross after the Happy Valley fiasco. Both times he'd left himself wide open to the enemy while firing his machine gun. Or so Chambers had heard. He'd never seen McCutcheon in action—hoped he wouldn't—but the crew chief's fanaticism came through in his tireless work on the helicopters every night and in his talk about extending his tour. He didn't even seem to be bucking for rank.

They flew west toward the Cambodian border, and Chambers leaned back against the firewall and let the cool morning wind blow on his face as the impenetrable green raced away beneath the ship. His left leg stuck out straight, resting on a box of grenades behind the pilot's seat. His right foot hung halfway out the door, the heel of his boot hooked on the floor, while the toe dangled down, occasionally touching the rocket pod suspended beneath the side guns. A machine gun lay across his lap, and he toyed with a smoke grenade hooked to the carrying handle of the gun.

Thoughts about Slagel ruined the clean, crisp feeling he usually got on the early flights. Tom hadn't been any different at chow this morning. A little nervous, but not at all sorry about murdering the prisoner—didn't even mention it. Maybe he wasn't aware of what he'd done. If anything, he was more exuberant than usual. The younger kids in the platoon flocked around him, and the older riflemen and NCO's gave him the respect accorded a seasoned trooper.

In Fulda none of them had thought about this kind of thing. They'd talked a little about what being shot at might be like, even about whether or not they could kill, but no one had ever mentioned shooting others for the fun of it. He should have seen then that Slagel might end up this way. He'd enjoyed beating up Germans, and he was the only one who'd been in a fight in Florence. But he should have seen a lot of things, seen enough to keep himself in Fulda. That was the trouble with war—no one ever let you see enough first, and the guys they got to fight it were too damn young to know the difference. How did anyone know what it would release inside you? Morgan would say, "Great, 'know thyself,'" Bullshit if it meant knowing you could be a ruthless killer. No one had the right to dump that on the world. With seven months to go things could really get out of hand.

The chopper flew in a slow circle around the day's area of operations, then Captain Hobart radioed back to the field base that the AO was clear for artillery prep.

"Take it down on the deck, Mr. Patterson," Hobart said to the warrant officer at the controls, "and head it west."

"Down we go."

The ship slowed, drifting smoothly down to the treetops, then sped up again. Chambers shrugged off his fears, trying to enjoy the silky floating that he liked most about flying. The helicopter fit the air perfectly.

"Okay, Pat," Captain Hobart said as they neared the mountain barrier in the west, "let's be careful not to go into Cambodia."

"Yes, sir. Wouldn't mind drifting in there a few feet, though. Let fuckin' Charlie know what's up."

"Roger that."

"Roger that back here too," McCutcheon said.

Hobart turned to the cabin, his black-mustached lip curled in a nasty little grin. "You know those runts are right over there too, and we can't do a thing about it."

"What a way to fight a war," Patterson said.

All the peacefulness left the ship as the officers jabbered on and Cambodia came closer. The rage and grief over the big battle last November made them suddenly tense and bitter. More than anyone, more than the Vietcong and North Vietnamese, the pilots cursed the politicians at home who didn't know the situation, who wouldn't let them go over the border. They had all lost friends, and Captain Hobart had had his arm filled with shrapnel.

"I fired some over there anyway," Patterson said. "I tipped the nose up and squeezed three pair of rockets right over Chu Pong Mountain, and fuck LBJ if he don't like it."

Chambers had been enjoying his last day of leave in Berkeley about the time of the battle, and he didn't regret it.

"Take it up north about a mile, then let's head back," Hobart said.

"Roger."

The chopper banked left and he felt himself tipping slightly out the door. He studied the ground, seeing only green and darker green and pockets of black. He thought about Italy last spring, and the thought of someone rising out of the jungle to shoot him seemed absurd.

"Sir, I got a hooch," McCutcheon said as the ship banked into the turn that would take it back to base.

"Where?"

"Back about eight o'clock. If you want to turn I'll show you."

The chopper circled and Hobart shook his head. "Shit, McCutcheon, that thing was probably last used by Ho Chi Minh's granddad."

One wall of the faded tan hooch was nearly gone, and three large holes gaped in the roof.

"I think we should put some rounds in there, sir."

"If you want to fire, it's fine by me, but let's not pretend it has any strategic value. Chambers, lob a Willie Peter on it while McCutcheon's firing."

"Yes, sir." He picked up a white phosphorus grenade, pulled the pin, and watched McCutcheon's tracers. A few went in the hooch, then they sprayed wildly all over the jungle. He dropped the grenade behind the hooch. The roof flew off as the white smoke and hunks of liquid fire spat up from the ground. McCutcheon ceased firing and stuck his thumb up in Chambers' face. They circled the hooch once more, then headed back to the field base.

That night, after McCutcheon left him to help another crew chief with an inspection, he smoked a joint and lay on his sleeping bag on the helicopter floor. It had been a rougher day than usual. Flying by the border had stirred up bad memories in the rest of the crew. They'd been hateful all day, harassing peasants, making low passes to frighten children and scatter herds of water buffalo. But the worst thing had been the talk. By the time their second mission got under way they'd forgotten the politicians completely. Just a continuous babble on the intercom about gooks—any and all kinds of gooks. The Cong and NVA's were their enemy, but the South Vietnamese were just as bad. Stupid, shiftless, smelly. Giving aid and comfort to the enemy, therefore enemies themselves. Everyone knew that the VC controlled the ground at night, so the dumb-ass peasants had to be in cahoots with them. Why not kill the bastards? Why not kill the children too, since they were nothing but future VC? Why not the women, for that matter? Hadn't the first recorded kill of the division been a woman carrying grenades in Ia Drang Valley?

The talk had been a petty irritation at first, but by the end of the day it had become a weight that threatened to submerge him in a black pool of depression. Over the past few weeks he'd been able to push away some of the revulsion he'd felt after Happy Valley, but it had suddenly sprung back. Nothing done with, nothing forgotten. Pick the scab and find plenty of pus. He'd taken Captain Hobart's affable nature as genuine, rather than a cover for the hatred and frustration underneath. Maybe the captain would flip out someday and start blowing away women and kids. Christ, he didn't want to be around for that.

He should have gotten out of combat altogether. Building barracks wouldn't be so bad, except all the guys who did that were already flipped out. Burning shit would be too much, and from the looks of the men who worked in the mess hall, you had to be pretty crazy to land that job. No one ever said it, but they were thought of as chickenshit, probably more by themselves than anyone else. They always had the apologetic look in their eyes, at the same time searching to see if you judged them, praying you didn't. He wished he could type so he could land a clerk's job somewhere.

He dreamed that his father was yelling at him across a barbed-wire fence, but he couldn't hear what he was saying, then it seemed as if he was in the barracks in Fulda as the drunks stumbled in. Something clutched his legs, and he suddenly sat up, bumping his head into someone.

"*Was ist los, mein herr?*"

Morgan! It couldn't be Morgan. He reached to his left, touched the pilot's seat and his machine gun. He was still in Vietnam, and something held his legs.

"*Verstehen was ist los?*" Morgan said.

Hands slid off his legs and Padgett and Slagel rose up on either side of Morgan, laughing. "What the hell's going on? What are you doing out here, Will?"

"Got a special ride so I could celebrate our anniversary."

He lay back down. He had to be dreaming. Morgan in the field? Anniversary?

Padgett handed him a beer as Slagel hopped in the ship. No shit. They were all here. He pinched his arm. "It's no dream. Here I am in the middle of Vietnam with my three friends who convinced me to come." He drank from the cold can. "Gentlemen, come into my home." He shoved the sleeping bag against the left door, sliding back himself as Morgan and Padgett climbed in. "How'd you get out here, Will?" He felt terribly glad to see him, to see that all the bad feelings from after the awards ceremony were gone.

"Greene had to come out to see the colonel about redeployment."

"Already?"

"Division left the States last August, and they start sending the old guys home in June. Means I'm going to be working my ass off again. We go back in the morning. But I had to celebrate with my main men." Morgan stuck out his hand for Padgett and Slagel to slap.

"I'm glad you're here, but what's to celebrate?"

"April fourteenth, 'cruit," Padgett said. "You now in the presence of three over-two motherfuckers."

"Three over-two? What've you guys been smoking?"

"Two years, baby!"

"We're two-thirds of the way home."

"Two years together," Morgan said, "and we didn't even come in on the buddy plan."

"Congratulations." He saluted them with his can.

"One more thing," Morgan said. "I'll be joining you guys in six weeks."

Through the dark silence he could see Morgan grinning from up on the seat. "What do you mean?"

"I'm going to be a gunner in C Company. For Major Quinn."

"Really, Morg?" Slagel asked.

"Yup. Brooks is leaving June first, and I'm going to take his place. Brooks was a clerk before he came out."

"You sure you want to do that?" Padgett said.

"Hell, yes. That base camp's getting to be nothing but chickenshit. Starting next month I have to come up to S-1 every night between midnight and two to do a special report. That's *after* working seven to seven. It's not hard to learn, is it, Orville?"

"Guess not. Damn, Will, you ought to stay back."

"Sure should," Padgett said.

"Come on. If you had that job, you'd want out too. I don't want to talk about it anymore."

He didn't want to talk about it either. He didn't want Morgan coming to the field, but it wouldn't do to argue about it. Nothing would change, and a bad fight might get started. If Morgan wanted the experience so bad, he could come ahead on and have it. Chambers wouldn't interfere.

He lit a joint and passed it to Slagel as the three of them started in on their stories of meeting on the Trenton-to-Newark milk train in April of sixty-four. How many times had he heard the stories around the barracks and at the EM Club in Fulda? He felt as though he were a part of them, had been at Fort Dix with his three companions.

Morgan kept pulling beers from a waterproof bag he'd brought to the field, and Chambers brightened as the stories moved from Fort Dix to Fulda. He re-created the grubby post in his mind, the utilitarian pink, gray, and latrine-green barracks, the larger green buildings of the Regimental and First Squadron Headquarters, the benign gray sky day after day. The town with its ten funky bars blaring the latest American and English rock and roll. St. Boniface's grave. What a place for him to come alive.

He found himself laughing along with the others as the stories continued about the drunken clowns they'd known. He'd never found them so very funny, but sometimes he couldn't help laughing. What else could you do? Taking the sorriness and waste too seriously made for continual depression or led to an unadjustable discharge.

He told a couple of stories himself when they got on their trip to Florence, feeling high and excited remembering what had probably been the best two weeks of his life. He stopped when he noticed Slagel silent behind the ember of a joint. Maybe Florence hadn't been that good for him, although he'd never said so. He'd gone along with them to the churches and museums, but had always seemed nervous and impatient to get back to drinking and partying. But he was usually that way whenever they talked about serious things. Grunting assent or throwing in a line here and there, but mostly relieved when the conversation turned back to storytelling and general shit talking.

"Wonder where old Shipley's pissing his pants tonight," Slagel said.

"Down in Texas somewhere," Padgett said.

Shipley had been a cook, a stocky, rock-hard Texan who drank three quarts of whiskey a day. He stayed in the barracks every night, except for once a month when he put on his dress uniform and went drinking at the post bowling alley. On one of Chambers' first nights in Fulda, when he was talking in the barracks with Morgan, Padgett, and Slagel, Shipley had reeled down the hall, his drawers soaked with piss, and sat down beside them.

"Morgan, you been to college?"

"Yeah."

"What's twelve and twelve, then?"

"Twenty-four, I guess."

"Guessed wrong. It's twenty-five. You ain't so smart."

"How's that?"

"And equals one."

"What?"

"And is one. Twelve and twelve is like saying twelve, one, twelve. So it's twenty-five."

"Horseshit."

"I got your horseshit hangin'." Shipley lectured them on his mathematical theories for another half hour, then stumbled off to bed.

Shipley could barely write, and his wife, who lived in Texas, couldn't write at all. They drew pictures to each other. Last June Shipley had received a series of pictures of his wife fucking ten different men. After a few weeks of hassling he was given a compassionate reassignment back to the States.

On the night before he left, a week after the four of them

had volunteered for the war, Shipley had teetered into the shower room where they all were. "What you young queens doin'?"

"Getting ready for Vietnam, Ship," Morgan had said.

"What's that?"

Morgan explained, and as he talked, Shipley's face grew darker and darker. He stared at the four of them, shaking his head.

"I ought to whip all your young asses," he finally said. "You never known no combat, and you think it's funny now, but I been to Korea and I know. It's bad, and I know." Shipley turned and left the shower room.

When they came in from the club later that night, a few guys stood by the door to the cooks' room, laughing. Shipley lay on the floor, passed out in a puddle of his own urine. It was the last they saw of him.

"I hope he got his old lady squared away," Padgett said, passing a joint to Chambers.

"He probably caught the train to Sweden instead of Frankfurt," Morgan said.

Chambers dragged deeply, feeling it starting, not even trying to fight it anymore. He couldn't remember as others did, couldn't isolate his life into manageable fragments. It was as though some immense interior gasp shook loose a clot, a dam, in his brain, leaving him with no choice but to ride out the torrent of his memory.

He barely heard himself and the others making their half-hearted plans for drunkenness when battalion came in from the field. They left him. McCutcheon returned babbling about torque and mag plugs and servo mechanisms, then the crew chief fell asleep on the seat, his breathing as erratic and disjointed as his thoughts.

Chambers sat in the door, staring at the flight line and the phosphorescent moon, puffing a six-cent King Edward cigar. Just because Shipley had been to Korea and Chambers remembered.

Purple is the color of lilacs and love smell and all summer

long Grandma was there playing canasta and sometimes yelling at you and Roger to come in at night when Mother and Father were gone and always "come and listen to the convention" and happy Eisenhower a war hero and Stevenson the biggest crook in the country let alone Illinois and baseball proud being Roger's and Eddie's younger brother with all the letters they'd won and people saying you'll be as good as them someday, and seeing coach Crandall and telling him "Hey, coach, Eddie got another MIG," and Crandall, "Yeah, Ike'll stop it they shoulda fired Truman instead of MacArthur," and "No, Eddie ain't met Ted Williams 'cause Ted's in the Marines, but the Red Sox'll be something when he gets back," and every day riding the bike six miles to practice and six miles back to show Roger you weren't a sissy because he was gone at six thirty every day to work ten hours on the river bottom and never home but for half an hour at dinner and then out with the girls you guessed but they were always coming to baseball practice saying "How's Roger doing, little Orey? Is he gonna be quarterback in football this year?" and they knew he'd be quarterback and probably the best in the conference too but they liked to see you get red when they talked because everybody else laughed too and said "Maybe little Orey'll be quarterback too because he's the only one out of sixth grade starting on the baseball team now," and then you'd get red and pull the cap down over your eyes.

And after the ride home and Mother quiet and worried gets you lunch and most of the time after you'd ride the horse down to the lake always cool and fun and sleep a little and if you could steal a quarter from Mother you'd get pop and some peanuts, and at night from the window you could look all the way into Minneapolis lights and maybe you couldn't smell the lilacs but you thought you did and that was enough and sometimes you'd hear Roger come in but most of the time you wouldn't and all the days would go like that except Sunday when you'd mow the lawn or help Father paint with him not talking unless it was important and you seemed to be always doing something physical but never getting excited and then one afternoon Mother said you couldn't ride the horse which you didn't mind except when Father brought Roger home and they told you and everything seemed to stop for you because it stopped for everybody else at least Roger and Father and Mother was always pretty worried anyway but now she just cried a lot more and Father never saying hardly anything again.

Roger wasn't quarterback then and he didn't even go out with the girls that night or to the river bottoms the next day or the day after but the day after that he was gone and school started and the older girls were still friendly to you but they called you Orville now instead of little Orey and they didn't ask about Roger and no one even talked at dinner except Mother asking if football didn't interfere with your homework so you played quarterback instead but just on the junior high team and didn't do too bad and Ike got elected but it didn't matter since Eddie was burned up not even enough of him to send home for a funeral but they had one without a body anyway and everyone in the town was there but Roger and no one knew where he was at least no one ever told you but Father must have known because he never tried to find him or call missing persons, so the war started to end and they painted the mailboxes red, white, and blue and lots of people said we shoulda bombed them Truman or no Truman but you didn't think it would've done much good without Eddie even though they still had Ted.

Christmas didn't seem like much, hasn't since and pretty soon you'd almost forgot about Roger and just played sports and everything at home was quiet till spring when the snow half melted and the ground green and white and throwing the ball in the pasture and then the motor sound and the red flash slipping and spinning and sliding through the mud and unshaved-faced Roger getting out just a little before it stopped.

"You had that silly mitt on when I left, kid."

"Golly, it's Roger. Where you been, Roger? Where'd you get the

flashy car? I nearly forgot you'd ever been here. They really coulda used you in football this year—I did pretty good on the junior high team. Where'd you go?"

"Some other places. Is the old man home?"

"No, but Mother's in the cellar getting bulbs and seeds ready. Where'd you get the car?"

"One of the places I was gone to. I'll take you for a ride in it after I talk to Mother."

"Are you gonna stay home now, Roger?"

"Maybe. I guess so."

"Track and baseball season are starting in two weeks. You got time enough to get in shape."

But he was already walking away and laughing too but he still took you for the ride in the car but didn't say much about where he'd been or what he'd done but talked like a Southerner and drove fast and laughed especially when you told him that the girls never said anything but you knew they were thinking about him all the same.

At dinner Mother seemed happier and made a gooseberry pie for Roger and Father still didn't say much didn't even put up a fuss when Roger said he wasn't going back to school but was going down to the river bottoms to plant and Father said he didn't have to go to work but could just relax for a while if he wanted.

"No, the one thing I don't need—can't use—is relaxation because I need the money to get out and do and I can work down there twelve hours a day at two dollars an hour, and by the time planting's done I ought to have enough."

"To do what?"

"Just to do. I don't know, maybe it's just because Eddie's gone and I realize how much there is to do and see, and what little time to do it in, but after what I've seen in Houston and New Orleans and Atlanta I can't hardly go back to school and play baseball or just sit and relax either."

After that it didn't matter as much that Father bought you

the fifteen-dollar baseball mitt because you loved Roger, and even if the lilacs still smelled nice you couldn't take baseball as serious as before but he stayed way into the summer and was still gone every day by six thirty to work and out every night racing the car and the girls didn't say much to you at baseball practice anymore and every once in a while someone'd say something about Roger racing the car and chasing women at night and that if he didn't watch it he'd get in trouble and when you told him he'd just laugh and you finally had to beat Timmy Carlson half senseless because he cursed you and said Roger was a bum and everyone knew it, and there were more fights after that but summer wasn't a whole lot different from before just riding the bike and playing ball and riding the horse and swimming and smelling lilacs at night and sometimes the slow freight would go by at the bottom of the hill when you were in bed and the horn—short, short, long, short—seemed so lonely coming up through the woods and the bed the whole house shook and the metal horses rattled on the dresser, and you were glad when baseball season ended and you could play Daniel Boone and Jim Bridger alone in the woods all until that Sunday when you were riding and heard the slow freight coming so you galloped to the top of the hill to look and you saw the red car racing down the highway and it looked pretty much like it'd beat the train past the crossing but you (and you guess he) didn't think about having to slow for the turn so only the hood got to the other side of the tracks and the train didn't stop for another hundred yards.

You had to tell Mother and Father this time and it seemed almost like Father expected it but Mother couldn't take it you found out year after year, and the next day you went down there after they'd cleaned it all up but there were still some little hunks of twisted metal and shattered glass and dried blood and then you found it sort of dirty white and spongy looking and you remembered from Father's medical books that it was brains and picking it up then brushing off ants and squeezing it between your fingers and then the tingling coming all over you and you tore a little bit off and sniffed it and at that instant you went past where people should stop because it didn't smell that bad because it was still a little chilly out but when you put it in your mouth and chewed it was like what you figured an old piece of meat dipped in fresh cow's milk would taste like after being left to sit awhile.

There wasn't a body for the funeral this time either and nobody came this time either and the older girls weren't even friendly anymore when school started and people shied away from you as though you carried some bad smell and you didn't care as much about football but every once in a while you hit really hard and people started getting hurt until you were finally in twelfth grade and they'd switched you from quarterback to linebacker because they said you were built like a little gorilla and you were the toughest in the conference and after the third game and the second brain concussion you'd handed out it all quit making sense.

"That can't be helped, Orville," the coach said. "You gotta hit hard and can't help what happens."

"Can."

"What?"

"You can or you don't have to."

"But you're playing ball. You gotta play tough. We might win conference this year."

"So what?"

"So what?"

"Why hurt?"

"Not hurt—hit."

"Hit hurts."

"That's the game. Be a man, Chambers."

"Sure."

So you went and hit and hurt him and didn't play football or anything else anymore and got kicked out of school for two weeks Father not even blinking now but Mother getting thinner and maybe Elaine understood because she stayed by you and lost friends and didn't say much either, but maybe you stayed with her because you didn't want anything else and after four years you sure didn't want the baby God did you ever want anything after the baseball mitt? and with no money there was nothing left to do but ask Father and God it must have taken everything inside him to finally say yes and do it and you guess that's why he couldn't hold back the anger after putting two and a half months of life dead in a plastic bag so he just had to throw it on your chest you must have been the most worthless thing he'd ever seen lying there under the lilac tree but where else did you have to go? so he just had to yell at you "Let this day remind you forever that you don't squander life," so you left Elaine and him and Mother too to go dig graves and that didn't do anything because when you got back you just missed getting shot by Elaine's husband so here you are now for another seven, eight months and it looks like your chances of getting shot this time might be pretty good.

9

SLAGEL WOKE UP at five thirty, bad head, dry mouth, and bursting bladder. He slid out of his tent and stumbled over to the piss tube. He duck walked back, drained his canteen, then refilled it at the water trailer. By the time he'd finished shaving, his head still throbbed, but his spirits were high. He'd sweat out the rest of the beer this morning.

Morgan had picked a choice time to come to the field, and his visit had erased the bad feelings from after the awards ceremony. It'd be good to have him out permanently—someone else to talk shit with besides the know-nothing new guys. Morgan could handle the combat all right. Probably better than most of the fools they were getting.

He shouted greetings and mocks as the other riflemen crawled from their tents and stared stupidly at the morning. Christ, he felt good. He did a few squats and stretches, then shook his body all over. He laughed out loud thinking of characters from Fulda. What a pisser. When he really thought about it, he didn't have much to regret from his first two years. It was shitty, but it was supposed to be. Troops weren't happy unless they had something to bitch about. Fort Dix had been a gas, and even Fulda had had its moments. He hadn't been so crazy about the culture as the others, but he didn't mind seeing the paintings and churches if he could look at a woman and a gallon of vino when it was done. The broad in Florence had been just right. Rich bitch from one of those families in Connecticut where the father made piles in New York every day. Sopping up the culture because that was expected of her, going to Wellesley and all. But she didn't give that much of a shit and liked the grape and a hot time in the rack as much as he did. When it was all said and done, what did he have to kick about? So he could have played in the pros; he could've been born a clubfoot too.

After chow he was just saddling up when Morgan bopped over to his tent.

"Want to go on the operation, Morg?"

"I'm ready!" Morgan whipped the M-16 off his shoulder and brandished it in front of him.

"Shee-it! You fired that thing yet?" You could tell he was no combat trooper. Rusty gun. Two old magazines hanging out his front pocket, no pistol belt, clean fatigues. His face was pasty from too much beer and not enough sun and exercise.

"Hell, no. I'm supposed to go to the rifle range one of these days." Morgan fingered his bristly mustache. "That was fun last night. Good to be with my friends again."

"I'll be glad when you come out for good, buddy. We'll have some times then."

"Okay. I'll have the cold ones ready when you guys come in."

"That's talkin'. How's that little girl down at the laundry? You still see her?"

"Sure. Her old man can't launder worth a shit, but she's cool. I've got to go. Take it easy, Tom. I'll see you in a couple of weeks."

He watched Morgan go, then followed the rest of the platoon out to the flight line.

"Slagel!" Platoon Sergeant Trapp waved to him from the door of his squad's ship.

"What's up, Sarge?"

"New staff's coming out tomorrow to take your squad. You'll be team leader from then on."

"Good news." He eyed the already wide rings of sweat around Trapp's armpits. "You know, Sarge, you're going to be trim as me you don't watch it. How much you lost?"

Trapp stuck his thumb under his belt buckle, pulling it forward to demonstrate the looseness of his pants. "Maybe forty. I already changed fatigues once, and I'm getting ready for another set."

"Lookin' good." He patted Trapp's belly and climbed into the ship. He was starting to like the old sergeant after being sickened by his obesity when he'd joined the platoon. He hated fatness more than any physical shortcoming, mainly because of his lard-ass uncle who used to sit on him when he was a boy and make him cry. He remembered his uncle at the dinner table on Sundays, his white shirt cemented by sweat to the rolls of flab beneath it, and the big round fat face gobbling food. The forehead glistening with sweat. And the belching. Trapp was smart to slim down. His uncle never bothered and died of a heart attack at forty-six. The funeral was on Slagel's fifteenth birthday. As he looked at the still, doughy, bloated hunk lying on the satin of the coffin, he promised himself that the last thing he'd ever do was get fat.

The next morning the platoon stayed in, waiting for the new sergeant and a few other men to arrive at the field base. Slagel and Irwin walked over to the helipad as the supply ship, swirling dust and blowing bits of paper, hovered down. His apprehension over being replaced by a dud ceased when the giant Negro staff sergeant stepped off the chopper. "Would you look at that!"

"Big," Irwin said.

The new sergeant looked like some African prince who'd been thrown into fatigues to help out the U.S. Six feet four, two twenty-five, and not an ounce of fat on him.

Trapp and Captain Webber took him away immediately, and after half an hour Trapp called the other squad leaders over to his tent. "Gentlemen, this is Staff Sergeant May, new leader of the first squad." He introduced the three other staff sergeants. "And this is Slagel, who's been leading the squad for a month and a half. He's crazy, so you'll have to keep him in line."

"That right, Slagel?" May beamed and held out a massive hand.

"I've only been crazy since Trapp took over." May's hand felt like a shot put.

For the next three days he listened to May, watched him work. Christ, was he in shape, and no slouch either when it came to humping. He'd spent his last two years teaching camouflage and target detection at Fort Jackson, and he looked as if he'd pushed iron at the gym every night.

Slagel soldiered harder than ever. He wanted to show May that he knew the ropes, that he could make it no matter how rough things got. May made him feel better about what he did, made him feel that it was important and that he didn't have to mess up prisoners or anything like that to pass the time. The entire platoon came to life again, and morale in the first squad was higher every day. May circulated among the men each night, bringing beer and telling funny stories. He never got mad if he found a dirty rifle, but made it into a joke that resulted in the weapon getting cleaned. He didn't go near the other squad leaders much, and he didn't get close with the Negroes in the other squads. He reminded Slagel of some colored jocks he'd known at State. Always friendly and funny, but you never knew their private thoughts. He found out that May was married and that he wrote his wife every night, but nothing else.

Each evening when they got in they heard about action picking up in the division, and although they hadn't made contact with the enemy, platoons from the other companies had, so their turn would probably come before long. Slagel talked to both Webber and May, and they expected something to hit any day. Webber seemed worried that it might be bad, and May was apprehensive because he'd never been in combat, and he wasn't sure how the squad would react. Slagel told him that he'd never been in it with this squad either, but he thought they'd do okay.

A week after May took over they captured three North Vietnamese soldiers, and late that same afternoon B Company's rifle platoon had six men killed by an estimated company of North Vietnamese. The Air Force dropped a steady rain of napalm and seven-hundred-and-fifty-pounders all day, and at night the B-52's bombed constantly. It didn't make any difference. The jungle was too thick on the long mountain reaches, and a thousand holes in the canopy didn't make a dent in the number of hiding places.

Everyone seemed tense the next morning, and breakfast was businesslike and quiet. The first-light recon helicopters had spotted trails and hooches in Blue's area of operations. They'd made gun and rocket runs, and division artillery was firing into the area as the riflemen boarded their helicopters. In the air Slagel closed his eyes for a brief rest. Irwin nudged him and pointed to the ground. A small path ran along the edge of the valley, weaving in and out of the bushes at the base of the mountains. A small boy lay on the path, his hair the color of his pajamas, and his skin matching the packed khaki dirt on the trail.

"That's really shitty," Irwin said.

"Tell Westmoreland."

"That kid didn't do anything."

"He got in the way. That's what they'll tell you."

They flew over a small hamlet, and in another two minutes

the helicopter started down and the gunnery escort opened fire. They didn't leave you time to think about anything. He bolted from the ship, fired a clip into the bushes, fell in behind May, and started up the mountain ridge. They spent the day blowing up hooches and burning large caches of rice. Several sets of Ho Chi Minh sandal prints stood out clearly on the trail, but the platoon made no contact. When they got in that night, they found out that A Company had been ambushed, losing four men. "It looks like Charlie don't want to mess with Charlie Company," May said before going to bed.

In the morning the two North Vietnamese didn't fire, but turned and ran off through the dense underbrush. Both he and May fired as the bushes closed behind the men, but the crashing continued.

"Slagel, want to go after them?" May said.

"Why not?" Work up a little sweat before noon chow.

"Captain Webber, me and Slagel want to chase those NVA's."

"Don't go too far, and be careful."

May moved like a panther through the jungle, dodging trees, hurdling small bushes, sidestepping larger ones. He was pretty to watch, and Slagel felt a sudden burst of energy as he moved along behind him. He could follow May for hours. It brought back memories of his freshman year at State when he and Taliaferro, the Negro fullback, would go out running in the mornings. Five, six miles a day, and they could have done twenty with no sweat.

The grass caved in under May's feet. The muscular black sergeant turned, a look of utter surprise plastered on his face, and fell backward out of sight. A scream rose up from the hole and hung in the air. Slagel stopped, crouched, and fired a magazine into the bushes after the North Vietnamese. He clicked in a new magazine, then held his breath, listening. The trees swished with quiet indifference above him; the popping rotor blades sounded far away. Otherwise, silence.

He'd stopped three feet in front of the pit. He didn't want

to look, but couldn't help himself. The pointed bamboo stakes supported May five feet below ground level. His head was turned to one side, and his tongue hung out, the pink grotesque against his black face. The body did not move. But he couldn't be dead already. How the hell were they going to get him out? He whirled and nearly fired at Webber as the captain came through a bush behind him.

"What the fuck. . . ." Webber said.

"I think he's dead, but we gotta get him out of there."

Webber looked into the hole. "Oh, Jesus! How the hell can we get him out?" He bellowed for the medic.

The rest of the platoon filed into the tiny clearing, and Slagel moved off to the edge, feeling suddenly angry at the inquisitive faces gaping into the hole. None of them gave a shit, didn't care about May as he did. Even Padgett probably thought he was an Uncle Tom because he didn't act like a blood all the time. What a cheat. One fucking week, and he falls in a hole and dies. One chance in a million.

Irwin walked over from where Webber was on the radio. "Tom, you want to stay here until they get a medevac for him? Webber needs a squad to wait with the body."

"Fuck no! I want to get out of here. Are they going to pull him out with ropes?"

"I guess so."

"I don't want to watch it."

"I'll tell Webber."

"You do that." They'd probably tear the body all to shit. One of the gunnery helicopters hovered down above the clearing. The noise was deafening, and the wind whipped his fatigues. As the chopper pulled back up, Webber approached him.

"You don't want to stay, Slagel?"

"No, sir."

"Okay. I'm leaving a team from the fourth squad who'll go back in with the medevacs. After chow we'll keep chasing those NVA's. They're going toward our LZ anyway."

"Whatever you say, sir."

"You've got the first squad again."

"Roger." Big fucking deal. "First squad, form up over here!"

They found nothing all afternoon, and the platoon was nearly asleep when they approached the landing zone. A small clump of trees and bushes stood in the middle of the clearing. The lift birds would have to be careful. It didn't strike him as funny until the first two squads were nearly half way across the LZ. They were sitting ducks! No one in the zombie platoon even realized it. He opened his mouth to tell Webber as the fire started from the other side of the clearing.

"Into those trees!" he yelled. He turned, crouched, and pointed his squad into the bushes. The second squad was trying to get back into the foliage behind them, and three bodies already lay in the open field. He fired two magazines, then dived into the bushes, coming up between Irwin and Brady. Like all the other ambushes, the fire blasted from the front and one side. Luckily, they were covered from each angle by three fairly sturdy trees.

"Lynch and Henderson, get your chunkers firing! One on the front, one on the side. Keep your bodies behind those trees. Sherwood, get that machine gun up here to the front. I want three rifles firing to the front, three to the side." Webber's neck bled, and Trapp was tying a handkerchief around it. "You okay, sir?"

"Just grazed, Slagel."

"I'm going to tell the other squads where to fire." He crawled to the back of the bushes. The other squads were firing wildly out of the jungle. He'd be slaughtered if he tried to reach them. He yelled and pointed to the side of the LZ. If they'd fire there, he could concentrate his squad on the front. He finally got them to turn their fire solely on the side, then he crawled back to the front. Webber was on the radio, so he regrouped the squad, set up two sectors of fire, almost all of it going to the front and began firing himself.

None of his men was even wounded. How lucky could you get? Couldn't tell how many gooks were out there, but probably no more than two platoons. Off in the distance the lift ships circled like four lazy flies, waiting for their pickup. "Captain Webber, get some gunnery on those spots before we run out of ammo." He turned and squeezed off another magazine. No one knew what to do but him. He felt strange all of a sudden, as if this were hardly a battle. Just organize the people and fire into the woods. Sergeant May had died a hundred years ago. The rat-a-tat of the bullets grew soft like the swishing of the leaves above him, like the spongy popping of the rotor blades.

Explosion behind him and sharp heat in the back. He stiffened, listening to screams, moved, knew he was wounded but not seriously. Two of his men were dead. Lynch was alive but his right arm and that side of his face were hamburger. Then the gunships started. Total harshness now. Rockets, machine guns—another ten feet and they'd be firing on the platoon—grenades tossed by the gunners and the crew chiefs. Three times both ships ran across the clearing, dumping everything they had. Another NVA grenade exploded in their cover, tearing a hole in Trapp's stomach, filling Maxwell's leg with shrapnel, and slicing into the radio so it wouldn't transmit.

Moaning and screaming and crying surrounded him. But hardly any fire came from the jungle. One or two crazy gooks doped up and throwing grenades. Irwin tugged at his sleeve. "I'm going to get them. I'm going to get them." He nodded, fired another magazine, and watched Irwin crawl out.

"Fucking radio's out," Trapp yelled, clutching his stomach.

"Shut up, Sergeant," Webber said. "Lie still."

"My belly. My belly."

"Shut up! Slagel, how's it look?"

"Getting quiet."

"Lift ships are coming in after that fighter drops its napalm." Webber pointed in the air where the sun flashed off silver wings.

Slagel believed it before it happened. He turned and

flattened himself and yelled at Irwin, who suddenly looked like a small boy crawling across the clearing and throwing grenades into the woods. His voice drowned—he couldn't even hear himself—in the roar of the jet and exaggerated whoosh of the napalm canister's explosion. The blast heated his body; white and bright orange splashed before his eyes. The flaming body rose briefly, then slumped back to the earth. Between the flame and the squad hovered the shimmering wall of fumes that hung above pavement on hot days.

The lift ships landed in two minutes. No one in the squad could help him, so he ran after Irwin alone. He lay on his stomach, one cheek on the ground, his arms tucked up under his chest. His face was scorched and jellied. Padgett ran over from the third squad to help carry him. Gently, they turned the body over, Padgett taking the feet. As Slagel tried to grip him beneath the arms, he bumped one of the charred ears. It slid off as though whatever gravity held it there had suddenly ceased to exist. He vomited onto the puffy black face. He ran his sleeve across his mouth, picked up the corpse, carried it over to the medevac ship, and dumped it on.

The other lift ships were waiting for takeoff. Screams came from the side of his bird, and as he walked around the tail boom, he saw Brady lying in the dirt, clawing it furiously but moving nowhere. He laughed. Tubby little Brady, shrapnel in his arm, swimming in the dirt. "Shut up, you fuckers!" he yelled at the bellowing men in the chopper. He knelt down. "What's happening there, Brady old buddy?" He put his hand firmly on Brady's back.

Brady rolled his head from side to side, his glasses caked with dirt. "Sarge, if we can just get over this hill, we'll make it. Just this last hill."

"We're almost there, buddy. Look up. You can see the top. We're getting close."

"We got to get over it. Get away from Charlie."

"Here it is." He lay down beside him and pretended to

crawl too. "See, here we are. There's the plane to take us home. Let's go!"

"Thank God! Thank God we made it." Brady stood up and climbed aboard the ship.

An hour later Slagel was walking out of the aid station after leaving Brady and seeing his other men. The surgeon called to him as he started through the tent flap, saying that there was blood on the back of his fatigues. He'd forgotten about the shrapnel. He felt no pain. While he lay on his stomach, the doctor pulled seven hunks of metal from his back and stitched two of the wounds. The day floated through his head like a smorgasbord of images, none of which would sink in. May dead, Irwin dead, Brady bug-fuck. Eight men in the platoon killed, another twelve wounded. He tried not to blame himself for Irwin, but he shouldn't have let him go across. He hadn't been paying attention. He never should've gone into the clearing in the first place. But his mind had been on May, and besides, Webber and Trapp should have known better.

Walking back from the hospital, he realized that Webber might have had his mind on May too, that Trapp was probably thinking about all that chow back in the base, that everyone was hot and tired and hassled by the whole fucking thing. Because no one gave you time to think or feel anything until it was too late. He wanted to spend time with Irwin's corpse, talk to it, respect it. He stopped in the middle of the dirt path, tipped the steel pot and plastic helmet liner back on his head, and stared at the winking red and yellow lights of a helicopter sweeping the perimeter of the camp. No, he thought, the word forming itself on his lips, but no sound coming from his throat. "No!" he bellowed. The chopper disappeared to the left, leaving his eyes fixed on a black chunk of night. A pair of soldiers, obviously startled by his cry, approached him, but he shook his head and moved off in the opposite direction.

He crept quietly into the platoon area, crawled into his tent, closed the flaps behind him, and fell asleep in Irwin's sleeping bag.

The platoon didn't go out the next day, but they weren't sent back to base camp either. He slept through most of the morning, not wanting to see anyone. He even yelled at Chambers and Padgett when they tried to enter the tent. He didn't want anyone around Irwin's gear. By noon he was roasting under the hot canvas and finally faced the daylight. He took a whore's bath, shaved, and put on clean fatigues. Webber was the last person he wanted to talk to, but he couldn't avoid it when the captain came over to his tent.

"How's your back, Tom?"

"Not bad."

"I'm sorry about Irwin."

"Me too." Why go through all this bullshit? "Want me to bag up his stuff?"

"I guess so."

"What do we do from here?"

"Wait. The colonel told Quinn we'll have some replacements in three days. B Company's getting theirs today, going out tomorrow. We won't get a break, but things should be pretty easy the next few days."

"Any chance of me going to town?" No way he was hanging around here.

"Tomorrow?"

"Yes, sir."

"Okay. How do you feel about going back out?"

"Mox nix to me. I'll go. What the fuck, sir."

"I'd appreciate it. We'll need you."

He spent the afternoon neatly folding Irwin's things and putting them in his duffel bag. After a while everything he said to himself about death and how much he'd miss Irwin sounded stupid. Trying to feel reverent about someone while you were folding up the drawers and fatigues that he'd never wear again was almost laughable. Better to think of it as something to be expected in war. He wouldn't want anybody weeping after him if he got greased. Better they got drunk and laughed a little. That's probably what Irwin would want. Damn right! He took a pair of Irwin's drawers and put them in his own duffel bag. He'd wear them to the whorehouse tomorrow.

He and Padgett went to town the next two days, returning at night totally drunk, the big side pockets of their jungle fatigues filled with marijuana. Padgett was pretty fucked up too. Jerrie had cut him loose, and it made him sick of everything—the war, the dead people, most of the alive people. They were both tired of the whole fucking mess. Being in town made them realize that they had no great love for the Vietnamese. Their beer tasted like piss, their whores smelled and couldn't screw worth a damn, their soldiers were chickenshit, and the people in general were just a bunch of money-grubbing stupid pigs. Their kids ran wild, selling rubbers and dirty pictures outside of the whorehouses that seemed to spring up as soon as the American troops arrived.

He instigated most of the trouble, but Padgett followed along. On the first day they beat up six Vietnamese soldiers, took three whores apiece (paying for only one), and stole beer at will, challenging the scrawny barkeeps to do something about it. On the second they wrecked the insides of two bars and knocked a wall completely over in another because it was too far to walk to the door. They each got six packs of pot for four dollars a pack. Slagel thought that a hundred and twenty joints might see him through the next two weeks.

He didn't bother to notice the names of the new men in his squad when they started out the next day. He hurt from the heavy drinking, felt ready to throw up. The sweep had been extended another ten or twelve days, and if things followed the normal pattern, they wouldn't have any more contact. One of the infantry brigades had been in a major battle with an estimated four battalions of North Vietnamese who had since gone back into Cambodia and were probably moving north. Then they'd reenter the Ia Drang Valley, and division could go back up there and chase them back into Cambodia again. This shit could go on forever.

He stayed alone in his old tent and smoked a joint with his

coffee every morning. He felt far away from everyone except Padgett, and they were usually separated by two squads during the day. At lunch they'd sit alone together, puffing leisurely on joints while the greenhorns gobbled their C's.

After three days of no action he began to goof off, firing at birds, pretending great danger when nothing was happening. He was so loaded most of the time that he couldn't fake the seriousness, and he'd laugh after everyone was crouched in the dirt anticipating combat. Webber spoke to him a couple of times, but it didn't make any difference. The captain didn't have the balls to really go after him, so he kept up his antics.

When he wasn't stoned or drunk, he slipped into a nervous bitterness that was downright frightening. He'd think of Irwin's smiling baby face, and that would trigger a string of pictures of the people who'd been zapped, like the end of a fucking war movie when the camera pans down the line of troopers who've been through some grisly experience together. He'd see them trudging along, sweating, cigarettes dangling, rifles slung, chin straps from helmets bobbing tiredly at the sides of their heads while the hero music played. He thought they should be arriving someplace where there'd be comforting girls, booze, and slaps on the back from people who appreciated what they'd done. But they were all dead, marching nowhere and to no music, and if he didn't join them, he'd just go home to nothing but pats on the back from VFW drunks, while the smart people would look at him as though he had the plague. God, but it was a cheat.

A week after they resumed their missions one of the scout helicopters spotted a squad of North Vietnamese in a clearing about four hundred yards from the rifle platoon's position. It was right before lunch, and Slagel needed a joint to fight his boredom and nervousness. He volunteered his squad to chase the NVA's, but Webber refused him coldly and sent the fourth squad instead. Two squads from one of the infantry companies were lifted out to a spot on the other side of the NVA's, and a helicopter with a door full of speakers was sent up with an interpreter to persuade the enemy to surrender. The rest of the platoon stayed ready, waiting for the NVA's to come to them or to help the fourth squad if something happened.

He had to dig in next to Webber and wait. The Vietnamese mumbo jumbo floated over to their position as the helicopter circled round and round the place where the North Vietnamese were hiding. It reminded him of the loudspeakers booming out his name after he'd done something on the stadium floor.

"Blue, this is Four-seven, over," crackled out of the radio.

"Roger, Four-seven."

"Blue, they've come out in this little clearing with their hands up, and your squad's bringing them back to your position. You bring them out, over."

"Roger, Four-seven. Better send an extra lift bird to the Lima Zulu. Out."

"Looks like we got them, sir," he said.

"Yeah." Webber didn't look at him.

He got up and walked down the line of his squad. What a sorry bunch. Herbert and Cunningham, two new guys, bent over the machine gun at the end of the squad. "This thing all set?" he asked them.

"Yeah, Sarge," Cunningham said. "Expecting some trouble?"

"Never know. Better let me sit behind it until those gooks get here. You guys eat your C's."

Cunningham moved out of the way and he lay down behind the M-60, nestled the butt plate into his shoulder, and squinted through the sight. He ran his tongue over his dry lips. What the hell would Webber do if he did shoot them? Bust him? Bring charges against him? Hell, no. Webber was a candy ass.

The eight NVA's looked like little rag dolls someone had dug out of a moldy attic trunk, and when he shot them, he expected stuffing to come out instead of blood. On the periphery of his vision he saw panic spread through the platoon, and he stood up so everyone would know who was shooting. He fired nearly two hundred rounds, making the NVA's bounce and turn over as if they were on a trampoline. He threw the gun to the ground and began to laugh. He put his hands on his hips, held his head back, and roared until his steel pot tumbled to the ground. He stopped laughing and made an icy sweep of the platoon with his eyes. He dropped to his knees and began to sob, then fell forward, buried his face in his forearm, and pounded the earth with his fist.

He woke up hot and sweaty, lying on a cot in the aid station. Broad daylight outside. "What the hell am I doing here?"

"Hey, Slagel," Morris, one of the medics, said. "Relax. You've been getting some Z's."

"What time is it?"

"Noon."

"Noon? Jesus! What day is it?"

"Hell, I don't know. Wednesday, Thursday. They're all the same in the Army, right? Man, you put up some fuss yesterday. They had to give you morphine to calm you down."

"Bullshit!"

"I ain't lyin'. You been in here sleeping like a baby since three yesterday afternoon. Afternoon, sir!" he said to Captain McCloud, the battalion surgeon.

"Hello, Morris. How are you feeling, Slagel?"

"Not bad, sir." His body felt incredibly heavy. "Did they really give me morphine?"

"I guess you got a little out of control. Must be too much combat. Maybe you need a rest. If you feel okay you can go. Captain Webber wants to see you when the platoon gets in tonight."

"Okay, sir. Thanks. I guess I'll get some chow."

Captain McCloud walked outside the tent with him. When

they were beyond Morris' range of hearing, he took him gently by the arm. "Listen, Slagel, if you want to talk to someone, I know a good psychiatrist at division. It's nothing to be ashamed of. You've done your share, and if it's getting to you, maybe you should take a break so you don't hurt yourself or someone else."

Dr. Bowen's face popped into his mind, and his stomach contracted. "Thanks for the offer, sir. I'll let you know."

He stopped at the mess tent for coffee, then headed back to his own. The KP's and cooks looked at him strangely, as if they were afraid to speak. He must've done some crazy shit after killing the NVA's. That was pretty crazy too. McCloud might be right. But he couldn't face a shrink. He was done with that shit. Maybe he just needed a break, or maybe he'd be okay for a while now that he'd gotten a lot of it out of his system. He went back to his tent and lay down.

Jews had lots of money and held on to it. They were smart, worked hard, and the women had bigger tits than the gentile broads. That's what he believed until midway through his sophomore year. Susie Rosen was in his history section, had given him the eye a couple of times, and she was good-looking and nicely stacked. He figured she was a Jew because Al Rosen, who'd played third base for the Cleveland Indians, had been one. Susie was from Cleveland but she wasn't related to Al Rosen.

A week before Christmas vacation he came to history five minutes early. He sat down by Susie Rosen. She produced the school paper and pointed to a picture of him with his football gear on in the middle of the page.

"That's you, isn't it?" she said.

"I guess." He hadn't seen the paper, but knew they were doing an article recapping the season and talking about the prospects for next year. It was a good picture, him leaning back with a stiff arm out.

"So you're the hope for next fall?" she asked.

"Is that what it says?"

"Right here." She pointed to a paragraph and laughed. "Do you really like doing that stuff?"

"I think I hate it." It felt so good to say it.

"Why do you do it?"

"Have coffee with me after class and I'll tell you."

She took him back to the apartment she shared with another girl. The rest of that day amazed him. This girl actually listened to classical music for fun, and read poetry because she liked it, and had paintings hanging on the walls as though her place were some kind of art gallery. It made his own room at the frat seem like kid stuff. All he had on his walls were stop signs he'd ripped out of intersections, an eight-by-ten glossy autographed by Howard Cassidy, one each of the team and of himself, newspaper clippings, a neon sign advertising Miller High Life beer, and a couple of *Playboy* foldouts.

And the warm easy way she talked about herself made him feel how stiff his own life was, made him feel how stupid it was to hold in his emotions. She touched him differently from the sorority bitches, not just trying to feel his muscles or tease his prick. She wanted to be closer to people. She served wine with dinner—he thought only Frenchmen and Italians did that—loosening him so that he finally began talking. For four hours he overflowed with horror stories about his father.

He felt relaxed and exhausted when they finally went to bed, and he dreamed that he and his father were lying naked, side by side, on a large plywood slab. His father quit breathing, and Slagel covered him with a cold white sheet.

He didn't go home for Christmas and stayed alone in Susie's apartment while she went to Cleveland. She came back just before New Year's, and they were together constantly through final exams. He surprised himself by getting a couple of B's—first time he'd ever gotten above a C average. The coaches had always fixed his grades before. They celebrated after the last final, and he got drunk for the first time in a month. When he woke up in the morning, he remembered nothing. Both eyes were puffed, and a lump rose off his forehead like a giant acorn. Susie said it had taken three men to subdue him and that he had caused considerable damage in the bar. He didn't understand it. She said he had been like a volcano, erupting suddenly with yelling, beating his glass on the table until it broke, then breaking the table and several other glasses until one of the men hit him on the forehead with a beer mug. He felt ashamed and confused. They'd been having such a good time, and he couldn't figure out what had made him so angry.

It was after that that Susie started talking about the pyschiatrist.

Dr. Bowen was one of the youngest shrinks in Upham Hall, and except for wanting to talk about football, he was okay. Slagel had been doubtful and hesitant, but both Susie and her roommate went. He began to trust Dr. Bowen after a month, and during March and April he made a great deal of progress. He was able to accept his father's limitations, and although he still had sudden fits of anger, he could bring them under control much sooner and without the usual destructiveness. He had moved out of the fraternity and taken a small room, but stayed with Susie most of the time.

After he went through his struggle to quit football, he and Susie had a couple of fantastic weeks before the time came to begin studying for finals. He never thought spring could be so fine. They took trips to Canal Winchester and Lockport and up to the Chinese Gardens on the Scioto River, where the spring flowers and greenery were so much prettier than in Columbus. As it got closer to finals, Susie suggested that he move back to his room so they'd each be able to study better. He knew he bored her sometimes; she was so far ahead of him in many ways. He didn't mind that anymore, because he was making progress, and he thought the separation might even be a good chance to test himself alone.

The only times he had to watch himself were when he drank. Sometimes he and Susie would drink at Larry's Bar on High Street, a hangout for therapists and their patients. He had gotten partially drunk with Dr. Bowen twice and nearly went out of control the last time, just a week before he moved back into his room. At his next session Dr. Bowen told him that it would be safer not to go to Larry's anymore, and Susie agreed. No sense in testing himself when the results could be disastrous.

How right the doctor and the woman were! A week later, when he was sick of booking and Susie had gone to study with a friend, he went down to Larry's to have a couple of beers. He walked in the front door, and his stomach started thumping like the inside of a kettledrum before his mind accepted what his eyes were telling him. Susie and Dr. Bowen kissing in a booth near the back! Sure as shit. He watched them with a kind of dull suspense—as if they were a movie—waiting for them to look up and see him. Dr. Bowen saw him first, and faded white as Susie turned toward him and quickly lost her color. He toyed briefly with what was going through their minds, found it funny, grinned, and walked away.

He sat in his room for three days, not sleeping and moving only to the toilet and back to the big chair. Susie came on the second day, but he could catch only fragments of her sentences. He heard that he was too slow and that she was sorry and that a lot of it had been fun. She cried before she left, but he couldn't do anything but smile. On the fourth day he got out of the chair and ate and cleaned himself up. Then he realized he'd done it for his appointment with Dr. Bowen, and he sat down in the chair for another two days.

He went back to the gym to lift weights. Twice a day, three hours each time. He ate well, ran five miles every morning, and spent at least two hours a day in front of a mirror, flexing and feinting with his head and shoulders. At night he lay in his thin-mattressed bed, fondling the smooth muscles of his shoulders and legs.

Tired, he pulled the flap closed on his tent to block out the sunlight. He rolled over on his sleeping bag, thinking that if his parents hadn't been killed, he might still be living in that room and lifting weights.

He woke up again at dusk, Webber tugging at his foot. "Hi, sir." He got up on his elbows.

"How are you feeling?"

"Pretty well. I—"

"Good. Slagel, I'm going to make this short and to the point. You fucked up bad yesterday, and by rights you should be in jail now, but I'm going to forget about it. You've done a good job, lost a lot of friends, and it hasn't been easy for you. So what happened yesterday's forgotten. As for the future, I don't much care. You can come back with the platoon, be a squad leader or not, or go back to base camp and work with the self-help people. But I want to get one thing straight: You do one more thing like yesterday and I'm going to hang your ass, and hang it high. We're over here to fight a war, and I know that's shitty, but it doesn't give you a license to kill anyone you want. You think about it—hard. You're one of the best soldiers I've ever seen. But if you murder someone else, you're going to pay for just that—murder. You can let me know in the morning what you want to do. Do we understand each other?"

"Yes, sir. I'm—"

"Good. I'll see you in the morning. Try to get a good night's sleep."

His mind raced with hatred and respect for Webber. He resented being called a murderer. People paid for his bullets with their taxes, and their lives went on while his had stopped. It was too much to think about. He lit a joint and puffed it greedily, trying to calm down. They'd have killed the soldiers if they'd surprised them. Why was everyone so bugged? They usually wanted the prisoners killed, didn't they? But enough. It was done with. Nothing more would happen. He had to figure out if he'd go back or not.

He lay down on the sleeping bag, feeling easy as the pot took hold. Was Webber trying to tempt him? No. He'd been too pissed. He'd laid it on the line like a man should. But in a way it was almost a challenge. He suddenly realized that he *was* a good soldier, very good indeed. He'd always thought he was fair, but if Webber could still tell him after what had happened, then it must be true. He could even see himself reenlisting, going to OCS, and staying in for a career. It wouldn't be so bad. Nothing on the outside meant that much to him anyway. He'd have to stay with the platoon. Start acting a little more responsible, that's all. Besides, he really didn't enjoy killing. But they'd pushed him to the edge. Maybe if he quit taking the diet pills and smoking so much shit, he could keep a better hold on himself. He couldn't go back to the base camp now. Everyone would think he was nuts. After another week of soldiering he'd prove himself again, and everything would be forgotten. Only seven months to go anyway.

He lit one more joint before putting the ones he had left, and all his pills, in a bag to throw away. Lying back again, he drifted in and out of images of himself with the squad. They could be made into a good group, good fighters and full of fun too. It could be like the old days before they'd been wiped out in Happy Valley.

The whistling reminded him of a police siren he'd heard in a Bob Dylan song one night in Berkeley. He didn't even flinch at the first explosion, which was dull and sounded far away. Voices were yelling, "Incoming, incoming." He sat up and put on his steel pot. There was a bunker by the mess tent, fifty yards away. He stopped outside the tent to strap on his pistol belt. The fuel point at the other end of the camp was a bright orange ball of fire, silhouetting a jeep trailer a few feet to his left front. As he walked by it, a high whistling invaded his head. He turned his back to the trailer and began to run, then a tremendous explosion stopped his legs. He fell forward, unable to move his arms up to break the fall. It felt as though someone had buried an ice-cold ax head at the bottom of his back.

10

MORGAN STARED over the counter into the after-midnight blackness outside the tent. Quiet, finally. Greene had dragged him out of the club at ten when the first of the twenty-seven casualty reports had come in. Now it was finished, and the personnel daily summaries from each company lay in a neat stack on the counter, waiting for their consolidation and trip to division by two. Why they'd changed the time of the report from ten A.M. was beyond him. Maybe Westmoreland wanted it at a different time—maybe McNamara or LBJ himself. He saw the reports running like a million tiny tributaries into a gigantic river. He'd have a hand in what the President read. Hot shit.

Slagel's name stared up at him from C Company's report. Critically wounded, already medevacked to Japan. His stomach had dropped when he'd first seen the casualty report, his body helpless and nervous with the fact that he could do nothing but read and record. Recording calmed him. Writing the name in five different places reduced the event to a piece of information to be passed along. He saw no blood, heard no screams of pain. It still seemed as though Tom would be there when battalion came in from the field.

Or would be out there when Morgan arrived at the end of the month. He'd had his doubts earlier tonight, facing the stack of casualty reports. Corporal Stout, gunner on the colonel's chase ship who'd given Morgan a few lessons on the flight line, had taken numerous hunks of shrapnel and was now at the division base hospital. Zastrow, his crew chief, had been medevacked to Japan with Slagel. For an hour and a half Morgan doubted the wisdom of his going to the field, had nearly cried out to his sergeant and Captain Greene that he'd stay in S-1 for the rest of his tour. But now, driving through the quiet night, taking the report up to G-1, he knew he wanted to go. He'd made his decision and would stand by it.

He didn't know what he wanted more, to go to the field or to leave S-1. Greene, who'd been passed over for major again last month, was driving him batshit. So was Sergeant First Class Chase, the personnel sergeant. Morgan had liked him at first—Chase was young, competent, and not a dough-bellied alcoholic like most of the lifers. He worked hard and had resolved not to cheat on his wife during his year away. But the months told on him, and lately he'd become a bitchy old woman. Greene frustrated him continually, reading all the documents and blocking Chase's many shortcuts. Sometimes Chase reminded Morgan of an old neutered tomcat, concerned only with his chow and sleep. Being shut of Chase and Greene would occasion no sorrow. The three of them sat around the tent day after day, bitching at each other about nothing. Going to the field would be almost like going on R&R.

Back at Overhead he took a beer from Alexander's cooler and sat on the edge of his cot. He imagined himself in the helicopter door, in flight helmet and flak jacket, whizzing along the treetops. How much better than pushing paper, better than feeling pissed off at guys for getting wounded and causing him extra work. He knew the war had nothing to do with it, at least not fighting an enemy. The VC and North Vietnamese were no more of an enemy than Greene or Stubbs. They were people with whom you played the game. You had to accept the rules and the consequences. Maybe it was wrong, but he would go where his impulses led him. He needed input. His life had been too ordinary, too fucking dull.

You couldn't beat his life for normalcy. He'd been transplanted from the Midwest to Los Angeles in 1953. His father starved during the Depression, fought in World War II, worked demonically into a management position with an appliance firm in Van Nuys, gave his son too much, made life too easy for him. The son was ungrateful, of course. All through junior high and high school his grades were bad, and when he graduated with a C-minus average, his father (who'd had to quit school in the eighth grade) couldn't even buy his way into a university. But the son blossomed in junior college. He repudiated his former world of sports and clubs and student government, repudiated blazer jackets and ivy-league clothes and short hair. He read, thought about what he read, got A's. Father, of course, said B's were fine. Why not play a little ball or join a fraternity, do all the things he never got to do?

He went to Berkeley, did well, then something went wrong and he quit in his senior year, the week before Kennedy was shot. The summer before, he'd begun to feel an irresistible attraction to wildness, to getting drunk and going out of control. He spent three days in jail, loving it because he'd done it, not read about it.

Because reading was no longer enough. About life, yes, but not really living. He'd wanted to teach, but how could he, knowing nothing but what he'd read in books? So he decided one night, while reading the *Piscatory Eclogs* of Phineas Fletcher, drinking Gallo muscatel, and listening to Pink Anderson sing "I've Got Mine" on the record player, that he didn't need to go to school anymore.

He drank, chased women, hitchhiked, rode freight trains with pints of cheap whiskey in his green book bag, went to dingy bars in Oakland and San Francisco in search of experience, of suffering. He'd had an easy life and could neither feel whole nor accept his advantages until he'd at least tasted the miseries of others.

He hitched across the country, broke, experiencing fatigue and hunger and cold. Sometimes it all felt like a charade, as though he were a voyeur with no right to be there. He could always call someone collect, ask for money or a bus ticket. But he stayed on the road, had luck with people buying him meals, and even walking in the cold he felt proud of the wet socks hanging out the rotted front ends of his boots.

He arrived at Princeton late in March and immediately realized his error. He had thought everything would be all right, that after his suffering on the road the world would be his. But he had no money and had not calculated on its sheer and utter necessity. He leeched off his friends and hated himself. In three weeks he went to see the recruiter.

Experience, experience. From school to the road to the Army to Fulda to Vietnam. One more step on the ladder to go. Combat. Now that he was here, why not take it? He slid into his sleeping bag, tucking the mosquito net under it so the rats couldn't jump onto the cot while he slept.

In five days the latest operation ended, and as Morgan returned from a laundry run, the jeeps and trucks from the other companies were rolling up and down the battalion road, bringing in men from the flight line. He found Chambers in one of the tents, hanging his mosquito net over a cot.

"Orville! What's happening?"

"Hey, Will. You look good."

"I feel good." He'd been going easy on the booze ever since Chase said he could go to the field, and his body felt alert, cleaned out. "You glad to be in?"

"Sure, but we're going back out in four or five days."

"No rest, huh?"

"All set to come down to the line, Morgan?" Brooks, the former clerk, now Major Quinn's gunner, slapped him on the back.

"Hi, Brooks. Sure. I'm learning the guns right now."

"Good. See you later."

"On the first for sure." He had to calm down. It was still three weeks away. "Get some beer tonight, Orville?"

"Why not? You're all set for gunning, huh?" Chambers' beady eyes narrowed in his large head.

"I guess. How do you like it?"

"It beats humping, but still sucks. Too bad about Tom."

"It really is." He tried to feel sober, but it wouldn't come. "Did you see him after he got it?"

"No. Medics picked him up, then he went on to Japan. You heard anything more?"

"Just that he was in critical condition."

"He'll probably never walk again." Chambers said it evenly, with finality.

"What do you mean?"

"Medics said he couldn't move when they picked him up. Shrapnel—big hunks too—buried in his back. Probably messed up his spine."

"It's hard to imagine Tom not being able to walk." He shuddered as he saw Slagel strapped in a wheelchair. "They'll probably fix him up."

"I wouldn't bet on it. They fuck people up for good out there." Chambers moved his arm in a circle above his head.

Padgett came in before chow, and the three of them went to the club when Morgan finished work. He'd never seen LaMont in such shape. Fatigues spattered with dirt and grease, hair long, the bill of his baseball cap jutted comically to one side. His eyes were red and tired.

They each got a beer but could find no place to sit where they wouldn't be surrounded by fifty screaming people. A crap table stood by the bar, and the first one-armed bandits lit up the back wall where soldiers banged them and fed them coins, faces greedy with expectation. Too much like Fulda. The clothes were different, there were no waitresses and no shitty bands with fucked-out broads rubbing their snatches on the microphone, but the spirit was still the same. Hunger and desperation for women, companionship, forgetfulness. For success at anything, if only the slot machines. Three oranges and you won a couple of bucks.

"Let's get out of here," Chambers said. "I can't hear myself think."

They went to an old bunker at the end of the S-4 tents, its sandbags rotted open from too much sun and water. They crawled up on the bags and sat in a circle. Padgett seemed ready to fall asleep while Chambers talked about going to college. He'd written the University of Minnesota and figured that with an early out he could enroll for spring quarter the next year. That and his reading seemed to be his only interests. He got up to leave after finishing just one beer. "You coming, LaMont?"

"I'll shoot the shit with Morg awhile. See you in the morning."

They sat quietly for a moment, then Morgan lit a reefer, and they passed it back and forth without speaking. The night had come on almost unnoticed, and he could see Padgett's face only when illumined by the uneven red ember of the joint. Rotor blades popped as helicopters, winking soft reds and yellows, glided down to the helipad half a mile away. A sudden gust of wind rattled the palm fronds in the tree above them.

"Jerrie quit me, man," Padgett said.

"No."

"Ain't this a bitch? Left me for some jive jittybug I used to hang out with."

"Jesus. I'm sorry, LaMont."

"Ain't no big thing. It just made me think about when you and me and Tom used to tear up New York with her and his sister and my cousin."

"We had a lot of fun."

"Damn did. All gone now, though, huh? Tom's sister married, cousin married, and now Jerrie off with this clown."

Morgan got a hard-on just thinking about Patti Slagel. Smart little nurse who'd caught herself a doctor. "Maybe you can get her back when you get home."

"Fuck that bitch. Maybe I'll come out to California and we can get all smoked up and stand on the street corner talkin' shit. Tell 'em I'm like Donald Duck—got web feet and don't give a motherfuck!" Padgett laughed tiredly. "Me and old Tom tore us some pussy in Cheo Reo, though. I guess we were both of us three-fourths goofy. When I saw him zap those NVA's I was sayin', 'Yeah, baby, get one for me.' I've been feeling sorry all right. I hope I can get it together on this next operation."

"What happened to Tom out there? How come he did that?"

Padgett collapsed on his back and groaned. "Shit, I don't know. Maybe it seemed like a good idea at the time. You know, man, he probably had the ass from people fuckin' up and dyin' all around him. We nearly killed some ARVN's in Cheo Reo. Couple more drinks and we would have. I don't know, man. Why does anyone do anything?"

He couldn't answer, but it seemed as if there should be a warning before a person flipped out like that. Someone should've seen it, given Tom a few days rest. He felt revulsion for the act, but it cost him no sleep. Part of him remained awed by it, by the sheer immensity of being that far out in the zone of no control.

He'd run amok once in Fulda himself, but behind alcohol speeded through his veins by diet pills. He'd climbed a garage roof, leaped to the balcony of a house, and smashed doors and windows in pursuit of someone's wife until the MP's took him away. Slagel had gone crazy in Fulda a couple of times; so had Padgett. So had nearly everyone except old steady Chambers. How could you know when it might happen to you?

Morgan said good-bye to Padgett and Chambers, then drove Stout down to the flight line. Battalion was going back to the field, and Stubbs was making Stout go along. "You all set to get out there again?"

Stout shrugged his large shoulders. "I guess." He really looked like an old soldier, and he was only twenty years old. Deeply tanned, a large bushy mustache drooping off the corners of his lips and onto his jaw, he could've been in the war for ten years. "Only thing fucked up is my sleep. I had a dream this morning that I was on the flight line in broad daylight when this thing starts falling down from the sun. I know it's a mortar, but when it gets closer, I see it's really me—my face grinning down out of the sky at me on the ground. I woke up before the thing exploded, but I was on the floor yelling my head off. Other than that I'm okay. At least Stubbs seems to think so."

"That asshole." Stubbs had just come back from a thirty-day emergency leave stateside, because his wife had had alleged trouble with her pregnancy. Everyone knew it was bullshit. He'd probably phonied it up with the Red Cross just so he could get a little break. He'd hinted as much to Alexander on one of their trips to town, and Alex had told the others, admiration for Stubbs' cunning in his voice.

Stubbs was the fixer-upper, but he wasn't as swift as he thought. Alexander had been fooling him for two months, using the laundry runs made in Stubbs' jeep to trade greenbacks on the black market. He and Winston had made at least five thousand so far, and they'd been getting plenty of pussy too.

"Well, Timmy, take it easy out there. Say hi to Zastrow when he comes back. I'll see you on the first. Thanks for the lessons."

"Okay, Morg. Keep cool."

He sat in the jeep on the road in front of the helicopter, watching the crew get ready. Stout wore his flak jacket and flight helmet and looked knowing and nonchalant as he snapped the barrels into the guns, peered inside the step holes of the cowling for fires, slid into his harness, and climbed onto the seat. He raised his thumb to Morgan, then the ship jerked off the ground, rose ten feet, and hovered around forty-five degrees. The wind tore off Morgan's baseball cap and blew sand onto him and into the jeep. The chopper dipped its nose and headed north as he ran across the road to retrieve his cap.

The next day S-1 got a huge bundle of reassignment orders for the men who'd come over with the division and a flight manifest form that had to be filled out in four days. Greene supervised the job as though his life depended on it. The whole battalion became electric with activity. The first sergeants and company clerks were suddenly officious, making lists, revising them, revising them again, bringing them to S-1, and getting them to jibe with the battalion master list. Morgan, Greene, and SFC Chase spent fourteen hours a day in the tent, balancing the forthcoming losses of personnel with the projected gains. Going to chow or drinking became nearly impossible. People besieged Morgan with questions about their orders, begging and even offering bribes to get on the manifest as early as possible. Chase fumed with rage, screaming at anyone who came near the tent. He had Morgan bring him his meals, and he wouldn't leave except to go to division.

They got the list ready in time, and the day after they finished he decided to ask Chase about leaving. Only eleven days until the end of the month, and he didn't want to be left hanging with no replacement. He waited till late in the afternoon, when Greene was out, and just the two of them were drinking Cokes in the sweltering heat of the tent. "It's a relief to have the list done, huh, Al?"

"Sure is." Chase put his feet on the desk and flipped through the small notebook that contained the master list. "You did some good work on this, Will. I appreciate it. Hell, you and me could run this place fine without Greene."

"I suppose. Listen, Al, how about me leaving?"

"How about it?" Chase reached behind him and grabbed a notebook of regulations.

"I don't mean to bug you, but do I go or not?"

"You found yourself a replacement yet?" Chase opened the regs and stared at them.

"What do you mean?"

"Just what I said."

"You mean I've got to find him?" He couldn't be this chickenshit.

"You don't expect me to, do you?"

"It's your office."

"And I got a clerk I'm happy with. I don't want to change that."

"How the hell am I supposed to find one?"

"I'm sure you can figure that out."

He stormed down to Overhead but the talk was so intense about going home that they hardly noticed him. Same with his friends in aircraft maintenance. They were all leaving. They couldn't care less if he got what he wanted. What did going to the field have to do with anything anyway?

Greene was his last hope. He didn't want to ask him, but how the hell could he find a replacement by himself? He didn't swing any weight with the people at division, and he couldn't do them any favors. Chase had him, and if Greene wouldn't help, there wasn't much he could do.

At eight o'clock he drove alone to the division shower point. There were plenty of showers around the battalion now, but he wanted to get away from all the celebrating. He was glad his friends could leave, but it had nothing to do with him. If they offered him a plane ticket home tomorrow, he wouldn't take it.

At ten o'clock he stopped at Overhead to drop his dirty clothes. Alexander and Winston knelt on the floor, talking in quick whispers. They jumped when he walked in. The rest of the tent was empty.

"Morg, baby," Alexander said. "Come here and check this out quick."

He stuffed the fatigues in his laundry bag and walked over to the cot. A huge pile of ten- and twenty-dollar bills lay on a piece of newspaper between them. Big deal. "*Beaucoup* money you guys got there."

"Talk titty," Winston said. "There gonna be twice as much tomorrow when we finish downtown."

"Mama-san pay two scrip for one greenback now," Alexander said. "We gonna have ten thousand apiece by tomorrow night."

"You can buy some more liquor for Overhead."

"Overhead comin' down in a couple days," Winston said. "I'm sending this home to my old lady, and we gon' partyyyy when I get back."

Morgan stepped over to his cot, took off his thongs, and pulled on a pair of clean socks. "Your laundry runs paying off, huh, Alex?" He wished he could feel some excitement, but it seemed silly. Money couldn't solve any of his problems.

"You bet your booty. Old Stubbs think I'm really being helpful going to town for him every day."

"That motherfucker's some fool," Winston said. "Bet he'd be tryin' to make out too if he knew what we was doin'."

"Is that right, Sergeant Winston?" Stubbs stepped out of the darkness through the tent flap. His thick eyebrows grew together diabolically above his nose. Malicious triumph radiated from his face. "Do you have any idea how long you can spend in jail for black-market activities? And for taking an officer's name in vain?"

"I didn't mean it sir," Winston said. "You want the money, you can take it." He was totally panicked.

"And for trying to bribe an officer?" Stubbs had too much ego to accept the money. His sneering victory kept back his rage at being insulted. "Well, Alexander?"

"I don't know."

"You don't know *what*?" Stubbs roared.

"Sir! I don't know, sir."

"Morgan, what do you know about this?"

"Nothing, sir. I just came back from the shower point, and I'm going to do the PDS."

"Get up there, then. I'll deal with these two alone."

"Yes, sir." He wondered how badly Stubbs would burn them. He had a vindictive streak, probably from bitterness over his lack of education and having to grub after everything he got. He hoped Stubbs wouldn't be too rough on them, but their fate wasn't the most important thing on his mind right now.

Greene was rustling pages in the back when he came into S-1.

"Evening, sir."

"Evening, Morgan." Greene came around the bamboo partition with the manifest in his hand. "We did a good job on this redeployment. It should run smoothly from here on."

"Yes, sir. You're staying till August?"

"Have to make sure everyone gets out of here. It wouldn't look good if I grabbed an early seat."

"Sir, Sergeant Chase said I have to find my own replacement." Might as well jump right in.

"For what?"

Jesus. He isn't even thinking about it. "So I can go as Major Quinn's gunner at the end of the month."

"Oh, yeah. Explain that again."

He repeated what Chase had said, how he thought it was unfair and designed to keep him in S-1 forever. Greene listened patiently, although Morgan sensed that he experienced an inner glee.

"Well, Morgan, if that's what Sergeant Chase says, there's nothing I can do."

"But you're the adjutant, sir."

"That's true, but I can't cross Sergeant Chase. The S-1 clerk is his responsibility, not mine."

"But isn't it unfair?"

"Technically, no. You've still got ten days to find someone. That's not impossible. You can check the new troops as they come through here, see if any of them can type, and you should find some that would rather clerk than chase Charlie."

"That's it, then, sir?"

"I'm sorry, Morgan. You've done a damn good job, and we want to pay you back by letting you go to the field. But you'll have to do your share in finding a replacement."

He nearly tore the PDS report in half. He wanted to tear down the office, to yell at Greene and tell him what a sorry sack of shit he was. "Okay, sir," he said. "I'll start trying to find one tomorrow."

"Good luck, Morgan."

Alexander and Winston were talking by candlelight when he returned to Overhead after midnight. The lights had been turned off, and the rest of the tent slept. He shook his head and sat down on Winston's cot, facing them. "It's too bad, you guys. What's he going to do?" Both of them were as jumpy as cats.

"He gonna cool it," Alexander said. "Man, we ought to get some sleep." He and Winston nodded at each other.

Morgan took a beer from the cooler and went over to his own cot, glad they didn't want to talk. He wasn't up to it. At least they wouldn't get in too much trouble. He guzzled the beer quickly and crawled into his sleeping bag. Sleep would be a long time coming. He smoked for a while, then pulled the mosquito net down and tucked it under the bag.

They could drive him crazy with frustration. He wanted to murder Chase and Greene. His body was rigid as though electricity pumped through it instead of blood. What were they trying to pull? He was a good clerk, but that wasn't shit. Any idiot could do it. Follow directions and type. So why did they have to pick on him? Greene was jealous, that's all. Never got to fight. Couldn't even get promoted. Chase probably felt the same way. He was too smart to get his ass in the field, although it probably gnawed at him just the same. But why take it out on him? What they were wasn't his fault.

He dozed briefly, waking to whispers from the other side of the tent. Something moved by Winston's cot, then two figures ducked out beneath the tent flap. He listened to the snoring and muttering of the other soldiers in Overhead. What a crazy group of losers. A muffled explosion that sounded far away, maybe over the hill and past the perimeter, punctuated the snores. He hoped there wouldn't be an alert. Probably a night artillery salvo. He listened for the concussion but heard nothing. Footsteps pounded on the path outside the tent. From the moonlight he saw Alexander and Winston duck under the flaps, undress quickly, and slide into their sleeping bags. In fifteen minutes the entire rear echelon of the battalion was fallen out on the road. Someone had murdered Major Stubbs by throwing a grenade into the conex box where he slept.

The people from the Criminal Investigation Division

interviewed him at seven that morning. He'd been up late with the PDS, and he might have seen someone on the road or around the conex boxes behind S-3 where Stubbs had been murdered. No, he hadn't seen anyone. And he didn't know anyone who had it in for Stubbs.

The rest of the morning he stayed in the tent, filing regulations and bringing the casualty book up to date while the investigators conferred with the colonel, Greene, and other officers. By noon he knew Alexander and Winston would never be caught. No clues. No fingerprints on the door, and so many people had gathered outside after the explosion that no footprints could be traced. Stubbs must not have told anyone about the money.

When he walked into Overhead, Alexander and Winston were sitting on cots by the cooler, drinking gin and ice water. He got his mess kit, then plopped down next to Winston. As the gin boiled in his chest, he realized that they were waiting for his daily report on S-1 folly. If they knew he'd been awake, they'd probably kill him.

He took three long gulps of ice water and shook his head. "Looks like the culprit has escaped." He was careful to use the singular, to sound unconcerned, but not flippant either. No one pretended to give a shit for Stubbs, but no one laughed about it on the first day. "Whoever did it sure didn't leave a trace." He explained about the morning, trying not to notice Alex and Winston relaxing. The temptation was great to let them know he knew, but there was no way. He went to chow, although he would have liked to remain in the tent, invisible.

Stout's ship had come in with the colonel's that morning. Morgan went down to the flight line after chow and sat in the ship alone while Stout helped another gunner correct a malfunction. As he sat on the floor, smoking, his hands suddenly began to shake. He had really been a witness to murder and was withholding vital evidence. That made him an accessory after the fact.

His head jerked involuntarily as he thought of Stubbs. The conex box was about seven by seven by seven. They'd picked him off of the ceiling, floor, and all four walls. He wondered if Stubbs woke up before the blast, had a moment, when the door closed and he realized that he was trapped, in which his entire sorry life occurred to him in a split second. Maybe he lunged for the door and was caught in midair. Or did he shrivel into a corner? Perhaps he'd just laid in his bed, wondering why someone had closed his door.

He could still turn them in, say that after he'd thought about it for a while he remembered some people leaving the tent. This wasn't just bullshit Army games. Flat-out murder!

He turned and let his hand come to rest on the cool metal of a fragmentation grenade. He smiled to himself, thinking of Alex and Winston in Leavenworth forever or of them calling for gin and ice water before their execution. No way he'd be responsible for that. He argued his silence politically, racially, culturally, then nearly laughed. He liked them, for Christ's sake, and he hated Stubbs' guts. And nothing would put Stubby's guts back together again.

He raised the grenade and pressed it to his cheek. So cool, little olive-drab drop. He sat up in the seat and tested throwing motions—overhand, underhand, and sidearm. When you approached a target at eighty knots, the best thing would probably be to hold it up right below your eye, then let it go with a quick flip of the forearm, as though you were throwing darts.

11

PADGETT JUMPED off the helicopter into the waving brown grass, took two steps, and fell forward, pain shooting up his leg. He closed his eyes on a series of expanding red circles. "Fuck it! Medic!" His yell whispered against the clattering rifles and whining helicopters. The guns stopped and the choppers pulled pitch. "Medic!" The platoon started to move.

"What's wrong, brother?" Kelly said, dropping his machine gun and kneeling beside him.

"Punji." The pointed bamboo stake stuck in his right leg, through his fatigues, six inches below the knee. "That dude smarts."

Tuttle, the medic, tore the fatigues from around the wound. "Little scratch, LaMont. Nothing serious." He pulled the stake out.

The red shot up behind his eyes again. "Careful, man. Why you medics want to make a man feel so good all the time?"

Tuttle poured brown-orange fluid on a piece of gauze. "This'll sting a bit." He pressed the gauze over the wound.

The red circles popped purple. "Mother fuck you, Clyde. Damn!" He squeezed his rifle and ground his teeth, feeling hot all over.

"Get up and walk," Tuttle said.

"How's it feel?" Captain Webber asked.

"Okay, sir." Besides the stinging, it didn't hurt so bad.

"Tuttle, what's it look like?"

"Nasty little hole, sir. Might take a stitch or two."

"I'll call back one of the birds."

"Sit down, LaMont." Tuttle pulled the gauze off, dabbed the wound again, then tied a thick bandage around it. "That'll hold you till you get in." He winked.

"Thanks, Tut. Keep me out of this shit for a while."

Back at the medical tent Major Quinn came in as Captain McCloud put a bandage over the stitches. "How's it look, Mac?"

"He'll have to stay off it, except for some light walking to keep the muscle loose."

"Could you manage a few days' rest, Padgett?" Quinn's teeth were yellow, nearly the color of his face.

"I could handle it, sir."

"Supply ship's going back to base camp in an hour. Take

five days if you want. Just get back out here before I leave."

"Thank you, sir."

"That's okay, General." Quinn saluted him and left the tent.

The major was good people. Shot down three times, crashed and burned twice. Some fighter too. Only CO who'd kept his company for the whole tour. And he wasn't half-steppin' now that he was short either. Was working hard breaking in a new commander. It didn't help that much, but Quinn at least tried to keep up morale, getting to know the new men, bullshitting with you in the chow line. Wasn't the phony with the social scene like the other officers. Did his job and didn't make no big deal about it.

Using a stick, Padgett picked pieces of dried, red-orange clay from the lugs of his jungle boots as the chopper headed back to the base camp. He wasn't sorry to leave the ravaged Ia Drang Valley for a few days. Chances of contact were good, and he just wasn't up for it. They'd been operating around Plei Me Special Forces camp, on the eastern slopes of the mountains that divided Nam from Cambodia. Whole divisions of NVA's were laid up on the other side, and someday the rifle platoon would be caught in the middle and chopped to shit again, and his number was due to come up. Maybe today's punji would hold it back.

He missed the green from the other places. The trees in Ia Drang were gray all over, because the bombs and bullets had killed them and they didn't leaf anymore. He'd never seen so many craters, staring up from the ground like assholes. And dry. His fatigues carried a faint tinge of orange from the dust. He'd almost be glad when the rainy season started again.

The jungle grew greener as they approached the base camp. The chopper cleared the last mountain and started down the pass to the helipad. He relaxed, nearly falling asleep. Maybe he'd just stay in his tent and blow Z's for a few days. He didn't miss anyone from his squad, and he felt pleasantly unconcerned with whatever happened in the field.

As the truck dropped him off in the little parking space between C Company's orderly room and S-1, Morgan bounded out of the tent. "LaMont! Got another punji, huh? How do you feel?"

"Okay, man." He wasn't ready for no barrage of questions. "How you makin' it?"

"I'm still here. Sorry bastards. Still looking for a replacement." Morgan's face flashed his pissed-off look, then got sad. "Looks like I'm not going to gun for Major Quinn."

"He hattin' up in a few weeks anyway."

"I just want to get out of this fucking place."

He left Morgan and fell out on his cot in the big tent for the rest of the afternoon. Unlived in for a week, the tent was musty. The air seemed month old, stale, and unbothered by human life.

That night, walking to chow with Morgan, he noticed the rectangular cement slabs covering the ground where Headquarters Company's tents had been. "They tore down Overhead, huh?"

"Tore down all of B Company and Headquarters. Guess A and C are next."

"You all down in the chapel?"

"Supposed to be. I was so oiled last night I passed out in the ditch next to Fisher's tent."

Morgan could go to sleep in a fire when he was drunk. "Gettin' back on the juice?"

"What am I supposed to do? You want to get some tonight?"

"Doc says I can't. But I guess a couple beers wouldn't hurt." He didn't go for Morgan getting out of control. It was a stupid way to drink, and the way Morgan did it would probably get him killed someday. He couldn't just get high and enjoy himself. And when he was done, he couldn't remember if he'd enjoyed himself or not. Maybe it would be better if he did go to the field. Have something to keep his mind on.

"No action last week, huh?"

"Punjis and boobies. Pretty slow." It seemed as if they'd been out for a year.

"You like it better that way?"

"Ain't no way I like it." He was all of a sudden mad. "I'm sick of the whole routine! The waiting gets to you, like you almost wish Charlie would come out, because you know he's around any damn way. Everybody kind of jittery. I'll be glad when it's done."

"We're halfway now. A year ago we were just getting ready to volunteer."

"Let's not talk about that. You hear anything more about Tom?"

"Got some orders transferring him to Walter Reed. I wrote to Patti, but haven't heard back yet."

After chow Padgett went to the area behind Fisher's tent, where Morgan had been drinking since Overhead went down. He nursed the beers slowly, smoking dope and saying little. The others talked about Stubbs and about the botched-up investigation by the CID. He'd only heard about Stubbs through Morgan, had never had direct contact with him. When news of the murder reached the field, he'd thought Morgan might've done it. But Morgan would've told him, and even if he didn't tell, he'd give it away in his actions. He couldn't hide a thing.

Damn! None of it fazed him anymore. People gettin' blowed away, murdered, losing their ever-lovin' minds. Uh-huh, so what's for dinner? He tried thinking about C Company. Only people came to his mind were Chambers, Webber, Todd, and Major Quinn. Four grays, the last two stone Crackers. And here he was sitting with a bunch more, listening to their jive. White jittybugs. Talkin' about all that cunt they going to lick back in the world. He finished his second beer, started a fresh reefer, complained of pain in his leg, and went up to his tent, where he could be alone and sleep.

He was supposed to walk to relieve the stiffness, and it was a good way to stay off detail. Parts of division he'd seen only from the air, so after chow the next afternoon he took a right off the battalion road and headed north on the division perimeter road. Next door the two infantry battalions were deserted, but seemed ready for a parade. Gleaming brass artillery canisters made a little fence around a large replica of the regimental crest, and a white flagpole grew out of the green grass, the stars and stripes hanging limply in the windless air. The regiment had had a series of hotshot commanders over the decades or centuries, and the battalions were always outdoing each other getting the most men killed. Both had had something like three hundred percent turnover so far, and the brigade commander had been awarded a couple of Silver Stars. For sure! Keeping his ass five thousand feet in the air and directing the battalions into the shit.

He walked slowly up the incline by division aircraft maintenance, unable to see the end of a line of tail booms and tail rotors sticking out nearly to the edge of the road. He tried counting up the row, but quit at fifty. There was another row inside the first—not so many choppers, but a shitload anyway. When he'd flown in from the field, aircraft maintenance hadn't looked like much more than an anthill off at the northeast corner of the pad. Up close it was out of sight. The cowlings torn away from the shiny engines and the shafts that drove the tail rotors, the birds tipped at all kinds of angles while grease-stained dudes crawled over them with wrenches and cans of oil. Other cats were tearing parts off choppers that had been mangled in wrecks and lay lopsided, like decomposing birds, on the oil-soaked helipad.

He felt a sudden urge to paint. If he'd had some paints and canvas, he would've sat down in the goddamn dusty road and started to work. He wanted a canvas as big as a football field or a wall a hundred yards long. The shapes in front of him began to extend infinitely, then became grotesque. He could make *Guernica* look like a country fair by the time he was done. Crazy. Crazy. He could make everyone see the crazy hurt of the whole thing. The faces of the mechanics didn't seem to mind. Safe job. Probably get a good job back in the world. But if he painted them, showed them to themselves as they really were—building cords of muscle into the weak birds—they'd know they were crazy, were uncontrollably out of proportion.

If he only had a sketchbook with him. That would really be out of proportion. Walking around a combat division painting pictures. But that's what the news photographers did. Driven around by some private so they could snap pictures of the helicopters and the troops. As though a photo said a thing about what was really going on. They never had any of the troops boozing or smokin' shit.

He made a slow turn around the curve at the northeast corner of the division, and the road declined until the next curve, a quarter mile away. Everything grew quiet, and then he realized it was only in his head. The excitement about painting seemed to die as quickly as the object to paint disappeared. There hadn't been much noise by aircraft maintenance. A few clowns yelling, a few helicopters being run up. Walking along the north side of the perimeter road he could still hear the ceaseless pop-pop-pop of the rotor blades, could still see the choppers coming in overhead to the helipad.

He was in second-brigade territory now, and he knew people would be scarce. Only the barest rear-echelon force—clerks, personnel sergeant, a few commo and supply people, mess people from one company, a few losers who'd gone scared or nuts or who'd been fucked up not quite bad enough to be sent home. They hadn't even put in cement slabs for barracks yet.

"Hey, brother!"

He looked all around but didn't see anyone. On the left side of the road was a broad empty space, then the dreary olive-drab rows of GP tents. To his right was a thin band of trees, parallel to the road. Beyond them the perimeter defenses were set up. A raggedy outhouse sat a few feet back in the trees. He heard silly laughter.

"Up here, brother. In the shithouse."
"What you want?"
"Come here, man."
He walked up to the latrine door. The giggling was crazy. "What you want, man?"
"Come on in."
He opened the screen door and entered. The dude looked like a spider all hunched up in the corner of the shit stool. Two holes gaped in the board.
"Have some, man." He held out a canteen and giggled. He couldn't have been more than nineteen, but his eyes had that shiny craziness in them like the old men on the corner in Newark who were always rapping their tired shit to the young bloods.
"What's in it?"
"Taste and ye shall know."
This dude was out of his frame. Muscatel. "Where'd you get the musky?"
"My man bring it from Qui Nhon."
He took another pull. Soft rotten syrup.
"Shit's out of sight, isn't it?"
"It ain't bad."
"I drink it all day too. You quit the field?"
"What?"
"I say, you quit the field, man? Like me. Lay up, drink pluck all day, smoke shit all night. Better'n the field."
"Why you in the shithouse?"
"My job after I quit the field. Burn shit. But don't burn no one's but my own, 'cause don't nobody else shit up here." He threw his head against the wall and laughed insanely.
"You nuts, man. How'd you *quit* the field?"
"Just told 'em. In the firefight, my main man blowed away, my next buddy can't move, I hat up right back to the CP. Told 'em I quit, I motherfuckin' *re*sign. Gave them my weapon and sat down. Wouldn't get up. They sent me back, told me to burn shit. You quit too?"
"No, man. I just got a punji and came in for a rest."
"You ought to quit, brother. Nigger crazy to stay out there.

Make 'em think you nuts like me. They think you crazy enough, they get scared and leave your black ass alone. That's right. They mess with me again and my shit's ready. Look here." He dropped to his knees and pulled three boards off the floor. An M-60 machine gune and an M-79 grenade launcher lay on a cloth next to five cans of bullets and three bandoliers full of grenades. Another box of hand grenades was set farther back in the trench.

"You ready, ain't you?"

"I stay ready. All I need now's an M-16, and I'll get that soon. I got a little tunnel back there and everything. Got me some C rations too."

Poor dude. Half out of his head and probably be all the way before he got home. "Thanks for the pluck, brother, but I got to get on the road."

"Where you goin'?"

"Back to my unit."

"You remember what I said, hear? Act crazy, man. It's the only way out of that shit. They fuck with you, come on up. There room for two here."

He was glad to get out of the second-brigade area. Too desolate, like a goddamn ghost town. It would be a good place to paint anyway, but right now the sparseness made him feel weird and lonely. Fuckin' Jerrie. Bitch layed up with some bullshit jittybug while he wasted away in a rice paddy. He walked up a hill by the support battalion. Inside a barbed-wire fence were stacked coils of more barbed wire, miles and miles of it. And piles of sandbags and hundreds of conex boxes and folded-up tents. Farther down the road were the five tents of the pathfinder unit. After having their asses dropped in the jungle for days at a time, they were coming out now with thumbs and fingers and ears swinging from their belts. Across from the pathfinders a small road led up to the division tactical operations center and G-1. Weird the way the two little green and white houses sat on the hill, surrounded by tents. For the CG and his deputy, looking like a pair of suburban cracker boxes.

The medevac ship flew so low that a jeep couldn't have gone under it. The medics were waiting by the helipad, and as soon as the skids touched down, the stretchers were pulled out, and the bearers jogged into the hospital with them. He stood on the side of the road, held his cap, and watched. Like a needle stuck on a record. Four bodies per ship. Five ships. What unit was it this time? Maybe his squad. The last chopper pulled off the pad, did a half turn, stared at him like a giant grasshopper, then flew away toward the fuel point. Through his fatigues he felt the hard roll of scar tissue on his side. Three motherfuckin' wounds, and he'd be going out again in a couple of days. He didn't mind that, didn't even mind the wounds so much, but at least they could let him get some pussy before he went back out. He was suddenly hungry for a woman.

The next day he got the first pig to put him on a pass list, and he went to town with Alexander and Winston for ice and laundry. The MP at the division gate squeezed the laundry bags, turned them over, and squeezed again. "You guys got anything in here besides clothes?"

"No, man," Alexander said.

He waved them through.

"He didn't check our pockets none, did he?" Winston said.

"What you cats holdin'?"

"Little dust to trade with Mama-san," Alexander said. "You ain't tellin' me you didn't trade none in the field."

"Never did. I hear the dudes on R&R makin' out real good." He thought he'd trade a few greenbacks when he finally got to go.

"Three for one in Nha Trang," Winston said. "Only two for one here."

"How much you got?"

"Thousand."

"Damn! Where'd you get it?"

"White boys like to lose that money at poker," Alexander said. "You get in a game and watch us—you'll win some."

That's all he needed. Start cheating grays at cards. It

always got him hot listening to splibs digging on fucking over whitey. So small. You could waste your whole life thinking about that. "You sure I can get some pussy today? I need that more than money."

"It ain't much," Winston said.

"It'll be something else when this place open up," Alexander said. He pointed to the right of the highway where a bunch of Vietnamese worked while a few Americans supervised. There must've been fifty rectangular block-houses going up in a square. Government whorehouses to regulate the clap.

"You know there gonna *be* some cock down there," Winston said.

"They be open in a month," Alexander said. He took a left at the road that went into town, then made a quick right into a laundry. Three young boys crawled on the jeep, yelling and begging.

"Deedee!" Alexander said and got out of the jeep.

Everything was brown except the aluminum roof. Two old men ironed while the boss ran around like it was a Chinese laundry in New York. A little girl played on a table by the brown mud wall of a hooch.

"Papa-san," Winston said. "Bring beer."

"Bring some boom-boom too," Alexander said. "You want it, Padgett, you better get it now. Motherfuckin' MP's be by here in a little bit."

"Lang!" Papa-san screamed at the little girl, then said something in Vietnamese and shoved her into the hooch. He directed Padgett through a door in another hooch, taking four hundred piasters from him.

Inside was more brown, the air a dead dusty gray. The woman, brown and gray herself, came through a side door that connected to the main hooch. She looked too old to even have the juice flowing anymore. Her smile made him think skeleton head, and as he screwed her, he kept expecting his joint to grate on little pebbles or grains of sand. She tried to be friendly, but he couldn't handle looking at her and got up and went outside as soon as he was done.

"Damn, breeze," Winston said. "You about set the record."

"Chest was heavy, man. That bitch's cock was filled with dust." He stuck his hand out and Alexander slapped it.

"I hate to admit it, but I thrown yards of dick into that motherfucker."

Some relief. Not much, but a shot was a shot and better than getting it off in your hand. An MP jeep cruised down from town, Alexander picked up the clean laundry, and they headed back to base. At the town ice plant, where they swapped their greenbacks, the blocks of ice cost eight dollars apiece.

"Old Morgan gonna be jealous of you," Alexander said. "Been a long time for him."

"He don't care about no pussy," Winston said. "He just want to get out to that field. That's some kinda crazy dude. Where'd you hook up with him?"

"We've been together since basic."

"And you all volunteered to come over here?"

"Yeah."

"Damn!" Alexander said and shook his head.

"He work his booty off up there," Winston said. "One night he didn't get done till nine thirty. Just got down to Overhead for some taste when these two dudes come in ask him will he go to division and get R&R orders for them. Said Chase wouldn't do it and that Chase said Morgan could do it if he wanted, but he wasn't gonna make him. Morgan like to shit. Start yellin' around about how they drivin' him crazy with work and motherfuckin' this and motherfuckin' that—you know how he carry on. The cats couldn't go in the morning unless they got orders that night. So he finally drove up there and got 'em. Said he had to bribe the division clerk with a pair of fatigues 'cause he didn't want to do no work either. I admired him after that, though, boy. I never seen no one in the Army do anything like that."

"He'll help you out if he can."

"That's right, Padgett," Alexander said. "But he fuck up behind that juice. Oooo-wee! Dude slept clean through alert one night he was so oiled. He'd probably fuck up in the field."

"I'm hip," Padgett said. "He still think they only playin'. But I guess he'll never think different till he gets out there."

"How about you, man? Why don't you get out?"

"I been thinkin' about it, Alex. Maybe after Quinn leaves I'll go my damn self. It's gettin' sorrier and sorrier the more new guys come in. I'll hang it up after the next operation." Why not? Both Quinn and Webber were going. No one depending on him anymore. He swallowed hard realizing that Webber was the only one who'd been in the platoon longer than himself.

"You ought to," Alexander said. "You could pick up one of these easy jobs when the old guys leave and make yourself some extra dust besides. You might get in at the club. Old Sergeant Wiencek made him some heap running that place."

He fingered the Combat Infantryman's Badge on his chest. Yeah, he was proud of it. And proud of his Bronze Star and Air Medal and three Purple Hearts. He saw himself in his uniform on the block, walking by front porches and waving at the old folks. Maybe they'd forget about him cutting up the heat and about the other crazy things he'd done. He'd earned the medals anyway, and probably a couple more they hadn't given him, so it wouldn't be no big deal for him to quit. He'd humped for six months, and by the time he got out it'd be seven or eight, so why not? He thought everyone should do his bit, but there was no sense overdoing.

He stayed in the base for two more days, sleeping sixteen hours per, walking and shooting the shit. His leg felt fine and base camp bored him, so he went back to the field. Morgan was getting too hard to handle anyway. Drunk and yelling about having to stay in S-1 and about how combat ready he was. It might've been funny for the rest of the base-camp chumps, but he didn't need to hear that shit. He'd been through enough of it.

He got to the field base, an abandoned tea plantation near the eastern end of the valley, late in the morning. The rifles were already gone for the day, so he prepared himself for tomorrow. Got new bullets, cleaned his rifle and put a thin coat of oil on the bolt, taped grenades to his ammo pouches and suspenders, filled his canteens with fresh water, and put two bottles of insect repellent beneath an elastic band around his steel pot. Combat ready? Does a brown bear shit in the woods?

After chow he went down to the flight line when he saw Chambers' ship coming in from a mission.

"Hey, dude! How's the leg?" Chambers squatted in the door, collecting shell casings.

"Ready to run. You guys fire?"

"Just prep for the rifles. No contact today, but they've had minor shit the last three days. No one hurt."

"I heard."

"This is Ia Drang, you guys." McCutcheon walked over from the tail boom, where he'd been tying down the rotor blade. "This ain't fuck-off time like some of the places we've been." His hound-dog face was dead serious. "Glad you're back, Padgett. They need you out there."

"Sho' 'nough!" He did a little dance and strutted. "I'm gonna lead my team over the mountains and into Cambodia."

"You might not have to." McCutcheon looked at the ground as though he were going to cry.

"Why's that, Cutch?"

"Because they'll probably be in our laps any day now. I've seen it before."

He eyed the crew chief for a moment. "And I bet you can't wait for it to happen again."

"What do you mean?"

"You dig this shit, man."

"Don't get funny, Padgett. This is serious."

Chambers elbowed him as he prepared to tell McCutcheon off. "Forget me, I just had too much of that good base-camp life." McCutcheon was like a preacher or something.

"That's okay. I'm going to chow. Orville?"

Chambers waved him away. "I'll skip till dinner."

McCutcheon walked toward the mess tent, his roly-poly ass swaying from side to side like a fat whore's.

"What's with that clown?"

"Like you say, he loves it. Too bad he has to act like he really cares." Chambers shrugged. "Maybe he does. He extended."

"Shee-it!"

"How was the base? Morgan didn't kill Stubbs, huh?"

"Guess not. He really whoopin' it up about coming out here." He threw his hands out helplessly. "If he comes, fine; if he don't, fuck it; but I just wish he'd keep his mouth shut. Same with McCutcheon."

Chambers nodded. "I know what you mean. I'll be glad when it's over."

"You all set to go back to school?"

"Yeah." Chambers' body all of a sudden had springs in it. He brought his duffel bag around from the baggage compartment, pawed through it until he produced the fat catalogue of courses from the University of Minnesota. He lit a cigar, then flipped pages, explaining classes he'd made little X's beside.

Padgett listened and watched, drifting back to the snowy December morning when he'd first seen Chambers. He and Morgan and Slagel had been on an overnight pass that Saturday, going up to Frankfurt to see the town and to try for a shot of cock. They'd walked from bar to bar most of the night, but the women were only coming on free drinks. They finally gave in and bought some pussy about midnight, drank until they were almost broke, then took the train back to Fulda.

There were two cafeterias in the Fulda *Bahnhof*, one for regular folks and another, cheaper and dirtier and dimly lit, where GI's and town drunks hung out. They were drinking and eating in the latter place when ten new guys burst through the door. Six o'clock in the morning, and all the lushed-up soldiers were looking for a laugh. Suddenly it was as though they'd been there three years instead of a couple of months. The new guys were young, dripping with enthusiasm for exotic foreign places, great beer, easy women. One of the clowns even had a box of Hershey bars tucked under his arm—he'd heard he could get laid for some chocolate.

Padgett and Morgan and Slagel had joined in the jeering too. They were Fulda vets—they'd come to expect nothing from the town but booze and boredom. They'd stumbled into the lobby half an hour later, with barely enough dust for cab fare back to the base. One lone new guy sat on his duffel bag by the main door, smoking a cigar and staring at the floor. They all made some jive remark to him about being new, and he'd smiled just enough to let them know he didn't want any trouble. Two nights later he'd been in their barracks when they'd teetered in from the club, and it didn't take long before he'd begun to run with them.

Damn, but Chambers had changed! From a lump who didn't seem like he could take in anything—like an old man, really—to this new young kid who couldn't wait to get back to school and learn. Morgan had pushed him, talking about books, dragging him to the record room at the library to listen to classical music. Chambers didn't move for a while, then all of a sudden the lump dissolved. Couldn't get enough of the buildings. Then it was him trying to drag Morgan to the library at night when Morgan wanted to drink. Even at the club he'd bring his book along, sneaking peeks while the rest of them got blowed away. He saved his money, and on weekends when the others stayed at the base and fucked their bread away on booze, he'd take trips to look at the architecture in other towns.

For the next three days Padgett was hardly part of the rifle platoon. His body went through the motions—he even captured a prisoner—but his head wasn't there. He couldn't feel afraid of the enemy, but only think of how sorry he'd become, how if he didn't get it together he'd just be one more jive ass when he got home. He couldn't stop thinking about painting, like how he was letting it go because he didn't give a fuck anymore. At night he lay on his bag and smoked dope and tried to see colors, but there wasn't nothin' but the night. And during the days he couldn't get it to come, couldn't let his eyes move in the colors and shapes in front of him. He only thought about how it wouldn't happen. It was like being in a sinking boat—he was so surprised at the water coming in that he didn't have the strength to bail.

On his fourth day out they moved into the northwest corner of the valley. He kept telling himself that it was greener, that the grass was thicker and the ground softer, but the words simply dropped in his head, without echo or reverberation. He talked to his men as though in a dream where he stood far away watching himself be a soldier.

As the first shots of the ambush were fired, he knew he was responding perfectly. Behind a tree, organizing the fire from his team, he dropped three khaki uniforms hiding in a clump of bushes. He calmed his panicked grenadier until his shots were placed precisely on the enemy positions. He dragged two wounded men behind the tree, fired clip after clip, dropping a body here, one there. The moisture from the ground soaked into his thighs and groin, chilling them. The sounds of battle were very far away.

The helicopters dropped in a hundred meters north, on the other side of a small stream. His team covered as the fourth squad ran behind them, dragging the wounded. The tree cracked as he stood up to run, and a low branch knocked his pot to the ground. He bent to retrieve it and streaks of yellow light tore though his eyes as something thudded on the back of his head. Some giant lay on his back, pushing his body into the soft grass.

12

"Wake up, Chambers! Let's go!"

Lying on the floor of the helicopter, his legs dangling out the door, he opened his eyes and looked back over his head. McCutcheon, upside down in the other doorway, was strapping on his vest.

"Come on, Orville. Blue's in the shit!"

The pilots clambered into their seats and the engine began running up. He struggled to his feet, grabbed the barrels from behind the seat, and clipped them into the side guns. Rotor blades were spinning all over the flight line. Jesus Christ! Blue was in it again.

He plugged in his flight helmet as the bird pulled pitch, gave the all clear, then arranged his machine gun, bullets, and grenades. His late-afternoon tired and heavy feeling was gone. The radio said that there were already several casualties from an estimated enemy company, and Blue was trying to get back to the landing zone by the stream. The afternoon in Happy Valley flashed through his mind—men dropping in the clearing, the mad scramble back to the LZ, helicopters shot and falling out of the sky. He swallowed a mouthful of panic and steadied himself against the fire wall.

The four lift ships circled the LZ while Major Quinn's and another gunnery ship sprayed bullets and rockets and grenades into the surrounding bushes. Red smoke crawled up through the foliage above the firefight.

"Four-one and Four-three, this is Six," Major Quinn said. "Dump everything you've got west of that smoke."

The pilots clicked their microphones in acknowledgment, then circled to the east to start their run. The riflemen stumbled across the stream, dragging the wounded, stopping to fire wildly back at the bushes. The noise from the bullets rose in low pops, like heavy paper tearing along a perforated line.

The side guns opened up as a pair of rockets tore out of the pod beneath them. He squeezed the trigger automatically, overshooting the target by a hundred meters before adjusting with the tracers. He feared shooting short and hitting his own infantrymen.

He saw nothing in the bushes but an increasing volume of smoke. He moved the machine gun a few inches to the side, a few up and down to cover as large an area as possible, then threw out two frags and a white phosphorus grenade as the helicopter turned beyond the enemy line. He bent to pull more bullets from the wooden box at his feet. His head shot back as something sharp pricked his cheek just below the eye. At the same instant the ship jerked violently to the left.

"Oh, shit!" Warrant Officer Patterson yelled. "My legs! They got me in the legs."

"I got it." Captain Hobart released the infinity sight and grabbed the stick in front of him. "You okay, Pat?"

"I got a bullet in my leg somewhere," Patterson groaned. "I'll make it."

Chambers' hand went up to his face, and the pin suddenly felt like a nail. The fat pad beneath his thumb came away bloody.

"Everyone else okay?" Hobart turned around. "Chambers, you're bleeding."

He pushed the mike button. "I think it's Plexiglas. I'm all right." It didn't hurt unless he touched it.

"Four-one and Four-three, this is Six. Take it in again. Out."

"Can you make one more, Pat?" Hobart asked.

"Shit, yeah." Patterson stiffened in his seat. "Let's bring *smoke* on those fuckin' gooks!"

As they completed the circle and started their second run,

the lift birds rose to their right, turned, and headed east. At least what was left of Blue was safe.

The chopper banked to the left, and he leaned out the door to fire a final burst. He thought he saw tracers flying under the tail boom. He looked to McCutcheon and his stomach dropped. The crew chief was gone! He scrambled across the seat. Outside the door McCutcheon's body hung over the pylon, his arms holding the machine gun below and firing furiously beneath the tail boom at the unseen enemy.

They were all at the aid station—Padgett, Todd, and Myles—sitting on the cot like prisoners waiting for interrogation. He nodded at them, then sat on a wooden stool beside the cot.

"Be with you in a second, Chambers," Captain McCloud said. He pushed his needle and thread through the purple skin on one of the new infantryman's legs.

"What you got, Orville?" Todd put his hand on his shoulder and squinted at his face.

"Plexiglas, I guess. How's it look?"

"Not bad. Dripped a little blood. Mine ain't nothin' but a scratch." Todd held up his bony, bandaged forearm. "Reckon I'll go out again soon enough."

Padgett giggled, stopped, all the time staring at the floor.

"What's up, LaMont?"

Padgett continued to stare at the floor, shaking his head an inch or so to each side. His lips were pushed out; he was more bug-eyed than usual.

"Tree fell on him," Morris said, handing Captain McCloud a thick piece of gauze. "He hasn't said anything since he got here."

"Fuck you, Morris." Padgett's voice sounded like a record running slow. He raised his head and stared insolently at the medic. "I said mother fuck you, chump!"

Captain McCloud got up; Morris sat down and began taping on the gauze.

"Shit!" Padgett's hands went to his waist, and he resumed staring at the floor.

"Okay, Chambers, you're next." Captain McCloud motioned him to a stand beside a table. "I wish you guys would break this habit of coming here."

Chambers shivered as the Plexiglas came out of his face. The dried blood was washed away, the fresh blood mopped up, and the cut dammed with gauze and tape. Another inch and he would have lost his eye. Had the bullet been fired half a second later, he could've lost his balls, or they could've crashed in a nest of NVA's.

He left Padgett sitting with the others and went back to his ship. Captain Hobart and McCutcheon had gassed it up and filled the cabin with rockets and boxes of machine-gun bullets. The chopper was deserted. McCutcheon had already gone to help another crew chief with a periodic inspection. The other gunners were gathered at Webster's ship, where Hancock, who had been shot down this afternoon, was drunk and bellowing the stories of his four crashes.

Chambers liked the other gunners well enough, except for the ones who kissed the platoon sergeant's ass all the time. But he didn't feel like talking to them, didn't feel like telling or hearing war stories at this time of night. What the hell was happening with LaMont? Why couldn't McCutcheon have loaded the side guns and the rockets? What would his parents say if they knew about this shit?

He flipped on the cabin lights, filled both pods with rockets, then crawled in the ship to load the boxes for the side guns. He knelt on a casing that sprung a nerve in his knee, nearly causing him to cry out. Just clean them up, Orville. You might get attacked tonight and have to go out again. How stupid, this continual loading bullets in little boxes so they could get sucked out the sides and into the ground. Besides that, he could've been dead.

He finished loading, adjusted the seat over the boxes, tested the slide of the bullets in the chutes to the side guns. All right. Everything all right. He spread his sleeping bag on the cabin floor, lay down, then thought of LaMont again. He couldn't just leave him like that. A friend needed to talk when he was down. His head jerked with guilt. He could've gone to see Slagel the night they'd been attacked instead of leaving him alone in his tent. But Slagel's murders had left him so outraged that he never wanted to see him again. For a moment he'd even felt glad that Tom had been wounded so badly, felt that he deserved the punishment.

He hopped out the door and nearly bumped into Padgett, who stood still in the darkness outside the ship. "LaMont! I was just coming to get you. You all right?"

Padgett shook his head and scuffed the ground with his boot.

"What's the matter?" In the moonlight moisture glistened on LaMont's face—a solid streak beneath each eye, phosphorescent beads of sweat on his forehead.

Padgett shook his head again, then extended a shaking hand that clutched a can of beer.

"Thanks, buddy. That's just what I need. Come and sit down." What the hell was happening? He was afraid that LaMont had gone insane. "How about some dope? I got a lot of sticks left."

"Yeah," Padgett whispered, his head nodding seven or eight times. He took two steps forward, turned, sat down in the doorway as though he weighed a ton. "I don't know, Orville."

Chambers got his pack of joints from the baggage compartment, then came back around to the door. After a toke he said, "Better?"

Padgett exhaled as though he would never stop. "It'll be right."

"Should I get some more beer?" The first swallows had made him realize his thirst. Starving too, but that could wait till morning.

"That's good."

"I'll be back."

A fifty-five-gallon drum of cooling beer cans sat in the

middle of the mess-tent floor, First Sergeant Bugelli standing beside it. Chambers was amazed to see him. He could remember only one other time the topkick had been to the field. Bugelli mumbled a few words of commiseration, then handed him four beers.

He got outside the tent and stopped. Maybe he should go tell McCloud about Padgett. He obviously wasn't right, and he might do some harm to himself. McCloud could give him a sedative or something to knock him out for the night. But what would LaMont say? He might really flip if Chambers went talking about him as if he were nuts. Besides, he had enough good dope at his ship to keep him quiet. The beer would help too.

LaMont would probably be okay by morning. This was his fourth wound, and five guys in the platoon had been killed. Another nine wounded, six of those sent out of country or back to division base camp. His own pilot had been medevacked with what looked like a broken leg. Maybe he should be worrying about himself, not Padgett. Going about his business on the ship as though nothing had happened. But you had to, if you weren't going to lose your mind.

"First pig even made it out tonight." He set the beers down by the ammo boxes.

Padgett snorted, almost laughed. "I seen him." He handed Chambers a fresh joint.

"Thanks. Feel better?"

"Some."

He'd always admired LaMont's spirit. No matter how bad things got, he could always laugh it off or at least lash out against it. Tonight he was whipped. Didn't look like he could even talk.

Chambers wriggled his behind in between the side guns and the door, then leaned against the pylon with his feet crossed on the ground. Padgett puffed and drank, seemingly watching Chambers' feet. They said nothing for at least twenty minutes. Finally Padgett crushed a beer can in his hand, dropped it to the turf, and sprawled back on the sleeping bag.

Chambers took his P-38 opener and cut the top completely off his can. Sloshing the contents around, he tried to catch the moonlight in the amber fluid, but got only a dull reflection on the inside of the can. The other gunners continued to holler and curse at Webster's ship.

"LaMont?"

Nothing.

He moved off the pylon, careful not to bump the dangling legs. What the hell was he supposed to do now? He pissed beneath the tail boom, came back, and stared at the slumbering body on the cabin floor. A slight wave of irritation passed over him. He was tired and wanted to go to sleep. He'd had a rough day too. Was it wrong for him to feel he needed a break? He grabbed the last beer and sat cross-legged on the hard ground. McCutcheon would be back soon, and if he woke LaMont there might be trouble. He'd finish the beer, then roust him.

Leaning over on his elbow, he wished he'd stayed in Fulda. Maybe he could have made it without his friends. Besides, Slagel was gone, he hardly ever saw Morgan, and now this happening to LaMont. It would be early summer in Fulda, when the sun at least came out occasionally. He'd just be getting back from his spring leave to Italy. He'd planned to go to Rome this time, maybe stopping in Florence for a few days on the way back. He could be studying St. Peter's instead of lying in the dirt drinking beer and smoking dope.

He policed the cans and dumped them in a trench full of old ammo boxes and casings in the middle of the flight line. Back at the ship, he hovered over the sleeping Padgett.

"LaMont," he whispered. "LaMont!"

Padgett groaned, rolled his head to the side, and lay still.

He covered the knee with his hand and shook it gently. "LaMont. Wake up."

"Whaaat!" LaMont screamed, rising so quickly that their heads nearly collided. His face was terrified, as though he were seeing ghosts. "Oh, man!" He fell against Chambers, his solid arms hugging him tightly.

Automatically, Chambers started to withdraw. The grip,

however, was strong, then something else caused him to stop. He suddenly glimpsed how lonely they all were, how utterly impoverished, and it shook him profoundly. "It's okay, LaMont," he muttered, feeling his face go hot as his throat tensed with emotion. He tried to raise his arms but LaMont held them firmly, as though he wanted nothing more than to cling to something for a few moments. LaMont breathed violently for a full fifteen seconds, then suddenly broke away. He rubbed his finger hurriedly across and back beneath his nose, shook his head, and raised the corner of his mouth in an exhausted grin.

"Whoo! Damn, Orville, I'm sorry."

Still moved, he reached out and touched his shoulder. "What's to be sorry for?"

"You know, man. We hard soldiers, huh? Ain't supposed to act like no babies."

"I guess we both know better."

"Ain't it the truth. I better hit it. Thanks don't seem like enough."

He raised his hand, not needing to hear any more. "I got you, cool breeze. See you in the morning."

Padgett stood up and shuffled. "Sho' 'nough will."

Chambers watched him trudge toward the rifle platoon's tents, then crawled into his own bag and pretended to be asleep when McCutcheon came back.

The entire rifle platoon left for the base camp in the morning, and the expansive feeling with which he'd awakened shrank as he watched the lift ships rise from the flight line and fly eastward. Now who would he talk to? McCutcheon? He had lain awake for at least an hour last night, anticipating conversations with Padgett or Todd, spending time with them in the evenings. But they'd be back in a few days, so what's the big deal? He tried to fight—or forget—the growing sense of depression, but somehow it felt as though some precious opportunity had been lost forever.

He spent the day on his machine guns, cleaning all six

more thoroughly than ever before. He used a fresh pail of avaiation gas on each one, scrubbing the parts with wire brushes until every speck of dirt and carbon disappeared. Then he oiled them carefully until they gleamed. He left his sleeping bag hanging over the tail boom to air out and late that afternoon took all his dirty laundry up to supply, where he scrounged some new drawers and socks. After chow he showered for fifteen minutes, shaved, then smoked a joint while changing into fresh clothes at his ship. He felt so good that he nearly ran to the mess tent to buy beer.

"How's the face, Chambers?" Staff Sergeant Hart, gunnery platoon sergeant, leaned on the drum of beer cans, the wax on his handlebar shining in the light of a naked bulb.

"Still there, Sarge."

"Have one on me." Hart handed him a beer.

"Thanks, but I want a whole case."

"You can't have that on me." Hart's gallery of kiss asses laughed from the makeshift table where they sat. "Don't tell me you're turning into an alkie too."

"Just buying for the platoon."

"Then you'll probably need four cases." Again the gallery laughed.

"One should do it." He paid, then left the tent hurriedly, carrying the cold cans in a sandbag.

"Chambers, you old sack of shit," Webster hollered as he approached the ship. "What you doing up this late?" Webster reminded him of Slagel with his cockiness and muscular athletic presence. He held up the sack of beer, then set it on the cabin floor, between Hancock's feet. The fat gunner from West Virginia leered at him while digging his hands into the sack.

"You get promoted or something?"

"Just felt like buying a case."

"A case!" Robinson said. "Shit, that won't last five minutes." The loudmouthed Texan leaned over and grabbed a can.

He'd disliked Robinson since the day he'd come to the

platoon. White trash, mean, bitching all the time, he was supposed to have thrown a prisoner out of his helicopter in January, although no one talked about it anymore.

"How you doing, Chambers?" Brooks said, grinning at him from beneath thick glasses.

"Okay, okay." He handed him a beer. "Getting short, huh?"

"Two days." Brooks drank deeply. "What happened to Morgan? I thought he was due out yesterday."

"Last I heard he hadn't got a replacement yet. Just as well with me." Hancock, Webster, and Robinson went back to talking among themselves.

"Why's that?"

He shrugged. "I don't want to see him get hurt."

"That's true. But you don't know what clerkin's like. It gets to you. I've felt a lot better since coming out here. S-1's even worse than being a company clerk. You might as well get a piece of the action while you're here, right?"

"Guess that's what he thinks."

"I'm going to get another case."

"Well, hurry up, god damn it," Robinson said. "You should've bought two already."

Brooks shook his head at Robinson and walked toward the mess tent.

"No shit," Robinson said, "that bastard pays those bitches just so he can eat 'em out. That's crazy if you ask me. What do you think, Chambers?"

"About what?"

"About Mallison. Guy been in the rifles about three months. He don't fuck when he goes to town, but he pays four hundred p. to eat that nasty pussy."

He shrugged off a faint wave of nausea. "Each to his own, I guess."

"Each to his own? Jesus, man, that's some funky-ass snatch to be goin' down on." Robinson cracked another beer and gulped it furiously. "I mean, I'll yodel in the canyon myself back in the world, but here I feel I'm doing these broads a favor just to fuck 'em, let alone chowing down. After I got the clap the second time I quit these cunts altogether. I'll be glad when they get that whorehouse built so they can supervise the bitches. Man, these people are fuckin' dirty."

"I reckon they stink bad enough," Hancock said.

"That's what I mean." Robinson nodded and held his arms in the air. "But can you imagine lappin' it after she's fucked thirty guys? That's low-lifed, boy. Think you could handle it, Chambers?"

He nearly gagged on his beer, then tried to wait out the silence. "Like I said, each to his own."

"Oh, man!" Robinson whipped his head back against the fire wall. "You probably gobble it yourself."

"So what if I do?"

"What'd I say? Chambers is a gook lapper."

"I didn't say that."

"Bullshit. You said it."

"I said so what if I did. I don't guess it's your business what anybody does anyway."

"Oh-ohh, listen here. Gook lapper's getting shook up. Come on, Chambers, why don't you just tell us?"

He hadn't felt so mad since the days in the hospital after Happy Valley. "If you're so damn hot to know, Robinson, I don't, but if I did, I sure as shit wouldn't let people like you say anything about it. You got that?"

"Oh, come on."

"Come on, shit! Why don't you keep your nose in your own business."

Robinson shuffled on the seat. "Why don't you go back to bed?" he muttered. "No one asked you over here."

"Anytime you want to take me, let's go." He was suddenly ready, almost eager to brawl, to kick the shit out of Robinson if he could. Then Brooks arrived with another case of beer, and the tension dissolved.

Chambers leaned back on his elbow, drinking quietly while the others continued to bullshit. He drank for two hours, talking only briefly with Brooks, then Webster. The truth of

Robinson's last words stung him. No one *had* asked him over, and they'd probably just as soon he hadn't come. Christ, what was he anyway? The platoon deadhead? Sit around his fucking ship and read and sleep. Well, that was better than trying to talk with a bunch of assholes. He'd have no use for these people on the outside anyway. So why not get ready to do what he was going to do when he got out? But he was sick of that for now. He needed people, but where was he supposed to find them?

He felt the slushy weight of drunkenness for the first time in Vietnam, at the same time realizing why he hardly ever got drunk. The booze made him crawl deeper into himself until it seemed as though he weighed a thousand pounds. He moved beneath the tail boom to piss, then staggered back to his ship. Utterly confused, he fell asleep immediately.

They flew first light in the morning, the cool air sobering him slightly, but even after the flight, after he'd reloaded and had two cups of coffee and a Coke, he still felt heavy. The sour smell of beery sweat on his body did nothing to make the morning more pleasant.

With the rifle platoon in the base, gunnery flew only occasional recon. Hart made a commotion about maintenance, so the crew chiefs were busy at their ships, readying them for full-time flying. The gunners had been admonished to clean their guns, replace worn parts, and straighten up their weapons systems generally. Having done his yesterday, he spent the rest of the morning dozing.

Webster woke him at noon, jangling his mess kit. "You going to eat, Chambers?"

He sat up, shuddering like a horse. "I don't think so."

"Okay. You want to come over to my ship and play some cards this afternoon?" Webster smiled. "Friendly game of nickel-dime."

He began to nod his head, then shook it slowly. "I don't think so."

"Why not?"

"I don't know. Not much good at gambling."

"Is it because of Robinson?"

"Not really."

"If it is, you don't have to worry about him none. He's just a whole lot of fat mouth."

"It's not him. I'm still hung over and need to sleep. I'll come over if I feel better."

"Do it, man. Catch you later."

"Thanks, Web."

For an hour he sat in the doorway, debating with himself, watching the gunners and crew chiefs walk back and forth. They talked, made each other laugh. For a while he thought he'd go—Webster's offer had obviously been friendly, an attempt to make up for Robinson's behavior last night. So what? What would the afternoon turn out to be after all? A stupid card game, with more of the same crap about battles and pussy and getting drunk. He could live without it.

Couldn't he, though? He had all his life, at least since Roger had been killed. His years in high school flitted through his mind as though they'd taken five minutes. Sure it had been hard getting used to people shying away from him after Roger's accident, them thinking he was weird, that his family was cursed. But he'd adjusted to that, and by the time ninth grade began he expected nothing from anyone. Why Elaine liked him—loved him—he couldn't understand—he wasn't even good-looking. But she had, making the time a little easier, a little less lonely. Five years! What had he been doing all that time? How did it pass by and leave him with nothing?

And the six years after high school had been no different. Three years working on the assembly line at the Ford plant, then three more digging graves. Again it seemed like five minutes out of his life. He hadn't done a thing, had made no friends, gone nowhere. Work all day, watch television in his rented room, or take long walks around Lake Harriet or Calhoun at night. He had thought about nothing. On weekends he'd go back to his father's farm to do a little work and talk to his mother.

Maybe life wasn't supposed to be happy. What evidence

was there to prove otherwise? The people in high school who'd had more fun than he had died after graduation. Wives, kids, payments, and jobs they hated. And working. The guys were bored to death, bitching about their wives' sandwiches, about niggers and Jews, having to spend an hour in the bars after work so they could face the old lady and kids for the rest of the night.

He'd been happy for a few months in Fulda, and perhaps that's all a man could expect or hope for. The river flowed, then dried up again. Simple as that. He'd had good times, been close to people, done the things that he'd wanted for a while. Just wanting to do something had given him more joy than he'd imagined possible. All gone now; the people were changed, and there was nothing he could do but wait to get out. Then school, and it would be hard for that to let him down.

He got his duffel bag from the baggage compartment, brought it into the helicopter cabin, and closed the doors so the breeze wouldn't disturb his treasures. Digging beneath his fatigues and underwear, he felt the thick plastic cover, then pulled out the small bundle. He unwrapped the plastic carefully, smelling the invisible funk, but happy that the mildew hadn't wrecked any pages. For the rest of the afternoon he contemplated his hoard, flipping through pages of Pevsner's *Outline of European Architecture* and Wolffin's *Principles of Art History*, which he'd bought in Berkeley, studying the reproductions in the small paperbacks on Masaccio, Michelangelo, and Botticelli that Morgan had given him before they'd left Travis Air Force Base last Thanksgiving. From a four-by-five tin file box he took a thick stack of postcards, went through them slowly, making sure he still remembered the titles, artists, and galleries. He'd collected them day by day in Florence, hesitatingly at first, then more and more up until the last few days when he'd become obsessed with getting cards of everything he'd seen.

McCutcheon and the pilots came down before chow for a recon flight. For a moment he was completely flustered—as he'd been the first time he'd flown—trying to get the cards and books back under cover and into his duffel bag before they took off. He barely got the barrels clipped in and his body into the harness before they pulled pitch. The first few minutes airborne he felt angry at having been disturbed, but he soon forgot it in the excitement of thinking about his future. He knew a lot about art history now, and by the time he got to college he'd have all the basics down, plus quite a bit beyond. He could spend his leave in the library in Minneapolis, and he could buy some new books to keep himself busy at his next post. And he'd have money saved too, enough to travel and see places he'd missed, like England and Spain.

They took fire a mile from the Cambodian border. Automatically, he squeezed the trigger, at the same time twisting the smoke grenade off the carrying handle of the gun and tossing it into the wind. He ceased firing as they circled to the left, the pilots jabbering idiotically on the radio as though it really mattered. No one was visible on the ground. Probably some lone NVA on a scouting mission. They came in again, lower this time, and again he fired one long continuous burst until they'd completed banking. Captain Hobart radioed the field base and was told by the operations officer to come back. Air strikes would be called in later.

He hung a fresh smoke grenade, then leaned back against the fire wall, cocking his head to the side while the ground raced away beneath him.

As they landed, Webster, Hancock, Robinson, and Brooks were walking from the flight line to the mess tent. He decided to clean up the ship and reload before going to chow. Brooks would leave in the morning, and there'd be a drunken short-timer's party tonight—the last thing he had any desire to attend.

The mess tent was nearly deserted when he went to eat. He sat alone at a free table, thinking about the reading he'd do that night, what buildings he'd try to memorize.

Brooks came into the tent as he was sopping up his gravy

with a piece of bread. "Come on, Chambers, all the beer you want on me tonight."

He covered his stomach with his hand, grimaced, and shook his head. "Can't handle it, Brooks. I'm still sick from last night."

"Come on, man. You can choke down a couple."

"I don't think so. I'll see you in the morning, say good-bye then."

"Okay, Chambers. You must be sick to pass up free beer."

Later the din from the party was so loud that he had to smoke two joints before he could fall asleep.

For the next three days he spent every free moment reading. Eating and excreting were necessary interruptions, sleep a welcome end to the day. He hardly paid attention on the five missions he flew, losing himself in postwar plans and in the ideas and images of what he'd read. The urgency of firing was gone, and as the machine gun jiggled in his armpit and his hand, he felt no more involved than a man holding a hose above a garden and watching birds in the trees beyond. On the third night, after studying his Michelangelo book again before going to sleep, he dreamed of a time in Fulda when Morgan had shown him a picture from a funny art book. A reproduction from the Sistine ceiling, only with God holding a Zippo lighter to the cigarette in Adam's outstretched hand.

In the morning another crew took first light, so after chow and a shave he was able to go back to sleep.

"Wake up, Orville. Here they come."

McCutcheon's voice sounded far away. "Okay." He opened his eyes for a moment, saw ten o'clock on his watch, then closed them, drawing his legs closer to his body.

"Another raft of new guys. Don't you want to see them?"

Rising slowly, he watched the four lift ships whip up dust in the southwest corner of the helipad.

"Rifles are back. We'll probably be in the shit again this afternoon." McCutcheon tried to look serious, but excitement danced in his eyes, and he seemed to be straining to keep back the smile. "Come on, let's go check out the new guys."

"You go ahead. We'll have plenty of time for that later."

"Don't you even want to see your buddies?"

He dismissed McCutcheon with a wave. "Let them get settled first. We've got nothing but time, right?"

"Says you. I'm gonna check 'em out."

"Later, then." He rolled his sleeping bag, put it away, and had just relaxed on the seat with a book when Padgett appeared in the doorway.

"What's *los*, papa stopper? How goes the war?"

"Hi, LaMont." He glanced back at the page to finish a paragraph.

"Morgan says hello."

"How's he doing?"

"Oh, man! Blowed out of his ever-lovin' every night. Still ain't found that replacement yet. He *stayin'* fucked up. How about you?"

"I'm all right. Been doing a lot of reading and going over my postcards."

"I been poppin' pussy outside the base. My chest is so light I had to sleep with a duffel bag on me so I wouldn't float away." Padgett burst out laughing and extended his palm.

Chambers slapped it lightly. "What do you think? Was Michelangelo a greater painter or sculptor?"

"Say what?"

"You heard me. What do you think?"

"What you been smokin'?"

"Come on. Don't you think it's an important question?"

Padgett dug the toe of his boot in the ground next to the skid. "I reckon. So is what we're having for chow or how much beer we can get tonight. It'd be more important back in the world."

"That may be true, but really, what do you think?"

"Shit, baby, I don't know. Look here, I got to go get my gear together for this afternoon. Platoon goes out at noon, and I got two green fish to look after. I'll talk to you tonight."

He went back to reading, but was interrupted in half an

hour by the rest of the crew. He quickly folded the book in plastic and stuffed it behind the ammo boxes under the seat. "What's up?" he asked McCutcheon.

"Recon and prep for the rifles. We're chasing Six. You ready?"

"Sure." He slithered into his harness and climbed up on the seat. He was beginning to like flying chase more and more. While not as exciting as flying lead—especially when the lead ship did treetop recon—it was more relaxed, giving wider panoramas of the jungle and the mountains. LaMont should have been a gunner; the prospects would help his painting.

They flew west to the border, then turned south, flying over the red-orange clay of the Plei Me Special Forces camp where a few hulking Americans stood in front of four platoons of scrawny Vietnamese. The trees on the border mountains were bare and gray, reminding him of mist. Major Quinn's ship went low, circling the camp twice before heading east again. The jungle became immediately greener, deepening in color and density the farther east they flew. Open spaces appeared after a few miles, then hamlets flanked by rice paddies.

"Okay, Four-three," Major Quinn said over the radio, "we're on Charlie's food supply right now, so watch out."

"Roger, Six," Captain Hobart said.

"Four-three, Blue's starting from this deserted hamlet about eight hundred meters up. Follow me up the south side with machine guns. Save your rockets for another run."

"Roger, out."

The side guns crackled and he turned to watch the oil burn off the barrels. He squeezed the trigger on his gun. He couldn't see the hamlet on the left side of the ship, only the increasingly dense vegetation that fell away to the right. The orange tracers tearing into the green were pretty.

"Hold it, Four-three! Cease firing!"

"Roger, Six. What's up?"

"Got a live one down here. We'll try to take him that way.

We're going down on the deck. Cover me in a tight circle clockwise."

"Roger, Six."

The ship banked to the right, putting the hamlet in front of him. The walls and roofs of the hooches were scorched black. The small dirt area between the hooches and the paddies, usually crowded with children waving at the choppers, was empty—not even any dogs or chickens. McCutcheon bumped against him, then leaned over his lap to get a good look.

A sudden cloud of dust whipped up from the ground as Major Quinn's ship hovered down. In the sunlight the dust became sparks of gold. A North Vietnamese soldier stood on a dike fifty feet in front of the ship, looking like a scarecrow. He had no weapon, no pistol belt or helmet—nothing but his khaki uniform.

Major Quinn's gunner stepped out on the skid and motioned the soldier toward him. The man turned and ran to the side.

"No sweat, Four-three," Quinn said. His ship jerked off the ground and floated to the left, passing the NVA and setting down in front of him once again.

Chambers' ship continued to circle. He lay his machine gun across his lap and rested his chin on his fist. Again the crew chief beckoned, and again the man turned and ran. The ship picked up and once more blocked his escape. Twice more it happened, reminding him of the way he and Timmy Carlson used to chase geese on the farm. They were hard to catch, but you could always keep them surrounded.

"You want any help down there, Six?" Captain Hobart said.

"Negative, Four-three. We'd probably collide. We'll keep after him."

The ship landed, the man ran, and the ship pulled pitch again, cutting him off at the edge of the hamlet.

"This is getting old in a hurry," Quinn said. The ship picked up and slid sideways to the far side of the paddy. The soldier moved farther out, toward the jungle, then whirled and made a dead run for the hamlet. Quinn's ship jerked wildly, tilting to the side, then leveled off directly behind the fleeing figure.

He ran low, leaping two dikes. He was going to beat the ship to the hamlet this time. Orange flashes tore across a third dike as the soldier leaped to clear it. His body seemed to stop in midair, then sped forward and up briefly, almost like a basketball player's going up for a difficult shot, before landing in a heap on the edge of the dirt yard.

They circled once again, low this time, and already a glistening crimson blanket had spread in a large circle beneath the NVA.

"Sorry about that," Quinn said over the radio, "but he's probably got a weapon in one of those hooches. Let's finish our prep."

"Roger, Six."

They fired all their rockets and nearly all their machine-gun bullets before flying back to the field base.

13

MORGAN leaned against the counter in S-1, watching the sun descend toward the top of Titty Mountain at the perimeter's western edge. For a moment it seemed to balance like a giant balloon. then the nipple carved an ugly little black mouth into its lower side. Behind him Sergeant Chase yawned and groaned, flipping pages in a fat notebook of regulations.

Morgan drummed his fingers on the counter, nervous with anticipation. The sergeant who made assignments at division had called him an hour ago with news of a new man on his way to recon who might be a replacement for Morgan. Christ, he hoped so. Every day for the past three weeks new troops had processed through S-1. Not one man had known how to type. One had replaced Brooks as Major Quinn's gunner, and another would be replacing Stout. Division had been short on clerks, and new ones went to needy units.

Earlier in the afternoon he'd flown to Qui Nhon with Greene, the captain logging some hours so he could remain on flight status. Morgan had sat in the door, practicing moves with his M-16 and snapping pictures of the mountains, rice paddies and the busy harbor at Qui Nhon. They'd come back at treetop level, the chopper speeding along like a race car as Morgan waved to the peasants and studied the terrain. The weight of the flak jacket had felt pleasant on his shoulders and around his back, and he'd pulled the sun visor from the flight helmet over his face and dreamed of the day when he'd fly full time. He'd come back to the base two hours ago, feeling more alert and lively than he had in months.

If this new guy didn't work out, he didn't know what he'd do. Some days his body felt so tense and hot, his mind so full of loathing for Chase and Greene, that the least provocation could have driven him beyond anything he knew of sanity. Once he had almost turned to Chase and begun a tirade, stopping only because he knew they'd keep him here forever if he did.

He bent down to straighten some forms on the shelf beneath the counter, then jumped back up as he heard a duffel bag drop on the straw matting. The new man handed his records to Morgan.

Orton DeWolf was white and fat and puffy, with a moon face and pale blue bags beneath his eyes. Sweating and breathing heavily, he looked totally disillusioned. He was a tanker and had finished one year at a junior college in South Carolina.

"Do you know how to type?" Morgan tried to keep the nervousness out of his voice.

"Yup."

"Do you want to go to the field or be a clerk?"

"Don't care."

"You don't care what you get assigned to?"

"Nope."

Incredible! He looked back at Chase. I got him, you fucker! I got him. "Al, I got a possible clerk here."

Chase looked up and nodded. "How fast can you type, soldier?"

"Thirty-five, forty a minute."

"Sounds okay. Will, take him down to the club for a beer and tell him about the job."

"I'm gone." He turned to DeWolf. "Leave your gear. We'll pick it up later."

"I like beer," DeWolf said.

He was so nervous that he chain-smoked the entire hour that he and DeWolf talked in the club. DeWolf didn't say much. He seemed much more interested in beer and listened passively while Morgan lied, coaxed, cajoled, and ran down the many benefits that accrued to the S-1 clerk.

"If it's so good, why do you want to quit?" DeWolf asked at one point.

He nearly shit. "I'm tired of it. Thought maybe I'd go to the field and give someone else the easy work."

DeWolf remained skeptical and uninterested, but finally agreed to give it a try. Morgan left him at chow and returned to S-1 alone, feeling quietly elated, as though he'd just finished final exams. He walked slowly in the twilight, studying tents, pebbles and ruts in the road, the naked concrete slabs that covered the ground in C Company's area. The camp was becoming civilized. Soon the old troops would be gone, and new bodies would live comfortably in barracks without rats and bugs and the stifling heat of the canvas tents. He tried to feel sentimental about the old days, the old guys, but too many other thoughts rushed through his head. He turned around to watch a helicopter wink its way down to the flight line. He couldn't wait to get on one.

"He'll take it," he said to Chase, then jumped up on the counter.

"Good. We'll check him out tomorrow."

"When can I go?"

"Don't get antsy. It'll take awhile to train DeWolf and make sure he's up to the job."

"What do you mean? When I came here you didn't even have a clerk."

"Times are different now. We got a lot more work."

"Christ, Al, I've got to get out there if I'm going to get a ship."

"Don't worry. There'll be plenty of ships."

"But you promised."

"I promised you'd go to the field, and you will. But we've got to train DeWolf first. Efficiency reports on eighty officers and warrants are coming up, and they'll have to be perfect. You'll go—and as a gunner too—but for God's sake, don't bug me about it!"

As he broke in DeWolf over the next three days, he thought he might explode from nervousness. He lived in continual fear that the new clerk would fuck up or see the job for the utter heap of shit it was. He liked DeWolf, but after a day it became apparent that he didn't give a damn. Morgan was used to doing the jobs once and perfectly and would get flustered like an old woman if DeWolf botched an efficiency report or a piece of correspondence. DeWolf would lean back and laugh, saying that he reckoned the war would go on anyway.

He was a wise-ass too, joking familiarly with Greene, calling Chase on mistakes. Never enough to get himself in trouble, but right on the edge nevertheless. Morgan sensed Greene's occasional irritation and worried that he might cut the new clerk loose. On the third day he mentioned it to DeWolf as they drove to town, but DeWolf brushed it aside. "Morgan, you got to keep these people on their toes. They ain't shit, and you got to let them know it."

They drove down the deserted main street, then stopped at Lang's father's laundry before heading back up the highway toward the new whorehouse and the base. Papa-san fetched the laundry while they drank beer and Morgan talked to Lang as she sat quietly on his lap. As usual, the boys attacked their boots with shoeshine kits. If he did go to the field, this would be the only place he'd miss.

Papa-san put the laundry in the jeep, and DeWolf suddenly grew impatient. "Come on, Morg."

"Wait a minute."

"What for?"

"I don't know. I like it here."

"Man, you're nuts. I'm ready to get with some of this sideways pussy, and your girlfriend there's too young."

Once they got to Sin City, he thought he'd never get DeWolf to leave. The new clerk had been in one of the small back rooms of the Carolina bar for half an hour when Morgan went to knock off a shot himself. Maybe they'd send him to the field in a couple of days and he wouldn't see a woman until the end of his tour. Worrying about getting back to the base on time, he hardly paid attention to the whore. He didn't know if he should bring up his leaving with Chase again or if he should wait for the sergeant's next move. So many things could go wrong.

He came out of the back room to find DeWolf sitting like a decadent caliph—Morgan could almost see him with satin robes and curly-toes shoes—in a chair made of plastic strips, flanked by two whores. "Come on, lover boy, we've got to get back." He walked past DeWolf and out the door.

"I was just waiting for you, boss. See you gals later."

"What'd you think?"

"Their women ain't much better than their beer." DeWolf scratched his chin. "But I reckon it's the only game in town."

"You got that shit right."

At seven that night they went down to aircraft maintenance to drink. Morgan was anxious to see Stout, who'd come in with Zastrow earlier in the afternoon. Both were through flying and would be in base camp until they went home.

He missed his friends in Overhead, but was glad the tent had come down when it did. Things weren't the same after Stubbs' murder, and Alexander and Winston now spent their evenings gambling at the club. Cement slabs had been laid in the Headquarters Company area, the tents put above them and personnel shuffled so that Morgan now lived with the other clerks and drivers while more fuck-ups filled the cots in New Overhead.

"Tell me a big old lie, Morgan," Fisher said, twirling the waxed ends of his black handlebar.

"You're pretty." Fisher was the chief scrounge for aircraft maintenance, and if you gave him an hour, he could come up with anything. Morgan generally needed beer, and Fisher always came up with that, driving to Qui Nhon every three or four days and bringing back fifty cases. He'd come over with division and one day in Ia Drang last November had crashed twice, been wounded twice, and won the Bronze Star and Distinguished Flying Cross. He'd never gone back to the field again.

"What'd you say your name was?" Zastrow asked DeWolf.

"DeWolf."

"No, your first name."

"Orton." DeWolf's moon face gave off a friendly smile.

"Well, fuck you, Orton."

DeWolf's grin collapsed as the others burst out laughing. Zastrow's laugh was controlled, his eyes beady—nearly slanted—and he looked like a mad Oriental scientist. Morgan handed DeWolf a beer and patted him on the shoulder.

Zastrow grabbed one of the little monkeys sitting on the shaving table, spun it on its leash, and threw it about twenty feet. As he reeled in the leash, the monkey put out its feet to break the slide down the tent roof where it had landed. Its lips were drawn back over yellow teeth, and its body twitched with fear.

"Why don't you cool it with the monkey?" Fisher said.

"What for?"

"He ain't hurting anyone," Stout said.

"Neither was that woman you killed," Zastrow said. "Or maybe the fucking monkey's more important."

"What do you care about the woman? You got enough of them."

"I don't care. I don't care about no cunt-lapping monkey either."

"I wish I had some cunt to lap," DeWolf said.

"Thirty-five days and I'll be all up in it." Fisher stuck out his tongue and wiggled it from side to side. "What I lack in dick, I make up for in tongue."

Morgan's mind went away as the other talked about going home. All the people leaving got him down. The new colonel was supposed to be big on the chickenshit, and there was no way battalion could keep from going downhill.

"Still dreaming about the field, Morgan?" Fisher yelled.

"Nope." The monkeys sat quietly on the shaving table, the female searching for lice and tics in the male's fur.

"I didn't think you thought about anything else."

"I'm still thinking about your tongue."

"You should be going any day, huh?"

"Could be."

"You dumb shit."

"Leave him alone," Stout said. "You wanted to get in it just as much as him. We all did."

"He should be able to learn from other people. He should thank God he's not out there."

The male monkey leaned back on his haunches, and the female licked and sucked its little pink prick.

"I think Morgan's a potential kill-crazy," Zastrow said. "Just like Stout here."

"I'm going to take a shower," Fisher said. Fisher had been jumpy for the past few weeks, especially when the others talked about combat. If he drank too much, he raved bitterly about the action he'd seen, about how unfair it was. Maybe his showers kept him sane. At least they got him away from the others.

"Did you ever kill anyone, Morgan?" Zastrow asked.

"No."

"Would you like to?"

He wanted to say yes, but knew Zastrow was playing. He shrugged and spread his hands.

"At least you're curious, huh?"
"I guess."
"You'll like it. It's fun, right, Stout?"
"It's nothing special."
"You thought it was pretty funny a couple days ago."
"You did too."
"I like it. I'm not ashamed to admit it."
"Then why talk about it?"
"I don't know. Rather talk about religion? Morgan, you went to college. Want to talk about religion?"
"Let's just drink beer." He didn't like Zastrow being so morbid. He looked up at the table as the monkeys began fucking.
"I want to talk about religion. Just one thing. When I have kids, I'm going to take them out in the woods, squash some shit under a piece of glass, hang it on a tree and tell them that's God. And you know they'll believe me, and if I tell them to, they'll kill anyone who messes with that piece of shit."
The male monkey jumped off the female and did a quick spasmodic dance around the table.
A scrawny black and white cat walked into the area between aircraft maintenance and division road. Zastrow held out one of DeWolf's Vienna sausages. The cat ate the sausage, then Zastrow took it in his lap and stroked its head. "Anyone got a knife?"
"What for?" DeWolf said.
"I'm gonna cut its tail off."
"No way." DeWolf shoved the Swiss army knife back in his pocket.
"I need a dull one anyway." Zastrow got a mess knife from the tent, then sat back down. The cat tried to scratch him when he held it by the tail, but stood still after he swatted it twice on the head.
Morgan pulled his arms into his body, like wings, and contracted his neck until his chin rested on his chest.
"Come on, man," Stout said.

"If you don't like it, leave." The cat mewed pathetically. It pulled forward suddenly, recoiled, and scratched him. "Motherfucker!" Zastrow slapped the cat three times across the head, then went back to cutting.

Morgan couldn't stop watching, wincing and jerking as Zastrow cut and the cat whined. No one could be as hard as Zastrow.

The cat let out a piercing howl and somehow escaped Zastrow's grasp. Its tail flopped up and lay briefly on its back, then fell down and dragged on the ground as the cat took off for the road. "Fucking pussy! I'm going to take a shit." Zastrow stomped off toward the latrine.

They sat drinking quietly, then someone pulled Morgan's foot and he woke up.

"C'mon, Morg," DeWolf said. "It's almost midnight. We got to do the PDS."

"Okay." He stood up and bent over the monkeys. They hugged each other and shivered in the cool night air.

"Wake up, alky." DeWolf's voice sounded filtered, far away. "Come on. Time to celebrate my one-week anniversary."

He opened his eyes on a can of Bud inches from his face. Behind DeWolf the white door of the little icebox gleamed. They'd bought it yesterday for sixty dollars. It held fifty-six cans of beer and two trays of ice. He drank half of the can before putting his feet on the floor. "How'd I get back here?" He remembered riding to G-1 with DeWolf and Stout at midnight, but his memory had stopped in the jeep.

"I brought you back from Fisher's about three, when I woke up. Another two feet and you'd have been in the road. Stout stayed there all night. At least he said he wanted to."

"You should've left me too." It was becoming a point of honor to lay up in the ditch all night.

"I *will* leave you from now on. Hell, if I'm gonna stay out there with the rats and skeeters."

Greene leered at them skeptically as they entered S-1 after

chow. "Glad to see you two made it back alive from last night."

DeWolf moved around the counter and farted. "Pardon me, men, for being so bold, but that was one fart I could not hold." The air filled with the smell of rotten garbage.

"Vy-ennies and beer leave a beautiful scent," Morgan said. DeWolf ate about ten little cans of the sausages every night.

Chase looked up from the morning reports. "You guys drunk again last night?"

"Yes, Sergeant!" DeWolf yelled.

Chase turned on the counter and leaned on one elbow. "I'm telling you for the last time; I want at least one of you sober when you take that report to G-1. You fuck it up and my ass swings. You could mess up the jeep if you ran it into a ditch."

"I was sober," Morgan said. He could do the report in his sleep. He slid into the chair behind the desk and began typing an officer-efficiency report. He had done so many, both here and in Germany, that he knew how to do them better than anyone in the Army. Big deal. Someone was the best KP too.

That afternoon he went to the flight line with Stout. DeWolf worked alone in S-1 while he was gone and could do everything pretty well except the efficiency reports. There wasn't enough work for the two clerks, so either he or DeWolf did shit errands while the other typed. God, he wished they'd let him go. But they didn't trust DeWolf because he couldn't take the strain. Two days ago he'd stalked out of the office saying he was through, and Morgan had to spend an hour pleading to get him back. It scared him. It could go on for weeks, or DeWolf could flip out and shit-can the entire thing.

"I don't know why I did it," Stout said. His face was solemn and puzzled, and he seemed to be thinking very hard. "I guess I'll wonder about that all my life."

Morgan pushed down on the butt plate of the machine gun, pulled the buffer yoke, and eased out the innards. He put the butt plate and buffer on the chopper floor and dropped the other parts into a pail of aviation gas at his feet. "What did you feel like?"

"Nothing special. We were just flying along. I was bored and pissed about the mortar—but that wasn't it."

"You really didn't think about it then?"

"I don't mean to talk any of that unseen-hand shit, but it was automatic. I was sitting in the door, I saw her, then I fired at her." Stout threw up his hands. He tried to grin, but looked utterly baffled.

"It must have been weird." He wondered how much the forty pieces of shrapnel Stout had taken had messed up his mind. Small scars stood out all over his arms and chest. But Stout didn't act mean. Not like Zastrow. Zastrow had taken over seventy hunks of shrapnel. A scar ran like a zipper from the middle of his thigh to the middle of his calf. He was the meanest person Morgan had ever met. "Did you feel bad afterward?"

"I thought it was funny. Zastrow laughed and gave me the thumbs up, so I figured it was okay. The pilots liked it too. Even now I don't feel much. It was shitty to do that, and I know I'm supposed to feel something, but I don't."

"But it wasn't the first person you'd killed." He scrubbed the pieces of the gun with the gasoline and a wire brush. "Was it?"

"Only one I know of for sure. That's what's strange. When division got orders to come over here, a lot of guys bitched, but they didn't mind that much. Then someone said that he was glad because he wanted to know how he'd react under fire and what it was like to kill someone. That summed it up for me too, but what can I say now?"

"I guess I feel the same way." He sloshed gas down the inside of the gun, cleaning dirt and grease away from the ridges that held the bolt and operating rod in place. "I guess a lot of people do." It had been almost a year since the four of them had volunteered. They'd been the first in their regiment, and he'd felt weird at first, as though something was wrong with him for wanting to go. After all, he was reasonably intelligent and thought he cared about other people and their general welfare. But at the same time he had experienced those same feelings Stout talked about, and he felt them even more strongly now.

Three weeks after he'd volunteered, LBJ gave his speech saying the U.S. would stand in Vietnam and ordering the First Cavalry Division to the combat zone. In the next four days more than half of the lower-grade enlisted men in the regiment had volunteered too. Suddenly his weird feelings disappeared—he was just like everybody else. The guys who didn't volunteer had only a few months till discharge or had families and didn't want to risk their lives. Basically, almost everyone wanted to go. He regretted his loss of uniqueness, shaking his head hopelessly when his superiors called him a fine American boy, a credit to the service and to his country. What kind of shit was that?

But then what made him so different, after all? Three years of college? A few ideas that he'd taken seriously for a while? Those ideas had obviously done little toward changing the deep-seated values he'd grown up with. In college he'd learned and believed that war was a crock of shit, killing barbaric and insensitive, that proving one's manhood through violence was no proof at all but only an exciting way to avoid more pedestrian problems. His father had even thrown him out of the house a couple of times for his "rotten pinko" views. But had those new ideas ever really taken hold? He might have believed them partially—could argue them eloquently against barracks superpatriots—but when it got down to it, he was right there with the others, ready to pick up the gun and kill or be killed. As much as he believed in his idea of experience, he knew nothing could justify killing for it. But deep down it made no difference.

Maybe ideas were a game, although he certainly took some seriously enough. He remembered a morning in Fulda, shortly after he'd arrived, when the front-page picture of the *Stars and Stripes* had shown the students demonstrating at

Berkeley, the beginning of the Free Speech Movement. He couldn't take it seriously. Months later, after reading hundreds of magazine articles about it, even after reading letters from his friends who'd participated in it, he still couldn't see the point. He'd felt free enough while he was there, had done what he'd wanted—so had his friends. All the demonstrating and protesting seemed funny, something to pass the time with or a way of meeting new friends. He felt that there were more important things to protest about.

"I know you have to do it," Stout said. "I just hope it doesn't mess you up like Zastrow. Plus you could get zapped. I want us to get together back in the world and do some screwing around."

"Don't worry, I'll be back." He felt suddenly warm. "I'll miss you, man. I hope you'll write."

"As soon as I get back there."

He brought his coffee into S-1 at seven thirty in the morning. Chase leaned on the counter, nearly asleep, while his replacement, Sergeant Wallace, studied the morning reports. "You didn't look too happy at reveille this morning, Al." He knew Chase was bugged, and he wanted to rub it in. For the past week, since the new colonel had taken over, the whole battalion—officers included—had to stand reveille every morning and run a mile every afternoon.

Chase opened his eyes halfway and cocked his head. "I wasn't."

"Still got that run to look forward to." Morgan had thought he might die the first day they'd done the mile. His glee at watching Chase and Greene suffer had been the only thing that kept him going. The last couple of times had caused him no pain, even though he'd been half drunk. Another new rule was that no one could drink until five P.M. and only at the clubs. He drank at noon in Fisher's tent, and at night they stayed behind aircraft maintenance, swilling beer and whiskey until it was time to do the PDS. Then four or five of them would take the jeep to division, screaming like banshees and nearly crashing in the ditches that lined the road.

"Will, are you ready to go to the field?" Chase asked.

What was he trying to pull now? "I stay ready."

"I'm thinking of going myself."

"What are you talking about, Sergeant Chase?" Greene yelled from behind the bamboo partition.

"I said I'm thinking about going to the field, sir."

Greene came around the partition, put his hands on his hips, and stared at Chase. "And what's that supposed to mean?"

"Just what I said, sir. A Company's rifle platoon sergeant's leaving in a week, and he hasn't got a replacement. Sergeant Wallace has this job under control. I thought maybe I'd pick up a CIB before I go home."

"You shit too," Greene said. "What do you know about leading a rifle platoon?"

"Enough."

"You better get that idea out of your head, short as you are. You've only got six weeks."

"I know."

"It'd be foolish to screw yourself up."

"Nothing would happen."

"Let's forget it, Sergeant. If you want a break, take a three-day pass to Vung Tau. Or spend a couple of days in town or down at the river swimming." Greene went back to his office, and Chase laid his head on the counter.

"What about me?" Morgan said. "When do I get to go?"

"That's up to Sergeant Chase!" Greene snapped.

"How about it, Al?"

"How about it? How about it? How about getting your ass in that chair and typing some more efficiency reports—or are you too hung over for that?"

"No, I ain't too hung over. You find a mistake in one, you let me know."

He didn't ask after that. The morning became a protracted irritation, and on the flight line that afternoon he couldn't stop his bitter denunciation of Chase and Greene. Chase was crazy, flat out. Wanting to go out for a week to get a Combat Infantryman's Badge. What cheap shit.

Two days later, while everyone was at lunch, he found a request for orders for Aircraft Crewman's Wings that First Sergeant Bugelli had made up for Chase to take to division. Both Bugelli's and Chase's names were on the request. A person got wings for flying at least twenty-five combat assault hours as a crew chief or a gunner. Chase hadn't flown twenty hours as a passenger, and Bugelli hardly ever had his ass out of the base camp. Morgan laughed when he saw it, but later in the afternoon it began to grate against his insides. He didn't mention it to anyone, but the image of Chase sporting the wings and telling lies back home filled him with rage.

When he stumbled into S-1 the next morning, after downing four beers and a cup of coffee, Greene told him that the entire battalion would be in from the field that afternoon.

"What for, sir? I thought they were supposed to stay in Ia Drang till July."

"They were." Greene's face grew serious, nearly urgent, and Morgan wanted to laugh in it, spit coffee all over it. "Charlie's got his ass back in at Bong Son, and we have to run them out again."

We, shit. We don't have anything to do with it. "How long are they going to be in?"

"Just today and tomorrow. Things are getting hot up there."

He felt relieved that they wouldn't be in any longer. He didn't feel like seeing Padgett and Chambers—or at least he didn't want them to see him. At noon he stayed in Fisher's tent, drinking, until it was time to go back to the office. He walked fast on the road, trying to get steady, sucking a clove Life Saver to sweeten his breath.

Padgett sat on the big rock in front of the tent. "Hey, stiff plucker, where you been?" Padgett stood up and grinned.

"Laid in the ditch, drinkin' gin." They slapped hands. "What's happening?"

"Bong Son, I reckon. You comin'?"

"Shit!" He threw a hateful glance through the tent flap. "Not likely. Where's Orville?"

"Probably in a tent studying Caravaggio or something."

"Really?"

"I don't know, man. That cat don't talk no more."

Captain Greene appeared at the tent flap. "Come on, Morgan. You can bullshit later."

"Yes, sir. . . . Come on down to Fisher's after chow tonight. See if you can get Orville to come too."

"Okay, breeze. Later."

That night Chambers was weird. He sat with them for half an hour, then went back to his tent, claiming sleepiness. Padgett stayed with the rest of them behind Fisher's tent, drinking and playing with the monkeys.

About ten o'clock two flares went off over the northern edge of the perimeter, sparkling like weak, dirty suns and coloring the sky a pale orange.

"What's happening?" Fisher leaped out of his chair.

"Probably nothing," Zastrow said. "Some hopped-up gook trying to crawl through the minefield."

Pope, the company clerk, ran into the area.

"Ten-shun!" Morgan bellowed. "General Pope's about to address the troops."

"What's happening on the perimeter?" Fisher asked nervously.

"Some guy's gone crazy in a shithouse at second brigade. He's been firing on people since after chow. No jeeps to go in that area till it's all clear."

"You mean there's gooks in there?"

"No, Fisher. It's a guy from the unit. He's got a regular arsenal. Machine gun, grenades, and he's built up protection too, because they can't get him out. He killed a major and his driver already, and he hit a couple of other vehicles too."

Morgan almost laughed. It seemed totally logical to lay up in the shithouse blowing people away.

"What are they going to do?" Stout asked.

"Rocket him out," Morgan said. The helicopter hung like a

tiny dark speck in the pale orange of the flare, and it seemed to stutter back and forth as the rockets discharged in a faint whoosh. Seconds later the concussions floated dully into their area.

Another helicopter dumped a load of rockets, tracers spitting out both doors, then winked its way back to the flight line. The tracers had looked pretty in the night.

14

NOTHING HAD occurred to Padgett until the chopper ceased firing. The pale illumination of the flares was swallowed back into the night, and everyone stood or sat like figures in a frieze of darkness. Then a faint light of memory. "Pope, where's that dude at?"

"Huh?"

"The one blowin' people away."

"Like I said, second brigade. In a shithouse. Down around the curve from division aircraft maintenance."

"Uh-huh." He snorted, shaking his head.

"How come?"

"Just wondered. Must be all clear now."

"I'll check."

Pope left the area as new cans popped open. Fisher calmed down and the others went back to talking trash. Had to be the same cat. There couldn't be two people in the division with an arsenal in a shithouse. Little spider monkey twisted up on his pile of grenades.

"They nailed him." Pope's voice sounded triumphant in the darkness, as though he himself had put an end to anarchy. "You want to go up there, Padgett?"

"I don't guess. Could use some sleep, though, if I'm going to Sin City tomorrow. I'll catch you folks later."

"We'll really get oiled tomorrow night," Morgan said.

"You okay now, seems like." He stopped at the water trailer, drank, then doused his face and neck. Halfway up the battalion road he stopped, the giggling, musky-drinking nut job still on his mind. Fuck it. He could walk up there in twenty minutes. He was wide awake anyway and could sleep in tomorrow.

Three jeeps and two small trucks passed him on the road, covering him with dust. Division aircraft maintenance looked like a little tract of homes. Dim, warm light shone through the slits of tents and the windows of shacks built from old ammo boxes. The drunken screams and laughs were less desperate than those at recon.

Rounding the curve at the northeast corner of division, he found himself in quiet darkness, as though he were on some lonely country road. About a quarter mile down he spotted a fire through the trees with figures moving around it, and soon he heard voices, yelling, cursing. Like some strange religious cult, meeting secretly in the woods.

He stopped forty yards from where the shithouse had been. Men walked hurriedly back and forth across the road, carrying things, shouting orders to other men. The headlights of two trucks shone on the smoldering remains and on the white, powdery residue of phosphorus all over the ground. A deep cylindrical hole, big enough for a man, gaped next to a pile of charred lumber. Back toward the perimeter, broken boards, obviously shattered by rockets and grenades, lay on the ground and hung on bushes like shingles put up by a drunken carpenter.

He stopped next to a fat staff sergeant, about twenty feet from the hole. "What happened, Sarge?"

The sergeant eyed him for a moment, then shook his head. "The guy went crazy, that's what happened. I told them too, told them three months ago to get him to the nut ward."

"You knew him?"

"Knew him? Shit! He was in my fuckin' squad till he quit.

Can you imagine that? He quit. A little bit of combat and he throws down his gun, cries like a baby, and says he won't fight no more. And what do they do? Let him quit. I told 'em, chief. I said to get his ass back in the field, 'cause that's the only way you cure chickenshit. Either that or send him to the nut ward and let the headshrinkers fix him. You don't send them back to the unit and let them lie around. That really makes them crazy. I told them too, so they sure as shit can't blame me."

"He just started firing on people?"

"Didn't he? Killed Major Blake and his driver, messed up a couple of others too. Look at that shit." The sergeant pointed to the hole. "He had a whole fuckin' tunnel system under there, little dugouts filled up with five point five six, seven point six two, grenades, pistol, everything. Had it rigged so just his head and weapon stuck out. If that chopper hadn't made a direct hit with Willie Peter, he'd still be in there firin'."

"He's dead, huh?"

"Dead, shit! Evaporated, man. Chopper jockey dumped four WP's on him at once. Nothing left but a few spots down there. Grease, that's what he is. Grease and a few bones." The sergeant shook his head and shrugged. "Like I said, they should've sent him back out. That or the nut ward."

Padgett drifted off to the side, then made a complete circle of the shithouse, staying in the light so no one would shoot him. The area reminded him of Ia Drang. The ground pocked by grenades and rockets, trees oozing juice from bullet punctures, debris all over.

When he completed the circle, the sergeant was still staring at the hole and shaking his head.

"They really blasted the area," Padgett said.

"They should have. He had the whole battalion pinned down. I thought a company of Charlies had sneaked in."

"Why do you think he picked tonight?"

The sergeant turned toward him, squinting. "I don't think, chief, I know. He was supposed to go back to the field tomorrow. I told him. He told me no. I told him either the field or jail, and he says, 'We'll see about that.' I guess we did. They should've listened to me a long time ago. Let a guy sit around and think too much, he's bound to go nuts. I mean, it's not my fault. Half my squad's been killed. I needed him out there."

"No one'd blame you." Padgett patted the sergeant's shoulder, knowing he didn't believe it.

"You never know, crazy as this place is. At least in the field you got some idea who you're fightin'. Sometimes even that ain't true in this crazy fucking place."

Padgett stood beside the sergeant for another minute, then slipped off with a few others who were headed back to their unit. As he walked, he wondered what they'd tell the dude's folks. His body tingled with thoughts of the cat's burning flesh, of his last desperate moments. The rockets must have killed him instantly; if not, maybe he was at least insane enough so that he couldn't feel pain. Didn't crazy people put cigarettes out on themselves without feeling it?

He stomped his foot down hard thinking that maybe he could have prevented the whole thing. Could have reported the clown and got him sent to the iron house or the funny farm. The thought had hardly crossed his mind before it disappeared. What the fuck. He felt a cold admiration for the dude, same as he'd felt for Slagel the day he'd blown away the NVA's. It took something to do that. Being crazy, he guessed.

It was close to midnight when he heard the gunshots coming from recon, and when he got back to his tent, everyone was sitting on his cot. What looked to have been fear was slowly giving way to laughter. Platoon Sergeant Givens and Captain Webber were talking with Collins at the far tent flap. The machine gunner stood in his drawers, a forty-five in his right hand, gesturing furiously.

"What's up?" Padgett sat on his cot facing Kelly, not really caring what had happened. No one looked dead, anyway.

"Rat, man. Ran over Collins in the rack and he just opened up. I thought Charlie had our ass, boy."

Padgett crawled in his sleeping bag, tucking the mosquito

net securely underneath. He was afraid that if he started laughing he'd never be able to stop.

He got back from Sin City about six the next night, half oiled and three shots of cock to the good. Or the bad, depending on how you looked at it. To the neutral, really. Bitches didn't do a thing for him, besides saying that they'd rather be with black soldiers than with white. Whites get too drunk, have to fuck too long, and get all nasty when they can't bust nut.

Sin City was already segregated, seemed like. Splibs here, Crackers there, hip California and New York here, clean-cut Midwest there. Just enough overlap so that the splintering off wasn't total. No big thing anyway. Maybe he'd go ahead on and get blowed away tonight.

Morgan said he'd be down at Fisher's tent after seven. Sometimes old slick-ass Fisher gave Padgett a pain—too much always being cool, knowing the angles—but he guessed he'd have to put up with him if he wanted to spend some more time with Morgan.

He went to the club to have a couple of beers with his squad before going up to Fisher's. The young bloods made him feel old, and he couldn't get all worked up about learning the new dances they were doing back in the world.

Morgan came in the club a little after seven. "You coming up, LaMont?"

"In a few minutes." He didn't want to seem eager to leave. He sipped his beer slowly for five minutes. "I guess I'll catch you cats back at the tent." He got up.

"Y'all be careful not to bleach out up there," Kelly said, looking at the top of his beer can.

He didn't have to take that shit. He banged his fist on the metal top, rattling the cans. "You got something to say, Kelly, maybe you want to step out and say it."

"That's okay, man." Kelly didn't look up.

"I figured it was. I'll see you dudes in the squad tent." Fuck if anyone was going to tell him who his friends would be.

Maybe he didn't want to be with Fisher and the rest of them so much, but he did want to see Morgan. Tomorrow he'd be back chasing Charlie's funky ass around Bong Son, and Lord only knew when he'd be back in again. He'd have plenty of time to bullshit with his squad.

". . . niggers . . ." he heard as he walked along the side of Fisher's tent. He stopped and looked up as if someone had hung a red neon sign blinking "NIGGERS" in front of his face.

"You just had a bad experience, Fisher," Morgan said. "You can't say it for everyone anyway. Why don't we quit this talk? Padgett's coming up here."

"We can listen to him run his mouth too," Fisher said.

He sat down in the semidarkness, between tent ropes and pegs, to listen.

"You gonna say he's chickenshit?" Morgan said. "He got it four times, and he's going back out. He saved Slagel's ass once and got himself shot for it."

What kind of shit was this?

"Okay," Fisher said. "Maybe Padgett's all right, but he's one in a hundred. Just like in the world. You meet one you can call a Negro in a blue moon, but the rest of them are niggers."

"That's crazy, man."

"You wait. You never been out of college and you never been in the field, so you don't know. Wait and see. Man, I wish I'd been in Watts with the national guard so I could've got me a couple."

Padgett kicked a tent peg. Dudes in a war didn't talk this way.

"You just had a bad experience," Morgan said again. "Plenty of white guys turn chicken too."

"Not the same percent," Fisher said.

"Come on, man. Anyway, a lot of those guys been in more shit on the street than they'll see over here."

He split. He almost popped around the tent and knocked Fisher out, but it wouldn't have done no good. Mother fuck all these clowns. He bought a quart of rye from Sergeant Neeley in S-4. The scrawny white sack of shit sold it for ten dollars a bottle, after buying it in Qui Nhon for a dollar and a dime. He went down by the club and sat at one of the little tables outside, but a bunch of howling new guys from A Company soon drove him away. He went up to the movie and found himself in the middle of some stupid-ass beach flick with Frankie Avalon and Annette Funicello. Morgan caught up with him as he was on his way to take a shit.

"LaMont, where you been, man?"

"Boozin'." He took another swig from his jug.

"Your buddies in the club said you'd gone up to Fisher's. Weren't too friendly either."

"Why should they be?"

"What's wrong? Where have you been?"

"I got as close to Fisher's as I needed. I heard that shit you chumps were talkin'."

"What do you mean?"

"You know what the fuck I mean!"

"I didn't say anything, man. You heard me."

"You stayed there talkin' to him, didn't you?"

"I was trying to change his mind. You know where I stand." Morgan lit a cigarette, and his sagging cheeks made Padgett think of a lovesick cow. If he hadn't been so pissed off, he would have laughed.

"I still don't see what you gotta hang around clowns like that for."

Morgan threw his arms up and stamped his feet. "Jesus Christ, who else am I going to hang around with? I spend plenty of time with Alexander and Winston too."

"Not so much anymore you don't."

"Are you trying to say I'm prejudiced?"

"I didn't say nothin'." He wanted to stop but he couldn't. "I suppose you and Fisher talk about them too."

"And you never talk about white cats, do you?"

What the fuck was going on? LaMont raised his fists, and as the tears came to his eyes, he dropped them. "Mother fuck it, then, man. I don't need to listen to your shit." He spun on his heel and headed for his tent.

"Go ahead and leave. But you know what's happening, and let's not pretend that you don't."

Chambers came to his tent about nine thirty. Padgett had been planning to go see Morgan, but was drunk enough so that when Chambers suggested it, he got mad all over again. "I don't need nobody tellin' me what to do, Chambers, you dig?"

"I wasn't telling you. You and Morgan are good friends, and there's no sense having a silly fight about something someone else said."

"I don't care what you think, man. Why don't you go look at your pretty postcards, and don't bug me with no shit."

Chambers looked at him for a moment, turned, and walked out of the tent.

LaMont took three long swallows, nearly throwing up, then almost broke the jug in his hand. You couldn't trust no fuckin' body in the motherfuckin' world. He should've learned that by now, many times as he'd had it stuck to him. But no, he always kept comin' back like a baby boy, dropping his guard, inviting someone to go up side his head. Fat cats and thin cats, whites and blacks and sergeants and bitches. Motherfucking dogs would bite him if he tried to give them some food. Maybe he'd go lay up in the shithouse his goddamn self before this war was over. No way he'd let down his guard again. Wouldn't pull no punches neither.

He said good-bye to Webber after two days in the field. Nice days. Activity, no contact, and the captain feeling light because he was leaving. They reconned areas near the beach, and the blueness of the water reminded him of the Mediterranean. Even when he walked in the sand that gave way like mush under his boots, he felt good. Strong and full of energy. He watched with little emotion as Webber climbed on the chopper and left that night. The captain had been gone since March, really. He'd kept going okay, but had tightened up and kept aloof from the riflemen. Probably just as well. Too damn many of them were gone now.

Padgett went back to his tent and wrote Morgan a letter. He apologized for being so unbending—hearing that shit from Fisher set him off. But then he'd blamed the whites when Captain Davis had led them into an ambush and had of course cursed them all when he heard Fisher talking that shit.

In some ways Morgan was the best friend he'd ever had. All shit aside about white dudes not being able to understand a splib—who really understood anybody else any damn way?—they'd at least tried with each other, and you didn't meet many cats who even did that. The fat cat might have dug his shit more, but he was in it for a whole different reason. Mother fuck it anyway—he and Morgan had had good times together and talked heavy shit too, and you couldn't ask for much more than that. Just because the world was screwed up, they didn't have to let that affect them.

Morgan's reply came two days later, gushing about their friendship, about how nothing should ever get in the way of it—at least not any petty racial stuff. He went on and on with plans for when they got back to the world—traveling to Mexico, laying up in California or Jersey. Morgan said he didn't care about seeing his old friends anymore because they wouldn't understand him anyway.

At the bottom of the letter was a note saying that he'd heard from Slagel's sister and that Tom was still in Walter Reed, was quadriplegic, and would probably be moving to the Bronx VA Hospital after a couple more months. She'd just got married, and it would be too much trouble to keep Tom with her and her husband. It wouldn't be good for anyone concerned. But they'd be living in New York, so they could see him often.

Bitch! Slagel's sister was some bitch. Loved to party, and Morgan said she screwed more ways than Carter's got pills. But, man, was she out for number one. She hadn't known anybody that summer they were all at Fort Dix and up in

New York on weekends. But she finally found herself some doctor clown, and she wasn't about to let nothin' bust up that scene. Even old Tom laid up, unable to move.

He couldn't think about it without wriggling his body and shaking his head. Some people he could almost see like that, but the image of Slagel moving nothing but his head was too much. Cat was all body. His mind formed a grotesque image of Tom strapped to a hospital bed, withered and yellow like a plant without water, his thoughts growing out of his ears and hanging in some mocking chorus above his head.

The next day, the Fourth of July, started with a bang. Hancock from gunnery dropped a grenade in a hole to wake up the company. After breakfast they began reconning the small mountains by the river, the same ones they'd done in January. The many shades of green were now an almost uniform pale brown, and the mountainside was filled with bomb craters. Captain Jones, new blood platoon leader, was a humper too. As they dragged down the mountainside that afternoon, they passed a place that reminded him of where Slagel had iced the crippled prisoner. The image came back clearly of the little moaning dude in black pajamas, all red around the balls. He tried to put down the thought of divine retribution, but it kept popping up in the way his mother and the churches had taught it, and then in the more educated form like the fat cat talked. You had to pay back for what you did. Bullshit! But it was scary to think about anyway. No, man, it couldn't be right, otherwise the leaders would've got it long ago.

Every day guys left. Except from the rifle platoon. Anyone who would've gone had already been sent in a bag or bed. But plenty of pilots and crew chiefs in the scouts and gunnery were going, along with dudes who worked in the mess hall, supply, and operations. A week after Webber left there was a change-of-command ceremony after supper. Major Quinn was leaving the next day, and Major Singer, the XO, would take over. Morale had already dropped because of the way Captain Jones ran the rifles. Singer wasn't bad, but he lacked Quinn's looseness—more the gentleman type.

After the ceremony he went to his tent with a beer, had a joint, and lay down to rest before his shower. Fuckin' Jones was tiring him out. He woke up to darkness and someone giggling outside his tent.

"Wake up, Padgett, god damn it!"

"Who the fuck is that?"

"Who the fuck is that, *sir*, you mean."

"Hey, Major Quinn, what's happening?"

"You and me. The officers' party got to be too much, so I thought I'd bring my longest-lasting rifleman a drink. Todd!" Quinn bellowed. "Get your ass over to Padgett's tent."

Quinn was pretty well oiled. He used to come to the enlisted men before the Happy Valley massacre, to drink and play cards when he couldn't sleep, but he'd stayed away after that. When Todd came, Quinn passed the bottle around and followed it with a Coke. "You two some good old boys, and I'm gonna miss you after tomorrow. I'll stop in D.C. and see Slagel too and give him your regards. I already told Chambers. I just wanted to say that it's been a pleasure having you in the unit, and I hope you make out okay with these new fish. They might get chickenshit on you, but don't sweat it, because you're too short to get in trouble. If you get stationed at Benning, come and look me up, and I'll square you away."

He sat with them for another half hour, and when he left, all three of them were crying. Dude remembered everybody who'd been killed or wounded, and he thought about them all the time, like they weighed heavy on him. Quinn was a fighter—that's what the cat knew best—but he couldn't dig what had happened to the other guys. He thought he'd been trained to accept it, but he couldn't, and he'd gone on fighting hard right up to the last minute because he didn't know what else to do. What was he going to say when he got home? That they were still reconning the same hills they were doing six months ago? He'd always accepted that it wasn't his job to think about why, that people qualified to do that would, but now he wondered if anyone really did.

Padgett and Todd sat silently in the tent for another ten minutes. Todd touched his shoulder. "Reckon I'll hit the hay."

"All right, brother. Catch you in the morning."

The company didn't go out after breakfast. Singer delayed everything until Quinn left. Quinn came back from battalion S-3 about eight thirty. Everyone shuffled quietly as he walked to his chopper with Warrant Officer Fitch (a new pilot), the crew chief, Guillory, who was also going home, and Lowry, the new gunner. As the ship pulled pitch, Quinn stuck his thumb out the window of the door, and everyone on the ground returned the gesture. The helicopter rose about ten feet facing north, then turned to the east, dipped forward, and rose quickly. Padgett lost it in a glare of sunlight, then the ship appeared like a speck above the hollow glimmering spot in the sky. Padgett waved again, scratching out a little hole in the ground with the heel of his boot.

"Okay, rifle platoon," Captain Jones yelled. "Form up."

"Wring it out good, Padg," Kelly yelled from the hooch he was setting on fire.

Padgett squeezed and turned the chicken's neck, and the crunching was like twisting off carrot tops. The tension in the dumb animal relaxed, and he dropped the limp carcass to the ground. Chickens were the stupidest things he'd ever seen. He hated their dipping heads and necks as they walked and squawked around the hamlets, dropping little dribbly shits behind them. He picked up the carcass with the barrel of his rifle and lobbed it onto the roof of the flaming hooch.

"Gooks be gettin' with some fried chicken and rice tonight," Kelly said.

"We better hook up with the squad before we get left."

At the edge of the hamlet two old women and an old man stood quietly near the doorway of their hooch. They stared at him and Kelly without visible emotion. He grinned at them, then looked away. He hated the scrawny chumps. Sit there and let you waste their home. During the four days since Major Quinn had gone the platoon had been sweeping in an extended arc around Bong Son and the coast. They'd been through about fifteen hamlets so far. The interpreters questioned the villagers while the GI's searched the hooches, looking for too much of anything. No one had specified what too much was, but if it looked like too much, it had to be destroyed. They burned rice and wrung chicken necks, and Jesperson in the second squad had iced two old men who tried to run from a hamlet when the GI's came.

The white cats were a little too sentimental about dogs—even Jesperson didn't want to hurt them—and refused to shoot them even if it seemed that there were too many. The gooks ate dog and rice and chicken and got fish and other vegetables at the marketplace. If there was too much, it meant the Cong were eating it at night. He wondered why it couldn't mean the people were saving up for when the rice paddies weren't producing, but the bosses said that they wouldn't do that. He figured that the bosses must know about the habits of the people, then he realized that the bosses didn't know dick. But it wasn't his show. Why rock the boat? He'd gotten in with Captain Jones and Platoon Sergeant Givens, and it looked like he could get out by the end of the month. He was sick of humping, and for the last few days he'd been scared. In the open all the time, moving through the hamlets and along roads and rice paddies where the peasants were planting. His shit could get blown away anytime.

He stayed pretty straight during the day. Maybe half a joint in the morning and again at noon. To ease the tension. At night he smoked himself out of his ever-lovin' mind. He couldn't handle the dudes in his squad. Too much like the jittybugs back on the block, talkin' shit about how bad they were, about how they were gonna get their shit together back in the world. Like they'd all make it hustling. They dug Staff

Sergeant Peters, the squad leader, and that was cool, because they didn't bother Padgett as much. It was too much when a couple of them had bad-mouthed Major Quinn after he'd gone. He knew Quinn was from the barefoot country, but he was more than that too. He dug Quinn, that's all there was to it.

Chambers seemed like a villain. Everything that happened made him more tight, more locked into his own little world. Every night reading the fucking art books and always wanting to talk about painting and buildings, like if he let go of it he'd go nuts. The fool must have memorized the college catalogue by now. The last three times Padgett had gone to his ship he'd come away mad. At himself for not painting or not being interested and not wanting to rap about it and at Chambers for not admitting to what he was doing. His interest was genuine enough, but at least he could admit that a lot of it was defense. Cat acted as if there wasn't even a war going on, that people weren't dying and falling to pieces all around him. LaMont wanted someone to share the negativity with, to wallow in it as they'd done in Fulda. That always seemed to help, but Chambers wouldn't come on it anymore.

He felt deserted. His mood was like an undersea movie, where a thin beam of light illumined murky shadows but revealed nothing.

That night he dreamed he was home rapping with some people. Some of the same dudes who'd first bad-mouthed the fat cat to him, some of the jittybugs, and a few of the dudes from Germany. He was the center of attention, talking funny and making them all laugh. The fat cat sat watching from a corner of the room, bitterness behind his eyes, watching for him to fuck up, to reveal traces of his corruption. Whenever LaMont looked at him, his voice would weaken and fade away, but the animation would return when he faced back at the group. Still, knowing the fat cat was there watching made his throat dry and filled his belly with fear.

He woke in the morning and smiled involuntarily.

Somehow he knew that he'd never dream about the fat cat again. He remembered the main dream vividly, but in the back of his mind was a faint image of another dream with the chubby chump bowed in front of him, LaMont's hand resting softly on the fat head, forgiving, almost blessing.

The lines of peasants reminded him of pictures he'd seen of African villagers on the move. At least the Vietnamese carried things on their heads like the Africans. But they were short and shabby in their black pajamas, and their tiny steps were totally without the grace of the Africans. They were a sorry lot when you got down to it, but they were getting hip enough to move out of the hamlets before the GI's came through. For the next two days the roads were full of them. No one knew where the hell they were going. Bong Son? Qui Nhon? North to Quang Ngai City? Maybe they didn't even know themselves. The villages were empty—no rice, no chickens, no too much of anything. The platoon burned some hooches and blew up others with grenades. On the second day they found that the villagers had burned their own hooches before they left. Padgett found it funny, but everyone else was pissed.

They shook down the peasants on the road, rifling through their bundles and leaving them strewn in the dirt or letting the chickens out of the handmade wooden cages the peasants carried on their backs. You couldn't say that any of them carried too much rice, but a few bags were slit anyway. The gooks reminded him of Charlie Chaplin as they spun around in the road trying to recover the grains that splashed in the dirt. Even a couple of dogs were butt-stroked by rifles until they lay twitching, with their heads crushed, in the road.

He didn't do anything, but he let his fire team do what they wanted. It wasn't up to his sorry ass. Jones or Givens or Peters could say something if they didn't like it. But they probably had their orders too. The division wasn't bringing in the body counts it used to, and word was out that the head dudes had the ass and wanted some action. The word, or maybe just the feeling, trickled down, and the GI's were provoking the shit out of the villagers. If any of the peasants tried to retaliate, they'd be dead in a second, and they seemed to know that because they didn't do anything. The operation probably wouldn't end until the brass had some big news to report to the bigger brass.

The next day they made a move to fox the Cong. They went back to a hamlet near the beach, one they'd been to before that was still occupied. There were three hamlets along a five-mile stretch of road that wound through rice paddies and beside some small hills and eventually went into Bong Son. The peasants had begun to pack up before the choppers touched down, and the hamlet's population was on the road before the platoon finished going through all the hooches. They found nothing and burned all the mud-and-straw huts.

He forgot his men as they walked up the road to the next hamlet. The faint sea breeze fanned the back of his neck and rode up inside his helmet liner, cooling his entire head. He thought of the Mediterranean, of Florence, of how hard it must have been for the old painters to get the effect of the light haze that hung over all of Tuscany.

The peasants from the second hamlet were a mile ahead of them when they passed those from the first. Someone in the second squad pushed over a man with a cage of chickens strapped to his back. The cage broke and the chickens hopped crazily on the man and in the muddy ditch where he lay. The whole platoon busted up. After the second squad moved on, Padgett walked into the ditch and helped the man up. He couldn't have weighed more than ninety pounds. He smiled at Padgett and quickly bowed his head twice.

They burned the second hamlet, had chow, and began the two-mile walk to the third. The line of peasants was endless. It didn't seem that the ten or eleven hooches in each hamlet could hold so many. The platoon was turning right off the road when a machine gun opened up from the small hills about a hundred yards to their left.

Only a couple of weeks, he thought. Only a couple of

weeks and the operation would be over and he'd be done with this motherfuckin' shit. He dived into the ditch, scrambled around, and looked up. Two soldiers lay in the road. Others, kneeling in the ditch, were gunning down peasants. He fired a clip toward the hills, reloaded, and waited. He found himself staring at the turned-up face of one of his dead comrades whose name he didn't even know. The face seemed to be straining to come back to life. It could be one of a series of paintings about the war.

"Into the hamlet," Sergeant Givens yelled. "Take cover in the hooches."

"Let's go," Peters said.

The gooks ran into the hamlet for cover too. Some were shot from behind by the machine gun. More were shot or butt-stroked with weapons by the GI's. He found himself with Kelly inside a dim hooch, looking out the window. He counted fourteen bodies between the hamlet and the road. He heard firing from other hooches, but he didn't know if it was going toward the machine gun or into the peasants. Suddenly he realized that Kelly was staring at him expectantly.

"Cover that door," Padgett said.

"What do I do, brother?" Kelly's yellow face was paler than usual.

"Just watch out. Ain't nothin' gonna happen unless every goddamn body goes nuts." He could feel it in the air. But he wasn't scared like he used to be. He was bored and tired and wanted the operation to be over.

The gunships went in low over the hill, dumping rockets and grenades and orange dashes of machine-gun fire. Both ships went over three times. It looked as if they'd knocked out the gun, but the noise in the hamlet kept getting louder. Yelling, gook babble, rifle popping all swirled senselessly in his head.

Captain Jones and Platoon Sergeant Givens and the first squad headed out of the hamlet toward the foothills. LaMont didn't know anyone in the first squad anymore. Weird, but he was getting out. They moved across the road and didn't take any fire, so it looked as if things would be all right. The rest of the platoon could get some rest. The dark wall cooled his cheek.

Tuttle squatted at the entrance to the hamlet, treating one of the men. Six GI's were down but no one else was helping.

"Get your ass in there, bitch!"

He turned. Thomas pushed a girl through the door. Her pajamas were down around her knees, and the white top flapped around her nearly bald pussy as she stumbled into the hooch.

"Deedee, mama-san!" Thomas yelled and slammed the door. "Keep them motherfuckers out of here, Kelly. I'm gonna knock me off a shot."

"Okay, but I'm next."

A couple of weeks—three at the most—was all he had to go. They weren't taking fire so he could go help Tuttle with the wounded. As he went out the door, Thomas pulled down his fatigues and drawers. The crack in Thomas' ass seemed to hang in front of his eyes, even as he stepped into the sunlight.

Outside, a mama-san beat at his chest with both hands. He pushed her aside. "I only got a couple weeks, and I got to help the wounded." He ran to the next hooch and peered in the window. Jesperson looked up at him over his shoulder and grinned. His pimply white buttocks rose and fell slowly over a squirming figure beneath him. LaMont pushed another woman away and looked into the sky. A helicopter circled the hamlet slowly, the gunner sitting loosely in the door, the dark sun visor covering his face beneath the milky enamel of the flight helmet.

The mama-san grabbed his arms from behind, locking them in the crooks of her elbows. Her arms felt like dead twigs, thousands of years old. If he moved, they would shatter into hundreds of dead fragments. He relaxed and almost began to laugh. As he brought his eyes down, a hand scythe rose past his chest, the sun showering sparks along its sharpened edge. The old papa-san held it above his head, his face filled with an outrage that would have been a challenge for the painter to convey.

15

As THE chopper flew west, away from the South China Sea, Chambers remembered the day they'd gone swimming in a small cove beneath a Mediterranean villa. Slagel had found the only Catholic in Italy who screwed before marriage, and she'd taken them all from Florence in a Volkswagen bus. The nearly turquoise water had been ice cold, and he'd never had a more invigorating swim.

The soldiers swaggered sloppily down the road by the hamlet, gaining (he didn't know how) on the Vietnamese who moved away with determined staccato steps. A pair of GI's lurched and fell as if they were too drunk to continue. Orange flashes tore across the road and into the hamlet. McCutcheon opened up, and the casings from his machine gun clattered against Chambers' flight helmet. The pilots jabbered, and everyone on the ground went crazy.

He tightened his grip on the machine gun, but could do nothing. The firing came from the other side. The hamlet looked like a movie being run too fast. People scampering, stopping, falling, disappearing into hooches, olive drab colliding with black, continuous orange flashes. He shook his head at the stupidity of the moiling bodies on the ground.

"I got 'em zeroed!" McCutcheon bellowed into the mike as the ship banked high to the left. "Swing out wide and let me get 'em!"

The new gunnery platoon leader, Captain Sanders, and his pilot, Warrant Officer Eastman, didn't know what to do. They finally agreed to fly straight at the target in order to use all the ship's fire power.

"Okay, Orville," McCutcheon said, "just put your tracers where mine are going. And throw some grenades, for Christ's sake!"

He tensed as two tracers from the ground sailed fifty yards to the right of the ship, but couldn't get infected with McCutcheon's enthusiasm. He fired, he tossed two frags out the door, but what did all this have to do with him anyway? Three times they went over, and on the last pass his bolt slammed forward and nothing happened. The wooden box at his feet was empty.

"We got them, we knocked the fuckers out!" McCutcheon bellowed. "Four or five confirmed kills, sir."

"Red, this is Six, over."

"This is Red," Captain Sanders said.

"Good work, Red. Looks like you got 'em. We'll take it from here."

"Roger, out, Six."

McCutcheon slapped him on the shoulder and gave him the thumbs up. He nodded, then got down on his knees and checked the ammo boxes beneath the seat. Empty too. Christ, he'd be reloading for forty-five minutes.

After landing, McCutcheon left him to load by himself. By the time he finished, the ground outside his ship looked as though a squad of drunks had been through it. Eleven empty wooden crates were strewn on the ground among forty-four olive-drab metal ammo cans. Sweating profusely, he carried and kicked the boxes and cans over to the garbage pit, growing furious with the thought that he'd have to clean the carboned-up guns tomorrow.

He arranged two boxes of grenades behind the console, then climbed on the seat and lit a cigar. The lift ships landed in a veil of dust, and he watched disinterestedly as maybe twenty-five men got off the four ships. About fifteen had been sent to the hospital then, and that meant the company would be lying around for a few more days, waiting to go out. Normally he would have welcomed the break as a chance to do more reading and sleeping, but now the thought irritated him because it broke the rhythm and meant he'd have to readjust again. He wanted the days to go in a continuous pattern. The war for him would be over sooner that way.

The other gunners and crew chiefs walked toward the lift ships. For what? To see who was missing? To see who was left for next week's list? He fumed as the helicopter crewmen and riflemen met, his platoon helping the infantrymen carry their weapons and web gear. They were strong enough to carry their own stuff. Why all the false camaraderie anyway? Even Robinson was helping someone—maybe Mallison the pussy eater. He turned and hurled his cigar out the door, then groaned aloud as he went to retrieve it. He stomped out the ember that winked at him like an accusing eye and tossed the soggy, crumpled butt into the garbage pit.

In half an hour McCutcheon stumbled through the faded orange dusk, his head bent, his shoulders stooped as if they carried the entire burden of the war. "Hi, Orville," he said, raising sorrowful eyes.

"How they doing?"

"Seven dead. Orville, LaMont got it."

"He did? Must be his fifth wound." He couldn't remember if it was four or five. "Bad?"

McCutcheon's face suddenly turned cold. "It wasn't no wound. He got the max."

Chambers' right leg rose involuntarily, then stomped the helicopter floor. "Uh-uh."

"Some slope cut him with a scythe. Right through the heart."

"I don't believe it." His head burned as though hot ointment had been smeared on his scalp.

"It's true. I'm sorry, man. Want a beer or something?"

"No. No." Suddenly panicked, he jumped to the ground, then stood still for a moment. His body tried to go in three directions at once, and his mind ran with more than he could make sense of. He had to get to LaMont and apologize. He spun and faced McCutcheon. "Where is he?"

"What?"

"LaMont. Where's LaMont now?"

"I don't know, Orville. Probably on a chopper back to base camp."

"I have to see him." He moved away from the ship.

"Wait!"

He turned.

"Where you going?"

"I have to see him. I can't leave it like this." McCutcheon blurred in front of him.

"I know how it is. Maybe someone'll fly you in. I've lost a lot myself. You better take your pot and weapon." McCutcheon held out his pistol belt and grenade launcher.

"Thanks."

Major Singer's ship left in two hours. The new company commander had to fly back to base for a meeting with the colonel and agreed to take Chambers as long as he'd be ready to return in the morning.

As the ship rose in the black sky outside the field base perimeter, Chambers closed his eyes and leaned back against the fire wall. He felt like a mass of inert jagged rock hurtling through the cold regions between planets distant from the sun. Where was he going? What was the point of his futile gesture?

He opened his eyes onto the green phosphorescent glow of the dials and gauges on the dashboard of the ship. The pilots, silent and still, seemed like robots locked into position in their seats. Were it not for the engine drone and for the yellow and white lights winking outside the cabin, the helicopter could have been a statue frozen in the sky. Even the spinning rotor blades, the lights reflecting off them as from a scratched mirror, seemed solid, still. Beneath them, the jungle brooded—unfathomable darkness.

His mind slid backward over the past few weeks to the night when LaMont had clung to him in the darkness. What had happened since then? Why had he let LaMont go? He banged the palm of his hand against his flight helmet, then shook his head. Maybe if he hadn't been so distant, LaMont would be alive right now. The thought tortured him for a moment until he let it go, waving his hand into the cool, windy blackness outside the ship. War didn't take any of that stuff into account. He wasn't guilty.

Still, he had deserted his friend, given up talking with him because LaMont wasn't interested in art anymore. How stupid could you get? You couldn't isolate yourself in the middle of a war, not when your friends—or you yourself—needed someone to loosen up the time with. Hadn't he learned that in Fulda? Learning about art had given him great pleasure, but the contact with the others had been the most important thing, had made him feel the most alive. Lately he seemed to have been drifting back to the lump he'd lived in before going to Germany.

Suddenly the air beneath the ship blazed with white light; they were already at division base camp, hovering down to a parking space on the helipad. The landing light spread over the road where a driver in a three-quarter-ton truck held on to his hat, waiting to take them to battalion.

The truck stopped on the short stretch of road between C Company's new wooden mess hall and the S-1 tent. Morgan leaned on the counter, a coolie hat shading a light bulb above his head. He shuffled pieces of paper, making occasional notations with a pen. From twenty feet away his face looked puffy and tired, as though he'd just awakened from a bad drunk.

Chambers walked down to his platoon's tent. He hung his mosquito net above a cot, then spread his sleeping bag beneath it. At the water trailer he brushed his teeth, washed his hands and face, then went back to the tent and put his toilet articles beneath the sleeping bag. He lit a cigar on his way up to S-1.

He stopped in the opened flaps of the doorway. "Will?"

Morgan started, then turned his head to one side. "Orville. How'd you get in ?"

He tried not to wince at the stale beer breath. "Major Singer. You heard?"

"Didn't I? It all comes through me, you know. See, I got it right here." Morgan held up a sheet of paper and rattled it. "Your company strength, right here. You had ninety-one enlisted men present for duty at midnight last night, and at midnight tonight you'll have seventy-five. Tomorrow's morning report will say, 'Padgett, LaMont, from duty to KIA. . . .'"

"Cut it!" Orville slapped his hand on the counter. The ash from his cigar dropped onto one of the white forms.

"Careful, the CG don't like his paper dirty." Morgan backhanded the ash off the counter, onto the bamboo matting where Chambers stood.

Something rustled in the back of the tent, then Captain Greene stepped around the bamboo wall. "Morgan, take off if you want. DeWolf can do the report."

Morgan didn't turn, but grinned at Chambers. "It's okay, sir. It never rains in the Army."

"It's up to you. Hello, Chambers."

"Good evening, sir."

"I'm sorry about your friend."

He nodded to Greene as the captain walked past him out of the tent.

Morgan raised his middle finger to Greene's back, then made a few more marks on the papers. "What happened, Orville?"

"I don't know." He walked around the counter and sat down on the edge of the desk. He hadn't even questioned it. LaMont cut with a scythe? How the hell could that happen? "They got ambushed next to a hamlet."

"Were you flying?"

"Our ship knocked them out. I don't know what went on in the hamlet."

Morgan shrugged. "I guess it doesn't matter."

"Can we see him?"

"Who?"

"LaMont."

"Shit, I don't know."

"Can we find out?"

Morgan pulled a can of beer from under the counter, drank, then wiped the foam off his mustache with his sleeve. "Let's go to S-3. I think Greene's there."

First Sergeant Bugelli sat next to Greene at a table in the complex of conex boxes that made up S-2 and S-3. "Hey, Chambers." Bugelli stood up and slapped him on the back. "Rough day today. Too bad. Guess it proves you can't trust no fuckin' friendlies."

"What do you mean?"

"What do I mean? Hell, you were there. Reports I got said they lured Blue into a trap, then turned on them in the hamlet."

"I didn't see what went on."

"Radio report said the gooks attacked them with anything they could find—hoes, scythes, old sticks of wood. Killed Padgett and cut up four others. Platoon killed all the sorry bastards once it started, though. Body count of forty-three."

"What do they do with the bodies?" Morgan asked. "Ours, I mean."

"They should be at the hospital," Greene said. "They fix them up in the morgue room to send home."

"Can we see him?"

"I don't know. No harm in trying."

They went back to S-1, and Chambers sat in the chair behind the desk for an hour. Morgan stood at the counter, taking the individual PDS reports from the company clerks, joking with them, all the time guzzling beer that came from some seemingly bottomless hole beneath the counter. After the last clerk came in, Morgan quickly tallied the various categories included in the Personnel Daily Summary and filled them in on the battalion master copy. He seemed completely detached from what he did, as if the report were just another piece of paper, an ordinary letter.

Chambers turned and stared into the bottom of Morgan's typewriter, which had been tipped on its back to leave room on the desk for writing. Neat rows of metal keys and springs. The whole office was neat. The empty "in" box on the left corner of the desk, a few typed forms in the "out" box awaiting Greene's signature. Behind the desk regulations were filed away in notebooks in metal and glass cabinets. The day had been checked off on Morgan's calendar; a small pile of letters sat on a table beneath it next to a silent portable radio. The office might not be a bad place to work, but its lack of warmth gave him the creeps.

"All set," Morgan said, shaking the piece of paper. "Now the war can go on for another day."

They didn't mention Padgett on the ride to G-1. Half drunk, Morgan talked only about old times in Fulda or about his friends at the base. He raved about going to the field as though nothing had happened out there, then sentimentally described the combat experiences of Stout, Zastrow, and Fisher. Stout had been teaching him about gunning, and Morgan felt ready for the field anytime.

Irritated, Chambers said nothing and was relieved when the jeep pulled into the G-1 parking lot and Morgan took the report to the tent. He leaned back in the seat, watching the stars, realizing that his feeling for LaMont was gone. His body begged for sleep. He didn't want to listen to any more shit.

Morgan seemed calmer when he returned from G-1 and said nothing on the short drive to the hospital. In the parking lot they both got out of the jeep. Morgan walked up a gravel path while Chambers stood still for a moment, taking in the night. A generator crashed somewhere like a giant waterfall. A lone helicopter winked red and yellow as it circled the perimeter, trying to draw fire or spotting with an infrared scope. They never stopped.

"Come on, Orville."

"Okay."

An orderly wheeled a corpse into the Quonset hut that served as a morgue. A small portable radio, encased in black leather, stuck out of the front pocket of his fatigue coat, playing cool jazz.

"Can we go in there?" Morgan asked.

"What for?" The orderly eyed them pleasantly.

"A friend of ours got it today. We want a last look at him. We've been together over two years."

"Who was it?"

"Padgett. LaMont Padgett."

"Colored guy?"

"Yeah."

"He's in there. Just let me put this one in place, then I'll leave you alone with him. It's too bad. That scythe would've been a quarter inch to the side, he'd have been all right. Got him in the heart, though."

Eighteen mummy sacks lay on tables in utter stillness. The orderly wheeled his cart down to the far wall, left it, and strolled out of the hut. "Don't be too long. Docs might not dig it if they found you guys here."

The tag said, "PADGETT, LaMont," followed by his rank, service number, unit, and home of record. Orville fingered the tag and felt afraid. What if he zipped it down and LaMont jumped out and started to boogie in front of him? Boogie. A guy from Maine at Fort Knox called Negroes boogies.

He looked over his shoulder at Morgan, turned back, and pulled the zipper down two feet. The dark brown of LaMont's face had faded to a nearly olive drab—the color of the bag he was zipped in—and seemed on its way to gray. He looked strange with his eyes closed. Orville touched his cheek—hard, clammy, reptilian. The face had been tilted up, the lips slightly puckered in that arrogant and insolent attitude that LaMont so often wore. He drew his hand back and smiled. He felt a sudden urge to kiss him, but what would Morgan say? Besides, it wouldn't look too cool if the orderly caught him. He zipped up the bag and left.

Two down, two to go. The thought occurred to him involuntarily as he flopped wearily in the jeep. He felt sick of himself for thinking it, for being so tired and worried about not getting enough sleep. Maybe he didn't even care. He felt jealous of Morgan's being alone with LaMont now. But then they'd been the better friends. They'd shared the cubicle in Fulda where he and Slagel would come every night to shine boots, listen to music, and tell stories. LaMont and Morgan were the ones who kept people laughing. Maybe they were childish, but at least they hadn't been dead. Slagel had never acted mature either, had never taken anything too seriously, but his nonchalance was different, as though something inside him that was supposed to feel had dried up.

LaMont and Morgan had helped make Orville feel alive too—why else did he follow them to this place? Suddenly he was back in Fulda, back in their cubicle that Sunday afternoon in late June when they'd all resolved to do it. "Let's go, then," Morgan had said, and off they went. Down the small road that circled the barracks, up the stairway between the chapel and dispensary, over the cobbled walkway to the regimental headquarters, up to the personnel office where Morgan typed the 1049 forms requesting service in Vietnam. More than a year ago now. One of them crippled, one of them dead.

Morgan walked briskly out the door of the morgue, fired up the jeep, and drove it back to S-1. He killed the engine in the parking space, then sat still for a moment. "Want to have a beer and talk awhile?"

"I better not. Not much to say anyway, I guess."

"I guess. See you in the morning, then."

"I'm leaving first thing."

"When'll you be back in?"

"I don't know. End of the month, probably."

"Take it easy out there, Orville. I hope this doesn't get to you too much."

"Nothing to do about it." He walked away, wishing it had gotten to him more.

For the next five days the gunnery platoon flew meaningless flights, guiding the rifles through areas Charlie had occupied and that were now deserted. The hamlets along the road where Padgett had been killed contained not one living creature nor ounce of rice nor inch of documents. As the old pilots left, the flights turned into training missions for the new ones—knocking down walls with rockets, pinpointing tracers from the side guns on smoke grenades thrown by the gunners and crew chiefs.

Chambers didn't mind. Besides the relief of knowing Charlie had disappeared, he was glad to get Captain Sanders and Warrant Officer Eastman trained. He'd been feeling easier around the other gunners and had even had a few beers with them the last two nights before going to read. Robinson was arranging an emergency leave with the Red Cross because his father was supposed to be quite ill. Once that loudmouth left, things would be a lot better.

Chambers took it slower this time, dividing his time between the gunners and his books and postcards. He had to guard himself against his comrades' foolishness, and if his irritation became too great, he'd go off and relax with his books.

After finishing lunch with Hancock and Webster, he was dunking his mess kit in the garbage cans full of hot water when Staff Sergeant Hart strode up, his pink face tight with seriousness.

"What's up, Sarge?" Webster asked.

"You men got your gear together?" They all nodded.

"Then get your asses down to your ships and wait. We're leaving this afternoon. Charlie's back in Ia Drang and we're heading down there. We'll spend tonight at division, then leave first thing in the morning."

He went to his ship and began cleaning guns, figuring he could get a couple done before the pilots were ready to leave. He cleaned them slowly, and by four o'clock, when he'd finished all six, nothing had happened. The company officers had spent the afternoon like drones, running in and out of the operations tent as though a new war had begun in some faraway land.

Horseshit. They were entering the southwestern spasm of the Bong Son-Ia Drang syndrome, and it probably wouldn't last for long. When the chopper finally pulled pitch at five o'clock he was so disgusted that he nearly told Sanders how dumb the movement was. Their fearsome enemy, who fought helicopters with crossbows and who had one thirty caliber for every two men, pulled them around as if they were some big dumb goofy puppet. They could go back and forth between Bong Son and Ia Drang forever, until their helicopter and guns wore out, and they had to walk and eat snakes and roots and rice. The Twenty-fifth was already in Ia Drang, knocking down trees with armored personnel carriers. Maybe with a hundred helicopters and a hundred tanks they could flush out a platoon or two. The enemy, more than likely, would be on its way into Cambodia by the day after tomorrow. Sometimes it seemed as though the U.S. Army was being held at bay by no more than a squad.

Back at division base he set up his mosquito net and sleeping bag, then had a sandwich at the mess hall before going to find Morgan. He tried the club first, seeing nothing but unfamiliar faces from A and B and D companies guzzling beer and howling like crazed savages at the metal tables. For a moment he wanted to howl back at them, to wave his arm and send them all flying home to Ohio and Georgia and Texas. He turned on the sticky floor and walked out.

When he got up on the knoll behind S-4, he heard Morgan laughing, heard other voices bellowing. He crept between the S-4 tent and the one where Fisher slept and stood back, watching the group for a few minutes. Fatigue grabbed him, and he wanted to go back to his tent and fall asleep, then wake up, clear post and leave. But this would be his last chance to see Morgan for a month. "Anyone got an extra beer?" He stepped out from behind the tent.

"Orville!" Morgan yelled, jumping to his feet. "What the fuck is *los*?"

"Drink up, Chambers." Fisher handed him two cans. "From me and Zastrow. We're deedeein' in the morning."

"Congratulations."

"How long you in for?" Morgan asked.

"Till morning. Back to Ia Drang."

"Fuck Ia Drang!" Fisher screamed. "And fuck Bong Son and Westmoreland and Ban Me Thuot and Cheo Reo and Pleiku. Fuck the gooks and fuck the Army!"

"Sit down, Chambers." Stout made room between himself and Morgan, then handed him a joint.

"Thanks. How you doin', Stout?"

"Two days, and I'll be just fine."

"I'm glad for you." He wished he had gotten to know Stout better.

"You better write, Fisher," Morgan said. "We'll get together when I get back in December."

"I may be in Oakland when you get there."

"Fuckin' A. We'll get a place in Berkeley and join the VFW. Protest on Saturdays, drink booze and tell lies on Sundays."

Chambers leaned back and relaxed with dope as the others went on talking. Morgan always planned to get together with someone somewhere. If he followed through, he'd be traveling for a hundred years. Chambers wanted to see Morgan back in the world, but he didn't care about anyone else.

"You gonna re-up again, Zastrow?" Fisher asked.

"Guess so. Done twelve years now, might as well do twenty."

"You ought to get out and go to Bangkok. Crew chief good as you could make two grand a month working for Air America. I met a guy on R&R who offered me seventeen hundred a month to be a load master on C-130's and

Caribous. I still might go back there. The living's cheap and the pussy's good. What more do you need?"

"I'm thinking about it," Zastrow said.

"Shhooooort!" Fisher bellowed. "I'm a short motherfucker!"

They all smoked and drank to shortness. Although he felt detached, Chambers also felt a certain warmth for Fisher, Stout, and Zastrow. Maybe because they were Morgan's friends, but also because of what they'd been through, because of the exhaustion that seemed to weigh them down. For another hour they joked and reminisced, rehearsed evenings back home filled with steaks, soft beds, and sex, then everyone fell silent.

Fisher blew out an immense breath. "I'm going to take my shower and go to bed. I'm not going to let you guys get me drunk and make me miss my flight." He stood up, stretched, and fell over backward.

"I think you've *been* fucked up," Zastrow said.

Fisher stood up again.

"You have to leave us something to remember you by," Stout said. He reached out, slipped his fingers in Fisher's back pocket, and pulled down, tearing off the pocket and ripping halfway down the trouser-leg. Morgan reached out and grabbed the other pocket. "I need my share too." He ripped. "I still got a hundred and thirty days."

Fisher protested, but very lightly. It seemed to be part of some ritual. Others jumped up, and soon Fisher lay on the ground and they were all over him, tearing his clothes, shredding them in little pieces, and screaming like wild men. Morgan ripped a piece of cloth from a leg, crawled out of the thrashing pack, put it in his pocket, then pounced back on top of the heap.

Chambers went cold. The pile of bodies filled him with disgust. Grown men acting like idiotic kids, rolling around in the fucking dirt.

"Get off! Get off me!" Fisher's voice was filled with panic.

"Come on, man," Stout said.

"Didn't you hear them?"

"Hear what?" Two flares went off high above the perimeter, sending a pale pink illumination into their area. Tensed muscles stood out on Fisher's neck.

"Oh, no," he moaned. "They're going to get me! They're not going to let me out!"

"It ain't nothin'," Stout said.

"No. They're attacking. I know it. Gotta hide! Gotta hide!" His voice trailed off into a low pathetic moan. He jerked his head suddenly. "Let's get to the bunker."

Zastrow grabbed Fisher as he prepared to run off. All he had on were his drawers and combat boots. About two inches of pants hung ridiculously from his belt. "Cool down, Fish. Nothing's gonna happen."

"Let me go! Come on, Zastrow. You're going home tomorrow. You want them to get you too?"

The flares had gone down, and Zastrow and Fisher looked like a two-headed bear outlined in the darkness. A series of explosions shook the ground, and the figure began to squirm.

"What'd I tell you?" Fisher yelled. "Incoming rounds. For God's sake, let me go!"

"I should know what incoming rounds sound like," Zastrow said. "That's 105's going out. You've been here long enough to know that."

"I've been here long enough!" Fisher shouted defiantly.

They sat in silence for fifteen or twenty minutes. Fisher squirmed against Zastrow's grasp for a while, then relaxed, and the two of them sat like a pair of confused lovers huddled in the fearsome night. Zastrow finally let him go, and Fisher stumbled away to take his shower.

Chambers felt so tired he could barely stand up. Ia Drang tomorrow. He had to get some sleep. He muttered feeble good-byes to Stout, Zastrow, and Morgan, then walked heavily to his tent.

16

"MORG! COME ON, man. Wake up. It's time for reveille."

He opened his eyes and stared at DeWolf for a moment. "Okay," he croaked. He lay still for another minute, then sat up, one leg in his sleeping bag, the other out. He still wore his boots, and mud caked his whole right side. "Christ, I stink." He swung his legs over the side of the cot.

"You could try a shower," DeWolf said. "Even though it ain't the first of the month. Let's go to formation."

"Fuck formation. I'm sick of it." He stood up as DeWolf left the tent, grabbed his shaving kit and a change of clothes, and walked over to the S-4 shower. He could afford to miss reveille once—he'd stood it every morning so far. Besides, he hadn't had a shower in a week, since before Fisher's short-timer's party. He'd been dead drunk every night. Since Stout had left five days ago, he hadn't even stayed in the battalion area. He'd wandered the division road after work, a bottle of whiskey and a pack of joints in his pocket, stopping for beer at the dingy clubs along the way whenever he got too hot. Twice he'd awakened on the grass of the flight line and had barely made it back for reveille.

Everyone was gone, including Padgett, but he could hardly believe that, even though his lips had touched LaMont's dead ones. He kept expecting to run into him on the road or find him drinking in the club.

After shaving, he scrubbed at the new yellow stains on his teeth until they disappeared, then stepped into the shower. He couldn't get a heavy lather from the soap, but enough to remove the stench from his funky body. Salmon-colored rings of irritation covered his thighs— jungle rot moving out from his crotch. His balls were going to fall off one of these days. Little red heat-rash pimples speckled his ass. He rubbed the bar of soap over and over his flaccid buttocks, sometimes scratching with his fingernails to dig beneath the irritation. Too much sitting around in S-1. If he were moving, it wouldn't be so hot and stale inside his pants.

He dried himself, peeling away the dead skin between his toes until they bled, then covered his body with baby powder and got dressed. Voices laughed and joked outside the shower, boots stomped on the dirt, mess kits clanged. Back at the tent, he downed two beers.

Chase glared at him as he approached S-1. "Where the fuck were you this morning, Morgan?"

"At least let me get in the tent before you start up."

"I asked you a question, soldier. Why weren't you at reveille?"

"I was taking a shower."

"Why didn't you take it last night?"

"Come on, Al. For Christ's sake."

"Why not?"

"Because I was laid drunk in the fucking ditch like I have been for the last three months."

"I told you I wanted that shit cut out."

"And I'm telling you that I shouldn't have to stand reveille when I work till two in the morning."

"You don't tell me a goddamn thing, hear? You do what people tell you, no questions asked."

If he said anything more, he wouldn't be able to stop. He eyed Chase for a moment, then looked down at the desk. Behind his hot face, the tears strained to get out. "Okay, Al. I just feel shitty because of everyone leaving."

"What are you gonna do, cry?"

"No!" Rage straitjacketed every muscle in his body, and he felt as though his throat and mouth had been stuffed up with rags.

"Then start typing."

His mind rushed with such confusion that it took a few seconds before he could move. He sat down, counting the objects he could use to murder Chase. The typewriter would cave in the back of his head. The .45 hanging on the tent pole would be good. The letter opener; pens; shoelaces; paper clips through the eyes and ears. It could be done. In his mind he did it. With the typewriter. Bashed his head into the counter over and over again. He smiled as he listened to the bones crunch and crackle, watched the shaped head turn into an amorphous crimson blob. Squeeze it like chicken giblets. Hold the bloody hands upward in salute. He typed perfectly for the rest of the morning.

After lunch he walked down to the flight line alone. Stillness everywhere—not even any jeeps raising dust around him. Two helicopters took off from the far corner of the helipad, but he barely heard them, and the only other choppers were distant, swinging like toys in the bright blue sky. He felt light and strangely unoppressed. His rage had dissolved, and he'd even begun to feel relieved that he didn't have to say good-bye anymore. His friends were gone, but also the tension from watching them leave. The only good-byes left were for when he went home himself, and those wouldn't be hard.

With all the aircraft maintenance people at Sin City for the afternoon, the flight line was deserted. He'd just as soon be alone anyway. That's the way it would be from now on. He still had plenty of drinking buddies, but things wouldn't be the same. They weren't like the old guys. Obeyed the rules and didn't do crazy shit like lying in the ditch all night. They took their malaria pills and ate the shitty chow and wrote regularly to the folks back home. What a pile of crap.

He pulled back the canvas flap and looked into the maintenance hooch. No one. A padlock stared blindly from the parts-room door, and old rotor blades, pylons, and drums of fluid lay strewn around randomly. A broken pilot's seat sat in the middle of the floor surrounded by cigarette butts. The breeze flapped his fatigues, and he turned away.

A strong steady wind blew against his face, and a giant black cloud raced over the hills on the eastern side of the camp. The blue in the rest of the sky faded, turning gray, then growing darker. He ran to the nearest helicopter, making it to the cabin as the first raindrops hit him.

Outside the front window the rotor blade bobbed up and down, causing the whole ship to undulate gently. The wind tore violently at the canvas flap of the maintenance hooch, and thick sheets of rain danced across the shiny brown road. A spear of lightning ripped through the western sky. The thunder exploded deafeningly and rolled off into silence as though a whole world had been split apart and crumbled into nothing. He leaned back and imagined the S-1 tent blowing through the sky like a magic carpet.

In a minute fog covered the Plexiglas windows of the ship. He opened the door a crack, then flung it back and leaped to the ground. He spread his legs and arms, opened his mouth, and let the rain wash over him like a tidal wave. He'd never seen a harder rain. He thought it might knock him flat. After a few minutes he turned, letting the water beat against his back. A small stream already tumbled through the ditch on the side of the road.

The wind died down and the air around him lightened. The storm ended as abruptly as it had begun, the sky becoming white, light blue, then moving toward a darker blue. Blackness hung in the west. The rain stopped and the sun sparkled in the drops that hung and fell from the rotor blade. A rainbow rose out of the foliage on one side of Titty Mountain, arched over a slope, and disappeared into the side that faced away from the division.

He woke up the next morning still slightly drunk from the night before, and after three beers he was mellow without staggering or being incoherent. He worked well until ten, then left for the rifle range with a herd of new guys. He filled his canteen with beer and passed it around on the firing line. He fired his M-16 for the first time since coming to Vietnam, and although it gave him no thrill, it beat typing.

The next day he went to the rappelling tower with the new troops after a lunch of four beers. Sliding down the thirty-foot rope was trickier than he'd suspected, and the second time panic nearly made him fall. But he didn't let it show. Kept up a steady stream of shit-talking and laughing. By that night he'd become a legend around the camp. People sought his company and bought him drinks, and DeWolf had overheard a group of soldiers talking about his craziness.

Spurred on by the exhilaration, he spent that night going from tent to tent, boozing, smoking dope, but somehow managing to keep his head, so he didn't forget what happened. He felt called on to perform, and he didn't mind at all. He gave everyone the poop on the war, on the chickenshit in the base camp. You could beat it like him by staying fucked up all the time.

In the morning S-1 became responsible for burning shit for the next week. Morgan and DeWolf drew straws, and DeWolf got the detail for the first day. One would burn shit, the other do the PDS on alternating days for the rest of the week. When DeWolf left, Morgan wished he'd volunteered for the job. He was nervous and needed to get out of the office. He kept giggling and telling stories, almost uncontrollably.

Luckily Chase had some extra work to do, so Morgan took the morning reports to division.

On his way back he picked up a hitchhiker, a young Negro sergeant with a thick pile of papers under his arm. "Where to, Sarge?"

"Artillery battalion."

"I'll take you." He'd have to go around by second brigade, but on such a nice day he didn't mind driving. The sky was bright blue, covered in one spot by a thin, partly transparent group of tiny clouds that looked like dead cracked flesh on the palm of a hand.

"Thanks. You sure it ain't out of your way?"

"This whole place is out of my way. You got a lot of papers there."

"I'm the personnel sergeant."

"Where's your jeep? Our PSNCO never walks."

"Clerks took it to Sin City. What unit you in?"

"Recon. I work in S-1."

"Sergeant Chase?"

"You got that shit right. I'm his clerk."

The sergeant laughed. "That's some readin' fool, boy."

"What?" Chase never read anything but regulations and the daily bulletin.

"That cat put away some cock books. Some of 'em pretty good too."

He couldn't figure it. "How do you know?"

"I don't want to put the bad mouth on my man, now, but almost every day between eleven thirty and two you find him sittin' right inside the finance tent, face buried in a book. I usually read between one and two my damn self."

Morgan shook his head and thought about the last illusion. He'd always admired Chase's devotion to this work. Not because it meant anything, but because Chase believed in it and because he always strove to do a good job. Sitting around reading cock books. "How long has he been doing that, Sarge?" Could be short-timer's fever.

"I been here six months and he ain't missed too many days. Don't be tellin' him about that now, hear?"

"I won't say anything." Sham motherfucker. Like all the other dough-belly lifers. Shamming. Waiting for their twenty years to be up so they can sham full time. And always talking about what worthless kids the Army got nowadays. Three tears in the bucket. At least tomorrow he could burn shit.

He dropped the sergeant off and took the long swing

around second brigade and divison aircraft maintenance, arriving at S-1 at eleven thirty. As he parked the jeep, he saw Chase drumming his fingers on the counter, his big envelope full of papers beside him.

"Where the fuck you been, Morgan?"

"Bullshittin' with a guy in the morning report section and reading a magazine. Then I drove a sergeant back to second brigade."

"We ain't runnin' no goddamn taxi service, and you ain't got time for bullshittin' or reading either. A little more bullshit and you'll be in hot water! I'm so damn late now it'll take me till three thirty to get done."

"I'm sorry, Sarge."

"I bet you are!" Chase stormed out of the tent, fired up the jeep, and drove away.

He felt someone tugging his arm, but in the dream he had dived beneath a speeding car and died and was sitting in a living room telling people about it. "How'd I get here?"

Matthews, a crew chief, was looking down at him where he lay on the maintenance hooch floor. "We brought you down in the back of a three-quarter ton. You were going to tear up Chase's tent. We just fixed that old bird and have to test-fly it. Want to come?"

"Sure. What time is it?"

"Four thirty."

"I was pretty fucked up, huh?"

"You weren't pretty anything."

He sat on the benchlike seat that ran along the back wall of the cabin, fastened his seat belt, and yawned, too ruined to get excited about the flight. He still had to do the PDS tonight. Maybe he could go to sleep when they got back to battalion.

Matthews put on his flight helmet, and Morgan watched his lips move as he talked to the pilots while they ran up the engine. Outside the door the grass rippled away from the chopper in the wind of the rotor blades. He tasted shit in his mouth.

The helicopter jerked off the ground, hovered back, and turned ninety degrees until it faced north. The pilot glanced at him and nodded out the door. Seeing no other close aircraft, he stuck his thumb up close to the pilot's face. The chopper dipped slightly, then sped away to the north. He looked eastward as they rose, trying to find the battalion area. The green lawns and white decorations gleamed from the infantry battalions next door, then he caught sight of the headquarters mess hall just as the helicopter broke west.

The sky had turned gray during the afternoon. The altimeter said two thousand feet. He was cold, his body ached, and he wanted to stick his finger down his throat and puke. It started to come in waves, then a deadening sense of fatigue enveloped him completely. He leaned his head back and closed his eyes. He wanted to lie down on the seat and go to sleep. He had no strength left.

The helicopter shook and he thought it might crash. He opened his eyes and saw the pilots laughing and talking into their microphones. Matthews looked out the door, immobile. If it was going to crash, surely they would know. Highway 19 crawled with GI's and black-pajamaed bodies. Dump trucks had lined up by the gates of Sin City to take the drunken fucked-out soldiers home.

Christ, it was cold. The chopper still shook, making an awful racket. The pilots laughed and joked. Maybe they didn't know the fucking ship was about to break in half. He wanted to close the door to shield himself from the cold, but they'd think he couldn't take it. He'd have to start eating right pretty soon. His whole body had gone to shit. Nothing but liquor in his veins. He wanted to go back to his tent and sleep..

The rain pricked at his face like tiny pins. Matthews leaned back and slammed the door on his side of the ship. Much relieved, he did the same. A dirty gray layer lined the clouds.

The racket diminished, but the ship seemed to shake more and more. Maybe he should jump. The chopper couldn't possibly make it back. He started when Matthews touched him, offering a cigarette. He took it, thinking his face must have looked crazy with fear. He puffed greedily, knowing he'd die if he jumped. Better than being mangled in a crashed helicopter. His hand toyed with the seat belt, then he sat on the hand in disgust. What the fuck was wrong with him? Nothing would happen. The pilots would be panicked instead of talking shit. He wished he could hear what they said.

He lit one of his own cigarettes from the the other, then steadied himself against the fire wall. He couldn't remember being so afraid. It didn't have anything to do with crashing. Some nameless dread that nervous energy alone couldn't cope with. It had to be tied to his body. Rest and food. He wouldn't feel so weak and scared with them. If he went on like this much longer, he'd wind up a shriveled maniac, huddled in a corner gnawing his fingers and shitting all over himself.

He was calm when they circled back over the division perimeter and hovered down to the parking slot. The ground felt good, maybe too good. Could he make it as a gunner? They had to fly between six and eight hours a day, and a lot of the ships went down from mechanical failures. Screw that. Too depressing to think about. But what if he did get a gunner's job and then turned chicken? He wouldn't. He couldn't.

He found DeWolf at a table in the mess hall, his mess kit filled with barbecued children. The thick smell in the air made his stomach feel more hollow.

"What's happening, alky?" DeWolf said.

"You." He filled his mess kit with chicken, mashed potatoes, and green beans, then sat down by DeWolf.

"You all sober now?"

"Don't I look it?"

"Who can tell anymore? Man, you were out of your head this afternoon. Said you were gonna shit in Chase's mess kit."

He nearly spit out his potatoes.

"Me and Matthews had to hold you down while they got the truck. You'd be in the iron house now if we'd let you go."

"Thanks, man. I appreciate it." The food tasted so good, warmed his belly so much, that he could think of nothing else. But it satisfied him to know that he had been outrageous, out of control.

"No sweat. You don't have to go back to S-1 after chow. Al said we could have tonight off—except for the PDS."

"It's about time he lightened up. I found out today that he's been reading cock books at division all the time."

"More power to him," DeWolf said. "Me and Sergeant Wallace gettin' things set up so we can half-step all the time once you guys leave. You ought to stay on. We'd have it dicked. Probably make E-5 in a couple months too."

"Thanks, but no thanks. I *will* shit in a mess kit if I don't get out of there."

They left for the club in half an hour, stuffed. He could almost feel his digestive system going to work on the chow, breaking it down and distributing it to the needy portions of his body. His fear dissolved, and things seemed funny again. A couple of beers, then he'd go to sleep.

He finished one beer, slid back from the table, and belched. No good drinking on a full stomach. "I can't handle it, DeWolf. I'm going to the tent. Come and get me in a couple of hours."

"Roger."

When he lay down, he knew he'd be asleep within five minutes. He lay on his stomach, arms tucked under his chest, and let the drowsiness overcome him like a curtain between himself and the world.

DeWolf, leading a pack of new guys, woke him at eight. One of them handed him a half gallon of Early Times before he even got his feet on the floor.

"Come on, Morg," DeWolf said. "You only got three hours to get oiled for the PDS."

He drank and chased the whiskey with beer. "I can't get too drunk tonight. Chase is liable to hang my ass." He looked at the new guys and drank again. "But then I don't much give a fuck."

"I don't know how you do it, Morg," one of them said.

"Walk the dog!" he yelled, remembering an old song. "Let's go down to the club."

He went to S-1 at eleven, half drunk, but steady and in good humor. Chase sat at the desk writing a letter while Greene read a magazine at the counter. "Good evening, happy people," he said. His voice came out clearly—no signs of drunkenness.

"You drunk?" Chase asked.

"Can a cat whistle? Can a rooster dip snuff?"

"What?"

"Can a bulldog lay eggs?"

"I reckon not."

"Then I reckon I ain't drunk." He steadied himself against the counter, pulled out two blank PDS forms, and slid a piece of carbon paper between them.

"You're pretty happy for not being drunk," Greene said.

"I like doing this report, sir," he said without looking up. His eyes kept crossing. He heard Greene close the magazine, then walk out of the tent. "One sack of shit gone for the night."

Chase laughed. "He'll be back. He sits in here reading half the night now. Guess he doesn't like the officers' tent too much since he got passed over."

"Where's A and Headquarters companies' reports?"

"A's right here." The clerk stood in front of him.

He grabbed the report and checked it while the clerk and Chase yelled back and forth over the counter. Pope brought the Headquarters report in five minutes and talked with Chase while Morgan checked the figures. The report being correct, he stacked it with the others, preparing to tally all five. "Guess motherfuckin' Greene ain't coming back tonight." He liked to ridicule officers in front of Pope because the clerk took them so seriously.

Chase leaped from his chair as if someone had shot him in the chest. One index finger was perpendicular across his lips, the other pointed at the wall of bamboo matting separating Greene's office from the front.

"What's the matter, Sarge?" He wasn't back there. "That sack of shit ain't back there."

"Shut up!" Again the finger on the lips, the other pointing at the bamboo, the arm shaking back and forth.

"You saw that clown walk out of here ten minutes ago. If he's back there, you have *really* fucked up."

"He came back," Chase whispered. "Now shut up!"

If he was back there, it was too late to shut anything. Morgan looked at the counter. No magazine. Pope stared at him, his face tense with expectation. Maybe Greene had returned. "He ain't back there." He laughed. "And I don't give a fuck if he is."

"Yes, he is," Chase said. He looked like he wanted to be anywhere but in the office.

Morgan took three steps toward the entry to Greene's area. He stopped and let out a silly soprano giggle. Here I come, ready or not. He poked his head around the entryway and Greene looked up at him from the chair where he sat reading. His face showed no feelings whatsoever.

It was all over. It metabolized suddenly to every cell of his body as he stood grinning into Greene's immobile face. The light from the captain's table was so hot it made him think that he was on stage. "What's happening, babyyyyy!" he screamed and did not wait for an answer. He spun back to the counter and looked at the PDS reports. His heartbeat seemed to have doubled. Like a grenade with the pin pulled, he stood waiting for his heart—or something—to explode. Chase stood in the corner by the filing cabinet, shuffling his feet back and forth. "Sarge, you were right. He is back there." He wanted to laugh, but it wouldn't come.

"Get out of here, Morgan," Chase said.

He looked at Chase, his eyes blurring as though an optometrist were flipping different lenses from the machine in front of them. He couldn't leave. He didn't know why, but the stakes had risen too much for him to leave now. "I ain't leavin'."

"You're too drunk to do the report."

"I can do it standing on my head."

"I said get out of here."

"I'm doing the goddamn report because that's my motherfucking job!"

"Morgan, if you leave now you might get out of this without too much trouble, but if you stay I can't say what'll happen."

"I don't give a fuck what happens!" Hatred and rage stormed out of all the places he had hidden them. "I'm a goddamn man and I'll do my shit-ass job, and all I ask is for you people to leave me alone. Haven't you fucked with me enough already?" He turned to the report. Pope backed into the shadows, still watching everything.

"For the last time, Morgan, I'm ordering you to get out of here."

"I ain't leaving until I've done this report."

"I'm giving you a direct order, soldier! Now you better get the hell out of here!"

He turned around and leaned back on his elbows. "Run it up your ass, Sergeant. I'm sick of you and your shit and him and his shit and of this whole piece of shit operation, and I hope you don't like it."

"Morgan, I'm warning you—"

"You ain't shit to me!" he screamed. "You got no right to tell me a thing. You've been promising me since I got here that I could go to the field but you keep holding it back and holding it back, telling me I got to do all this work. Well, that's a bunch of crap because DeWolf can do everything I can and if you weren't on your ass at division reading cock books all day, you might do some of it your goddamn self.

I'm on to you, man. Hard-working Al Chase! I got your hard work hanging from the hairs on my ass. And then you finally decide you want to go to the field too, but Greene won't let you, so you take it out on me, then get yourself and the C Company first pig put on orders for wings when neither one of you even been near any combat assault.

"Can't you see my ass has had it?" He was yelling so loud his throat had dried, and he began to cry. "You can fuck with a man for so long, then you drive him out of his tree. I've done nothing but stupid, silly bullshit since the day I got here starting with that asshole Stubbs and all these asshole officers sucking ass for their cheesy little medals, and it's been nothing but the same crap day after day, and I'm tired of it. I even admired you for not being a drunk and not cheating on your wife, but look what it's done to you. You ain't even human anymore. I swear to fucking Christ, you don't let me out pretty soon, I'll bring my gun up here and do whatever I feel like doing." Tears dripped off his chin onto his fatigues and his lips quivered.

"You finished?"

"I could go on for days, and you know it."

"You could go to jail too."

"Send my motherfuckin' ass to jail! That doesn't make anything I said less true. But that's how you assholes keep going, isn't it! Someone peeps your hole card, you send them to jail." It didn't matter anymore. Even jail would be better than S-1.

"So you're not leaving?"

"You got that shit right."

"We'll deal with this in the morning."

He laughed. "I'm burning shit in the morning."

Chase left the tent, and he and Pope disappeared into the darkness.

Morgan was cold sober. Exhausted, but clearheaded too, and rage provided the energy to do the report. He'd do it perfectly, like always, but this was the last time he'd do anything in this tent. So he only had four months to go. He still wouldn't go back inside S-1 after tonight. He hoped he'd finish the report before Greene went to bed. But fuck it if he did come out. He wouldn't take shit from these people anymore.

He finished the master report, stapled the carbon together with the separate company reports, punched holes in it, and put the whole mess in the PDS notebook. As he checked the report once more, Greene walked out of his office.

"Hope you feel better in the morning," the captain said.

"You won't see me in the morning."

Greene hesitated a moment, but barely broke his stride. Out of the tent and into the night.

Morgan neatly put the notebook away under the counter. He picked up the possessions he had left in the office—letters, books, an old pair of boots—and put them in the jeep. He didn't walk around the counter when he came back, but stood in front of it, like a customer, and looked at the gray metal chair where he had sat for so many hours. No more. His calendar, with each day carefully blocked off, hung from the wall of bamboo matting by a twisted paperclip. July had one more day. Fuck it. A memento for DeWolf. He raised his hand and switched off the light that hung above the counter. He savored the darkness momentarily, then left.

Driving up to G-1 and back, he felt freer than he had since leaving Fulda for Vietnam. It didn't matter what lay ahead. He'd finished something bad—he wouldn't eat that shit again—and it made him feel inexpressibly free. And calm and strong. He no longer felt the need for belligerence, yet felt he could face Chase and Greene when he saw them without backing down and begging forgiveness. He wasn't even concerned with what they'd do to him.

In the morning he burned shit. DeWolf brought the jeep down by the mess hall, and from there Morgan drove it to the division fuel point. He got a five-gallon can of regular gas and another five gallons of diesel fuel. When he got back to the battalion, he carried the cans to a little knoll beside the shithouse. Then he went to his tent for a beer, his first of the day. He was going to quit, but the gas cans were heavy, and he was, after all, just burning shit, so why not have a few?

At the back of the shithouse he raised the three trap doors at the bottom of the wall. Breathing through his mouth, he pulled the half barrels into the sunlight and onto the knoll. When he got back for the third barrel, he noticed a small pile of shit and paper on the concrete floor where the first barrel had been. He started to curse, then laughed. He walked around to the front and put a note on the door to check for barrels before shitting. He went back and pulled out the third barrel, then cleaned up the mess with an entrenching tool.

He poured an even mixture of the gases in each barrel, regular to get it started, diesel to make it burn slowly. When he dropped the matches, each barrel burst into flames and sent out a steady sheet of black smoke. DeWolf said to stir it for the best results, but Morgan thought he should let it get hot first. He went back to his tent and had three beers and brought a fourth back to the knoll. He drank it standing, his body glistening with sweat as he stirred the barrels of burning shit with a long wooden pole.

At eleven o'clock DeWolf came down and told him that neither Chase nor Greene had mentioned last night. He came down the next day and said that he'd asked them and they'd told him to mind his own business. The next afternoon Morgan ran into Greene on the battalion road. "Hello, sir," he said, saluting, and kept walking.

"Wait a minute, Morgan." Greene stopped and looked at him for a moment. "How are you feeling?"

"Fine, sir." He'd been drinking all day.

"You know you said enough the other night to go to the stockade in Okinawa and have them throw away the key."

He stiffened. "I meant what I said."

"Okay, Morgan. Don't start up again. You've done a good job—the other night excepted—and we want to pay you back for that. So I've talked with Major Singer in C Company, and he's got an opening for a gunner on one of his ships for you."

He couldn't believe what he heard. "You serious, sir?"

"I wouldn't joke about this, Morgan."

"Jesus Christ. When do I go?"

"If you can get packed in forty-five minutes, the maintenance ship's making a special flight after chow."

"Roger, sir. Thank you, sir." He spun around and headed for his tent on a dead run.

17

"HEY, CHAMBERS," Webster yelled, "there goes your main man." He pointed his mess kit at an eastbound chopper.

Chambers, bloated with his lunch of four peanut-butter sandwiches, nodded. Robinson gone, at least for a month, on emergency leave. "Praise the Lord."

Webster squatted in front of him. "He wasn't a bad gunner, but I sure ain't sorry to see him go."

"I'll drink to that." Chambers raised his canteen cup of coffee, then dragged on his six-cent cigar. "Nights'll be a little more peaceful now."

"Unless Hancock finds some Old Crow," Webster said.

McCutcheon popped out of Hart's tent and loped toward the ship.

"Oh, shit!" Webster said. "Looks like up in the air again."

Four pilots strode out of the operations tent.

"I figure about a hundred and twenty days," Webster said.

"I figure about a hundred and fifteen." Chambers stood aside so McCutcheon could hurl his gear on board. "What's happening?"

"Get ready! One of the companies from third brigade got contact." McCutcheon ran to the rear of the ship and untied the rotor blades.

Sanders and Eastman jumped into their seats, the engine was run up, and they pulled pitch and headed west. The grid coordinates sounded about midway between their camp and the Cambodian border. Couldn't be too urgent with only one pair of gunships going out. He arranged his bullets and grenades on the floor, braced himself in the door, and tested the swing of his machine gun. They'd been up only ten minutes when he spotted the smoke.

"There it is," Sanders said. "Four-five, we've got it in sight at one o'clock."

"Roger, Red, got it in sight."

Chambers looked up and to the rear where the other ship gleamed in the sunlight. His left eye picked up a sudden flash, and he turned quickly as a mushroom of smoke rose from the ground. The sun flashed off the silver wings of a jet as it sped upward and circled to the west. Another jet roared in from the south, got lost in the cloud, then emerged on the north side of it, leaving a second small mushroom behind.

"Looking pretty crowded down there," Sanders said. "Let's circle to the east until I find out what they want."

"Some artillery just went off," Eastman said as the ship broke left, away from the battle.

"They're throwing in everything," Sanders said. "I don't know what they want with us." He flipped buttons on the console.

Chambers relaxed in the seat, wondering if they'd be struck down by a badly placed artillery round or if they'd collide with a jet whose pilot had forgotten that other things were in the air. Perhaps they'd end up firing on the

American infantry. It had all happened before, for sure. It was amazing that anything ever got coordinated.

"Long Rifle Six, this is Noble Rider Red. Do you read me? Over."

Static crackled. "Read you loud and clear, Noble Rider Red." Intermittent rifle fire punctuated the transmission.

"Long Rifle Six, I've got a team of gunships up here and ready, over."

"Roger, Red. Request you hold your position zero-five minutes until these jets get done. They'll be coming through twice more, then you follow."

"Roger, Six. Throw out some red smoke. We'll run south to north."

"Will do, Red. Anywhere north of the smoke is fine."

They circled once while the jets dropped their bombs, and halfway into the second circle McCutcheon grabbed Chambers' harness and pointed out his door. Red smoke rose from the ground at two points, diffusing into a hazy pinkness. At least it looked as though a clear line of battle had been drawn.

"Got your smoke in sight, Six," Sanders said.

"Come and get 'em, Red. Out."

They completed the circle, broke to the right, then to the right again. Straight ahead the smoke and dust from the battle hung over the ground in a sooty yellow cloud.

"Take it in at a descending angle, but don't get below two hundred feet," Sanders said to Eastman. "Use three pair of rockets this time. Okay back there. Keep your fire north of that smoke."

Chambers flipped the safety switch, braced his left foot in the door, and hung his body out in the wind. A fresh smoke grenade went off as the others dissolved into the sickly yellow above the battle. The side guns barked out beside him, the oil burning off the barrels in a sudden puff of smoke. He worked his own gun up and down, then made S-like motions to the side. The gun jammed and he quickly cocked it, pulled more ammo from the box, fired with his right hand, feeding with his left.

The side guns quit, and he released the trigger on his own as the ship broke to the right and circled back. As usual, he'd seen no one on the ground. They ran over the battle twice more, and he found himself concentrating on firing more than he had in a long time. He didn't feel the fanaticism or blood lust that he knew motivated the other gunners, no insane love of combat that glassed McCutcheon's eyes. The firing simply came easier; the job was laid out and had to be done. He had to protect his comrades, and it would be silly not to do that as effectively as possible. At the ammo point, as he lugged rockets and crates of bullets to his ship, he felt a sense of pride that he could not understand.

Back at the field base he stepped more lightly, and as he and Webster walked to the mess tent for coffee, he found himself nearly swaggering as they passed the new pilots and crew chiefs. Looking at their starched stateside fatigues or at their jungle uniforms that had not yet been washed (or even dirtied), he felt the veteran's disdain for the first time. Even though he *was* closedmouthed and tired, he felt he had to act that way too, to maintain the aloof and cynical pose of the farm boy giving directions to the flustered city slicker lost on a back road. He nearly laughed at himself, thinking that for all his reading and his lonely nights of serious contemplation, he was probably not much different from Hancock, who'd quit school in the eighth grade and who could barely read or write.

Hardened vets. On their second or third day in Saigon, when they'd still been dressed in fatigues stiff with starch from a German laundry, when the toes of their Cochrane boots still gleamed with layers of spit and polish, he and Morgan had gone to the Camp Alpha snack bar while Padgett and Slagel pulled KP. Most of the tables had been crowded with new guys nervous with anticipation, trying to talk or yell or boast or lie their way around the fact that many of them would be dead within the month, let alone the year. In wrinkled khakis a group of tanned veterans about to go home had sat silently around a table near the back, their boots scuffed or covered with a hasty coat of polish, their badges and ribbons pinned on above their pockets. Chambers hadn't noticed. Too busy wondering why he was here, what he would tell his parents when he finally wrote them, he'd simply been staring into the top of a can of Coke when Morgan had pulled his sleeve.

"Look at them," Morgan had said.

"Look at what?"

Morgan nodded toward the table in the back. "You can tell they've really been through it."

"Two weeks in this sun and you'll look the same." And that had been all. The veterans hadn't struck him as particularly impressive. He'd meant what he'd said about being in the sun. But now, as he squatted on the floor of his chopper, laying the belts of bullets in the boxes for the side guns, the picture came back to him vividly, only this time with himself seated at the table, silent, scuffed, two rows of ribbons beneath his Aircraft Crewman's Wings and Combat Infantryman's Badge.

He finished reloading, then carried the empty crates to the garbage pit. The Headquarters Company maintenance ship floated down to the helipad, rotor blades popping wildly, making its daily parts run. He dumped his refuse among the ammo and C-rations cans, the bandoliers and plates that lay in the six-foot hole near the middle of the helipad, then returned to his ship and sat in the doorway, staring at the ground. Could he really, after more than two years, be turning into a soldier?

The last thing he'd ever been accused of was being a gung-ho all-American boy. He sure didn't look it with his fat head and barrel-shaped body, and he'd never been a cheerleader for anything. Playing ball in high school had been something he could do—he was strong and fairly quick—but he'd never felt much about winning or losing. The Army and the war were things to be gotten through. Being with his friends and surviving were more important than who won.

His friends were—had been—about as all-American as you could get, even LaMont. Their stories made it seem as if they'd tried to be the best in basic and infantry school, and in Fulda, despite their continual scoffing, they'd shined their boots and worked hard on their jobs. The energy they expended in pretending not to care could mean only that they cared more than they wanted to admit. They wouldn't have come here otherwise. Christ, maybe beneath it all he was the same, although he never would have thought so until now.

He felt someone staring at him, and he looked up into Morgan's grinning face. He bit down hard on his cigar, looked away, then back again.

"It's okay, Orville. You're not hallucinating. It's me."

"Are you here?" Morgan looked ridiculous, his bushy mustache running in twelve directions, his duffel bag dropping one shoulder a good three inches below the other.

"No, I'm there." Morgan pointed to the air beside him. "Yeah, I'm here. What does it look like?"

"I mean for good." Morgan's eager smile made him sick.

"Until I get my shit blowed away."

"I don't see anything funny about that." He thought of Slagel, Padgett, of himself on his last flight. All of this couldn't have happened, be happening now.

"What's the matter, man? Aren't you glad to see me?"

The pleading tone made Chambers scowl disapprovingly. "No, I ain't glad to see you. Out here, anyway. Why did you come?"

"What?"

"You heard me. Why?"

"I was always coming. We made that agreement the first day."

"First day, shit!" He stood up, ready to drive his fists into Morgan's face. "We made plenty of agreements on the first day and on other days too, but a lot's changed since then. Or doesn't that affect you either?"

"Come on, man." Morgan sniffed, then stared at the ground.

"Don't give me no 'come on,' Morg. I'm sick of losing people, and now you come out here joking around as though it doesn't make any difference."

"Get off it, Orville!" Morgan's head came up suddenly, defiant. "You know I take it as seriously as you. How come you're still out here? You can quit flying anytime and you know it."

Chambers crumpled in the doorway like an untied balloon. He bit off the soggy end of his cigar and spat it on the ground, then stuck the butt back in his mouth. His hands squeezed the floor of the ship until his knuckles went white. What could he say? What the fuck could he possibly say? "I'm sorry, Will. It's been a long day. I am glad to see you. Just wish it wasn't here."

"I'm glad to see you too."

They shook hands, then Morgan sat down next to him in the doorway. "You don't smell so hot, Will."

"Been burning shit. I'll get a shower tomorrow."

"Your face is all puffed up like you've been on a drunk for a month."

"Make it three or four and you'd be about right. I finally flipped out, and they let me go."

"Really?"

"Greene could've put me in jail or kept me back there. I never figured he'd let me out. He's fairer than I thought. Or else he thinks he can kill me off."

They talked for another half hour, Morgan reciting the details of his last night in S-1, his drunkenness over the past few weeks, and anticipating flying as though it were manna sent down from heaven. Chambers' anger deserted him. He listened, nodding, filling in Morgan on where they were and all the time growing more and more tired. When he stood up, his body felt as if someone had hung lead weights all over it. "You better go talk to Hart and get your gear squared away." He felt a sudden desire to leave, be alone. "It's chow time anyway."

He went around to the baggage compartment, got his mess kit, then walked across the helipad, knowing he could fall down in the dirt and be asleep instantly. They stopped in front of Hart's light-green teepeelike tent. "New man, Sergeant Hart," Chambers yelled.

Hart's square, pink face appeared between the flaps. Beneath his bulbous nose a neatly waxed handlebar gleamed.

"This is Willard Morgan, Sarge. He's new from Headquarters Company. I'll see you over at chow, Will." He left the two of them staring dumbly at each other.

After filling his mess kit with liver, onions, mashed potatoes, and pale-green canned peas, he went to the far back corner of the tent and sat on the ground. He wanted to eat fast, get away before Morgan came, but his inertia barely allowed him to raise his fork. Opening his mouth required effort. Besides, the food tasted like shit. Rubbery liver, greasy onions, lumpy potatoes. He wanted to hurl the whole garbagy mess on the babbling soldiers around him. He'd only half finished when Morgan appeared in the front of the tent, searching the crowd for him. He looked pathetic—rummy, puffy, lonely, and timid, not knowing what to do. His face brightened when he spotted Chambers, then he worked his way to the back.

"How'd you like Hart?" Chambers asked after Morgan sat down.

"Typical lifer asshole."

"Right. What'd he say?"

"I'm supposed to gun for Barry and sleep on his ship. Who's he?"

"I'm Barry." The new crew chief sat right next to them.

Chambers stood up. "Well, I'll leave you guys to get acquainted. I have to fly last light. See you in the morning, Will."

"Morning? I'll see you tonight."

"I'm going to sleep when we get in. I'm tired."

"Okay." Morgan looked at him questioningly.

Chambers turned away, ducked under the tent flap, and hurried to his ship.

As the helicopter screwed its way into the blank, gray-blue evening sky, he found himself wishing that this would be his last flight. He wished that every day, was sure nearly every GI spent at least part of the day wishing it would be his last. But this time was different. He didn't feel that he could put it aside any longer and simply wait out the next four months. He wanted it to be finished now and didn't see how he could make it through another day, let alone a hundred and fifteen. Had he really been doing this for eight months?

The chopper circled the scene of that afternoon's battle. Desolate and quiet, bomb craters gaping up at the sky like toothless mouths of old men. Nothing had happened there this afternoon. Some infantrymen killed, maimed, and wounded, a lot of money spent on ordnance and gasoline, but nothing had happened. The B-52's would go over tonight, the trees would be all gray and brown in a week, but nothing had happened.

He looked inside the ship as McCutcheon pulled the pin from a smoke grenade. Chambers flipped the intercom to private so the pilots couldn't hear. "What the hell are you doing?"

McCutcheon jumped in his seat. "Gettin' ready. Those NVA's are around here somewhere, and when they fire, I'm going to get that smoke right out there."

"I guess I'll keep the pin in mine." He flipped the intercom back, then stared out the door. A few miles to the west the mountains sprawled along the Cambodian border like a giant dead man, the dying sunlight a worn blanket of faded pink on his back. They flew right at him, turning north as the flat land commenced sloping upward into the carcass. Dry like a mummy.

As the chopper crossed a stream, he remembered that it was where Padgett had nearly been brained by the falling tree. What difference would it have made? Even a drooling, brainless idiot had life. Even Slagel, staring at the ceiling in some ward for cripples, had life. Even that for what? To think about his murders without being able to squirm.

"NVA on the ground!" McCutcheon bellowed. "Red smoke on the way!" The crew chief opened fire.

"Four-five, this is Red. We've spotted the enemy. Shoot the red smoke."

"Roger, Red. We're on your tail."

Chambers stared out the door, seeing nothing, caring less. A wisp of red smoke curled around his belly. He turned inside the ship. Fucking McCutcheon had put the grenade on the floor! Red smoke streamed out both doors.

Sanders turned around and for a second looked as if he might faint. "Four-five, don't shoot the red smoke! We're the red smoke!"

"Got you in sight, Red."

McCutcheon bent over sheepishly and lobbed the smoking grenade out the door. Chambers turned away and leaned into the wind, clearing his nostrils of the acrid stench.

"Sorry, sir," McCutcheon said. "Guess I got a little excited."

"It's okay," Sanders said. "Let's make one more run, then head in. How many did you see?"

"Just one."

They finished the run and pulled up to leave. Chambers hadn't bothered firing.

"Sir," McCutcheon said, "how about setting me on the ground to look for that gook? He might be heading for a whole nest of them."

"Don't be ridiculous."

"I feel bad about it, sir. If it wasn't for me, we might've had him."

"We may have hit him anyway," Sanders said.

"Put me on the ground, sir. I'll just take my bayonet so if they do get me, they won't get any weapon."

"We're going back in."

"Come on, sir. It's my fault. He could have value as a prisoner."

"I said we're going in."

"The hell with it, then! I was only trying to help."

Chambers looked inside again, unable to believe what he heard. McCutcheon's pouty expression made him look like a child—the fat kid on the playground that no one wanted on their team.

"Shut up, McCutcheon !" Sanders said.

McCutcheon put his feet up in the doorway, folded his arms over his chest, and dropped his head. He wasn't even going to look out the door.

To hell with all these crazy people. Chambers leaned back out the door and tried to concentrate on the trees. Nut jobs! Those would have been LaMont's words. Trapped in a world of nut jobs. The fucking helicopter was full of them, the platoon too. He was led and followed by nut jobs, him the biggest of all for being here.

Hendricks' black face hung out of the window of the fuel truck at the gas and ammo point. The ship hovered down next to one of the dark-gray fuel bladders, and Chambers leaped off and headed toward the stack of ammunition crates. He lugged two of them back to the ship, then ran to the truck, clutching a ten-dollar bill in his fist.

"What's happening, Chambers?" Hendricks said.

"Shit. You got any?" He handed the money through the window.

"Not this much."

"Can you get it?"

"Goin' to Pleiku tomorrow. I'll tighten you up then. Take these in the meantime." He handed a half-full Pall Mall pack through the window. "Should hold you till tomorrow."

"Thanks." He stuffed the pack in his front pocket and returned to the ship.

Back on the flight line, he reloaded quickly before spreading his sleeping bag on the floor. McCutcheon had gone away to tell war stories with the other crew chiefs, and Barry was instructing Morgan at his ship. Chambers closed the left door that faced the flight line and lay on his stomach with his head hanging out the right door that overlooked the perimeter. Propped on his elbows, he leisurely smoked two joints, slid into his bag, and tried to sleep.

18

MORGAN FINISHED soaping his naked body, upended the water can above his head, and watched the lathery residue roll onto the dirt beside the helicopter. He dried himself, noting the faint odor of burned shit that still clung to him. He pulled on a clean pair of drawers, put fresh socks in his boots, and made a pillow of his clean fatigues.

The sleeping bag warmed and soothed his weary body as he lay on his stomach and gazed out the half-open chopper door. Fifty feet away cigarette embers darted in the cabin of another ship, and muffled voices drifted across the flight line. None of the other gunners had said anything to him tonight. A few nods, but no overtures of friendship. He had to expect that, being a new guy and a former clerk—a clerk and jerk, as the combat soldiers called them. He could worry about making friends later. Right now he had a new job to learn. He turned on his side and tucked up his legs, full of the anticipation he used to feel the night before a new semester.

He jerked awake at ten, a brief and irritating dream escaping before he could remember it. He sat up again at eleven, vivid pinks and purples and reds blurring in his mind, fuzzing into gray and then to nothing as he shook his head. He smoked, wishing for a drink, wishing he had brought a bottle. But whiskey in the field was a court-martial offense. Besides, maybe the time had come to dry out.

It sprinkled off and on all night, and he dozed and dreamed and woke over and over. Faces popped into his dreams—his parents, college friends, old girlfriends, Army bosses from Fort Dix and Fulda, Chase, Greene, and Stubbs. He stood before them, trying to explain his new role, his need. They seemed drunk, their faces bloated with laughter, and with the drunkard's disregard they dismissed him, waving their hands as though he were too trivial for words. Near morning the rapid oscillations between sleep, dream, and waking made him feel plugged into his watch: dozing and dreaming on the tick, waking on the tock.

When Staff Sergeant Hart woke him at six thirty, his head was buried in the mound of twisted fatigues. Again the dream outlines faded. The dayroom in Fulda? He and his friends being mocked by the first sergeant? Or was it his living room at home where they sat in fatigues, listening to his father's World War II stories? Scenes and fragments from his life swirled aimlessly in his head. Must be like what drowning men feel.

"All set to go?" Barry smiled down at him from the seat. He had large, soft, dark-brown eyes, and his face was the gentlest Morgan had seen in a long time.

"I guess."

Barry slapped him on the back. "Don't look so nervous, man. It's no big thing."

After chow, as Morgan wiped the rain from the side guns

and brushed a thin coat of oil over them, Barry explained what he'd have to do on their first mission. Too many things. His mind, sluggish from the sleepless night, couldn't process all the information. His hand shook, and he wanted whiskey in his coffee to take off the edge. He sat in the chopper and smoked, wondering what the hell he'd do if they got contact on the first flight.

Barry climbed down from the top of the ship and stuck his head in the door. "Let's get it ready, Morgan."

"Huh?" He didn't know what Barry meant. His own voice sounded stupid, and he probably looked like an utter boob.

"Here come the pilots."

His body came to life and he jumped on the ground, his heartbeat doubled. He clipped the oily barrels into the side guns and yanked them to make sure they were secure. He opened the pilot's door, and after Warrant Officer Woolsey got in, he pulled the armor plate forward to protect his side, then closed and latched the door. He hung his own armor shield in front of his stomach and chest and arranged his harness on the seat. Captain Sloane looked over from his seat and waved. Morgan remembered him processing through S-1.

Woolsey's gnarled hand flipped switches on the ceiling, and with a long strident whistle the engine started to wind up. The main rotor spun slowly over his head once, and he closed the cabin door, pushed down the little step-hole flaps in the cowling, and watched for leaks or fires for ten seconds. He released the flaps, whirled, stepped around the rocket pod, crashing his thigh into the back of a machine gun. Pain shot through his body, turning into a throb as he stood on the skid and tried to slide into the harness. He couldn't get it over his shoulder and tore at it furiously, worrying they'd take off and drop him. He got it on, latched it, and jumped up on the seat.

Sweat trickled down his sides as he put on his flight helmet and looked out the door for other aircraft. It seemed as if he'd done a hundred things in thirty seconds, and he must have fucked up somewhere. Maybe he'd missed a fuel leak, and the ship would explode when they were two hundred feet in the air. Or he'd put the barrels in wrong, or they were clogged, and when the guns fired, the bullets would fly into the ship. This wasn't him, wasn't Willard Morgan doing all these things.

"How's it look, Morgan?" Captain Sloane said over the intercom.

He pushed a black button on the cord. "Nothing in sight, sir."

"You about ready to go, Four-two?" Sloane said.

"Ready, Four-one," another voice said over the radio.

"Pulling pitch," Sloane said.

Morgan looked back out the door—to the front, to the side, to the rear. He wasn't going to be responsible for any midair collision. The helicopter jerked off the ground, rocking slightly from side to side as it rose ten feet. It reminded him of a gymnast doing a difficult strength move on the rings. Such a graceful strain. He could almost see the muscles of the machine bulging while its face turned red. The chopper tilted to the front, then sped forward and up. It broke south, turned slowly, and headed east. He leaned proudly out the door, wondering if the tiny soldiers on the ground envied the gunners.

Barry yanked his harness and pointed at the machine gun leaning against Woolsey's seat. Morgan reached for the gun, his mind surging into frenzy once again as his arms moved, trying to remember. He brought the elastic cord down from the ceiling and ran the carrying handle of the gun through the loop at the bottom. Bracing the stock in his lap, he turned a switch on the right side of the gun, raised the cover, and flipped down the feeder tray, which held the bullets in place for the bolt. Twice the belt of rounds fell to the floor before he secured the first four beneath the cover. He draped the linked bullets over his knees and hung a smoke grenade from the carrying handle. Before looking out the door to scout the ground, he stared at the explosive instrument in his hand, wondering if it would blow up in his face when he finally squeezed the trigger.

"Four-two, we're going down on the deck," Sloane said.

"Roger, Four-one," came over the radio. "Got you covered."

The chopper slowed, tilted back, and floated toward the lush green below. As they speeded up again, he leaned into the wind and loosened his grip on the machine gun, trying to relax, to fall into the rhythm of the chopper as it chugged along. His fear left him, exhilaration taking hold as they raced down the side of a small valley of densely layered green. He wanted to wave, to shout at people that he was free at last. He'd felt the same way riding a freight train from Oakland to Los Angeles on a sunny Saturday morning two and a half years ago. He'd overcome his terror of the hobos, and with his spirits raised by a swig of Ten High, he'd lounged in the boxcar door, saluting cars on Highway 101 as the train barreled through the Salinas Valley. Children in a small town had pelted the boxcar with rocks.

Maybe the VC would fire at him now. He swept his gun from left to right, then stretched the cord and pointed the barrel straight down. The ship jerked up suddenly, almost stopping as it turned nearly a hundred degrees, then fell forward and down. He brandished the gun at the treetops rushing toward him.

"Okay, Four-two," Sloane said, "let's light up the back of the valley."

"We're behind you, Four-one."

They were really going to fire! His chest pounded and his stomach went hollow as he made checks on his gun. He held up the belt of bullets, making sure they were linked together as far as he could see.

Again the helicopter swung to the left, this time making a wide sloping arc over the valley floor and up to the top of a small mountain on the other side. Captain Sloane pulled down the infinity sight from the ceiling and twisted it in his palm, causing the side guns to rotate laterally.

"Okay," Sloane said, "bank it up and run it straight across. You fire the rockets, Mr. Woolsey. I'll do the guns. Once we're on the other side of the valley break to the left, but fly it so we get the fire in the trees."

"Yes, sir."

"Heads up, back there," Sloane said to Morgan and Barry.

Morgan jumped when the side guns fired and jumped again as a rocket tore out of the pod beneath the pylon. He squeezed the trigger on his gun. It didn't move. He flipped the safety switch and squeezed again. Three or four bullets and it quit. Another rocket tore out of the pod. He cocked the machine gun and fired again. It jammed again. He pounded the top of the gun before cocking it, his face hot with frustration. He fired again as the third rocket smoked toward the ground. The ship turned; they'd stop firing any second, and he was jammed again. His whole body burned with embarrassment. He cocked the machine gun and pulled the trigger. The gun jerked out a few rounds and quit. The side guns, which had been tilted so they fired nearly straight down, ceased, then rode upright to their normal positions. He looked inside as Sloane fastened the sight back on the ceiling.

He cocked the gun and put it on safe, knowing he hadn't fired more than twenty rounds. He turned out the door so no one would see his face. What an incompetent asshole he was.

By the time they landed at the gas and ammo point he wanted to run away and hide. Maybe he should quit right now, go back to S-1 and his pencils and paper and typewriter where he belonged. What a sorry excuse for a combat soldier. His muscles were so shot that he could barely carry the rockets and crates of ammo to the ship. Sweat poured from his body, spotting his fatigues, and the smell rising from his armpits was stronger than that of the fuel-soaked ground. Flying back to the company helipad, he stared dully at the hills and valleys, wanting to dive out of the ship and break his ruined body to bits.

He and Barry reloaded in silence. When they finished, Barry said, "Hey, were you having trouble with your gun?"

"It kept jamming."

"Could be the way you hold the ammo. Let me show you how to make it feed better."

"I'd appreciate it."

Barry seated himself on Morgan's side of the ship, hung the gun, pulled the trigger so the bolt slammed forward, then put in the belt of bullets. "You're probably getting them hung up on your leg or at an angle so they won't pull freely. What you want is a lot of them on the floor, so they'll pull straight up rather than over your thigh." He draped a long belt over his left thigh, piling the remaining bullets in a stack on the floor, the top layer going up into the gun. "When you fire, those'll pick right up without any resistance. Your right leg'll be clear most of the time anyway. When you fire to the side, brace the stock in your right armpit and fire with one hand. That way you can feed the bullets with your left if you have to."

"Sounds simple when you talk about it."

"Mine jammed every time the first few days. It'll take a couple of times, then it's like brushing your teeth."

He struggled through the first week hour by hour, eking out a few more rounds on each mission, performing his preflight duties more smoothly, with less panic. He slept more every night, but it took the entire week before he could sleep straight through. After flying each day, he'd eat as much as possible, take a shower, then lie in his bag and wait. His nerves and dreams cried out for drink, but he wouldn't allow them even one beer until all the old and rotten booze had been wrung out. This experience was too important to go into it with a sluggish mind and a flabby body.

The sense of importance kept him going, made him try harder when he wanted to give up in despair. Sometimes he shook as he saw himself back at S-1, standing before Chase and Greene in utter humiliation. He sensed that failure would bring a lifetime of regret, a morning in his forties when he would wake in panic and press the razor to his throat.

When he woke up on the morning of his seventh day, after sleeping through a dreamless night, he knew he'd made it; the strength acquired from sleep told him so. On first-light recon that morning he fired a burst of more than two hundred rounds, and although he put only fifty near the target, he knew he'd won the main battle. At the ammo point he didn't huff and wheeze beneath the bullet crates, and on the flight line he reloaded quickly without asking for Barry's help. He felt cleansed, as though for a week he'd been wrapped in hot blankets sweating out a tropical disease.

The confidence made other things come too. Now that he could fire more than twenty rounds at once, he had time to practice his aim. By the end of another week he was zeroing targets within three tracers. It took a third week to put everything together. There were so many things to think about that no matter how much he got right, he usually screwed up something. Sometimes the gun would jam if he moved for the target too quickly. Twice he forgot about the barrel, once knicking the edge of his boot with a round, another time putting seven holes in the doorjamb as he dragged the gun inside the ship. But the other choppers on the flight line were full of holes too, and not from enemy rounds.

He felt relaxed and easy on the flight line now, cleaning his guns or reloading or simply sitting on the skid and smoking. He'd been so tense at first that he could barely walk straight, stumbling and tripping like a freshman late to a midterm. He didn't push things with the other gunners, saying hello and nothing more unless they made conversation. Familiarity came gradually—a joke here, a friendly comment there—

and during his third week Hancock and Webster stopped at his ship to drink a beer and tell stories. He'd known them only on paper or as faces seen occasionally in the base camp. He sorted awards for them, typed citations for their bravery. Their ordinariness shocked him—perhaps he'd expected wild men—and he kept looking for signs of insane heroism in their eyes and gestures.

But how could you tell anything about anyone? From the outside every flight looked the same—the gunners and crew chiefs strapping on their gear, the helicopters taking off and sailing into the distance. Even the riflemen looked bored in the chow line or holding their rifles and waiting for the day's mission. Slagel must have looked the same on the morning of the day he'd killed the squad of NVA's. What about himself, for that matter? Who knew how he'd respond if they ran into a nest of Vietcong? That didn't matter now. What did was that Hancock and Webster accepted him, seemed to like him even though he'd faced no enemy.

By the third week he realized that his weapons system was one of two or three that worked perfectly nearly every time. If he had a malfunction, he corrected it between flights. He cleaned at least two of his six guns every day. The other gunners let malfunctions go for days, and some cleaned their guns only once a week or when excess dirt and carbon caused them to jam. He saw that he worked harder than the other gunners, surely more than the three old low-rank lifers who spent their time drinking coffee and bitching. The three youngest gunners were busy sucking Hart's ass when they weren't flying, and Hancock and Webster whiled away their free hours playing blackjack and acey-deucey and planning drunken fucking sprees in Sin City. Maybe he hadn't faced the VC yet, but at least he'd be ready when it finally came.

With Orville he had next to nothing. At first he'd hardly noticed— Chambers usually flew with the team that replaced his, so they weren't together on the flight line that much, and at night he worked on his guns while Chambers slept. But during the third week the strain in their conversation became apparent, and if he talked with Webster and Hancock, Chambers would grow silent, then slip away. The last two nights he'd mentioned the pot he'd smelled on Orville's breath, but Chambers had shrugged it off and gone back to his ship to sleep.

Perhaps the unfriendliness would pass. He knew better than to prod Orville during one of his moods, knew that he was the last person who wanted to hear progress reports on gunning. He missed the closeness with his friend, but things were different now. The four of them volunteering was no longer relevant. He was beginning where the other three had started eight months ago, and his own death or mutilation seldom crossed his mind. Orville had to see it differently, probably struggled to just hold on.

But Morgan couldn't take the sullenness right now, didn't want to talk it out. His own seriousness about the job was enough, and he welcomed Hancock's and Webster's carefree banter as the only relief that soldiers got outside of drunkenness. In the end it made the Army tolerable, kept you laughing until discharge. The cab driver at Fort Dix had told it right to him and Tom and LaMont one Sunday after they'd gone successfully AWOL: "You know what I used to say when I was a young soldier? There come a time in every young man's life when he must cast caution to the winds, and fuck it." Maybe none of them believed it, all having their private reasons or obligations for being where they were, but the pose had to be adopted, if only for survival.

After lunch he came down to the chopper and sat in the doorway sipping coffee while Barry dozed on the seat. He took out his pocket calendar and counted backward from November twenty-fourth. He was beginning his fourth week in the field, and in ninety-three days he'd be on his way home. It should be time enough. The fullness of the first three weeks made him feel as if he'd been flying for a year, made the repetitive months in S-1 seem like a few days.

Sloane and Woolsey stepped out of the operations tent with another pair of pilots. He shook Barry's foot. "Come on, man. We're going up." He worked so fast and easily that he even had his machine gun hung by the time they pulled pitch.

They flew southeast into a large valley, different from any he'd seen so far. Several Vietnamese squatted in a giant rice paddy on the valley floor. A hamlet of about fifteen hooches nestled in a corner where the terrain climbed into a tangled bright-green jungle. Across from the hamlet a finger of uncultivated land jutted out from the hillside, covered with tall palm trees. About a quarter mile away over a low hill, a small South Vietnamese Army camp stood surrounded by barbed wire. Close to a hundred soldiers milled around inside.

They flew over the palm grove, swung past the hamlet, and started up the other side of the valley. He took his hand off the gun and folded his arms on top of it, pulling it down on his thigh.

"Four-one! Four-one! This is Four-two. We just got sniped at from that banana grove. Nobody hit."

"Roger, Four-two. You sure where it came from?" Captain Sloane's voice was cool, unruffled.

"I saw the tracers, Four-one. Want me to mark it with smoke?"

"Do that, Four-two, and I'll radio it back to base."

As the excitement flashed through him, he sat up straight, tucked the gun in his armpit, released the safety, and made sure he had plenty of rounds on the floor. The yellow smoke billowed up through the green palms. He saw no snipers, no bananas either.

"Four-two, this is Four-one. Smoke on target?"

"Roger, Four-one. Are we clear to fire?"

"All clear. You go in first. We'll follow."

He didn't pay any attention to the tracers from the other ship's guns. Someone was really down there shooting at them! He felt a sudden clarity as he leaned into the rushing wind and squinted at the banana grove. A thin wisp of yellow smoke hung above the palms, a white cloud from a phosphorus rocket rising into it. The other ship broke left and he squeezed his trigger before the side guns even started. He was thinking too fast because the gun seemed to be firing too slowly. He shot systematically at every tree, but saw no one. As the ship broke to the left, he pulled the machine gun around to the right, firing under the side guns until the pylon blocked his view.

He turned back inside the ship, yanked more rounds over his thigh, and piled them on the floor. He hung a frag and a white phosphorus grenade on the carrying handle and braced his left foot against the doorjamb as they leveled off for another run. Again firing at every tree, he leaned out as far as he could, wanting to see the sniper, wanting the sniper to see him face to face. Thirty yards before the grove he twisted the WP off the handle and lobbed it out the door, following it immediately with the frag. He turned in time to see the white and gray explosions, and two soft reports came through his flight helmet a second later. He raised the gun and tried to fire over the pylon, but the angle caused it to jam. He turned, recocked the gun, and leaned against the fire wall to rest.

They made two more runs, still without seeing anyone or drawing more fire, and headed back to the base. He wondered if a sniper had really been there. The other pilot said he saw tracers. He'd been here for a while so he should know. At the ammo point he exuberantly hauled bullets and rockets to the ship, finishing in time to help Barry refuel. He'd been in danger today and hadn't been afraid. He couldn't wait to get back to the flight line and tell Hancock and Webster.

After the helicopter shut down and Woolsey and Sloane left for operations, he walked over to the other ship. "What'd you think of that, Crockett?"

The gunner dropped a handful of spent casings into his steel pot. "I think we fired too damn many rounds." Crockett was an old lifer who'd been in eighteen years and had the same rank as Morgan. "I hate reloading this fucker."

"That's the first time I've been shot at."

"Won't be your last. Wasn't nothin' anyway. Probably some farmer with a thirty caliber."

"Could you see anything down there? I couldn't."

"I wasn't even looking."

"How did you know where to fire?"

"I was firing into that South Vietnamese Army camp over the hill. Them bastards should've been after that sniper."

"You were shooting into that camp?"

"That's what I said." Crockett looked up and shrugged. The tiny blue booze veins around his nose blinked like lights as his laugh degenerated into a phlegmy cough. "Does that bother you, Morgan?"

"I don't think so." He stared at Crockett , suppressing a laugh. "I've got to reload."

19

CHAMBERS SAT straight up out of sleep, shook his head, and looked at the luminous dial of his watch. A little past midnight. He lay back and closed his eyes, knowing that it wouldn't work. He usually didn't wake up till three or four. McCutcheon slept on the seat above him, breathing heavily like a dog dreaming of the chase. Chambers slid out of his sleeping bag, spun on the cool metal floor, and thrust his legs into the night. He put on fresh fatigues, socks, and boots. A thin cloud blew in front of the moon as he walked to the water trailer to fill his canteen. No one else was up in the gunnery platoon. Muffled voices and laughter wafted out of the mess tent. Not unusual. The cooks were always up boozing.

Back at the ship, he sat on the skid and lit a joint. Forty feet in front of him the guard stopped momentarily, glanced in his direction, then resumed his slow walk along the concertina wire. The bright moonlight kept all but the brightest stars from shining. Good to get a clear night. He hated sitting outside in the poncho when it rained. During the summers in Minnesota, after Roger was killed, he'd sleep alone in a tent in the backyard. After his parents' light went off, he'd walk for miles on the cool dirt roads that were always so dusty in the daytime. He liked them best in the full moon because it made everything eerie and the night seemed so much quieter than when the stars were out. The cows stood or lay silently, the geese only honked if he got too close, and sometimes a dog would howl from a long way off. He wondered how far he'd get now if he crawled under the concertina wire and walked away.

He finished the joint and lit a cigar. Same feeling as when he woke up. The dope wasn't going to work. Morgan's coming to the field had balled him up enough, but tonight had been too much. Morgan all excited about Crockett shooting at the South Vietnamese. "I finally realized what the war was all about, Orville," he'd said. Morgan really dug Crockett, old, sorry, wasted, fucked-over Crockett. Eighteen years' service and already Spec-4.

He didn't need to hear Morgan rave on. He didn't need to see him or even think about him. He didn't want to see or talk to anyone about any more stupid Army bullshit. Peace. All they could give you was three or four hours. Then, bingo! Kill it. He'd thought the torture was finished when Robinson left. He'd been looking forward to quieter evenings on the flight line, talking with Webster, even listening to Hancock's preposterous tales about West Virginia moonshine. He'd felt good for three hours, then Morgan's silly, puffed-up boozy face had to be there staring at him.

To hell with the whole damn thing. For a while he'd thought it might be worth it, but what, really, was the sense of all the being pals and joke telling? He'd avoided it before, and he could again. McCutcheon was too crazy to get close to anyone, so he didn't have to worry about him. And now that he and Todd had been in different platoons for six months they didn't talk that much. So what? Todd would probably be dead before too long. And Padgett was dead and Slagel was all but dead and Morgan had turned into a rummy, so why get close and then worry about losing someone else? He was surprised at how easily he could fade into the woodwork. Almost natural. He hadn't looked at an architecture book in three weeks and could probably get along without that too. He had, before the Army. Maybe they'd have a catastrophe in S-1 and call Morgan back to clerk.

He smoked another joint but it still didn't work. He wouldn't be able to shut Morgan off. He'd tried with LaMont, but that hadn't worked either. Something kept nagging at him to loosen up, but then it was too late because LaMont was dead. He couldn't let that happen with Morgan. The chances of a gunner being killed were pretty slim, but you could always get sent on a crazy mission or have mechanical failure or get your whole face shot to bits like that gunner in B Company. Or you could get mortared or shot by a drunk or die in your sleep. All those things had happened in the battalion, but they wouldn't happen to him. Maybe he'd try talking to Morgan. He'd have no peace otherwise.

The next day he went to noon chow with Morgan and told him that maybe they could have a beer that night, but after dinner he felt so tired he could hardly move. Walking back to the ship with him, he thought he might topple over. "I'm sorry, Will, but I've got to go to sleep. I really feel dead. Maybe we can talk tomorrow night."

Morgan's face drooped with disappointment. "Sure, man. I know how it is. I need to clean my guns anyway."

He awoke at two in the morning, breathing hard. He couldn't remember ever feeling so panicky. He sat on the skid and smoked his dope and worried that Morgan would quit caring about him. Hadn't the other guys in the platoon? They'd tried to get him into their groups, but after he'd stayed away a few times, they'd given up. No one was pissed off, but they didn't try to include him anymore. He hadn't wanted to be included, so no big thing. All he wanted was to sleep through the next three months and go home. It hadn't seemed like so much time, but now it stretched before him like years.

For the next two days he kept trying with Morgan, but every time they got near to talking about anything serious, he backed away and found something else to do. And Morgan seemed to care less and less. He was getting friendly with Webster and Hancock, and when Orville retreated, Morgan let him go.

When he came in from flying the next day, a letter from his father was waiting, the first since he'd been in Vietnam. His mother wrote once a week, but the only word from his father had been a stiff note at the bottom of her Christmas card. What was this all about? Maybe he was happy that his son would finally go to college.

The letter from the Department of the Army fell out first. He banged his forehead with the heel of his hand. The fuckers had written to his folks at the end of May about his being wounded. About all three times. His mother had never mentioned it.

His father had sat on it for two months. Sat and brooded until he exploded like the crazy man he was. He could see the stumpy, dumpy old man raging and fuming in the study as he wrote out his outrage and his grief. How could Orville do it? How could he go to the war and kill people and take the chance of being killed himself? Hadn't his parents been through enough with two dead sons and all the trouble that the third had caused them? Didn't they deserve something for what they'd suffered? If he had to be in the war, then he could damn well get a safe job. At least for his mother's sake.

He finished the letter, pulled a pad of paper from his duffel bag, and wrote. Apologetic, he said he'd been out of combat since this third wound and now worked with a couple of friends in the mess hall. He spent his nights boning up on different subjects for college. They had no reason to worry about him anymore.

He sealed and addressed the envelope, wrote "free" in the upper right-hand corner in place of postage, took it up to the first sergeant's tent, and dropped it in the ammo can that served as a mailbox. It only hit him as he walked back to the chopper. Why the fuck was he in the war and fighting? Why wasn't he in the mess hall and why didn't he have a couple of friends? And why had he quit reading?

Morgan sat alone in the door of his ship, a pail of aviation gas at his feet, running a wire brush through the gas cylinder of a machine-gun barrel.

He sat down on the grass. "Keeping them clean?"

"Hi, Orville. Past your bedtime, isn't it?"

"I thought I'd stay up awhile tonight. How about you?"

"Just cleaning these barrels. You do yours often?"

"Never the bore. First round knocks the dirt out. I get the gas cylinder every couple weeks."

Morgan pulled the shiny gas piston from the pail and scrubbed it with a toothbrush. "This carbon's a bitch."

"That one's pretty clean. Mine never look that good."

"I guess it doesn't matter too much."

"Flying's been kind of dull lately, hasn't it?"

"I'm glad for the time to learn. I think I could do pretty well now if we got into something." Morgan put the piston into the cylinder and screwed the nut into the back end. He attached the gas cylinder extension to the front end, then ran some safety wire through the two small holes in each piece.

"I sure don't need to get in any shit right now."

"Why's that?" Morgan didn't look at him, but turned the wire into a tight double strand with needle-nose pliers.

"The Army wrote home about me getting wounded. My father just wrote, having a shit fit too. Aren't they supposed to check with you before they write? What if someone in the family had a heart condition?"

"I don't know. I remember something about it from S-1, but not which way it went. At least no one's telling you to kick ass, like my old man."

"That might be easier to take. This one shook me up."

"There we go." Morgan held up the barrel, admiring the neatly wrapped safety wire. "Not bad, Orville, huh?"

"Pretty good." He tried to fight the sudden fatigue.

Morgan stood up, shoved the barrel behind the ammo boxes, and sloshed the gasoline on the ground. He half filled the pail with rags and brushes and tools and put it in the baggage compartment.

"That aviation gas sure smells nice."

"It's all right." Morgan sat down in the doorway of the chopper. "Sorry to hear your old man's got the ass at you. What's his beef?"

"My being here, I guess."

"I thought you'd worked that out with him."

"Until Sam wrote. I'd told them I wasn't in danger."

"It's weird about parents. My old man's real happy now that I'm fighting."

Morgan's father had told them war stories at breakfast the day they left California for Vietnam. He'd even told a couple of fuck stories when Morgan's mother and sister were in the john. "I guess my father doesn't need any more dead sons."

"I think mine would almost dig one. Give him an excuse to beat up demonstrators. They really piss him off."

"He was pretty gung ho."

Morgan snorted in disgust. "Your old man's got a point, Orville. You ought to get out if it bugs you—and him—so much."

"I wrote him and said I was working in the mess hall."

"I don't mean that. Why don't you get out, period? You don't dig it, you don't especially dig the guys, and you don't need the experience. Why not work in the mess hall? I would."

"Sure you would."

"I won't, but I would if I were you. Seriously, why don't you quit flying?"

"They'd send me back to the rifles."

"Horseshit! They'd put you in the mess hall or give you a job in the base camp. I bet I could get Sergeant Wallace to take you on as a driver." Morgan narrowed his eyes and flicked the ash from his cigarette. Being in the field had actually done him good. He didn't look so boozy anymore, and his mind seemed to be quick and sharp.

"From what you said I don't think I'd like S-1."

"Driver's got it dicked. Wallace and DeWolf are bullshitters too. You want me to write him?"

"I don't know." Somehow quitting didn't sound so good.

"It's up to you, but like I said, I don't see much reason for you to stay. Or maybe you do dig this stuff."

"Not hardly."

"Well?" Morgan seemed to be getting irritated.

He shrugged.

"Look, the only reason you came here was so the four of us could be together. Well, Padgett and Slagel are gone, and you and me haven't been the tightest twosome lately."

"I'm sorry about that. I've been trying to change, but I don't want to lose anyone else."

"So why not quit so you don't have to see it? Turning into a vegetable won't do any good. Christ, man, you don't belong out here. You've got things you want to do on the outside. None of these other guys gives a shit."

"Not even you?"

"I'm doing what I want right now."

He couldn't think of anything to say. They stared at each other for a moment, then he looked down at the ground.

"What makes it so hard for you to quit?"

"I don't know."

"Bullshit."

"Maybe it's because of my brother."

Morgan stared at him for a minute, then dropped his eyes. "You mean you'd be hung up quitting because he didn't?"

"Maybe. I just thought of it. Kind of stupid too when you think of what happened to him. Don't you feel that sometimes you have to do what you don't want to because it's expected of you?"

"You mean by the country?"

"Yeah."

"Fuck the country. That's the last think I'm hung up on. Are you serious about that stuff bothering you?"

"I think so. I never really thought about it before."

"Jesus!"

"Come on, Will. It's no different than you rubbing your face in the shit of the world because somewhere you got the idea you had to experience it all. Remember, I never went to college to get all those ideas about what a shitty country it is."

"But you got brains."

"So do the rest of these guys. Ask them what they think."

Morgan turned his head and stiffened his lips. "Maybe you're right. But still, you know better now."

"It's hard to get over a lot of those feelings. Maybe you should know better by now too."

They talked for two hours until Barry came back from maintenance. Then he went over to his ship and read an architecture book for another hour before getting into his sleeping bag. He hadn't felt so alive since before Slagel was hit. He'd been running down slowly since then, pushed by LaMont's death and finally by Morgan's arrival in the field.

Tonight Morgan had been the Morgan of the early days in Fulda. Sober, alert, interested. Making him think about himself as never before.

Could he really be a patriot? After more than two years in the Army? No way. He kept thinking about Eddie's funeral, without a body, but with the band and the flags and the Distinguished Flying Cross. Eddie must have done something special to deserve all that. The funeral was the most exciting thing he'd ever been to. It changed only at the end when the speeches were done and the trumpet man had played taps and Mother cried while Father stood stone-faced as always.

He wasn't doing anything special in the Army. He'd joined to avoid being shot, not to serve his country proudly. But quitting was another matter. When he'd quit the rifles, Captain Webber had offered him a job in the base camp. But he couldn't take it. Just shrugged it off and took the gunner's job. Even now it would nag him too much to quit, though he didn't know why.

The week after he talked to Morgan went smoothly. Only sporadic rain, no contact, and he'd managed to wriggle out of his shell. He'd had fun bullshitting with the other gunners. He'd quit smoking dope, but kept a pack of joints in his duffel bag for hard times.

He exhaled the cigar smoke, savoring the smell as it blew back in his face. They had just replaced another gunnery team flying cover for the rifles over a small mountain range east of the field base. The afternoon sky was a pale blue, and the wind warmed and soothed his body.

"Four-five, this is Red, over," Sanders said.

"Roger, Red."

"Four-five, we're going to recon up to the north end of the valley. You take Blue and guide them to those hooches. They're only a hundred yards away now."

"Will do, Red."

The helicopter turned slowly to the left, slid through the air down to the valley, then turned right and started along the floor. He flipped his cigar butt out the door, turned, and watched it whiz past the tail boom. The other chopper twisted up the mountainside, the sun reflecting off the spinning rotor blades like a wheel of fire.

The black movement at the edge of the tree line caught his eye as he turned back to the front. His head shot around in time to see two black-pajamed bodies duck into a clump of bushes, the sun winking off the barrels of their guns.

He turned to the front and dropped his chin onto his armored vest. He didn't have to tell them. But that wouldn't work. The VC were on their way to ambush the rifles or shoot down the gunnery ship. They might link up with another platoon or company. He pressed the black button on the cord. "I got two VC in a bush back here."

Sanders' Adam's apple went quickly up and down. "Are you sure, Chambers?"

"Positive. They got guns too."

The bush was about ten feet from the tree line, and Eastman did a figure eight around it so everyone could see the black clump beneath the green.

"Red, this is Four-five," the radio said. "What's going on down there?"

"Four-five, this is Red. Two Victor Charlies in a bush. Give Blue the word, and tell them to be careful of those hooches. My gunner'll take care of these."

His stomach flipped and he pushed the mike button, then let it off. He couldn't tell them that he didn't want to do it. But why not let McCutcheon kill them? He liked it.

They flew by again, keeping the bush on the left side of the ship so Sanders could see. McCutcheon had his gun aimed out the door, and Chambers wished he'd fire. He didn't.

Eastman banked the ship to the right, and for a moment it seemed to stop. Chambers hung in the door looking directly at the bush. The ship came around and started slowly down.

"Okay, Chambers," Sanders said. "Kill them."

He looked at Sanders and couldn't take his eyes off the wart. The hairs must be as stiff as a pig's.

Sanders whirled and leered at him. "Come on, Chambers. What's the matter?"

His saliva had nearly cemented his lips to the mike. He pushed the button. "I lost the bush for a second. Better go over it again."

"Okay, let's get it in sight and kill those bastards before something happens to Blue."

"Yes, sir." The ship banked around and he fired a steady stream of bullets into the bush. Blue couldn't get into shit because Todd was in Blue and he'd been in Blue and too many people had died in Blue already. They flew directly over the bush and he stood and fired straight down. Something black boiled beneath the green leaves. The man broke through the foliage like someone rising through water from the bottom of a lake. One-eyed, he looked up at the ship, the other half of his face totally crimson. His mouth hole gaped, but nothing sounded except the popping of rotor blades and the incessant report from the machine gun. He stopped firing and the man fell back, drowning in the green.

"Good shot, Chambers," Sanders said.

"You sure brought smoke on him," Eastman said.

He turned at the tug on his harness. McCutcheon's lips were pursed triumphantly, his thumb raised at the end of his stiff arm.

He was glad to fly last light that night because he wouldn't have to go to chow, and when he got back it would be dark so maybe all of the gunners wouldn't be around. No, they'd be waiting. At least Morgan and Hancock and Webster. Waiting to pat him on the back and hear the story. He'd been able to avoid them this afternoon because of the need to reload and fix one of his machine guns, but tonight they wouldn't let him alone.

For the first few minutes after landing he thought he'd escaped them. It had begun to rain during the mission and the other ships had their doors shut when his hovered down to the pad. Maybe everyone would stay in and sleep tonight. He took the barrels off the side guns, dried them, and brushed oil on the cold steel. He covered the guns on one side with his poncho and put a waterproof bag on the other pair. After tying down the rotor blades, McCutcheon left to help another crew chief with a periodic inspection. He could work in the rain and suffer late into the night.

Chambers went to the mess hall for coffee to wash down the C-ration peanut butter and crackers. He returned to the ship, closed the door, and was attacking the C's when he heard the pounding and laughing. The door slid open and a flashlight blinded him. Three people climbed into the ship, then the light went down on Morgan, Todd, and Webster, each holding an unopened can of beer.

"You're a goddamn shame, Chambers," Hancock said.

Webster flipped on the cabin lights as Hancock stepped into the ship and slammed a fourth beer can on the floor.

"We brung you your four beers," Hancock said. His pudgy face shone with rain, and his white T-shirted belly hung out between the sides of his unbuttoned fatigue jacket. "First pig says you get two extra for killing those guys. Was you scared?"

"Yeah. You guys can have the beer. I don't want it." The air vibrated with popping cans and mumbled thanks. Good thing they'd come. He'd been preparing to shut off. "Blue got out okay, huh, Todd?"

"Reckon we did, Orville, thanks to you. Them Charlies woulda got up there, they'd've had our ass in some bind."

"Let's drink to Chambers," Webster said, holding up his can. "For bringing smoke on Charlie and saving Blue's ass."

They all cheered and drank. Maybe he had done the right thing today. He wouldn't worry himself anymore. If he kept flying, he'd have to take what went with it. "What was in those hooches, Todd? I got so shook I never found out."

"Rice and documents. Might've even been a trap. Anyway, Orville, everyone in Blue says thanks."

The door opened again and Staff Sergeant Hart stuck his pink face into the ship. Everyone laughed. Without a mustache his upper lip looked six inches wide.

"Don't be so quick to laugh," Hart said. "All of yours are coming off in the morning. Chambers, I brought you four beers. It's on me." Hart pulled the cans from under his rain jacket.

"Thanks, Sarge. What's this about the mustaches?"

"New order from Colonel Snider."

"But they're the unit mark," Morgan said.

"Under Billings they might have been," Hart said. "This is Snider's unit now. I want those womb brooms off by zero eight hundred."

Hart left, and Todd and Hancock and Webster left after finishing the beers that Hart had brought. Morgan sat cross-legged on the floor, flicking ashes into a can.

"You want to go to sleep, Orville?"

"I'll stay up for a while now."

"Christ, I'm almost drunk. First time I've had more than two beers in a month. Do you always get extra when you kill someone?"

"I don't know. We never had this two-a-night rule until Snider took over." He wondered if Morgan might go kill-crazy to get more beer.

"How'd you feel about that stuff today?" Morgan yawned.

"I didn't want to do it, but I had no choice. I wish everyone wouldn't make such a big thing about it. No cause to celebrate. It's over with now, and I'd like to forget it."

"I guess. I wonder if I'll ever have to do something like that. It must be weird."

"Hope you won't." Morgan's head nodded sleepily, and Chambers felt at once a loathing for the banality of their talk and a sympathy for Morgan's juvenile desire to know. How could someone get that way? Then he thought of how

Morgan talked about what reading had done to him, about his gung-ho father. Maybe that was part of it, but not the whole story. "Hey, Will, let's not go to sleep on me now."

Morgan's head jerked up; he seemed to come back from miles away. "I better hit it, Orville. Can't handle all that beer. Are you going to shave your mustache?"

"I guess. Not worth getting in trouble over. It's not that pretty anyway."

"You're right. Fuck it. No one else seems to care very much."

Morgan left and Chambers spread his sleeping bag on the floor. That would have been almost par. Picking something as trivial as mustaches to raise a stink about.

20

MORGAN STEPPED up to the full-length mirror, wondering who this fool was. The skin where his mustache had been was still tender, gleaming against his tan face, speckled with small dots of dried blood. Tan, mosquito-bitten arms hung from the sleeves of a new white shirt. The cuffs of his slacks fell perfectly over the tops of shiny black shoes. As he walked to the door, there seemed to be no friction between the unscuffed soles and the soft white carpet of the hotel-room floor.

Rest and relaxation. Intercourse and Intoxication. He'd almost squandered his first twenty-four hours, but still didn't feel rushed. The plane had come in the previous afternoon, and buses had carried the sweating, howling troops into the city, dropping them at hotels. He'd been tired from the previous night's drunk in Nha Trang, tired from the day before that, which he'd spent drinking and fucking in Sin City. He'd paid his hotel bill in advance (as all GI's were required to do), eaten a huge meal in the hotel restaurant, bought the clothes sold by lobby hucksters at outrageous prices, and gone to his room. There he took a steaming shower for half an hour, then sprawled on his soft bed with a copy of *Newsweek* until he fell asleep.

Now, past noon, riding down in the elevator, his main concern was whether or not he could still get breakfast.

He tried to eat slowly, savoring each bite, but couldn't help hogging it in less than ten minutes. He ordered the same again, restraining himself this time, relishing the freshly squeezed orange juice, the bacon, eggs over easy slopping around his plate, toast, and most of all the ice-cold milk, the first he'd had in nine months. Stuffed, satisfied, he drank coffee for forty-five minutes, smoked, and watched the miniature, handsome Thais scurry about the dining room.

He left the restaurant at two, peered in the bar filled with shouting, boisterous soldiers, then moved toward the street door. He wanted to be alone and walk around the city.

As the soggy heat enveloped him outside the hotel door, he realized that he didn't know where to go. He became aware suddenly of how light his feet were in the nearly weightless loafers. There were no tents in front of him, no flight lines, no sergeants to dodge. He didn't know how he should walk and wondered, for a moment, if he shouldn't drop to his knees and crawl, just to get the feel of things again.

Wandering through the city, he knew that he didn't want to do anything. The shops he passed made him think that he should buy things—Hong Kong suits, jewels, Seiko watches, Pentax cameras, stereos. He should be bribing cab drivers with Salem cigarettes for cheap tours of the city. He could've hooked up with another GI and been out lining up some women in a bar. For a moment he felt a vague desperation, a sinking feeling that he always got when alone in a big city where he knew no one.

He walked by a couple of temples, was unimpressed, not bothering to remember their names. A sudden monsoon cloudburst drove him into a bar, where in less than fifteen minutes he was fleeced for twenty dollars by a wily mama-san and three young girls who drank colored water at his expense.

Angry at himself, he stumbled into the street at the tail end of the storm. He remembered his first three-day pass from Fulda. Disgusted with the prospect of spending two and a half years in the gray, Catholic German town, he had taken the train to Frankfurt with the idea of going to Mainz and trying to transfer to an airborne unit there. He figured that at least the field maneuvers and continual physical activity would give him something to do. He'd gotten to Frankfurt late Friday morning, walked around the city for hours stopping here and there for beers, feeling too depressed to go to art galleries or the university, too afraid to try to pick up a woman, too tired to go on to Mainz and talk with some brainless airborne first sergeant. When it turned dark, he took the train back to Fulda and got drunk with Padgett and Slagel.

Sweating and tired, he walked into the hotel bar, relaxed under the air conditioner, and ordered a gin and tonic. The soldier sitting next to him looked up from his shot of whiskey and bottle of San Miguel beer.

"What's happening?"

"Heat and rain," Morgan said.

"You in the crotch?"

"I don't think so. What's the crotch?"

"What are you? Air Force? Army?" The soldier gave him a hard look.

"Army."

"Shit!" He turned to the man on his right. "Hey, Smitty, we got an Army boy here."

"Great," Smitty said, not looking up from his whiskey.

"The Army sucks," the other said, staring at him again.

Morgan sipped his drink, realizing that he might have to fight. "It sure does," he said. "You in the Marines?"

"Yeah, I'm in the crotch. What of it?"

"You guys got it a lot tougher than us."

"You ain't said shit. Where you stationed?"

"Highlands."

"Nothin' compared to Con Thien. That's some shit up there."

"I know. We don't have it too bad."

"It ain't right they treat the Army better than us. You guys get everything."

"You're right." He finished his drink and rose to leave. Fighting on R&R would be too stupid. "See you later."

"Come on, man. Have another. I'll buy." The soldier said it in such a way that Morgan's refusal would surely have brought a fist to his mouth.

"Thanks." He sat back down. "What's your job up there?"

The other downed the shot, cowboy style, then swilled some San Miguel. "Commo. I work in commo. But we get shelled a lot."

Morgan looked seriously at the young man, trying to figure him. Did he really want to be in the infantry, or was he afraid and just trying to talk tough? "Any job in the Marines is rough."

"You said it. What's your job?"

"Door gunner." He mumbled it as though it were nothing.

"You guys got it easier there too with the Hueys. All we got are them old thirty-fours that ain't worth a shit."

"They should give you better equipment. You do most of the fighting." He rose to leave again. "I have to go now."

"Got some hot twat waiting, huh?"

"I need a shower and a nap."

"Shower and a nap? This is R&R, you dumb shit. Boozin' and fuckin' is what you should be doing."

"I guess so. Thanks for the drink." He began to walk away.

"What are you, some kind of Army fag or something?"

He hesitated a moment, then moved quickly into the lobby, his heart thumping as he nearly ran for the elevator. The last thing he wanted was a fight. He got on the elevator safely, went up wondering what that soldier would be like back in the world. He could see him staggering from bar to bar in his small hometown, telling war stories and picking fights. Piss on that! It was enough thinking of his own sorry ass back on the block.

By seven that night, after showering, napping, and showering again, he found the whore whose name Fisher had given him back in May. She didn't remember Fisher, but after an hour of drinking colored water she agreed to spend the rest of the night with Morgan for twenty-five dollars.

"I stay next four nights, eighty dollars," she said as they walked out of the bar.

"We'll see." He cupped his hand over one of her buttocks. Not much bigger than a large grapefruit.

She slapped his hand away. "You butterfly? Want other girl?"

"No butterfly," he said. "I'll tell you tomorrow. Let's go eat someplace."

She took him to a restaurant, a floating barge on a canal, bathed in soft swaying light from Oriental lanterns. He guessed it was Thai music that tinkled steadily from somewhere. He could see no performers. The restaurant had class—obviously not a GI hangout, although some soldiers, probably officers, were spread among the tables with red-faced Occidentals and their elegantly coiffed wives.

Morgan leaned back in his chair, sipping gin and tonic, dragging on a neatly tamped Pall Mall. They'd really gotten him to where he felt privileged to have a cigarette that wasn't wrinkled or yellow with dried sweat. He sank farther into the soft chair, blowing smoke rings at the soft clay face across the table, feeling impossibly elegant. He downed a chilled shrimp cocktail, then, after another gin and tonic, ordered a cold bottle of white wine to wash down the hot Korean and Thai food. He toasted his whore, wondering if it would be this easy back in the world. He felt so relaxed that the Army and the war became ridiculous abstractions far behind him. Even in drunkenness he experienced no pull toward the belligerence that waited at the bottom of every Army glass.

They walked nearly a mile back to the hotel, Morgan feeling healthy and clearheaded even beneath the oppressive clouds of humidity—colored dirty pink from the streetlights—that hung above the city. This could be Berkeley on a Sunday night, and tomorrow he could be going back to school.

Up in his room, they stripped. Her small body was proportioned perfectly, firm, and the faint odor of her sweat mingled with perfume was heavenly compared to the funky whores in Sin City. They made love quickly, then showered together for half an hour. He wondered if the hotel seemed plush to her, if she was from a slum where she'd been forced to sleep on hard pallets in filthy rooms throughout her early life.

He ordered gin and ice, lime, and tonic from room service, had three drinks, then pulled her to him in the bed again. He went slower this time, exploring her tiny body, kissing, sucking, stroking the thighs that were smooth with short soft black hairs. She barely moved beneath him, moaning occasionally, but he knew she was faking. So what? Whores couldn't let themselves enjoy it. At least she tried to make him feel good.

He came in fifteen minutes, then rolled off, sweating profusely and breathing heavily. She lay beside him for five minutes, then invited him to the shower. He refused, wanting a drink. He started to mix another gin and tonic, then poured straight gin into one glass, ice water into another. A toast to the old days of Overhead, to Winston and Alexander back home in Anniston and Louisville. He swilled the perfume, chased it with ice water, then did it again.

"Outa sight!" he yelled, then collapsed on the bed in laughter, visualizing Winston's gleaming black drunk face, a towel tucked in the fatigue coat around his neck.

Only a fourth of the bottle remained when the whore came out of the bathroom. She sat on the bed, bent to kiss him, and he flipped his finger into her nipple. She jumped back, covering her breasts. His elbow slipped and he fell to the side, knocking her to the floor, then rolled off on top of her. She jumped up and hobbled away from him on a bruised ankle. He grabbed the bottle, downed two large mouthfuls, then greedily gulped more ice water. "Come here, girl." He lunged at her, sticking his fingers between her buttocks, then pushed his arm up.

"No!" she screamed, bouncing off the desk.

"Me going to eat you!" he bellowed, reeling toward her. "You going to eat me!"

"No!" She tried to run for the bathroom, but he caught her arm and hurled her onto the bed. He staggered forward, then fell in a heap on top of her.

He woke up alone the next afternoon. Fragments of glass covered the carpet. A large spot darkened the wall where the bottle had hit. He blinked at the ceiling as the confused images floated through his mind. His hand tugging on the head of black hair, forcing it down toward his crotch. He couldn't remember if the girl screamed or only moaned pathetically or if he hit her hard or just played with her. He got up to piss, then lay back down, sure the police would be there soon.

At nine thirty Morgan and Chambers left the other gunners and hauled forty gallons of water to the shower at the north end of the company area. Then they returned to their ships for soap, shampoo, and a change of clothes.

"Get yourself pretty, Mr. Combat," Webster said as they walked away.

"No sweat, breeze," Morgan said. He'd come back from

R&R in the afternoon, and his chopper had been hit on his first flight. The thirty-caliber shell had gone through a panel between the cabin door and the pilot's door. Had it been fired a second later, it would have hit him right between the eyes. Both Captain Sloane and Warrant Officer Woolsey had caught a few pieces of flying metal, but the wounds didn't even require stitches.

He hadn't felt afraid, had thrown smoke and opened fire immediately, even though he saw no one. Back on the flight line the other gunners had gathered around his ship, and he'd felt loose and nonchalant as they speculated about the shot, about the size of the enemy force building up in the west. Even Staff Sergeant Hart had bought him two extra beers after chow and had invited him up to his tent for more later. The invitation to join the suck-ass circle. He'd have to pass that up.

"Sure is nice here, huh?" Chambers said as they walked between the two lines of parked choppers.

"Yeah." A few stars glittered and winked before them, while from behind, the moon laid down a phosphorescent path on the short grass. "You're feeling pretty good, huh, Orville?"

"Not too bad. Keeps up like this, seventy-five more days'll be nothing."

"I can't believe that's all we've got left." He'd come back from R&R to find C Company moved two hundred miles south, to the outskirts of Phan Thiet, a big city on the coast about fifty miles north of Saigon. The rest of battalion had gone back to Bong Son. C Company had been dispatched here with two rifle companies, artillery and transportation support, probably because of the next day's election. But he wasn't sure—he didn't even know what the election was about.

The camp was prettier than the one in Ia Drang. It rested on a high palisade next to the sea where the air was cool and bugless, light with a faint salt smell. Beyond the concertina wire to the south and west a rolling plain of scrub grass and small bushes fell away for at least a quarter mile before turning into forest. A small shantytown began at the north end of their camp, growing more dense as it moved in to the city.

He felt freer than he had in Bangkok, where he'd spent his last three days cooped up in the hotel, reading, eating, sometimes taking a walk. He'd thought he'd go crazy if he had to stay another day.

The shower stall, built from wooden artillery-shell crates and a fifty-five-gallon drum, stood alone at the base of a small knoll. Someone had built a bench next to a wooden pallet so you didn't have to put your clothes or feet in the dirt. "Go ahead, Orville. Just don't use all the water."

"I won't."

He stripped to his drawers, then stepped onto the dirt as the water splashed on Chambers. Hart's tent stood thirty yards east of the shower, a candle flickering in the flaps. Hart read aloud from a cock book he'd finished while his lackeys laughed. To hell with them. What could they do to him for refusing to join their circle? A little extra KP or guard would be nothing as long as he flew the rest of the time.

"Your turn, Will."

He dropped his drawers on the bench and jumped under the cool water. He washed himself slowly for five minutes, rinsed for a few more, then stepped out on the wooden pallet to dry himself. A gentle breeze blew in from the sea, and he let it tickle his balls for a minute before pulling on fresh underwear.

The entire flight line glowed with moonlight as they walked back, revealing bobbing shadows and darting cigarette embers near the door of his chopper. He let out a little whoop and slapped Chambers on the butt. He couldn't believe how happy he felt to be back.

The next morning no one flew first light. The platoon ate

early, and at seven thirty the first sergeant stood the company at attention, then turned the formation over to Major Singer.

"At ease, men," Singer said, and the formation shrunk about two inches. "Today's election day, as you all know. Free elections are part of what we're here to promote, so you can be proud of this one. We didn't run any first light today, and Blue won't be going out till after noon chow. The VC have been harassing the people to scare them out of voting. So we're going to put on a little show of force to show the people they've got nothing to fear. The whole company's going. I've briefed the pilots on the flight order. We'll fly low, and I want everyone to have their guns out so the people on the ground can see them. But no firing unless you get the word. When you fall out, go straight to your ships and get ready to go. First Sergeant."

The topkick waddled in from the side of the formation, took over the company, and dismissed it.

The formation had been right in front of his ship, so all Morgan had to do was turn around and clip in his machine-gun barrels while Barry untied the rotor blades.

Captain Sloane finished pissing under the tail boom, walked up to the pilot's seat, and strapped on his armor vest. "Hey, Morgan," he said. "Ready to make the world safe for democracy?"

He looked up from his box of bullets on the floor. "Ready, sir."

They flew at the front of the formation with Major Singer, followed by another team of gunships, two scout choppers, more gunships, the lift birds with the riflemen, two more scouts, and four gunships bringing up the rear.

They flew west fifteen or twenty miles, dipping low over every hamlet and village so the trailing ships could drop old C rations. As they neared a mountain range in the west, the choppers made a wide arc to the north. Another ten miles and they crossed a paved road, turned, and followed it east.

Large, neat rice paddies flanked the road, going east as far as he could see. The peasants glanced warily at the choppers, turning only their heads while their hands remained fixed on the shoots of rice beneath the water. A few Vietnamese drove mule-drawn carts on the road to and from Phan Thiet, while others stepped briskly beneath poles that drooped bundles at both ends.

Two bubble scout helicopters broke out from the formation, one on each side, and suddenly red smoke billowed from the skids where someone had tied grenades. A few minutes later the other two did the same, this time with yellow smoke.

"Okay, gunships, this is Six. We're coming to a rice paddy that's already been harvested. I want all the guns pointed down and firing into the ground. Maybe a hundred rounds or so. I'll give the word when to start and stop."

The side guns tipped downward. Morgan stretched the elastic cord until his own gun pointed straight down.

"Okay," Singer said. "Let it go."

He squeezed the trigger but didn't watch the bullets. Across the road panic stiffened through the farmers like an electric charge. Only a couple ran. The rest knew better. The smiles and friendly waves that they'd been getting along the road vanished, and the faces and bodies were suddenly like stone.

He released the trigger a few seconds before Singer said, "Cease firing." The major's voice was tired, nearly empty of expression.

He pulled a few more rounds out of the box and hung them over his thigh, his preflight excitement evaporated. He didn't want to look at the peasants in the rice paddies. He felt like a big fucking bully in the chopper. Barry's chin rested in his palm while he watched the sky. Sloane hitched the infinity sight to the ceiling and lit a cigarette. Woolsey flew them straight ahead. Everything seemed quieter than before they'd fired.

The radio whir went on. "Let's take it back in," Singer said.

For the rest of the day the field base seemed to be enveloped in a sluggish cloud of tiredness. The men ate slowly at noon; the gunners flopped listlessly on the chopper seats waiting for the next flight. The crispness of the morning had gone limp and flaccid like old celery. Morgan didn't have to fly anymore because his ship was undergoing a periodic inspection and would be down for the rest of the day. Barry remained his usual cheerful self, but nevertheless seemed distracted, as though he didn't want to talk.

Morgan finished cleaning his guns by two, tried reading, then walked the quarter mile to the concrete shithouse at the end of the runway. Shabby children from the shantytown extended grubby paws across the concertina wire. The MP didn't even bother to shoo them away.

He sat on the commode, swatting at flies, trying to figure it. Had the door opened a crack this morning, letting in faint intimations to his comrades that they were doing nothing for the Vietnamese, dying for nothing? They had to realize it sometime. He had, before leaving Fulda, so he'd no illusions to lose that way. He wondered what would happen once the cat was out of the bag. Would the soldiers rebel and quit? Shoot their officers and turn the equipment over to the Vietnamese and Vietcong? Most likely they'd just go on drinking beer and counting days. He wiped himself, thinking that squatting in a shithouse wasn't quite the position for a philosopher king. What did he know about how the others felt? He walked back to his ship and fell asleep.

The quiet continued into the night. Chambers had one beer with them, then went to his ship to read. Webster went to bed about ten, and Morgan took a quick shower, trying to get back some energy. It did nothing for him. When he got back to the flight line, Barry still had all the panels off the cabin floor. He'd found complications that couldn't be fixed till morning. "How the hell are we supposed to sleep tonight?"

"We can odd-man for the seat or the ground," Barry said.

"And wake up with a snake in my bag."

"I don't mind, if it's female. I'll take the ground."

"I don't want you doing that. Hancock's crew chief's on R&R. I'll sleep in his ship." They both went over to talk with the gunner.

"You guys ain't never been in no crashes," Hancock said after a while. "And you been damn lucky. Sometimes I start feelin' too scared to go up anymore, but I reckon I won't give Hart the satisfaction of me quittin'." Above his cigarette ember, Hancock's eyes bulged, dark-brown bags beneath them. "Got shot down the first two times, once out there by Plei Me, then at Happy Valley. That's scary shit because you know the gooks is crawlin' all over. Then we had to ditch in Qui Nhon harbor once. Damn ship just quit. I dove out from about thirty feet and a gook sampan hauled me in. Last time was at Ia Drang. Compressor stall and we fell forty feet into the fuckin' sand. I like to cracked up that time, boy. You guys'll get yours."

"I think I'll get mine to bed," Barry said.

Hancock told stories for another half hour. The flight line was absolutely still, and down the path between the two rows of ships Morgan could see out beyond the perimeter where the eerie light from the moon covered the ground. Hancock was from West Virginia, where he'd done men's work from the time he was twelve until he'd been drafted at twenty. He'd reenlisted after his first two years and had fifteen months left on this hitch. They crawled into their sleeping bags at midnight.

"I reckon I'll try getting on with the post office when I get out," Hancock said. "Do something easy for a while. This war about made me stone blind, Morgan."

Morgan faded in and out of sleep. "Yeah," he muttered and rolled on his side and hugged his field jacket.

At first the muted buzzings going past the ship reminded him of the seventeen-year locusts that whizzed around the S-1 tent when he worked at night. But they went too fast. He listened to a couple more, then propped himself on his elbows. "Hey, Cock, I think that shit's coming in."

"Huh?" Hancock turned over in his sleeping bag.

"I said I think we're getting shot at."

Hancock sat up. "Ooooooh, Christ!" The moan rose from deep in his stomach. "Morgan, we're taking fire! They're shooting at us! Get out, god damn it!"

Morgan had never heard so much fear in a voice. He swung his legs outside the chopper and slid into his fatigue pants. "Incoming rounds!" he yelled.

Hancock jumped out of the ship and stood in front of him, shaking. "What'll we do? We can't let them get us!"

"What's happening?" Barry yelled from across the line.

"We're being attacked! Get to a hole somewhere." They hadn't dug bunkers. There weren't even any sandbags around the ships. There was one big pit a few feet down the line where they threw empty ammo boxes and casings.

"Morg, I'm hit," Barry groaned.

"You're shitting." He could see Barry's white T-shirt on the ground by the chopper.

"They got me in the leg."

"Medic! Hancock, what do we do?"

"Go take care of him. I'll get a medic. Medic! Man wounded!" Hancock crouched and ran toward the infantry tents where the medics slept.

Fifty feet separated Morgan and Barry, across the lane between the tow lines of choppers. Fuck it. Nothing else to do. Like waiting to dive into the ice-cold ocean. As he stepped into the lane, two bullets zipped past him like angry hornets. Halfway across two small puffs went up from the ground to his right front. Maybe they were inside the perimeter. He dived, rolled, and came up next to Barry. "You okay, man?"

"Here, in the leg." Barry pointed to his thigh.

He put his hand gently on the leg and felt the warm blood oozing through Barry's fatigues. He slipped his fingers into the hole and tore the material a few inches. "Take your pants off."

Barry handed him his T-shirt, then slid his pants below his knees.

"I forgot most of my first aid, but I'll tie this above the wound."

"Okay. Okay."

"Medic! Get the motherfucking medic out here!" He tied the shirt around the leg, letting one sleeve flop over the wound. He jumped into the helicopter and tugged at the first-aid pack that hung above the door. More bullets whizzed through the air outside the ship. "Relax, Barry, so your heart won't beat so fast."

"I'm cool, Morg."

He pulled the bandage out of the first-aid pack, jumped down, and tied it around Barry's wound. McCutcheon suddenly appeared in front of him, barefoot, two belts of bullets crisscrossed over his shaggy chest, his steel pot on his head, brandishing a machine gun.

"How's Barry?"

"I'm okay," Barry said.

"Come on, Morgan, let's move him around to the other side of the ship."

"Where's Chambers?"

"Manning a machine gun."

They carried Barry out of the line of fire and set up a machine gun to cover him.

"Morgan," McCutcheon said, "don't you think it's time to take off that white T-shirt?"

"I wondered why they were shooting at me." He took off the shirt and leaned back on his elbows. Flares popped outside the perimeter, covering the ground with orange light, while brighter orange tracers streamed through it into the woods beyond. "They must've been pretty close."

"I'll be back later." McCutcheon ran off toward Major Singer's tent.

"How you doin', Barry?"

"It smarts, but I guess I'll make it."

Hancock barreled across the flight line, pulling someone by the arm. "Here he is. Now take care of him." He nearly threw the medic to his knees.

They went separately to Hancock's ship to get their pots, weapons, and flak jackets, then came back and lay in the grass, smoking. An engine ran up behind them.

"Was you scared, Morgan?" Hancock asked. "I was. Still am. I know Barry was scared."

"Not me, Cock," Barry said.

"Another four inches he'd've had your dick. He gonna live, there, medic?"

"And get some time off too," the medic said. "I don't think this'll get you to Japan, buddy, but you should land two weeks in Nha Trang."

As a helicopter spattered the ground with bright-orange rain, the gunners and crew chiefs came out from their hiding places behind the skids and under the choppers to watch. Charlie wouldn't fire anymore. Charlie was home in bed by now. The spitting helicopter looked like a pale olive-drab ghost in the eerie orange sky.

A jeep rolled slowly down the airstrip, picked up Barry, and took him to the small medical building at the north end of the camp.

"Come on, Cock, let's go out so we can see better." Hancock still hadn't put on his pants and looked like a big kid in his unlaced boots, pistol belt, and pot.

The ship made a second run, showering the ground with tracers, many of them ricocheting into the pale-orange glow of the flares, then broke off and circled around the western side of the camp. Morgan and Hancock kept quiet while the others told their stories. One of Hart's boys had caught a piece of shrapnel in the cheek from a mortar that had hit farther up the flight line. Two men had been killed in the aircraft maintenance company on the eastern side. Barry had been C Company's only other casualty.

"Well, I'll tell you what," Hancock said. "Me and Morgan—"

A tremendous explosion went off above them.

"Oh, no!" Hancock screamed. He took two steps forward and dived into the trash pit.

Morgan fell down, laughing. The chopper fired two more pairs of rockets in rapid succession, went forward a couple of hundred feet, and fired four more pairs.

Hancock's head rose slowly to the edge of the pit, an empty bandolier hanging from his helmet. "Give 'em hell!" he screamed. "Give 'em hell!" He shook his fist at the sky. The others cheered and shouted as though they were watching a football game.

Morgan felt suddenly alone. Everyone was pissed off at Charlie except him. In a way, he'd almost enjoyed the attack. He looked at the ground and gave a feeble yell. "Kick the shit out of them."

21

"Good, Red! Good. Right on target. Keep those rockets coming."

Good, Red! Hot shit, Red! Fuck you in your mouth, Red! Chambers moved his arm in and out of the door so Sanders would think he was throwing grenades.

The ship broke left and McCutcheon eased himself out on the skid and fired two clips from his M-16. The Air Force L-19 Piper Cub flew across their path fifty feet up, then swung back to watch the other ship.

"Guns really talkin', Four-five. Looking good."

The L-19 dived toward the ground while the gunships circled to the west.

"Red, this is One-eleven. Got a couple in a hole waving a white flag. Think one of your ships could get in and take a prisoner? There's a small LZ right next to them."

"This is Red, One-eleven. Hold one. How about it, Four-five? You want to check it out?"

"This is Four-five. That's affirmative, Red."

They flew crossing patterns while the other ship went down. Webster jumped out of the door, stood around the spot by the people for a few seconds, and got back on the ship.

"One-eleven, this is Four-five. Over."

"Whatcha got, Four-five?"

"Man and his daughter. No weapon. My gunner says the man's head is messed up pretty bad, but he'll live. Didn't see anything else."

"Roger, Four-five. Okay, Red, that's it for tonight. Good job. Give yourself seven estimated kills."

"Roger, One-eleven. See you later. Out."

Chambers bit down on his lip, hunched over, and shook his head. Why did they always have to fuck everything up? Phan Thiet had been so good at first that he'd nearly forgotten about the war, but it had turned to shit in his hands. For the five evenings since the night attack they'd been flying up the coast to fire on suspected Vietcong that the Air Force spotter plane had seen. Ten confirmed and fifteen estimated kills so far. No one in the helicopters had seen anyone.

Webster came over to his ship while he was reloading. "They're putting me in for a medal for going on the ground tonight."

"Really?"

"What the hell? Twenty-fifth's giving away Bronze Stars for getting out of bed in the morning."

Morgan walked up carrying a can of beer. He and Hancock were both being put in for medals for helping Barry. "Got some ground action tonight, Webster?"

"All the kills we got ain't been nothin' but farmers and kids." Webster shrugged. "I know that dude tonight couldn't work no weapon."

"I'd like to get Sanders out there with no weapon." Chambers visualized the captain running through a rice paddy, his wart glowing while gunships bore down on him.

"I don't mind fighting," Webster said, "but not farmers and kids. I'd get out if there was something else to do. But they ain't sending nobody to the rear, and the mess hall's filled up with nuts from the rifles. Even if they'd let you sit around, you'd go crazy. Least flyin' keeps your mind busy."

All that was true. Chambers had been so nervous the last time his ship went into a periodic inspection that he'd been glad to start flying again. He couldn't read for much more than an hour at a time. The inactivity made him think about going home, and then he'd be counting minutes and seconds instead of days and going out of his skull.

"What the hell, Orville," Morgan said. "We'll be going in for good in a couple of months. Lot of us'll be leaving. That's probably why Hart won't let anyone go now. If one goes, everyone'll want to."

"Except you," Webster said.

"I'll hang around a while longer."

"Sixty days is still sixty days," Chambers said. It meant at least two hundred more missions, two hundred times he could crash or get shot through the face or the balls. Each time the goddamn bird took off could be the last. But everyone waved and joked and gave the finger and acted as if it was no big thing.

McCutcheon appeared out of the darkness, carrying the

ship's little green notebook of forms. "Two more days, you guys, and my ass goes on the ground."

"What's up?"

"I just talked to Hart, and he says a new crew chief's coming out, then I'll take over as full-time line chief. Might make E-5 this month too."

"Who's going to be my crew chief?"

"A guy named Maddin from Headquarters Company."

"Been here for about six months?" Morgan asked.

"I think so."

"That's some loon. I don't envy you, Orville."

"What do you mean?"

"I probably shouldn't say anything, but he got drunk and tried to do himself in a couple of times. I just heard about it. I never saw him try."

"That's all I need." He sat down in the doorway and squeezed his face between his hands, then jumped back up again. Brooding was no good. He finished reloading, kicked his debris in the garbage pit, and grabbed his soap and towel. "You going to get a shower, Will?"

"Fuck it. One more day's funk ain't likely to hurt none."

"I'll be back later."

Up at the shower he stood for a moment listening to the babble and drunken laughter coming from Hart's tent. He had no idea what the little sergeant thought of him. Just a body in the platoon, most likely. Hart had never chewed him out, but then he'd never slapped him on the back either. If he went to Hart now, wanting to quit, what would he say? Orville couldn't see himself sucking ass for the favor. He'd just have to ask him flat. One of these days he'd do it. Maybe tomorrow.

Walking back to his ship, he could hear Robinson bellowing from a hundred yards away. The Texan had come back on election day, two bottles of whiskey in his duffel bag, boasting that he'd be going home permanently in a week or two. The other gunners were still squatting by the door to

Chambers' chopper, passing the bottle and listening to Robinson. Chambers threw his dirty fatigues in the baggage compartment, then came around and climbed up on the seat.

"Fuck the gooks anyway," Robinson said. He took a swig from the Old Crow and handed it to Hancock. "Ain't none of 'em worth a shit. We ought to get out of here."

"You soundin' like one of them old demonstrators," Hancock said. "Take you some Oscar Charlie there, Chambers." He handed him the bottle.

"Fuck a lot of demonstrators too," Robinson said. "One of those faggy bastards came up to me in the Frisco airport. I'm waitin' to go to Texas to see my dying father, right? Minding my own business. This punk stops me, says, 'You been in Vietnam?' 'Yeah,' I say. 'Going back?' I say, 'Yeah.' Then the cocksucker just looks at me and says, 'I hope you die.' Now ain't that some shit?"

"What'd you do?" Hancock asked.

"Spit on him. Big lunger. Right in the face. Then I kneed him in the balls and walked away."

"I'd of killed him," Hancock said.

"I would have if there hadn't been no one there. Fuckin' communists. I don't mean we should let them have this place. There just ain't no goddamn gook worth dyin' for. Take that election shit. Those fuckers out there shittin' in the rice paddy are too damn stupid to vote. Probably can't even read. This whole country's a waste. Gimme that whiskey, Chambers."

"It's empty. It only had a drop in it when it got to me." He'd taken one swallow and was already feeling mellow.

"Shit! And I was just gettin' a little buzz. I want to get my head *bad* tonight. I shouldn't have brought it over for you guys."

"Where can we get some more?" Hancock said. "I'll put in five bucks for a fifth. How about you, Chambers?"

"I'll chip in a couple of dollars." What the hell. Maybe some whiskey would make him feel better.

"I'll bet the mess pig has some," Robinson said. "Give me the money and I'll go check him out."

In fifteen minutes he heard Robinson laughing, then he was standing beside the ship, shaking a bottle. "Ten bucks for a quart of this piss." He gave the Old Crow to Hancock.

They passed the bottle around two more times, then Robinson and Hancock kept it between them. Chambers didn't mind. He'd had enough and didn't want to make himself sick. Robinson boasted about the pussy he'd had on leave, about the barroom brawls he'd been in, then everything went quiet for a few minutes. Robinson never let anyone finish a story anyway, so there was no use talking.

"Well, fuck you deadheads," Robinson said. "Hancock, let's you and me go drink with them gooks."

"You want to give them our booze?"

"Maybe we can have a little fun with them. Come on."

They left with the bottle, and Chambers could hear them laughing far down the flight line where two Vietnamese sergeants, who were to pull some rotor blades tomorrow, slept in a wrecker.

"You drunk, Orville?" Morgan asked.

"Not me. How about you?"

"Just right. That's the first whiskey in a long time for me."

"Me too."

"Damn, Orville, I can barely see you up there." Morgan leaned against a stack of rockets on the ground. "Come on down with the folks."

"I'm comfortable here." He heard the laughing again, then Hancock and Robinson stumbled up leading the two Vietnamese sergeants. They all sat down, and Robinson handed the bottle to a Vietnamese. The sergeant grinned and nodded three or four times before drinking.

"We're going to give them a couple of drinks," Robinson said, "then kill 'em, throw 'em in the garbage pit, and burn 'em in JP-4." He smiled at the sergeant and had him pass the bottle to the other. "How about it, Hancock? Which one do you want?"

"Hell, I don't know. You pick first."

"I'll take the one closest to me. Who's gonna go first?"

"Maybe you should," Hancock said. His voice wavered, but the fear must have been put on.

Robinson took another swig from the bottle, handed it to the sergeant, and patted him on the back. "Drink up there, fuckin' little gook," he said, smiling. The sergeant beamed, nodded, and raised the bottle to his lips. "Because I'm going to kill you when you're done."

The sergeant handed the bottle to Hancock and nodded at Robinson again.

Robinson smiled. "You gooks are so damn stupid, you know, little gooky? Now I just said I was going to kill you and you go on grinning like a Chinese cocksucker."

"Why don't you cool it, Robinson?" Chambers filled with disgust for the gunner.

"Don't sweat it, Chambers. I'm just having some fun with little gook-ass here before I choke him to death."

"You better be joking."

"Sure I'm joking. How about it, Hancock, you going first or me?"

"I'll do it if you do."

Robinson turned to the sergeant. "Hi, gooky. Time for you to go bye-bye for good." His hands shot out and closed around the sergeant's throat. The sergeant gagged as though he might vomit. Robinson stood up, lifting the sergeant by his throat, then lunged forward and fell on top of him on the ground. "I'm going to choke your fuckin' gook ass to death!"

Chambers had never heard so much hatred in a voice. For a moment he watched Robinson, certain he would stop any second. Hancock had hold of the other sergeant's arm, and the Vietnamese squirmed, trying to get away.

"Jesus Christ!" Chambers exploded. "Isn't anyone going to do anything?" He flew out of the helicopter, dived on Robinson's back, and pulled him off. "What are you, crazy or something?"

They rolled over once and Robinson came up swinging.

"Fuck you, gook lover!" He ducked around Chambers, dropped to his knees, and hit the sergeant in the face. "Come on, Hancock, you chickenshit, get yours." He hit the coughing, gasping sergeant again, knocking him flat, then dived on him.

"Cut that shit out!" Chambers put his arms around Robinson's waist and pulled him off again.

Hancock slapped the other sergeant twice, but the man wriggled free and ran down the flight line.

"Turn me loose!" Robinson brought his elbows back hard, causing Chambers to lose his grip. He whirled and swung, but Chambers blocked it and punched him in the stomach. Robinson doubled over, spun again, and fell forward on the sergeant. "Help me, Hancock," he gasped and hit the sergeant feebly a few times. Hancock kicked the sergeant twice in the head, but stopped when Webster stepped in front of him.

"Help me with him, Morg!" Chambers grabbed Robinson, ready to break him in half. But the Texan's body was loose—all the fight gone.

"Okay, I'm through," Robinson said. His chest heaved and tears ran down his cheeks. "I won't do any more. Just let me alone."

They both let go. Robinson stumbled a few steps to the side, weaved, then fell against Chambers' pile of rockets. He slid down one side to the ground while the rockets rolled off on the other. He breathed deeply once and seemed to fall asleep just as the first sergeant and Major Singer arrived.

"I can't afford a bust," Hancock said. "I might have made sergeant before I left here, but now I'm all fucked up." He pulled hungrily on his cigarette, looking nervously at the others.

"I'm getting out anyway, so I don't give a fuck," Robinson said, although his voice wasn't quite so bold as it had been the night before.

"I might get out too," Hancock said. "But I might stay in. Then where would I be at?"

Major Singer was giving them all Article 15's for drinking whiskey in the field. No one had said anything about the Vietnamese sergeant last night, Singer accepting Hancock's and Robinson's version that the two of them were caught trying to steal from one of the ships. The sergeant had apparently regained consciousness early this morning, and the first sergeant had alerted the gunners that the Vietnamese had told the whole story to someone from the Criminal Investigation Division. It was now ten in the morning, and the CID would be on the flight line any minute. They were trying to agree on a story. Robinson reasoned that the word of five Americans was worth that of two Vietnamese any day.

Chambers hadn't said anything last night. He had been so full of rage that he thought if he started talking he'd never be able to stop. But today he felt different. "Fuck it, Robinson," he said suddenly. "I ain't tellin' no lies for you today. You tried to kill someone, and you can damn well go to jail for it. You make me want to puke."

"Come off it, Chambers," Robinson said. "We're all in this together."

"Fuck you in it together. I just tried to save someone from being murdered."

"What's it matter what we say? It's not going to change anything."

"It'll get you out of my sight. It—"

"Wait, Orville," Morgan said. "Come here." He steered him around to the other side of the ship.

"I don't want to hear it, Will. I want that bastard out of here." But he knew what Morgan would say and felt his resolve slipping as Morgan talked. He agreed that Robinson was a sorry son of a bitch, but who could say if he was naturally mean or if being in the war had made him crazy? Besides, he'd probably be leaving on a permanent change of station before long. And if pinned to the wall, he might report them for smoking dope or even say that all of them had tried to kill the Vietnamese sergeant.

Chambers argued with Morgan for fifteen minutes, finally relenting, even as his anger grew. He didn't want to feel any sympathy for Robinson, but after a while he couldn't help it. "Okay, Will, okay!" He banged his fist into the side of the chopper. "Maybe it is a little late to bring out the law book. But, Christ, this shit has to stop somewhere. I guess if they started charging people now, they wouldn't know where to stop, would they?"

As they walked around the tail boom, Robinson, Hancock, and Webster looked up at them. Webster looked loose as always, like he really didn't care. Poor Hancock was scared to death. Robinson's face showed at once apprehension and cockiness, and Orville realized that the Texan had no idea of what he'd tried to do, that to him, as to the rest of them, the Vietnamese sergeant was just a gook—not even half a person.

"You gonna red-ass on me, Chambers?"

"No, Robinson, but I'll tell you what. You ever try anything like that again and I'll put *you* in the hospital for a couple of months. I'm going down to my ship. You call me when the CID comes."

A week later, in the morning, Robinson left for good. Everything had been dropped. The CID had swallowed their story, then Robinson had told Major Singer that the mess sergeant had sold them the whiskey and that the pilots were buying it from him too. Rather than formally discipline the whole company, Singer dropped the charges against everyone.

As the twin-engine Caribou carried Robinson off the airstrip and into the sky, Orville felt a sudden relief. Maybe everything had gone to shit. His new crew chief was nuts, Hart had been turned down by a promotion board and was raising hell with the platoon, but at least Robinson was gone and Orville would never have to look at him again.

Late that afternoon they flew into the mountains about fifteen miles to the southwest to recon an alleged enemy buildup. Sanders predicted a turkey shoot—a whole battalion going up a hill that they could blow to bits. Plenty of Vietnamese crowded the roads, but they were all farmers and villagers carrying loads, and none of them ran. Many waved and smiled at the low-flying ship; others went impassively about their business. Sanders seethed. "Mr. Eastman, take the bird down on the deck, as close as you can get."

"Yes, sir." Eastman dropped it until they skimmed along the road no more than ten feet above the people. Understanding the contract, they still didn't move. Run, and you got shot. You might get it if you didn't run, but chances are you wouldn't unless you were alone.

"I'd like to search some of the bastards," Sanders said. "I'll bet half of those coolie baskets are filled with ammo. . . . Four-five, this is Red, over."

"Roger, Red."

"Four-five, keep your eye peeled for anything suspicious. Don't hesitate to fire."

"Roger, Red."

They rose five hundred feet and flew farther south into some small mountains thick with green. Chambers swung around in the seat, braced his left foot in the door, and moved the stock of the machine gun into his armpit. He closed his left hand around the smoke grenade just in case they did take fire, then leaned back to enjoy the scenery. He'd like to come back here to live when the war ended. The thought occurred involuntarily, pushing insistently into his consciousness. What the hell? Life could be good in the mountains, away from city crowds and the craziness in the U.S. But he still had to go to college first, get his education. Maybe he could build his own house here someday.

"Wake up back there," Sanders said.

He sat up in his seat as they cleared a ridge and hung a thousand feet above a valley.

"Will you look at that shit," Sanders said.

A giant stone Buddha, at least a hundred feet long, lay on the valley floor.

"Gooks all over down there," Sanders said. "Don't fire unless I give the word."

Antlike Vietnamese crawled around the massive stone. Buddha flat on his back in the grass. Fifteen feet thick from his back to his belly, his face almost grinning.

"See any weapons?"

"No, sir," Maddin said.

"Chambers?"

"What?" Most amazing statue he'd ever seen.

"See any weapons?"

"No. No, sir."

The Vietnamese cleared brush from around the Buddha's body, hacking it away with scythes and carrying it into the nearby jungle. It must be hundreds of years old. Impassive light-gray stone.

"They must have weapons hidden in the jungle," Sanders said.

Chambers looked up and smirked as Sanders turned around, red with frustration.

"It'd take a whole lot of grenades to blow old Buddha up," Eastman said as they circled the statue.

"We ought to blow the shit out of it," Sanders said. "Buddhists caused enough trouble during the election."

Chambers fingered the trigger of his machine gun. It'd be hard to keep from blowing Sanders' head off if he tried it.

"Red, this is Four-five. Anything?"

"Negative, Four-five. Nothing visible, anyway." Sanders ran his index finger over the map on the console, then jabbed it fiercely three times. "Let's take it back in, Four-five. We can't do a damn thing about this."

Dumb fucker's dying of frustration. Chambers resisted an impulse to cuff Sanders on the back of the helmet. None of the Vietnamese even looked up as they circled twice more.

He flashed a quick salute at the Buddha as they flew over it from head to foot and continued north to the base.

Sometimes, like tonight, he got so lonely that he thought he'd wake up frozen. After everyone had gone to bed and Maddin babbled off to sleep, he slipped the pack of joints from his duffel bag, sat on the skid, and smoked. He almost wished a bullet would come tearing down the flight line and smash his life apart.

The whole platoon had wanted to bomb the Buddha. The statue was the catalyst that brought all their hatred to a boil. Only Morgan had said that the Buddha wasn't bothering anyone, so why not leave it alone, but he had been shouted down immediately. All of them—Hancock, Maddin, Crockett, McCutcheon, even Webster—were ready to dump rockets and grenades on the harmless stone. And everyone was pissed off because the Vietnamese wouldn't show their weapons, wouldn't come out in the open and fight like men. But the statue was only a statue. It had nothing to do with anything.

He pulled his knees up to his chest and rocked back and forth, smoking. The thin crescent of the moon shone more intensely than a full moon. The stars glittered, but the ground was nearly black.

He didn't want to be a small-town character. One time when he and Morgan were in the club in Fulda, Morgan had screamed at him over the deafening band that he was like a small-town Southerner in some book he was reading. Morgan predicted he'd end up on a woodsy hill at midnight, trying to scream the moon out of the sky.

Even though he knew Morgan was joking, he'd taken him seriously. Because he already had the fear that like his father, he would become a prisoner of his outrage and someday go insane. He'd been trying to escape it, by being friendly with the others in Germany and by volunteering for Vietnam with them.

When they'd arrived in Florence on their leave, Morgan had immediately dragged him to the Academy to see Michelangelo's "David." He had been duly impressed, and as they left, he noticed the half-finished statues lining the walls on the way up to the "David." They nearly overwhelmed him, and he stayed to look at them while Morgan left. They seemed so much more true to life, less removed than the beautifully polished stone of the completed statue. They were so much like himself.

He stood in front of "The Awakening Giant" for an hour and returned to it twice more. The statue symbolized everything that had been his life and was happening to him in Florence. Although imprisoned in stone, the body seemed to be moving, freeing itself slowly from the confines that locked it in. He thought that if he stood there long enough, the rock would crack and the figure would erupt into life like a man breaking suddenly out of sleep.

During those two weeks in Italy he had pushed away the rocks and clouds that weighed so heavily on him. So what had it gotten him? He experienced only traces of that freedom now, like when he'd seen the Buddha. That massive rock had made him happy because it seemed free and wasn't hurting anyone, alive though solid stone. Maybe that's why everyone wanted to destroy it.

He heard footsteps in the grass behind him and quickly tucked the roaches under the front of the skid.

"Is that you, Orville?" Morgan came around the tail boom.

"Hi, Will." His voice cracked in his dry throat.

"I couldn't sleep. Thought I saw a match over here." Morgan sat down and patted him on the shoulder.

"I can't sleep either." He coughed.

Morgan sniffed a couple of times. "Man, you don't smell like no cigar. Got any more?"

He pulled out two more joints and they smoked silently for a few minutes.

"That thing with the statue really got to me tonight. These people are nuts." He suddenly blurted out his unhappiness.

Morgan took off his glasses and polished them on his fatigue jacket. "It's too bad it hurts you so much. It must be hard to go on from day to day."

"It was pretty good for a while, like when you got back from R&R. Then it all went to shit. First the crap on election day, then the night attack, then Robinson trying to murder that guy, plus shooting unarmed people for the Air Force to phony up the body count. I almost went up to Hart's tonight and quit, but I guess it's even too late for that now."

"It may be. Two more guys from the rifles went to work at the mess hall today. They don't need any new people. And I don't think they'll let you go back to base. Wouldn't hurt to ask."

"I still might. I like the guys in the platoon, but tonight I had to hold back from hitting someone. I guess there's some points where no one will ever understand you. Maybe you shouldn't even try."

Morgan nodded. "The day I joined I knew I was different, but I figured the guys knew things about life I didn't. I've learned a lot, but I'm starting to get tired of it now. Replacements should be here next month. At least by the beginning of November."

"I sure hope so. One or two missions a day wouldn't be bad, even with Sanders."

"I don't mind Sloane. He's straight and doesn't go for the chickenshit."

He yawned. "I'm beat, Will. Guess I'll try to sleep."

"Me too. That's good shit you're smoking. We could stay high for the next two months. I'm glad we talked. At least we've got that."

"It was good for me too."

"See you on police call. Assholes and elbows now that Hart didn't make E-7."

The next night Sanders gathered the platoon to tell them they were leaving, that division had been mortared at Bong Son, taking several casualties, and that C Company was needed to pick up some extra recon. The following morning the company flew up the coast at five thousand feet with the doors closed. The sun stippled itself insistently on the gently waving sea, almost like Morse code. When Orville was young, he used to sit in a tree by the lake and watch the sun on the water. One summer he became convinced that it was God's way of giving messages, and the secret would be revealed if he watched long enough. That summer Roger was killed.

As they flew north, memories of Happy Valley came back, and when they crossed the river near Bong Son, he felt as though he were having a bad dream. They hovered down and refueled, then flew west a few miles.

The helipad was a dark oval spot bigger than two football fields, bordered on the south by an airstrip. South of the runway a hill about a quarter mile long and two hundred feet high stuck out of the ground like a dinosaur's spine. On the other sides the helipad was surrounded by tents, and as they landed, he could make out the markings on aircraft from the other companies. The ground was spongy and sticky with oil. Ugly shit brown. Morgan left on a mission right away, and Hart gathered the rest of the platoon at the northeast corner of the flight line.

"I hope you all brought your shelter halves with you, because Colonel Snider says no more sleeping in the helicopters. Seven of them took shrapnel during that mortar attack, so everyone's moving into tents. We ain't got no squad tents here, so you'll do the best you can. I don't give a shit who lives together or what you make your tents of. But no more than four bodies per tent, with at least a three-foot wall of sandbags around each one and a good drainage ditch. A few other things, while we're here. Anyone not sleeping under a mosquito net gets an Article Fifteen. And I don't give a shit if you're going ten feet away from your ship—you *will* wear your pistol belt, pot, and weapon at all times. We ain't playin' no games up here. And when you get your tents done you can dig bunkers—everybody's got to have a bunker. Anyone fuckin' off will be down at the mess hall scrubbing stoves. Now get to it."

"Whaddya say, Orville?" McCutcheon said, grabbing his arm. "Want to bunk in together?"

He knew no one else would want to sleep with McCutcheon. He wished Morgan was here, but he might be too wild. He'd have some peace and quiet with McCutcheon. "I don't even have a shelter half." He'd left the field gear he didn't use in the base camp.

"No sweat. I got two of them and another two ponchos we can use. Make a nice tent with a little room inside."

"I got an extra poncho too."

The platoon settled on soft sand covered by small plants whose roots looked like a cross between carrots and peeled potatoes. They fixed the tent so there'd be a shelter half on each side, overlapped by the two ponchos, which also formed the roof. They had no trouble with the supporting poles, but the pegs kept pulling out of the sand, making the tent sag and wobble. After two hours Eastman got them for a mission.

Morgan was cleaning his guns on the flight line. "Take it cool, Orville. We got shot at twice."

"Nice to know. How come you're not back fixing your tent?"

"What tent?"

He told him about Hart's formation.

"You set up?" Morgan asked.

"McCutcheon needed someone to bunk with."

Disappointment flickered across Morgan's face. "I'll do it later. These damn guns got filled with sand at the fuel point. Two of them jammed on me."

"I've got to go. See you at chow."

He knew the terrain so well that for a while he thought he was home. They flew north a few miles, then east along the road where LaMont had been killed. The roofs on the hooches had been burned away long ago, the brown mud walls blackened along the tops. The tiny rooms were empty, showing only the dark-brown packed-dirt floors. The hills on the south side of the road were pocked from the tons of bombs dropped that day.

The sky had turned gray, the sea too, flecked occasionally by white as the small waves curled and fell by the beach, leaving a bubbly mustache on the sand. They flew south, crossing the river again and heading into the small mountains that he'd worked as a foot soldier in January. Push them out. Leave. They come back in. Back again. Push them out. Round and round she goes, where she stops, nobody knows. How long would it last this time?

Morgan had been fired at twice! He tightened his grip on the gun and grenade, leaned forward, and stared at the ground.

"Okay," Sanders said. "This is where they took fire earlier today. Hear that, Four-five?"

Two clicks of acknowledgment sounded back on the radio.

They flew south down the spine of the mountain, swung left, and came back lower, between the mountain and the sea. He couldn't see the ground, so he watched the water, thinking about flying over it, all the way home.

Plexiglas showered down on him, and Sanders squirmed in his seat as if he might bail out. Chambers automatically flipped the smoke grenade out the door, then froze. Two holes big as baseballs gaped in the window in front of Sanders.

"You okay, sir?" Eastman asked.

"I think so," Sanders stammered, brushing the Plexiglas off his front. "Four-five, this is Red. We just got hit."

"Roger, Red. Got your smoke in sight."

"Is the bird smoking?"

"Negative, Red. Yellow smoke on the ground."

Sanders relaxed. "Must've been fifty calibers. I guess they went right by my face and out your door, Chambers. Anybody cut?"

He checked his face, but found no blood. "No, sir."

"Damn lucky. Well, let's make a couple runs on them."

They got in at twilight, the camp winking at them with little white lights. He'd been able to make the gun runs without thinking, but as they flew back, he had become more and more terrified. He refused to go on like this. He'd done his fucking duty or whatever he was supposed to do. Two more months would kill him for sure, replacement or not. He'd made up his mind to quit. It was illegal to keep him on flight status if he didn't want to fly.

He loaded slowly, then trudged over to the platoon area. Morgan, Webster, and Hancock lay on the ground laughing, a crumpled heap of shelter halves, ponchos, and torn waterproof bags between them.

"Three tears in the bucket!" Morgan bellowed. "They don't flow, mother fuck it!" They all guffawed.

Hart stormed out of his tent twenty feet behind them. "What in hell's going on here? You guys drunk? Why ain't this tent up? Get off the goddamn ground."

"We can't get the tent up, Sarge," Hancock said, then fell to his knees laughing.

"You better fuckin' well get it up. I'll have your asses up all night. Everyone else is squared away and digging bunkers. Where you guys been? If you've been drunk, you're gonna swing."

Morgan belched. "We were cleaning our guns."

"Fuck your guns. They can wait. Now quit playin' grab-ass and get this tent up. You ain't sleepin' till you get three feet of sandbags around there."

"But we were fired at," Morgan said.

"And I just got back," Webster said. "We was fired at too."

"I don't give a shit!" Hart screamed. "Now get to work."

He turned and stomped back toward his tent.

"Sarge?"

Hart turned from the flap of his tent. "What do you want, Chambers? Is your tent up?"

"Yeah. Can I talk to you for a minute?"

"C'mon in. What is it?"

"I want to quit flying."

Hart sat down and popped open a beer. He played with the foam for a few seconds, then turned his head up. "What for?"

"Because I'm sick of it, and I'm getting short." He could see Hart wasn't going to bend.

"So are a lot of guys."

"But I want to quit."

"And do what?"

"I don't know. Work in the mess hall. Go back to the base and build barracks. Anything."

"Can't do it. Mess hall's got too many people already. They're sending guys out from the base to the rifles because there's too many of them back there."

"I'll burn shit, then."

"Brady from rifles is burning shit. We don't need no extra men. You better keep on flying. You'll have a replacement in thirty days."

"I won't fly anymore."

Hart looked up and grinned. "Yes, you will."

"You can't make me. You can't keep me on flight status."

Hart nodded, drank from his beer can, then swirled it around three or four times. "That's right, Chambers. You don't have to fly. So I'll tell you what. I'll let you out. I'll send you to the rifles in the morning. I'm sure they've got someone who'd be proud to be a gunner."

"I ain't going to the rifles. I've done that already."

"Then you go on flying. Seems like you're always quittin' something, Chambers. I'll give you the night to think about it. Let me know in the morning."

"But—"

"No buts, Chambers." Hart's voice was cool, totally confident. "Now get out there and help McCutcheon with that bunker."

22

THE HELICOPTER floated across Highway 19 a little after nine, and Morgan could see a few soldiers already trickling into Sin City. He'd be there himself this afternoon—probably his last time before rotation. After a couple of quick shots he'd go see Lang at the laundry. Maybe he'd stay there all day, drinking beer and playing with the kids.

The ship landed in the parade field behind the battalion. He lugged his duffel bag down to C Company, dropped it on a cot in one of the few remaining tents, and went up to S-1. He stood outside the tent for a minute, watching DeWolf at the typewriter. Another PFC leaned against the counter next to an unfamiliar sergeant. His old calendar still hung on the bamboo wall, check marks covering the first week of October. For a moment he thought of Chase and Greene, wondering what they were doing now. He'd never said good-bye to them. He wondered if they'd ever hear about how he did as a gunner, that he'd been put in for a medal. He felt a rush of sadness for them, brushed it aside, and walked through the tent flaps.

"You got a note from your first sergeant?" the sergeant behind the counter said.

"I just want to see DeWolf."

"Morg!" DeWolf looked up from the typewriter. "What are you doing in?"

"Went down in a rice paddy yesterday." He tossed it off as though the twenty-foot fall into the stinking brown water had been nothing. The crash had caked his fatigues and boots with mud, and he'd nearly shit his pants.

"Are you Morgan?" the sergeant asked.
"Right."
"I heard about you. Want to come back and clerk?"
"Nix. Looks like you've got two now."
"I'm going to aircraft maintenance in a week," DeWolf said.
"Let's get some coffee."
B Company's barracks had all been completed on the left side of battalion road. Farther down it looked as if the ones in Headquarters were finished too. "Damn, it's changed."
"You ain't said shit, Morg. Not just the barracks either. This place is nothing but chickenshit now. Well, at least the gooks'll have a place to live when we finally leave."
"What happened to Sergeant Wallace?"
"He got pissed off about reveille and got himself transferred back to the States. Don't ask me how. I think he phonied up something with the Red Cross."
In the barrack DeWolf produced a quart of Old Overholt from the foot of his sleeping bag. He took a drink and handed Morgan the bottle. "How's it going out there? Kill any gooks yet?"
"You never see anyone. I don't even know why they moved us up to Bong Son. We've been sniped at a few times, but nothing big." He doubted that he'd see anything big as long as he stayed. The eight days at Bong Son had been wild with rumor—that incendiary fact of Army life that had flared even in Fulda, where nothing ever happened. One day they were at Bong Son to protect the rice harvest, the next to secure the area for another Army division and two B-52 runways at Phu Cat. Two days ago a prisoner had been captured with twenty-five pouches of gold dust hanging from his belt, so now sweet rumor had it that Uncle Sam's sole purpose in the war was to beef up Fort Knox. He drank from the bottle and chased it with a beer from DeWolf's cooler. "Fuck it anyway. You want to go to Sin City?"
"I was down yesterday." DeWolf stroked his crotch. "I have to go back to work."

Morgan got his clean clothes and headed for the shower. Tents still covered the ground in the S-4 and aircraft-maintenance area. Probably not enough room to build barracks. Behind Fisher's old tent he stared at the spot where he'd been drunk so many nights. The benches, water cans, and warped shaving tables still lay haphazardly around the area like an old stage set, waiting for the players to come on for another act. A monkey shrieked at him.

He shaved, showered, and changed, then went to the mess hall. He sat down, enjoying a loose feeling. For being in the field only two months, he had seen a lot. His ship hit by snipers, the night attack, kills given by the Air Force spotter, now a crash in a rice paddy. He'd earned his wings and at least six Air Medals and was being put in for a valor medal too. He'd touched the blood of the wounded. The next two months would probably show him plenty more. He sipped his coffee, eyeing the new soldiers who walked in and out, greeting others he'd met before going to the field. He maintained a certain aloofness, kept his voice restrained and subdued as a combat soldier should.

He left for his tent at eleven and met Hart on the road by C Company. "Going to Sin City, Sarge?"

"No." Hart scowled. "Why?"

"Just wondered. I'm going down after chow."

"Like shit you are."

"I've got nothing else to do."

"You gotta clean the guns on that ship."

"I'll do them tomorrow."

"You're going back to the field tomorrow. You're cleaning those guns this afternoon."

He stared at Hart for a moment, unable to believe what he heard. What did the sergeant have against him? "Christ, Sarge, the ship crashed. Don't I deserve one afternoon off?"

"You're in a war, Morgan. You don't deserve nothin'. Those guns need to be cleaned. My platoon don't have dirty guns."

"Jesus Christ!"

"Keep talking, Morgan, and I'll bust your ass. You be down on that flight line at one or you're gonna swing." Hart turned and walked away.

Morgan stared at his departing back, then at the dirt in the road. He tried to calm down, told himself that Hart's maliciousness wasn't personal—the asshole was just pissed because he hadn't made E-7. But that didn't make it fair. He still deserved to go to Sin City for a couple of lousy hours. "Fuck it," he muttered, then went to DeWolf's barrack.

He pulled the whiskey from the sleeping bag, two beers from the cooler, and lit a joint. He took a deep breath, then went from whiskey to beer to reefer over and over, stopping only for a breath between each hit.

He opened his eyes and stared at the naked light bulb hanging from the barrack ceiling. Darkness outside. He bent forward into a sitting position, then fell back and groaned. He'd missed the whole afternoon.

DeWolf pushed through the screen door. "Sleeping beauty has finally roused his sorry ass."

"Don't tell me." He knew he was in big trouble.

"You better go see Hart. That's one pissed-off dude."

"What happened?"

"They were trying to roust you all afternoon. First that crew chief, then Hart, then the first pig, then our CO. I stopped in about three. All four of them had you standing up. They were yelling, shaking you, and slapping you. They gave up about four, I guess."

For a minute he couldn't talk for laughing so hard.

"You might as well laugh now."

"Three tears in the bucket, they don't flow, mother fuck it. I'll see you in the iron house." He walked out of the barrack, popped a piece of gum in his mouth, and headed up to C Company. All they could do was bust him, and he didn't care about that.

Hart sat on a cot, talking to Murdock, the crew chief who'd replaced Barry. Morgan watched them for a moment, shaking off his fear, then strode through the flaps. "Get the guns cleaned okay, Murdock? Sorry you had to do them alone."

"They're all done, Morg."

"Morgan!" Hart yelled. "What do you think you're doing?"

He turned to Hart and put out his hand to silence him. "Relax, Sarge. The guns are clean. That's what matters."

"You were drunk on duty! They could've dropped a bomb on this place and you wouldn't have known it."

"In that case, I'd have been better off passed out."

"You're really askin' for it, Morgan! I'm going to Captain Sanders first thing tomorrow and get you busted. I may even try for a court-martial."

"It's your show, Sarge." He sat down on a cot.

"Stand up when you talk to me! And call me Sergeant!"

"Yes, Sergeant!" Standing at attention, he couldn't stop himself from grinning.

Hart stood up, purple with rage. "God, I'm sick of you! Now you stay in this tent until morning."

"Can't I go to the club tonight?"

"No! You'll be lucky not to go to jail." Staff Sergeant Hart stormed out of the tent.

"I do declare," he said. "I think my platoon sergeant has a case of the gross ass." He pulled his sleeping bag and mosquito net from his duffel bag. "Well, Murdock, now that I've had my nap, I guess I'll go to sleep."

The next morning Hart said nothing when they met on the flight line and flew out to the field. He responded in kind, staring briefly at the sergeant, then sitting sullenly while the ship raced through the cool morning air. He felt futureless, not so much as if something had ended, but as though nothing would begin again. He tried to feel proud about yesterday's drunken episode, but it seemed like a static moment, years ago. He didn't even look forward to boasting of it to his friends. He felt no fear, no excitement. He knew he'd be a private by tonight, but he didn't care. They could send him to Leavenworth if they wanted. They could do anything. Even the thought of going back to S-1 caused him no consternation.

When they landed, Hart sent him to the flight line to wait. He found Hancock and Webster, their faces stubbly and dirty, their fatigues caked with dried mud, working in holey, oil-stained T-shirts. They seemed to have aged a year in the day he'd been gone.

In the afternoon he flew two missions, ate, and went to his tent. Captain Sloane came over at six. "Another mission, sir?"

"'fraid not, Morgan. Sounds like you really messed up yesterday. Sanders wants you at his tent. I don't know what he'll do. Try to play it cool, okay?"

"Yes, sir."

"I'll go with you."

Sloane pushed through the flaps of Sanders' tent. "Here he is, sir."

He faced Sanders and saluted. "Specialist Morgan reporting as ordered, sir."

"At ease, Morgan. What do you have to say for yourself?"

"Not much, sir. I did wrong, but I don't think those guns had to be cleaned right away. Besides, I crashed."

"I know it's rough, Morgan, but that's no excuse. Captain Sloane's told me that you're one of the best gunners in the platoon and that your guns always work perfectly. So we're going to let you off with no formal punishment. You'll get two nights' extra duty in the mess hall. Report to Sergeant Hart and he'll tell you what to do. Keep your nose clean from now on, because next time I'll throw the book at you. I know it's tough being short, but the only way we'll win this war is if everyone stays straight. Understood?"

"Yes, sir. Thank you, sir." He saluted Sanders and left the tent with Sloane. "Thanks a lot, sir." He tried to feel grateful, but only felt dull.

"It's okay, Morg. Why don't you cool the drinking? I don't want to fly with some no-time-in-grade PFC."

"Yes, sir. Thanks again."

Hart bellowed from the road by the gunners' tents, and

the platoon lined up before him. "You men are a disgrace! This is the sorriest bunch of soldiers I've ever seen. Morgan! Get in line with the rest."

He fell in between Hancock and Chambers.

"I go away for one day and come back to a shithouse. Look at yourselves. You're not men. You're pigs."

He nearly fell, rooting and oinking, at Hart's feet.

"Well, I'm not going to let you be pigs. No one's gonna say my platoon is sorry. From now on I want you in full uniform at all times. No more T-shirts or sunbathing. And starting tomorrow we'll have reveille every morning at five thirty and shaving inspection at seven. Anyone who misses reveille or hasn't shaved will spend the night scrubbing field stoves in the mess hall. Morgan'll start tonight because he couldn't conduct himself like a man when he got a couple hours off. I'll be waking everyone at five to get ready for reveille. That's all. Fall out. Morgan, report to the mess sergeant."

In three days Barry came back from the hospital in Nha Trang, claiming to have spent every night for the last week with a woman in a hotel bed, every day lolling on the beach. Talking to the gunners from the ship's doorway, he looked like a plantation owner addressing his field hands. His face and arms were deeply tanned, his fatigues clean and starchy. He seemed happy. The hollow-eyed gunners watched him dumbly, their fatigues wrinkled and splotched with grease, their faces sickly yellow as their tans faded beneath the monsoon clouds.

Every night Hancock and Webster drank at the other companies, returning late to the platoon area, where they woke everyone with loud cursing as they pulled out the pegs from Hart's boys' tent. Hart went after them, but could find no evidence that they'd exceeded their nightly allotment of two beers. When confronted by the sergeant, they said that they'd been sober for so long that just two cans made them drunk.

They kept the pressure off Morgan. He laid low, keeping

out of Hart's sight, hardly drinking at all. He knew that if he started now he wouldn't be able to stop. He felt an obligation to Captain Sloane, and he didn't want to go downhill.

Or he felt he shouldn't go downhill, but then again, why not? Why do anything—why not? He felt listless on the flights—even while firing—knowing they meant nothing. He had mastered the weapons system, and all the cleaning and loading and repairing now bored him. Even the thought of action, of experience, left him dulled. He knew it would never happen.

The nights made him nervous because of all the time to kill. He took showers, began stupid letters that he eventually tore up (what did he have to say anyway?), devoured news magazines that he immediately forgot, stared at the sexy pictures of Raquel Welch or Elke Sommer or Joey Heatherton in the *Stars and Stripes*, lost in visions of primitive lust.

He talked with Chambers, listened while he went over his plans for college, set long-range goals for his civilian life. That made him nervous too, nervous with thoughts of himself at home, free from the Army and having to choose something to do.

And he used to feel sorry for Chambers, for his hard life and lack of education. What a joke. Orville was so far ahead of him now that it wasn't even funny. He'd confronted the raw mass inside himself, had made sense of it, and was becoming a mature man. Sometimes, when Orville talked, Morgan's envy rose at his maturity, his sense of completeness. He wanted to snatch it away and keep it for himself. For the past two years Orville had been on a steadily ascending plane, while he had gone farther and farther down.

But how could he imitate him? Orville had had the experience in the world necessary for maturity, for curbing whatever silly impulses ran his life. He hadn't. He still felt as though he lived at the end of a burning fuse, waiting to explode. Perhaps he'd turn out to be a dud.

A week after his confrontation with Hart they flew cover for the rifle platoon in the mountains across the river from Bong Son. The chase ship guided the rifles while his swept along the ridge around the horseshoe of mountains, then reconned the edge of the valley floor.

"Sir! Sir!" Barry yelled as they came out at the northeast corner of the valley. "Two people running back there."

Sloane whirled and looked out the door. "Got 'em. They just dove in that big bush in the middle. See any weapons, Barry?"

"No, sir. Just the black pj's."

"They still might be armed. You see them, Morgan?"

"No, sir."

The ship swung around, bringing the bush into sight.

"Don't shoot yet," Sloane said. "We'll give it a couple of passes."

As they flew past the second time, Sloane asked, "You guys see anything?"

"No, sir," Barry said.

"I saw some leg, sir, but nothing else."

"Okay, Morgan. Fire on the ground by the bush. Maybe scare them out so we can take them alive."

"Yes, sir." He peppered the ground on two sides. No one emerged as the ship circled.

"Shit! They're not coming out, and it doesn't look like they're going to shoot back."

"We could go on the ground, sir."

"Forget it, Morgan. Then they probably would shoot."

"Maybe it's some kids."

"I don't think so. There's no village within five or six miles of here."

"They didn't look that small," Barry said.

"Mr. Woolsey, take it slow down to the south end of the valley, like we're going away, then whip it around and head back as fast as you can. Morgan, you fire straight in there, and maybe we'll get them on the run."

He restacked his bullets, braced his foot in the door, and leaned into the wind. The bush behind them stood alone and still.

Woolsey turned the ship so fast that he almost fell out. He stuffed the stock into his armpit and opened fire. The dirt kicked up in front of the bush, then the tracers went right in. They were two hundred yards away when someone ran out of the bush. He moved his gun a few inches to the right and the body went down.

"Cease firing!" Sloane yelled.

He relaxed his finger and the gun quit. His breath came fast. He'd actually hit someone.

"Jesus Christ!" Sloane said. "It's a fucking kid."

His stomach contracted and he leaned against the fire wall, looking helplessly at Barry.

"I'm sorry, Morgan," Sloane said. "It's my fault. At least he's not dead."

He looked down as they flew over the boy. He lay on his back, his mouth open in a silent scream of pain. Both his calves spurted blood.

"I'm sorry, sir."

"It's not your fault, Morgan. We're all to blame. I just hope the other one's okay."

He'd forgotten all about that. He wriggled in his seat, but what he'd done hung all around his body, allowing no escape.

Sloane called the medevac company at the field base and told them he was bringing in two wounded kids, then had Woolsey land by the boy. "Barry, you pick this one up. Morgan, go to the bush for the other one."

Somehow he quit thinking about what he might find. He leaned the machine gun against Woolsey's seat, unfastened his harness, and pulled off his armor vest. He unplugged his flight helmet and jumped out on the spongy ground.

Blood speckled the leaves inside the bush, and branches had been sliced away by his bullets. No one was there. A thin trail of blood ran out of the side, pointing toward the dense foliage a hundred yards away. At least the kid was alive. And probably moving pretty fast too. Relieved, he walked back to the ship.

Three days later, in the afternoon, they flew fifteen miles southwest to a wide flat plain, studded with small ridges. The ground looked rocky and hard, pale green with scrub grass—an unlikely place for the VC to hide. Farther west the green darkened in the dense jungle that ran into Happy Valley, melding with the blue sky at the horizon many miles away.

The kid looked as if he'd be all right. His shattered calf bone had been set, transfusions given, and he seemed to be enjoying the attention at the hospital. Barry took it harder than anyone, blaming himself for the whole thing.

Morgan had felt bad too, although no one in the platoon but Chambers seemed to mind. Most of them thought it was funny. At least the kid would be all right. He hoped the other hadn't crawled into the jungle and died.

He shivered and leaned forward to study the rocks at the base of the small spine they circled. A man came into his vision slowly, as though someone had focused a camera lens. His gun pointed straight up. He was going to shoot them.

Morgan squeezed the trigger on his machine gun and flipped a purple smoke grenade out the door. The tracers ricocheted around the rocks, lighting them up like a pinball machine. He thought the man went down, then the pylons blocked his vision.

"What's the matter?" Sloane asked.

"Man in the rocks. He had a gun. Smoke's out. I think I got him."

They went low over the rocks, seeing blood but no sign of the man.

"He's probably in a little cave or something," Sloane said. "Let's make a run head-on, then we'll go back in. One of you goes on the ground, you're liable to get shot."

They showered the mountainside with bullets and rockets, and each dropped a grenade as they crossed the ridge.

"That should keep him honest," Sloane said. "I think we can radio in one estimated kill."

Morgan drank with Hancock and Webster. For the next ten nights they made the rounds of the dingy tents at the other companies, where they filled sandbags with beer cans, dragged them to the flight line, and sat drinking and bitching in the dirt. He emptied the bullets from one of the boxes for his side guns, filled it with cans, and lay a belt of rounds on top of them for camouflage. He drank two every morning, another at lunch with half a joint. He didn't get hangovers. His skin turned mushy and his body felt sluggish as though it were filling up with pus. "I feel weak," he said one night, "but then I guess this is the only muscle I need." He flexed his trigger finger while Webster and Hancock roared.

He stayed away from Chambers as much as possible. They talked at dinner, joked during the day on the flight line. But at night he stayed out of the platoon area until he stumbled back to his tent near midnight. Chambers never said anything to him, but Morgan could feel judgment in his look.

A crew chief from Headquarters Company brought them bottles of Old Crow, which they kept buried on the flight line. He missed reveille once and spent a night in the mess hall scrubbing stoves. Combat activity had been restricted to shooting at campfires and searching old men along the road.

Chambers left for Hong Kong on the twenty-ninth, the day of a promotion board. Hart went up for E-7 again. The platoon had been given ten allocations for sergeant, but Hart had recommended only five men—two crew chiefs and his three lackey gunners. Neither Morgan, Hancock, Webster, nor Chambers had been mentioned.

On Halloween he came back from last-light recon after dark. He knew that Hancock had crashed again that afternoon, his ship falling fifty feet after a compressor stall by the fuel point in a near carbon copy of his last crash. He found the fat gunner sitting with Webster on a chopper skid, his left hand bandaged, his lower lip puffed.

"Fuck that motherfucker!" Hancock bellowed. "Morgan, can you believe this shit? Hart's not going to let me quit. Probably because he got passed over again. Fuck him. I ain't takin' but one more flight, and that's home. And I'll stay drunk too. Five crashes, and they won't take me off. Won't make me sergeant neither."

"Less than a month," Webster said, "we'll be out of here."

"And we ain't got no replacements. Morgan, I told the pilot he couldn't get that thing off the ground. We was barely pullin' five thousand RPM. I said, 'Sir, you can't fly this thing.' He said, 'No sweat. We'll just swing it around to the company pad.' Well, fuck him too. He damn near broke his back, and I'm glad of it. And that sorry-assed Hart won't let me quit."

Hancock drank and smoked and sputtered like a crazy man. He reminded Morgan of a bum he'd once followed through downtown L.A. In what must have been his last defense against the world, the man had given himself over completely to his rage and wandered the streets, directing a continuous stream of spit and curses at the sidewalk and the sky.

As the rain began to fall, Morgan quickly downed two beers, trying to plug in to Hancock's rage.

"I'll fly all the time," Hancock said. "I got enough Old Crow buried out here to keep me flyin'." He grabbed a stick and dug in the muddy surface of the flight line. "God damn it, Morgan, I know that Oscar Charlie's around here somewhere. Rain washed away my marking spot."

He nearly laughed. Hancock had probably marked it with an X.

"Gold!" Hancock brandished the bottle above his head. "I reckon we'll get drunk now."

In three hours they dumped the bottle and thirty empty

beer cans in the trash pit. They hadn't bothered to get out of the rain and were completely soaked. The monsoon had been so bad for the last week that all the platoon's bunkers had caved in. Even the huge one behind Hart's tent, reinforced with artillery canisters, had given way and was now nothing but a six-foot pit of water.

A candle flickered in the tent where Hart's boys—now sergeants—slept. Webster had to hold Hancock back from bombing it with a sandbag.

Morgan bent near the flap to listen.

"I got me a woman and a kid today," Alred said.

"That's all good!" Hancock bellowed. "But fuck you, Alred!" He kicked out a peg and the tent sagged.

Alred's head appeared between the flaps. "Cut that out! What are you doing, Morgan?"

He almost kicked Alred in the face. "What if it had been your mother, Alred?"

"What?"

"I said what if it had been your mother?"

"What are you talking about?"

"I asked you what if it had been your mother, you cheese-eating motherfucker!"

"You're lookin' to get your back busted, Morgan."

Webster moved in front of him. "Step out, then, you sorry sack of shit."

"All of you step out," Hancock said. "We'll take you on right now. I ain't afraid. I'll take all three of you myself, sergeants or no sergeants."

"Go to bed!" Alred yelled. "Before I report you."

"Report my ass," Hancock said. "I'm gettin' out anyway."

"Come on," Webster said. "Let's hit the fart sack. These lily-assed clowns ain't gonna do anything."

Morgan smiled at Webster, hit by a sudden idea. "I'm gonna tear Hart's tent down. He's driving Hancock crazy."

"Don't get yourself in trouble, man."

"I don't give a shit anymore." He ran for Hart's tent. He'd

dive on the top and collapse the whole thing. "Fuck all the cheese-ass sergeants in this platoon!" He ran into the pit of water behind the tent.

When he came up, Hart stood at the edge, laughing. "What the hell are you doing, Morgan?"

"Trick or treat, Sarge. Money or eats." He tried to grab Hart's foot, but only floundered in the muddy water.

"Are you drunk?"

"I'm taking a dip. What's it look like?" Seeing Hart had almost made him sober.

"Get out of that pool and go to bed. You got extra duty tomorrow night. You're really pushing it, Morgan. Keep it up and I'll send you home a private."

"At least I'm going home," he muttered.

"What was that?"

"Nothing! I'm going to bed."

He lay on his sleeping bag, cold sober. If Hancock and Webster hadn't been there, he would have cried. Only a few weeks left. Before long he'd be going in to clear post. But he'd just gotten here. No. He'd been here all his life. He wanted to go home, be free from all the stupid sergeants and officers. But he couldn't without the experience he'd come for. It had to be more than this. Getting drunk, shooting at people he couldn't see. Shooting kids. There had to be some moment when he would know he'd had enough.

23

CHAMBERS SAT on a sandbag in front of his tent, absorbing the twilight, relishing this quiet time of day when the flying was finished and the drunkenness had not yet begun. People rustling their letters and popping their cans of beer. The long, olive-drab barrels of the 175's rose slowly near the west end of the perimeter, recoiled violently, spitting orange flames and sending small puffs of smoke into the air, then glided down to their normal position. Just like giant pricks. Up. Shoot. Down. The sound of the explosion and vibration of the ground reached him a second later, and several seconds after that the dull concussion of the projectiles exploding several miles away floated into the camp. The aftersilence was nearly physical, as though the world were the inside of a drum beaten by no one. Like the cathedrals in Europe when they were almost empty. He wanted to rest his cheek against a cool stone pillar.

Webster suddenly plopped down beside him. "What's shakin', Chambers? Dip the old wick in Hong Kong?"

"Hi, Web. A little bit. Till I got rolled."

"Old whore got to you, huh?"

"British officer's daughter."

"You're shitting me."

"No, I'm not." He'd met the girl his first day after taking the tram up Victoria Peak. She seemed gentle, almost refined, and even talked with him about architecture during the days. At night she got wild with drinking and screwing, but always went home at midnight. On the third night she went home with his money while he showered. "I don't know why. I'm sure she didn't need it."

"She take every cent you had?"

"I'd left twenty in my shoe she didn't get."

"At least she was a round-eye," Webster said. "Looks like they made it in okay."

The lights flashed on Morgan's ship as it swung around the hill, the rotor blades popping like little farts.

"You coming out to the flight line?" Webster asked. "That's where we're drinking now."

"Maybe later. You guys been drunk a lot?"

"Not enough." Webster spread his arms. "Getting short, Chambers. You know how it is."

The tiredness washed over him as he watched Webster trudge toward the helipad. Not too much longer. No more than twenty days in the field. Christ, but Webster looked filthy. Chambers glanced at his fingernails, expecting to find them filled with instant grime. He'd arrived back at base camp this morning, then flown up to the field base an hour ago. Everyone looked dirty and crusty and half insane. He could feel it creeping over him too, as though being back triggered a gland that caused filth to grow in his pores. After the girl had rolled him, he'd spent a lot of time in the shower. Three times a day for at least an hour. Steaming hot until all the crap was boiled out, then ice cold to stop the sweat. He'd take the ferry across the teeming harbor, ride buses, then go up to Victoria Peak on the tram. He'd wander on the flowery paths overlooking the ocean and the harbor, reveling in thoughts of his approaching civilian life. He'd been able to sleep ten hours a night, and he felt rested now, ready to do his time standing on his head if they'd let him alone.

A week ago he and Morgan had received their orders, his for Fort Hood, Texas, Morgan's for Benning in Georgia. But no word had come on replacements, and the gunners couldn't leave the field until the new guys arrived and were trained. He'd do his time without a fuss. Between flying and the infantry, he'd have to take the air. If he made trouble, they'd surely find a way to fuck him.

He sat on the sandbags for the rest of the night, feeling too inert—too peaceful—to make the trip to the flight line. The clown show came to him eventually, reminding him of Brueghel's "Parable of the Blind," everyone stopping to inquire about R&R drinkandpussy before stumbling off to his lopsided tent and sandy sleeping bag. Morgan, Hancock, and Webster came last, cursing out Alred before collapsing in the dirt at Chambers' feet to tell the war stories of the last six days.

As they began, Chambers immediately lit a reefer. Is this what cavemen were like? Sitting around the beer cans as they would around a fire roasting meat, grunting, farting, scratching, and belching as they told the story of the day's hunt? It might be interesting, except it was so goddamn tiresome.

They crawled off to their tent in half an hour, leaving him to stare at the hazy sky, the faint pinpoint lights of the dim stars. A huge neon corona circled the moon. He flinched as the 175's boomed. McCutcheon moaned in his sleep, then everything went quiet. The air cooled. He was sick of all the people and glad they'd gone to bed.

Inside the tent he lay on his belly and unscrewed the top of the artillery canister that McCutcheon had buried in the sand and kept full of ice and cold cans. He took a beer outside, sat down again, and lit a cigar. A breeze had come up, and the moon raced eastward through the remaining wisps and puffs of clouds.

The breeze reminded him of Phan Thiet, the only thing about this place that did. Why was everyone so dirty? Morgan looked as if he hadn't showered in a week. Everyone in the platoon laughed more, but in a tense and nervous way, as if he'd lost the ability to even pretend to sanity.

He forced his cigar butt through the opening in the beer can. It hissed and died in the residue of foam. He crawled into his sleeping bag and put his hands behind his head. The 175's blasted off another salvo, and it seemed like an hour before the little pops of the explosions miles away drifted into his tent. Footsteps sounded on the road outside.

"Chambers, help me." The voice was muffled as though choking on something. "Help! Help!"

He slid out of his bag and pushed through the mosquito net into the night air. "Oh, Jesus!"

Maddin stood in front of the tent, the muzzle of a forty-five gleaming in his mouth. The hammer was back. Maddin's fingers played nervously around the trigger guard.

"Maddin, give me that thing."

"I have to do it. Pull the trigger for me. I can't do it myself."

He batted Maddin's hand away. He took the pistol around the trigger guard and yanked it back. Maddin bit down, and the barrel scraped eerily along his teeth.

"Give it back, Chambers."

He eased the hammer forward, released the clip, then cocked the gun, catching the ejected bullet in his hand. "What's the matter?"

"Gimme the gun." Tears glowed on Maddin's face in the moonlight.

"You don't want to do that." He tried to sound calm. "What's wrong?"

"My wife. She's fucking everything that walks. And she just had a baby nine months ago." Maddin sat down on the sandbags and bawled like a small boy. "She's been doing it ever since I got here."

He sat down next to him and put his hand on his shoulder. "Have you talked to the chaplain or the Red Cross?"

"I've never told anyone."

"Red Cross might send you home. I knew a guy in Germany the same thing happened to. They gave him a permanent change of station It's not your fault. Don't be so hard on yourself."

Maddin cried for five minutes, saying nothing. Then he talked for an hour, showing pictures of his wife and baby, of the house trailer they lived in by Fort Knox. He had a recent clipping from a Louisville newspaper that might result in a warrant for his arrest. His wife had got hold of some credit cards and spent nine thousand dollars. The furniture and appliances could be returned, but she'd also blown a lot in restaurants and had taken two trips to Miami with boyfriends.

Maddin finished his tale, his face sagging with exhaustion. The smell of stale whiskey from his mouth was nearly unbearable. "I figured there was nothing left to do but chamber a round and blow my brains out."

"That wouldn't help anything."

"It'd get me out of this mess."

Chambers almost agreed with him. "Why don't you get some sleep and talk with the chaplain in the morning?"

"Okay, Chambers. Don't tell anyone, okay?"

"Sure."

"I'll take the gun back now."

"I'll hang onto it till morning. Got any more whiskey?"

"You want some?"

"Let's pour it out."

"You can have it if you want. Stuff fucks my head up."

He brought the bottle back to his tent and took two long swallows before pouring the rest in the sand. He laid the bottle softly on top of the garbage can by Hart's tent.

Three days later Chambers' Huey B model helicopter was replaced by a new 540 model. The 540 had a shorter, wider rotor blade and held more fuel. Prettier, too. No nicks in the paint—not even on the skids. The old bird showed more silver and rust than olive drab, and the inside had been a stark shell without the slightest comfort. The 540 was nearly plush. Soft gray lining covered the fire wall and ceiling, and the shiny, bright-red vinyl seat shamed the torn and oil-stained one on the B model.

The new ship didn't have any side guns or rocket pods. The grenade launcher fastened to the front looked so much like a big cunt with a cock sticking out of it that all the gunners gathered around it and laughed and pointed and humped the air for half an hour. It hung beneath the nose assembly where the radios were housed, a half sphere with a slit about an inch wide running down the middle. Wire bristles lined each side of the slit. The barrel protruded from the slit and could be worked up and down, in and out, from the sight above the pilot's seat. A trough of linked grenades stood in the middle of the cabin floor, behind the console. The chute to the launcher ran over the console and to one side underneath the instrument panel and down into the gun.

It jammed all eight times they tried it the next two days. After every mission confabs were held around the launcher, the armorers disassembling, cleaning, and reassembling the complex parts inside the ball. The next day Chambers found a hunk of metal wedged in the chute that was hanging up the belt of grenades. On last-light recon that night Sanders dumped close to a hundred grenades into the trees on the side of a mountain, and Chambers reloaded as they flew. It was less hassle than loading the boxes for the side guns, and he didn't have to lug as much crap when they got to the ammo point.

After the flight Hart gave him a letter from his mother, the first serious one since he'd replied to his father's rage. He'd had a couple of trivial notes, but no mention had been made of what he'd said. In this one she actually apologized for his father's anger, saying he didn't mean it. Bullshit! He meant exactly what he said. But they were both relieved now that he was out of combat. She felt it was good that people did their part for the country, but he'd done his, and there wasn't any shame in not being on the front lines all the time. They were so happy that he was going back to college and that he would be home for Christmas. Too bad he couldn't be back for the nice fall colors. She was putting up lots of his favorite jams and jellies. She'd run into Elaine Banks at Neustadt's store and Elaine had just had a son.

He wondered who fathered Elaine's baby. Her asshole husband, no doubt. She wouldn't mess around. Except with old Orville. Yes, sir! And nearly get his ass killed. She'd married Tom Banks a year after the abortion, when she knew Orville would never be ready. Tom Banks had a good job in Minneapolis, wasn't shit otherwise, but she just said, "Orville, you'll never be ready," and that finished it. Until she called him two years after her marriage and met him by the lake on a spring night after Tom had passed out drunk. But when she came in at three in the morning, he woke up and beat her into confession. The next day she called again and said Tom had his gun out and would try to get him that night. And she even called when he came home from basic two months later and he hung up and finished it again. She'd better leave him alone when he got home this time.

At least his parents were taken care of for the time being. Now all he'd have to do was get himself killed. Not much chance of that. He knew of only one gunner who'd been shot to death while flying, and although the ship could always crash, the chances of that were pretty remote, especially with the new helicopter. McCutcheon was crewing again now that Maddin had gone home on emergency leave. He was a good crew chief and wouldn't screw things up.

He felt calm when he went to see Morgan and the others, even better after a couple of beers. But when he lay down, uneasiness crept over him like a fat, slow snake. His father knew he lied, knew he was trying to sleep before another day's flying, another day's possible death or killing.

The accusing, outraged face stayed with him during sleep, and he kept seeing flashes of it the next day during his first two missions. The sky was neutral, Fulda gray. He usually got some satisfaction from that. Comfortable, sobering. But today it made him edgy. He wanted either brightness or rain.

The infantry battalions were working Happy Valley now, and C Company's rifle platoon reconned the dense foothills just east of the valley, going through hooches hidden in the foliage and searching hamlets on the small valley floors.

Sanders had Eastman break off from the rifle platoon so he could fire the grenade launcher again. The chase ship took over the rifles, and Eastman flew down till the chopper skimmed the treetops where the jungle met the scrub grass and bushes on the valley floor.

"Better pull it up to a hundred and fifty feet," Sanders said. "We don't want to catch any of this shrapnel."

Two or three hundred yards from the tree line a hamlet sat out in the middle of the valley. Shaded by coconut palms, its light-brown huts resembled the toy dwellings where the kids played behind the Fort Knox dependent area. The hamlet looked deserted now, and no one worked in the valley—no telling where the people were.

He jumped as McCutcheon's machine gun went off, clattering casings against his helmet.

"You see him, sir?" McCutcheon said.

"Right. Ran in the tree line. We'll get him out."

"This one's mine, sir."

"Wait'll we see what's up there. Did you just see one?"

"Yes, sir."

"You see him, Chambers?"

"No, sir."

"Okay, we're going to circle the area until we get him in sight again. No one fire unless I give the word."

They dipped down on the treetops and circled twice and no one saw anything. As Eastman banked the ship out over the valley, something moved in the trees. Chambers pushed the mike button, but Eastman broke in ahead of him.

"Got him, sir." Eastman completed the turn and pointed the chopper at the woods. "Right at twelve o'clock."

"I see him," Sanders said. "Hold your fire back there. I want this one myself."

They flew over once more. Their enemy wasn't more than twelve years old. He hugged a tree with both hands, staring dumbly at the helicopter. Sanders already had the sight down for the grenade launcher and sat stiffly in his seat, rotating the sight up and down and peering through the glass.

"He's just a kid."

"How do you know, Chambers?" Sanders snapped.

"I could tell by looking at him. Anybody could. He didn't have a weapon either."

"You just didn't *see* any weapon. I'm surprised at you, Chambers. They start these VC young. You've been around long enough to know that. He may be alerting others in the trees."

"He was probably playing and got curious about the choppers."

"He should know better. He ran, didn't he?"

"Yes, but—"

"That's enough, Chambers. If it runs, you kill it. You know that. They start their whores at twelve, and the soldiers ain't much older."

Chambers released the mike button and slumped back against the fire wall. The muted chunk-chunk-chunk of the grenades being fired started immediately, and within ten seconds the little poppings started up from the ground. He didn't look. He hoped that Sanders would be as bad a shot as usual.

The chunking stopped as the ship began to circle.

"Hurry up, Eastman!" Sanders said. "We got him in the open."

He couldn't help looking now. The boy, weaponless, his black pajamas flapping wildly, made a dead run for the hamlet. Sanders fired before the chopper completed its circle, sending grenades flying haphazardly onto the valley floor, where they exploded in dark-gray puffs.

He could jam the box of grenades. He turned inside the ship but McCutcheon's hand rested on the thin metal box top as he looked intently out the front window. No way! He turned into the wind again, catching a faint odor of exploded grenades.

The boy was about a hundred and fifty yeards from the hamlet when a grenade went off a few yards behind him. He pitched forward, then the smoke of another explosion hid him. Chambers bent over and bit down on his thumb.

"Looks like you got him, sir," Eastman said.

"Circle around again. I want to make sure. This'll be my first confirmed kill."

Chambers looked around the ship for something to focus on to keep his eyes off the ground.

"Deader than a doornail, sir," Eastman said. "Even if he was alive, he couldn't move too good. Looks like you about took him off at the waist."

"One more circle. I'll put a few more on him just to make sure."

"Roger, sir."

A metal lining, filled with holes, ran between the ceiling and the gray cloth cover of the ship's interior. He unsnapped the cloth to check where the elastic cord for his machine gun hung from one of the holes and discovered that the lining was already bent. When the chunking started again, he reached up with his left hand to adjust the cord and accidentally squeezed off a few rounds. He jumped and released his finger. He took his right hand off the trigger housing, and the gun, held only by the cord, blew lazily off his thigh a few inches and dangled in the wind.

"Go ahead and get you a few licks, Chambers," Sanders said.

He pulled the gun back in and settled it across his lap. He looked up and Sanders grinned at him, his wart glowing like a bright-red Christmas light. He'd never seen Sanders smile before.

The helicopter lifted off the oil-soaked sand into the graying morning sky and headed west. Chambers watched the first-light crews from A and B companies getting ready for takeoff, then turned back for a look at the C Company gunners and crew chiefs shaving outside their tents. As the ship gathered speed, he faced front, hunching over to shield himself from the first-light chill. It had rained all yesterday, but today looked as if it would be sunny.

As they passed over the hamlet at the west end of the camp, he hung his machine gun and clipped in a belt of rounds. His movements were weary; the gun felt as though it weighed a hundred pounds. Three actionless days had drizzled away since Sanders had killed the kid. Orville didn't know if he could shoot back anymore. He'd been having trouble enough pulling the trigger when they prepped for the rifle platoon, and even then the idea that he might hit someone made him cringe. He thought he'd be able, if faced by someone on the attack, to fire and kill, but sometimes he even doubted that. It was as though the ship now had a debt to pay, even if it meant getting shot down.

Weird, the thoughts that floated through his head, the variety of moods he floated through. Sometimes he found himself tallying lists of wrongs in his mind, petitioning Senators like some earnest political theorist on the evils of the war, its total lack of respect for human beings. Before, he had thought mainly of himself, of not wanting to be in a position where he did stupid or unnecessary things. He didn't want to be killed, nor did he want to kill for sport.

Sport was where his speculations led him. The war was sport, the helicopters a new offense the coach needed to test, Vietnam a place to test it, where, even if it failed, the old plays could be used again to assure triumph. The country was a field that no one would regret chewing up; the people were insignificant—bush-league players whose loss would be felt by no one. And the coaches had their own eager young players who swallowed without question the platitudes about the importance of the game.

At times he drifted into the role of spectator, viewing events as if they could only be part of a movie or a television comedy, not real things in which he participated. Yesterday twenty people from a hamlet were nearly blown to bits by two jettisoned rocket pods that had been dynamited in a ditch by a demolition team. The pods had been rigged with a short fuse, the demolition helicopter pulled pitch, and the people ran furiously for the ditch. Luckily the pods blew before they got there.

Chambers thumped his flight helmet with the palm of his hand, trying to drive from his head the spastic images of the scurrying frantic people, trying to stifle his disdain for the peasants' lust over the tiniest bauble of American trash. He imagined them, long after the war was over, worshiping before some smashed rusty aircraft hulk as though it were Buddha himself.

"Still smokin', sir," Eastman said as the chopper skimmed a ridge and floated out above a small valley. A hamlet, discovered yesterday by the rifle platoon, smoldered on the valley floor. No one had been there when the rifles arrived, but one hooch had been full of rice, so the entire hamlet was grenaded and burned. The roofs of all the hooches were gone, some walls completely demolished while others gaped with large holes made by the boots of the infantrymen. Jungle surrounded the hamlet on all four sides.

The man stood directly in the center of the charred, smoking buildings. In black pajamas, his black hair plastered to his head, he stared at the ship for a moment before raising the thirty-caliber rifle he held in his right hand.

"God, shoot him!" Sanders screamed, pulling down the infinity sight. McCutcheon's machine gun went off as Sanders began firing grenades. The tracers hit to the left of the man, while the grenades exploded fifty yards behind him, knocking down the walls of a roofless hooch.

Chambers couldn't take his eyes off him. The man stood his ground, squeezing off rounds as the helpless ship flew over him.

"Four-five, this is Red. Get that man!"

"Got him in sight, Red."

They banked to the right as the other gunship let go with rockets and machine guns. The man whirled, ducked behind a wall, then sprinted to the southern edge of the hamlet, disappearing, a black flash in the green. For a moment Chambers expected the ship to crash, but they apparently hadn't been hit.

"Okay, Four-five," Sanders said. "Let's saturate those trees with everything we've got."

"Roger that, Red."

Each ship made three more runs, expending its entire load

of bullets, rockets, and grenades. Sanders called back to the base, and another team was on its way. Artillery would be called in in the meantime.

At ten o'clock Chambers' team of two helicopters went out again—to the same hamlet. The man had made brief appearances for each of the two teams that had since been there, squeezing off a few rounds before darting into the bushes. His aim was as bad as the Americans', and so far no one had been hit.

Eastman circled the hamlet while Sanders pumped a steady stream of grenades into the jungle. Chambers fired, but managed to get most of his bullets inside the tree line, into the thick grass that separated hamlet from jungle. Webster's ship followed theirs, dumping its rockets a pair at a time, lighting up the dark greenery with the tracers from six machine guns.

"I reckon that took care of him, Four-five," Sanders said.

"Hope so, Red. Grenades lookin' good."

Their ammunition spent, the ships rose and circled lazily, waiting for the new team.

"God damn it, sir!" Eastman said. "There the bastard is again."

Chambers whirled as the black-pajamaed body detached itself from the jungle cover and stood up next to a wall that seemed to be part of nothing.

"Holy Christ!" Sanders said. "And we're out of fuckin' ammo."

The man's barrel flashed three times, then he held his weapon in the air before turning and scurrying back among the trees.

"Let me go after him, sir," McCutcheon said.

"Forget that. I'm gonna get the whole rifle platoon out here to chase his sorry ass."

The new team arrived, and they flew back to the field base. The officers hurried away to the operations tent as Chambers began reloading.

At chow the talk was only of the man. He had earned everyone's respect, was almost a hero, but one who had to be killed. He seemed to excite the imagination like some Jesse James or Billy the Kid whose daring caused envy and admiration in those whose great satisfaction would be to kill him. For Chambers the man assumed heroic proportions. He hoped he was indestructible.

McCutcheon was the last crewman to chow. He'd been up to operations and heard all the plans. The hamlet was being bombarded with artillery once again, with napalm to follow before the rifle platoon went in. "We're gonna bring some smoke on that fucker, boy."

Chambers' ship went out again at one thirty. In the jungle just outside the hamlet deep holes smoldered from napalm at the four points of the compass. Smaller holes and twisted vegetation appeared randomly about the rubbled hooches. The rifle platoon had been on the ground forty-five minutes, had been fired on twice, the man appearing each time at the opposite end of the hamlet from where they were. No one had been hit.

Chambers' last mission of the day covered the extraction of the rifles at five thirty. They still had not found the harassing mosquito of a man. Chambers watched as the angry troops piled on the lift ships. A perfect opportunity for the man to spring from the bushes and kill three or four. But he didn't. The lift birds rose, speeding toward the field base while the gunships went round once again. The hamlet was completely leveled, the surrounding jungle a tangled mess. Once again they fired all their bullets and grenades, and the trail ship dropped its entire load. They circled a last time, then headed up and away. The B-52's would saturate the area tonight. Chambers looked back as the man, standing again in the center of the hamlet, raised his rifle and fired a parting shot. Chambers stuck his hand out the door, thumb up.

As the ship flew back to the field base, he began to tally up.

No lives had been lost, no men wounded, no helicopters shot down. His ship had fired at least six hundred grenades. He didn't know how much they cost. Even at five bucks a throw that was three thousand dollars. Add ten thousand machine-gun rounds at twelve cents each, and you were up to forty-two hundred dollars. Throw in gas and oil and salaries and wear and tear, and they'd easily used up five thousand dollars' worth today. He chuckled as he continued playing his game. Webster's ship had fired fifty-six rockets at sixty bucks apiece for thirty-three hundred and sixty dollars. Probably twenty thousand rounds from the machine guns for twenty-four hundred dollars. Add grenades, gas, and the rest of it, and you had a good sixty-five hundred. So eleven thousand five hundred between them. Add the other three pairs of gunships like Webster's, and you got a combined total, conservative estimate, of fifty thousand five hundred dollars, not counting postage and handling. The B-52's would surely push it over a hundred—making the man worth more than Willie Mays—and yet he knew, come morning, the man would be dancing on his pile of rubble after expending probably four dollars' worth of thirty-caliber shells. Even the dumb gorilla, watching the show from his grandstand seat, would be forced to turn away in disbelief and run deeper and deeper into the jungle, as far as he could go.

24

FUNNY NOW that a voice would start talking to him. Insistent. Every word enunciated perfectly. "WILLARD

MORGAN, YOU KNOW YOU'RE NOT GOING TO MAKE IT OUT OF HERE ALIVE." Coming the last few mornings as he pulled himself from his drunken sleep. The voice would rise from his brain, reverberate in some hollow portion of his skull, and sink back again. Fear, no doubt, because in only five days he should be on his way back to the world, although that seemed too crazy to think about. Standing on the street; social drinking in easy chairs. No. It made more sense to die now. Or the plane crashing on the California coast. Here I am, motherfucker. Maybe old Norma Bredon would be free. Nice. Soft, tan skin, light smell of perfume, silk nightie sliding over that round ass. Not here in the chopper, for Christ's sake. Lean out the door and put some wind on it, make it go down. It was getting so bad he could nearly come by thinking.

Sometimes the wind blew everything away, especially when flying lead like this on first-light recon. Closer and closer to the ground. Maybe they'd fly out over the sea and skim along the water. At least first light got him away from Hart and his silly shaving inspection. As though a clean face would win the war. Asshole sitting in his tent all day reading cock books and drinking rye.

They flew over a coconut grove and stretch of beach. Four mornings ago twenty dead VC were strewn on the sand, killed by an infantry bivouac they'd tried to assault. Water buffalo lay dead all around them, rigor mortis making their legs stick grotesquely into the air. Barry couldn't handle looking at it. He'd thrown up all over his boots while filling the ship's gas tank. Morgan was glad they were making him line chief when McCutcheon left.

"Hey, Morg," Captain Sloane said, "want to test-fire the guns over the water?"

"Roger, sir." Why not? Nice, the way they plunk up water, sometimes the tracers bouncing up. Orange skipping over blue; evaporating color.

"Four-two, this is Four-one, over," Sloane said.

"This is Four-two."

"Four-two, we're going to test-fire about a quarter mile out. You can follow if you want."

"Will do."

"Okay, Morgan and Barry," Sloane said. "Let's not hit any sampans. Just shoot straight down."

Pretty the way the oil burned off the barrels when the guns started. All six worked perfectly. Two or three tracers ricocheted off the water, burning out as they climbed the sky. He rested his machine gun against Woolsey's seat and picked up his M-16. The side guns stopped and he fired a clip from the automatic rifle. He wondered if the tracers kept burning when they got inside someone.

Woolsey pulled the helicopter up to the left. Morgan rested the machine gun on his lap again, gazing out the door as the other ship fired.

"Four-two, this is Four-one. Let's go up the coast a couple more miles, then we'll take it back in."

"Roger. We're right behind you."

He felt better and better as the ship sailed past the big rocks and hills that rose up from the shore. He'd managed to get down some breakfast this morning, and his stomach didn't feel so jumpy. He flipped the intercom to private so the pilots couldn't hear. "Five days, Barry."

"Well, I wish they'd get a replacement for you," Barry said. "You're happy as a pig in shit this morning. Still drunk from last night?"

"Just feeling good, that's all. Monsoon quit and the sun came out. Cool breeze blowing through the ship."

"Maybe you better keep your eyes on the ground. It was right about here Sanders took that fifty caliber through the window."

"Okay, man. I'll dig you later." He shuffled his feet in a little dance. Christ, he felt invincible. If he was going to get it, he should have gotten it by now. Maybe it was just luck after all. He'd always had plenty of that, or at least believed he did.

The voice didn't have him that scared. And he was never afraid when the shooting started. Finally an end to bullshit talk and lies. He'd almost welcomed it, that clear exhilaration of jeopardy.

"Let's take it back in," Sloane said.

"Might as well." Woolsey turned the ship west.

They hadn't even been out an hour yet, and he wouldn't mind staying out for another. Maybe he'd write Norma a letter when he got back in. Hell with that. He couldn't write worth a shit anymore. He'd get a little drunk and go see her as a surprise. She'd feel sorry for him, want to mother him. Maybe he'd get an early out and go to Berkeley in March instead of waiting till September—too far gone by then. He'd have two months at Fort Benning when he got off his leave, then out. Maybe he'd go to Mexico or to see Chambers in Minnesota. At least he'd be home for Christmas and have the money for a car.

"Four-one, this is Three," came over the radio. "How much fuel do you have left?"

"About five hundred pounds, Three."

"Roger, Four-one. That Special Forces camp about two miles north of the marketplace on Highway One is taking fire from the adjacent village. Go check it out. You can tune them in on your UH up one point six seven from this push. Their discretion on firing."

"Roger, out, Three." Sloane flipped a knob on the console. "You hear that, Four-two?"

"That's affirmative, Four-one."

"Let's head on up there, then."

The fucking Green Berets were always calling on them when they got into trouble. They might be tough, but he'd never seen them do anything but drink beer and test AK weapons on the rifle range. Well, they didn't have enough fuel to stay out long.

Woolsey banked the helicopter to the right, turning north as they crossed Highway 1. Tall palm trees flanked the road near the marketplace, where Vietnamese in black and white pajamas moved in and out from under the thatched roofs of several small huts. From both directions they converged on the road toward the marketplace, mostly women, carrying baskets on their heads or poles over their shoulders with bundles hooked on either end. Old men on bicycles wobbled down the highway, and an occasional motorbike raced by, flashing chrome and bright colors. North of the huts several children ran around a jeep, pointing and laughing at the MP's who lounged in it. One of the children crawled over the spare tire in the back and pinched an MP on the arm. The MP tried to swat the child, but he was out of the jeep and laughing by the time the arm came around.

Just like an old horse switching at flies. Fucking MP was probably tired from laying up with some whore all night while the rest of the troops had to stay on the base. And they'd report you sure as shit if they caught you downtown after six. He couldn't wait to clear post and go down to Sin City again. All of them would be going in together—him and Chambers and Hancock and Webster. Hell with the money too. When he got to Oakland, he'd only need a dime.

"This is Noble Rider Four-one. This is Noble Rider Four-one. Do you read me? Over."

"Noble Rider Four-one, this is Jungle Master Six. Read you loud and clear. How do you read me? Over."

"Lima Charlie, Jungle Master Six. What's the situation?"

The Special Forces camp looked like a cache for sandbags inside barbed wire. A few small huts with aluminum roofs, but the compound was mainly bunkers covered with layers of sandbags. Across a clearing, about a hundred yards north of the camp, stood a small hamlet of fifteen mud hooches, some shaded by palm trees, others blending with the tan ground around them. No sign of life.

"This is Jungle Master Six. We've taken fire from a hooch in that hamlet. I think they got a BAR and a machine gun. Can't figure out which hooch. You want to see if you can draw them out?"

"Roger, Six. Four-two, this is Four-one. We're going down on the deck and try to rouse these birds. You circle the hamlet and see if you can see anything."

"Roger, Four-one."

"I'll take it," Sloane said to Woolsey, putting his hand around the cyclic stick. "You take it if we get shot at so I can work these guns. Morgan and Barry, keep your eyes peeled and don't shoot till you're fired at unless you see VC with guns."

Sloane flew the helicopter back to the highway and banked it high to the right. For a moment the ship hung suspended—like a hawk poised to swoop for mice—then gradually fell back and around, gathering speed, until it headed directly at the hamlet.

Morgan braced his left foot against the doorjamb and leaned into the wind. Sloane completed the first pass and repeated the banking movement above a tree line past the west end of the village. White flash, then a long-haired woman ran from one hooch to another. "Sir, I just spotted a woman, and she wasn't carrying a BAR."

"I saw her, Morgan. Probably looking for a place to hide."

He looked over at Barry and shrugged. Barry grinned feebly, shook his head, and looked back out the door.

"Jungle Master Six, this is Four-one. We haven't seen anything but a woman going from one hooch to another, over."

"Roger, Four-one. Probably humping ammo for the others. Look, I got a Vietnamese interpreter down here who thinks he can spot the hooch. Why don't you take him up with you?"

"Roger, Six. Four-two, pick up that interpreter. We'll make passes and keep you covered."

"Roger, Four-one."

What the hell were they doing? How would the interpreter know a damn thing unless he'd been laid up in there the night before? He probably had. No sweat anyway. Only three hundred pounds of fuel left. Christ, why couldn't they just send a couple of scouts in on the ground?

"He see anything yet, Four-two?" Sloane said.

"Negative, Four-one. He seems more confused than us."

"Jungle Master Six, this is Noble Rider Four-one. That interpreter doesn't know which hooch it is, over."

"Roger, Four-one. Well, uh, maybe you ought to . . . no, what the hell. Why don't you make a couple gun runs over the whole hamlet? Try to get some in each hooch. You ought to smoke them out that way. Over."

"This is Four-one. You want me to fire at every hooch? There may be—"

"Roger, Four-one. You read me right. Every hooch. These people been helping Victor Charlie too long. Probably everybody's at market but them with guns and ammo. Make the runs from southeast to northwest. That'll probably be the safest. Out."

"Six, this is Four-one. But—"

"You heard me, Four-one. Southeast to northwest. I can't afford to lose any men because of some VC in a village. Out!"

"Roger, Six. Out!" Sloane flipped the radio switch. "Well, Four-two, you heard him. You follow me. Christ, if he wants it, let's give him the whole damn show—guns, rockets, the works."

"Roger, Four-one."

Maybe he'd read about this one in the *Stars and Stripes*. "Friendly village destroyed by accident." Fuck the lazy lard-ass Special Forces. He hung a fragmentation grenade on the carrying handle of his machine gun. He knew Sloane didn't want to do it, but probably didn't care that much. Neither did he. Experience, after all.

"Okay, Morgan and Barry," Sloane said. "You heard the man. He's a major and I'm only a captain, but I'm not telling you anything. I don't see any pigs down there, Morgan, do you?"

"No, sir." No pigs like they'd shot on last light a few nights ago. Just a woman. He wished it was Hart and the Special Forces major. Let them taste hot licks.

"Okay, Four-two, we're going in."

"Behind you, Four-one."

Woolsey couldn't bank as well as Sloane; probably nervous. The ship nearly stopped at the top of the bank, framing the village in the side door, then dropped suddenly, like an elevator.

When he fired, he realized he didn't have a target. Sloane twisted the infinity sight so that the side guns sprayed bullets all over. Morgan shot the ground, then raked the tracers across the roof of a hooch. Two rockets tore out of the pod beneath the side guns. He threw the frag grenade, then followed it with white phosphorus. He pulled more bullets out of the box on the floor, firing the machine gun with his right hand.

They crossed over the last hooch; Woolsey banked above a tree line on the west side of the hamlet.

"See anything?" Sloane asked.

"Nothing," Barry said.

"Morgan?"

"Lotta smoke, sir."

Woolsey laughed. "Hey, Morgan, you see that bird you hit?"

"What?"

"Guess it flew in front of your gun. You didn't see it?"

"No, sir."

"I saw it out of the corner of my eye. You must have hit it right in the chest because it just exploded into a puff of feathers. Looked funny as hell."

The other ship pulled up over the tree line. The smoke was so thick that Morgan could barely see any of the hooches in the village.

"You see anything, Four-two?"

"About ten chickens ran out of one hooch, Four-one. Didn't look too dangerous."

"Roger, Four-two. Let's hit it one more time, then you can drop that interpreter and we can deedee out of here."

Morgan was still breathing hard from the first run when they began the second. The more he thought about the bird, the more absurd it seemed, and he felt his mouth widening into a grin. With his first shots he began to laugh. He had fired about fifty rounds when three women ran from one hooch to another in the northeast corner of the hamlet.

"God, there's people all over down there," Woolsey said.

Something—perhaps the bumpkin's surprise in Woolsey's voice—made him laugh harder. His whole stomach seemed to be bubbling up. The knuckles of his right hand whitened around the trigger and trigger guard. He looked at Captain Sloane, bent intently over the infinity sight; Sloane glanced back, and their eyes met for a fraction of a second. His mouth was wide open and he couldn't get it shut. Sloane's eyes were like glass.

The rockets had destroyed a hooch midway across the hamlet. Two children peered up at the helicopter from the remains of one wall. He couldn't stop laughing.

He was standing, firing straight down, when a woman carrying a baby ran underneath the ship. She ran for the small hooch in the northwest corner. He watched the tracers from his gun hitting the dirt slightly behind and to the left of her. He watched them move over until they were directly behind her. She wore a white top and black pajama bottoms. The tracers looked better crawling up the black than they did when they got to the white. The baby looked surprised, then the woman did three somersaults into the wall of the hooch.

The ship banked, and he fell down on his knees and bumped his chin on the machine gun. Orange started out of the tree line. He moved into his seat and reached for the mike button, but Sloane was already on the radio.

"We're taking fire from the tree line! Four-two, they're in the tree line. Keep running straight over it and try to get some grenades in there!"

Morgan climbed outside the helicopter and stood on the skid firing into the tree line. The tracers returned like pinpoints, transforming into footballs as they sailed past the ship. The chopper turned right, blocking his view. Barry could do the firing now.

He looked down at the smoking village. The woman had rolled and the baby would probably remember his face. Something soft, warm, and moist hit the back of his neck. He put his hand behind his head and turned around. Barry lay on his back on the floor of the ship. One of the bullets had skinned the bottom of his nose before it split his front teeth and went through his mouth and came out at the base of his brain. Another had shattered his chin. Others had gone through his neck, taking most of it with them, and his head lay on a blanket of blood that kept growing larger and larger. A bright-red bubble welled up from where his Adam's apple had been. Morgan popped it with the index finger of his right hand, then he reached slowly for the mike button. "Barry's dead," he whispered.

He waited a moment, his body tense with silence, and as the pilots turned, his voice began low and guttural in the back of his throat. "Can't any of you motherfuckers understand that Barry's dead? Dead!"

Sloane turned to the front and flipped a button on the console. "Noble Rider Three, this is Noble Rider Four-one. My crew chief's shot up and I'm coming to the medevac pad and you better have it cleared and someone there to get him!"

"This is Noble Ri—"

Sloane flipped the switch again. "Jungle Master Six, this is Noble Rider Four-one. Your Victor Charlies are in the tree line, not in the hamlet, and one of them got my crew chief and I'm leaving. Out." He flipped the switch again. "Four-two, they got Barry and we're heading for the medevac pad."

"Roger, Four-one. They quit firing down there. I think my gunner got a grenade right next to them."

"Tell it to Three. Out. Okay, you take it in, Mr. Woolsey.

I'm going in the back." Sloane unfastened his harness and crawled over the console into the back of the helicopter. He pulled the cord from Barry's flight helmet out of the socket and plugged in his own. He switched the intercom to private.

The floor was almost completely red. Morgan knelt over Barry, legs spread so that each knee was a few inches outside the ears. He didn't move when Sloane touched him on the back and made no sign of acknowledgment when Sloane said, "I'm sorry, Morgan."

Barry's machine gun hung free from the elastic cord and bounced crazily in the wind as the ship moved toward the camp. A belt of a few hundred rounds, jostled out of the box on the floor, swung loosely from the gun outside the ship. Sloane crawled up on the seat and over to the gun. He pulled it in and secured it against the back of the pilot's seat, dumping the ammunition back in the box. Barry's calves dangled outside the ship, but there was no way to get them back inside without moving the entire body, so Sloane let them hang. Morgan watched the captain, then looked down at the corpse beneath him.

He reached back and let his hand rest for a moment on a fragmentation grenade. When they landed, he'd go to Hart's tent, drop the grenade, and hold him until they were both blown to shit. God! The woman rolled while he laughed and the child accused and now his knees were soaked with blood. Could he crawl in the mouth and get shit out by a dead man? No. Just use the grenade. The shaving inspection's done and Hart's laid in there with his morning shot. He'd blow them fucking both to bits. He didn't need the liquor this time—at least he'd come that far. He had his experience now. Pockets, three bags full, eyes forever branded on a somersault. Why couldn't the pinpoint footballs hit him? Barry didn't know or care or couldn't have thought of this and you couldn't expect his neck to be all hot on yours so you'll make Hart wet and hot too. Ten thousand Willard Morgan hunks go flying through the air. They'll tell the right lies. "Man and his sergeant killed in freak accident." Maybe it'll be in the paper and someone will drop it on the scattered bits of you no one cleaned up. The story can soak with the flies and ants, birds eating the accusing eyes plucked off your brain carrying the ever-rolling woman.

The medevac tents stood directly behind the gunnery platoon. Sloane leaned out the left door as the helicopter hovered in for its landing, gesturing frantically for the medics. Morgan took off his flight helmet and picked up a grenade. When the helicopter was five feet off the ground, he undid his harnesss, removed his armor vest, leaped out, and ran toward the platoon.Chambers rose in front of his tent, but he ran past him and screamed ten feet from Hart's tent. "Okay, Hart, you cocksuckin' motherfucker! You and me are gonna go see Dennis Barry together!" He burst through the flap, pulled the pin, and stopped. Empty. Any other time his sorry ass would be here.

He tore the flap and leaped outside. He nearly bumped into Chambers.

"Morg, I heard. I'm—"

"Where's Hart? Where's the bastard at?"

"What're you doing with the grenade? Jesus, Morgan. No!"

"I'm going to blow! I'm going to blow—there he comes from operations. Get out of here, Chambers. I'm gonna—"

"You ain't." Chambers grabbed his wrist.

"The pin's pulled, baby! I drop this thing, that's it."

Chambers pushed him slowly away from Hart's tent toward his own. "You don't want to do that, Morgan. You can't."

"I've got to! I can't go anymore, and I'm not leaving without him."

"You ain't leaving, Morgan! You ain't leaving me after the months of all we've been through. You think of LaMont and Tom and the others and tell me you're gonna go—look at me!"

"You got it out of you somewhere sometime but, man, I just shot a woman and her kid knew and Barry's neck was all over me! Please, please don't stop me."

Chambers had pushed him nearly to the front of his tent, pulling his arm in closer and moving his hand toward the grenade. "I ain't sayin' it's right what you did or that any of the shit Hart's done is right, or me either. But god damn it, maybe now you got your killing to think about. If you can't do anything more than do it again, you ain't no man to me!"

His arm gave way almost involuntarily. Chambers' hand slid over his, holding it and the grenade like a ball.

"Gimme the grenade."

"What's going on over there?" Hart said, standing by his tent flap.

"I got—"

"Gimme it!"

His hand loosened. "Careful, Orville, it doesn't have any pin in it."

"Everything okay there, Chambers?" Hart yelled.

"Sure, Sarge," Chambers yelled back. "Okay, Will," he whispered, "I got the handle of it. You can let it go now."

He let the grenade slip into Chambers' hand. Chambers tightened his fist on it and Morgan tightened his hand over the fist. He looked at Chambers again and blinked rapidly two or three times. He started to say "Thank you," but the words ground to a halt on the dry surface of his throat. His body relaxed. The first sob was nearly to his eyes when he choked it back. His chest heaved violently, and he shook his head as a second sob made his shoulders tremble. Chambers pulled his hand away and spread both his arms around him. Morgan pulled his own arms up and folded them on his chest and leaned against Chambers the way he used to lie on his bed as a child.

25

THE COMPANY quieted as Major Singer stood up behind a short table at one end of the tent. Chambers, leaning against a pole at the opposite end, slowed his chewing and dropped his arm to hide the half-eaten turkey drumstick. The tent's side flaps had been raised to let in the sunlight, and the three long tables where the soldiers sat were covered with white bedsheets and water pitchers full of jungle plants.

"I'm not going to give you a big speech," Singer said, "because I know you're anxious to get at that turkey and all the trimmings the mess hall staff has so beautifully prepared. Maybe a lot of you don't think there's much to be thankful for out here in the boondocks, but before you stuff yourselves, I want you to think about it for a minute. I want you to remember that if you didn't live in such a great country, these people in Vietnam wouldn't have anyone over here to protect them from the communists. Maybe we can't be thankful about having to do the fighting, but we have to give thanks for the fact that our country is strong enough to give aid to our less fortunate allies throughout the world.

"I want to read you something I got in the mail a couple of days ago, because it's intended for all of you, and I think it'll give you a good idea of how the folks at home think of us, even though we don't hear the good news all the time."

Singer pulled a letter from his pocket and unfolded it, then held it up so everyone could see the big, messy printing. "This is from a sixth-grader in the Eugene Field Elementary

School in Lakewood, Ohio. It goes like this: 'Dear Soldiers of C Company, Our teacher, Mrs. Daniels, got us all addresses of soldiers in the war. We are each adopting a company of the service. You are my company that I am adopting. I just wanted to tell you what a fine job you are doing. We are behind you one hundred percent and wish you will have the war won and be home soon. We say prayers for you every morning after the flag salute. I even say prayers for you during the weekend. My friends and me play soldier and I am C company with my toy M-16 my father bought me. I am only twelve and won't be able to come to Vietnam. I will still be a soldier when I grow up. [Signed] Mark Smith.' That about says it as well as I could." Major Singer sat down as the troops cheered.

Chambers gnawed off another mouthful, turned, and headed down to the garbage cans, where Morgan listlessly ran a wire brush over a charred pot. "Gettin' 'em pretty, Morg." He leaned against the water trailer and continued to eat.

"You got the next five, dishpan hands. This is good shit." Morgan pushed the sickly gray paste of soap and grease and small hunks of food off his forearm onto his boot. "Just like the pilgrims at Plymouth Rock."

They should have been on their way home today. They'd left the States last Thanksgiving, their dinner a hamburger and a couple of whiskeys in an Anchorage Air Force bar. But the platoon had no replacements, and the platoon had to supply two KP's today. They could have had the replacements a week ago for all eight of the departing gunners. There had to be eight men in the rifle platoon who could take the gunners' jobs, had to be eight men in the base camp to replace the riflemen. Training! Hart said the new gunners would need training. Chambers had joined the rifle platoon without ever firing an M-16, and Morgan had begun flying combat assault without having fired a machine gun in nearly two years.

He bit off another hunk of meat and hurled the bone into the garbage pit. He was done raging. For him the war had ended. They'd been flying in Happy Valley for close to a month, and the last fire they'd taken had been from his friend in the ruined hamlet. For the past few days he'd done nothing but drink in the scenery, stamping it in his mind so he wouldn't forget.

And baby-sit Morgan, who was dead drunk every night. Morgan had said nothing about Barry or the woman since Chambers had stopped him from killing himself and Hart. He drank at night, joked feebly with Hancock and Webster, then yelled—nearly cried—about the lack of replacements and not being sent back to the base to clear. He probably wanted to stay and couldn't stand that in himself. The booze was making him sick inside. He hardly ate, seldom changed his clothes, and his face puffed up more every day. His body seemed to be caving in on itself, unable to take the massive insults anymore. He reminded Chambers of sturdy alcoholic sergeants who'd suddenly gone to seed, aging years overnight like salmon after they've spawned.

Maddin had come back too, but in better shape than when he'd left. He'd returned all the goods his wife had bought, leaving him only fifteen hundred in the red. He couldn't lock her in a chastity belt, but had fixed it so no more credit cards would come her way. Maddin stayed sober and helped the other crew chiefs with their mechanical problems.

Chambers took the last shift of washing pots that afternoon, and when he finished, Morgan brought him a letter from Slagel that had arrived that morning—the first any of them had received. Chamber showered before taking it to his tent to read.

November 16, 1966

Dear Morg and guys,

Well, I figured it was about time to write you all, and hope you'll get this before you butt out. I'm dictating this to my buddy whose arms still work (I had one cute nurse who offered to take dictation, but she won't talk to me anymore since I bit her tit and asked her to sit on my face).

How are you guys doing? Short, I bet. You should be coming home about now, and if you're back this way don't forget to stop and see your old buddy. How's the fucking recon battalion? LaMont, I hope you got your black ass out of the rifles and Morg, I hope you didn't get yours in. Say hi to everyone for me and tell them I'm doing okay.

I'm doing pretty shitty, but what can you say? Besides not being able to move, I'm fine. Patti and her asshole husband used to come by, but I told them to fuck off a month ago. They came back a couple times since, but I just close my eyes and pretend they're not here. I could tell I was a burden to them, and I don't want to be that to anyone. Old Sam pays the medical bills anyway. Ain't he sweet?

I sleep about half the time and otherwise watch TV. My buddy holds smokes for me and flips pictures of the pussy in *Playboy*. Otherwise it's TV and war stories. I keep expecting to wake up and find myself fixed, but I guess that isn't going to happen. The bad part's watching yourself get loose and skinny and pasty yellow. I keep waking up from this dream where I'm running and my head is saying all these things but my body just won't react. Well, fuck that. It's pretty depressing. I just keep figuring they'll find a way to fix me up someday.

The room I'm in is a funky rat's nest. No shit. They actually have garbage cans in here, and the rats prowl at night, just like in good old Vietnam. One guy went crazy because a rat jumped on him. He can't move either, and the thing was on his chest staring in his face and all he could do was scream. He screamed for ten minutes, and now he hasn't opened his mouth for a month. Just stares at the ceiling.

Well, shit. Not too much else to say. Thanks for your letters. I don't blame you for not writing lately, but I'll try to write more from now on. I didn't feel much like it for a while there. Keep your tools cool in the motor pool, and let me know where you're reassigned to.

Love and kisses and all
that good shit,

T. S.

Chambers nearly cried when he finished the letter. He could never go see him. Morgan wrote a long letter, telling about LaMont and promising to come and visit when he got out of Benning. Chambers added on, saying he probably couldn't visit in the near future, but would try to make it next summer. He had the feeling that maybe Slagel didn't want to see them, had written the letter this late hoping they'd never get it.

The next afternoon, as Chambers' helicopter lifted off the ground, another chopper landed carrying the replacements. He waved to them as his ship sailed over the perimeter and headed toward Happy Valley.

The flight was nothing. Sanders grenaded a storage hooch and blew apart a canoe beached on the bank of the swollen stream that snaked along the valley floor. Back at the flight line, Orville loaded quickly and carefully—with a happy sense of finality—then walked to the tent area, trying not to break into a run.

He sat casually on the sandbags in front of his tent, savoring his cigar and beer, saying little as the gunners taunted the new guys and fed them war stories.

After chow Hart held a platoon formation. The gunners seemed ready to explode from anticipation as they lined up on the muddy road.

"At fuckin' ease!" Hart bellowed, quieting the platoon. "Okay, it looks like you'll finally be getting out of here. For the next two days the new men will be training on just two ships, and the rest of you will be flying as usual. Then they'll be shuffling around the other ships for three days after that. Four of you gunners will go in on December first, the other four on the second. I don't want no bullshittin' around just because you're short. We're still in a war. Anyone fucks up, I'll extend his ass another week. Fall out. New gunners up to my tent."

Chambers found himself cheering and screaming with the rest of them as they swatted and hugged one another.

He walked back to his tent and dropped his steel pot at McCutcheon's feet. "Six days, Cutch. What do you think of that?"

McCutcheon raised his eyes from a can of Bubble-up. "I'll be going home with you, Orville. I extended for six months and got a thirty-day leave. Then I'm staying till the war's over."

"How come, man?"

"You have to do what your heart tells you."

He rapped his knuckles against McCutcheon's pot. "If I were you, I wouldn't trust my heart so much."

"I've got to." McCutcheon looked like a sad basset hound. "What else does a man have?"

"Hey, what's the matter?"

"Sick of being line chief is all. I hate being on the ground all day. I miss the action."

"No, you don't. There's hardly any anyway. Why don't you enjoy the break?"

"I will until my leave, but when I come back, I'm going to start crewing again. Someone else can take over as line chief." McCutcheon bent the green can. "God, I love combat, Orville."

He wanted to call the men in the white coats. He thumped McCutcheon's helmet again. "You might change your mind on leave. You've been here a long time."

"I guess I need a rest."

"Don't we all?"

"Three motherfucking days!" Webster bellowed as the gunners left the platoon area.

"Big three and they can eat me!" Morgan shouted.

Chambers fell in beside him, behind Webster and Hancock. They were on their way to the hill across the airstrip, where one of the air-assault companies had built a club. The gunners had sniffed it out three days ago, after Hart had told the battalion beer concessions not to sell to any of the drunks from gunnery. Chambers liked the club better than the flight line, and if it wasn't raining, they usually showed a movie outside.

"Them whores in Sin City better be ready," Hancock said. "I'm gonna be layin' some pipe there when I get in."

"Probably take the clap home too," Webster said.

"Who gives a shit? Right, Morgan?"

"Right, Cock. Three tears in the bucket, they don't flow, mother fuck it."

Webster hooted. "You know Jody got that hometown pussy all sewed up anyway."

"Uniform'll get you some," Hancock said.

Chambers couldn't help laughing along with the others.

"Might be true," Webster said, "with them country-ass hillbilly gals, but in town this uniform and a dime might get you a cup of coffee."

"In a cheap cafe," Morgan said.

Hancock turned and shrugged. "You all come to West Virginia. I'll take care of you."

Until now Orville hadn't really thought of how he'd be received back home. He wondered if anyone even knew he was here. For a moment he saw himself being greeted by his old acquaintances from high school, being accepted again. For what? Because he had two rows of ribbons and a couple of tin badges? Because he'd dropped blood on foreign soil? Would that make him normal in everyone's eyes? But he hadn't done anything abnormal to cause them to reject him in the first place. He'd had a brother killed in Korea, another killed at home. It wasn't his fault. But people put the burden on him. He was the weird one because death clung to his family. Well, he wasn't going to win acceptance by parading things he knew were stupid, things of which he was nearly ashamed. He'd keep his uniform and medals in a mothballed closet, where he could look at them from time to time to remind himself of the waste and foolishness he'd seen, to keep alive in his mind even his father's outraged adage that it is wrong to squander life.

Three naked bulbs hung from the tent roof, dimly lighting the club. Two long tables, rudely built from ammunition boxes, faced each other down nearly the entire length of the tent.

"Looks downright bohemian," Morgan said, pointing at the candles flickering at regular intervals along the light, moisture-stained wood.

Two bartenders fished beers from giant tubs of icy water, dropped them on the tables, and collected the brightly colored denominations of military scrip.

Chambers sat for a while, listening to the others, to the endless repetitive nearly hysterical boasts of short-timer GI's the world over. How great the change would be, the promises the future held of bright, fast cars, curvaceous yielding women, clothes and booze and steaks and glasses of ice-cold milk. Mama's home cooking, good jobs, and adulation in the neighborhood. No more sergeants ordering them around.

He got a fresh beer, ducked under the tent flap, and found a rock to sit on in front of the movie. As Karl Malden brought the whip relentlessly over Marlon Brando's back, Chambers wondered how long the enthusiasm of the gunners would last when they got home. Maybe Morgan would escape. He'd had education and would probably get more. He himself hoped to escape the same way. But what about Hancock and Webster? Hancock would either stay in the Army or get a job where he'd be a private all his life. Webster worked construction in New York and could make the money for a modest home on Long Island someday, a paneled den in the basement where he could slurp beer and watch ball games and swap war stories with his friends. And the rest of them? Home to insane families, to payments on broken-down cars, to people who didn't care, jobs that didn't satisfy, death eventually.

He finished his beer as Brando took the butt of Slim Pickens' shotgun in his back as he was pushed up the jailhouse stairs. Brando whirled and kicked Slim down the stairs. Chambers ducked back under the tent flap.

"Hey, Orville!" Morgan shouted. "Come on, you guys, let's sing a hymn to Orville." He hummed the pitch, then the others joined him. "Hymn, hymn, fuck him."

He smiled back at them, trying to hide his disgust at Morgan's succumbing to the silliest of Army banalities. Morgan's eyes were bleary with drink, and brown nicotine stains, bright with saliva, spotted his two front teeth.

He sat down and drank another beer, trying to devise a way to get Morgan out before he got too drunk. Christ, he'd be glad when they went in from the field. No more baby-sitting. During a quiet moment he elbowed Morgan gently. "Want to go down, Will? I could use a shower."

Morgan looked at him uncomprehendingly for a few seconds, then slowly nodded his head. "Why not? I don't think I've showered in a week. I don't think I've even changed my boots." His voice trailed off into a pathetic laugh.

Chambers rose as Morgan bought two more beers for the walk down the hill. Hancock and Webster stayed. As they left the tent, a great cheer went up from the movie crowd. Brando, lying in the dirt, had gunned down Malden by a fountain in the center of town.

The low clouds had rendered the night completely black. Down below, in the battalion area, candles winked from tents, and flashlight beams bobbed erratically on the flight line. The helicopters they passed, parked in freshly bulldozed spots on the side of the hill, appeared like inert, prehistoric beasts in the surrounding gloom.

"Not too long now, Will, huh?"

Morgan gurgled assent between swallows of beer. "You're going to stay with me awhile, aren't you?"

"Probably a few days. I have to get home too." It would be no problem. His parents didn't know when he was coming.

"My sister'll take care of us."

"Good enough."

Morgan stopped to light a cigarette, and his eyes were sad and puffy in the orange flare of the match. "Guess I never will know what it's like to kill someone."

"What!" He couldn't quite believe what he'd heard.

"You know."

"But—"

"Not that. Real person. Like in combat." The drunken words slurred. It was as though Morgan spoke to no one.

Chambers remained silent for a moment, half angry, half confused, not knowing what to say. Finally he muttered, "It's no big thing."

Morgan snorted. "You know all about it, don't you?"

"About what?"

"About killing and what's right and wrong."

"I guess I've thought about it."

"So you pass judgment on everyone else, huh?"

"Have I ever done that? I've just thought it out for myself."

"Shit! If it weren't for me, you wouldn't even know how to think. I've taught you everything you know."

"Come on, man."

"Come on, man, come on, man," Morgan mocked. "Big moral Orville knows it all." His arm slapped slowly at Chambers' belly.

He caught it, dropped it. "What's the matter?" Morgan's arm moved toward him again, and again he grabbed it and shook it away. "Cut it out."

"You're too mature for that shit, huh?" Morgan danced out in front of him, his fists raised like a boxer's, then tripped and went sprawling in the sand. He lay on his back, staring at the sky.

"Come on, Will."

"Get up and be a man, right?"

"I didn't say that. Don't be so hard on yourself."

"Okay, Mr. Squared Away. Give me a hand."

He fought an impulse to leave him lying there. He bent down, arm extended. Morgan's arm came around, fist doubled. Chambers moved his head, and the fist glanced lightly off his shoulder. He grabbed Morgan's arm and yanked him to his feet. "You want to fight, why don't you at least stand up?"

"You're ready now, huh?" Morgan sat back down.

"It's not me wants to fight."

"Then what's your fuckin' beef!" Morgan screamed.

"It ain't my beef, Morg, you know that. I've never had a beef with you. You're the best friend I've got, and I just hate to see you doing this to yourself."

Morgan let out a low, sorry moan, then breathed in deeply, sucking the air between his teeth so that he nearly whistled. "If you don't like it, then leave me the fuck alone!"

Chambers eyed the dark form for a moment. In the night it could have been a pile of discarded rags. "Okay. I'll see you back at the platoon."

Back in his tent, he lay on his back and waited. He had to be ready in case Morgan did something crazy. He'd probably go back up and keep drinking with Webster and Hancock.

He was nearly asleep when he felt the light tap against his boot.

"I'm sorry, Orville," Morgan whispered out of the darkness, then he moved away, his boots scraping on the sand like the limbs of a wounded animal.

In the morning they flew cover for the infantry and in the afternoon went on recon with another ship. The small ravines beyond the north end of Happy Valley nearly hypnotized him. They appeared dense and impenetrable from above, but once the ship dropped near the floor a whole new vista opened, seeming to have no connection with the thick green of the treetops. The trunks and shafts of the trees looked like toothpicks next to the mammoth rocks, tipped at weird angles, that jutted out from the hillsides. Mossy splotches covered the rocks where little streams ran over and around them. Small fountains gushed through holes in a few of the massive chunks of stone. A narrow ledge wound through the trees near the spine of the mountain, and although they could see it was a path, they couldn't get close enough to look for footprints.

"Maddin," Sanders said. "Some caves coming up on your side. Put a few rounds in them."

Maddin fired three short bursts, chipping small hunks off the giant rocks, but not getting any in the caves.

"We ought to get the rifles in here," Sanders said. "Those caves are probably full of weapons."

He was glad they hadn't seen any footprints. At the rate they traveled, one VC with a thirty caliber could blow them out of the sky. He was sorry to leave the valleys—he'd never seen anything like them in his life—but he felt relieved too. There must be similar places in the States where you didn't have to worry about people shooting you.

They headed east toward the field base, slowing occasionally to run counterclockwise circles around wide deserted valleys. An empty hamlet stood forlornly among the bushes in the middle of each valley, and the surrounding fields, uncultivated this season, lay overgrown with weeds and scrub grass. In the third valley they swept, the burned hulk of a scout ship lay tilted on its side near the edge of the jungle, rusting in the sun.

Two casings clattered against his helmet as Maddin fired a short burst.

"He's coming under the ship!" Sanders yelled. "Get him, Chambers, before he makes it into the trees."

They were about fifty yards outside the thick jungle that ended abruptly at the valley floor.

"Try to hover it, Mr. Eastman," Sanders said, "so Chambers can get him."

The nose of the ship jerked up as the man ran underneath. An NVA with an AK-47.

"Get him, Chambers! Get him!"

He turned sideways, tucked the stock into his armpit, and took careful aim. He squeezed the trigger when the North Vietnamese was ten yards from the tree line. He fired straight into the trunk of a tree fifteen yards in front of the man. The chopper jerked forward a few feet, and he let the gun slip, sending the bullets wildly into the jungle. The khaki uniform disappeared into the dark green as he adjusted his bullets on the tree once more.

"Shit!" Sanders said. "He got away."

The tree shook, then toppled silently back into the jungle.

"Swing it around, Mr. Eastman. I'll put some grenades in there. Chambers and Maddin, I want you to spray the area as we go over."

He riddled the area on his side as they made their run. The man had gone somewhere to the other side and had doubtless found a hole to hide in. No infantry near the area, so it didn't make any difference. Blue had reconned this valley two weeks ago and wouldn't come back. The man was probably looking for a handful of rice. Orville leaned out the door and let a deep belly laugh escape into the wind.

26

MORGAN AWOKE from a dream in which he'd been a midget, a quadruple amputee with leather cups covering his leg stumps, hooks protruding from his biceps. Stubble-bearded, sitting on a small wooden cart, he'd been selling papers outside the PX in Fulda, an obvious favorite among the soldiers who walked by and joked with him.

He shook himself and sat up on the cot in the aircraft-maintenance tent. The thick, humid air wrapped around him like a rubber sheet, and beneath his fatigues his entire body felt moist. The rain clattered and popped on the thick canvas of the tent, dripped steadily into little pools and rivulets outside. He bent over and rummaged in his mold-covered duffel bag, then pulled out letters, some paperbacks, and his address book. He sniffed the last and wrinkled his lip in disgust, then rapidly flipped pages, squinting occasionally at a name blurred by mildew.

After hanging up his khakis, he dropped the wadded ball of slacks, shirts, socks, and shoes that he'd bought in Bangkok onto his pile of trash along with a set of greens and all the clothes that weren't absolutely necessary for the next few days. He upended the duffel bag, and a small pocketknife clattered on the floor. Besides its short main blade, the knife also had a corkscrew, now rusted shut. He'd bought it at the Munich Bahnhof to open a jug of wine he, Padgett, Slagel, and Chambers were taking back to Fulda. He stuffed the knife into his pocket as DeWolf burst through the entry flaps of the tent.

"Morg! When did you get in?"

"Hi, DeWolf. Little after lunch."

"How many days?"

"Four or five."

"Out of sight." DeWolf sat on the cot facing him. "What happened to your dogs—leprosy?"

"Gas burns." Purple welts covered both his feet, caused by a mixture of JP-4 and water. "I've been too wasted to take my boots off."

"I heard you was *stayin'* fucked up out there."

He shrugged.

"Let's go to the club. The guys'd like to see you."

"I have to sort this stuff and take a dump. I think I've got worms. My asshole's on fire half the time."

DeWolf left, rattling his mess kit. Morgan put rubber bands around the letters and dropped them back in the duffel bag. He bent over quickly as his stomach contracted, then rose, left the tent, and walked hurriedly through the mud toward the latrine. He hoped it wasn't an ulcer. He didn't think they made you crap all the time.

He entered the latrine, nodded at the unfamiliar PFC seated on the throne, then glanced down a hole in the rough wood plank before sitting. Flies swarmed on the multicolored heap of defecation and paper lying in the metal drum at the bottom. He recalled his shit-burning days after he'd flipped out in S-1 and another time, when Sanders and Hart had spent half an hour discussing the genius behind burning shit instead of burying it. He laughed out loud remembering the story of two new airborne troopers who, told to burn the officers' shithouse, had soaked the whole wooden and bamboo structure with gas and burned it to the ground.

The new PFC smiled at him and said, "Just get in from the field?"

"Yup."

"Got your feet messed up, huh?"

"VC pissed on me. They got strong piss."

The other looked at him for a moment. "Going home?"

"Um-hmn."

"Christ, I just got here. You'll be home for Christmas and everything."

"Ain't life grand?"

"Guess I'll go get some chow. See you later."

"Don't let the VC piss on you."

"Right."

He looked through the screen windows of the latrine, down the path between the ten neat wooden barracks with their shiny aluminum roofs. He felt like a stranger as he thought back to the time he had lived in the same area, in Overhead, months before the new regimentation and construction had begun. He couldn't believe how good those days seemed now.

When he'd left the field this morning, in a helicopter creeping through a thin blanket of fog, he'd wanted to feel some joyous sense of finality. He'd simply felt bored, as though he were taking another routine flight. Going home had been mentioned so many times that the expression had become meaningless gibberish, an attenuated group of words giving you nothing, like a piece of gold hammered to such a thinness that it finally blows away. I'm going home; it's over. He could say it to himself a thousand times, but he guessed now that there would be no feeling until he touched ground back in the world.

Through the screen to his left he saw Webster standing at the piss tube in C Company's area. "If you shake it more than three times, you're playin' with it."

"I was just coming to get you, Morg. Thought you might like to get drunk for a change."

He hitched up his pants and met Webster on the path, and they headed for the club.

"Morg, you're lucky not to be in C Company. They got me on KP day after tomorrow."

Morgan had never been officially reassigned from Headquarters Company, so the first sergeant had put him in aircraft maintenance for his last few days. "Doc said I can't pull any duty because of my feet. But he didn't say anything about Sin City."

They pushed through the brightly colored plastic strips that hung in the entrance of the club. One-armed bandits lined the back wall. A crap table stood a few feet from the bar, DeWolf rolling.

They got four beers and moved through the unfamiliar faces to a table in the back. They drank quietly for half an hour, then DeWolf came over from the crap game and set six beers on their table.

"So you guys all set to make the trip, huh? You're lucky." DeWolf's eyes swept the club. "There ain't shit around here no more."

"Bet they haven't run out of Vy-ennies yet."

"Short-timin' Cock!" Webster suddenly yelled. Hancock nodded from the bar, his pudgy face haggard and worried-looking. An unlit cigarette dangled from his lips. He wasn't due in until tomorrow.

He walked over and set the can on the table. "C Company got in the shit this afternoon." He sat rigidly in a chair, resting his chin on his fists.

"What?" Morgan asked. "Who, where?"

"Rifles ran into a platoon of NVA's in Happy Valley. Got tore up bad. Captain Jones got it right off. Man, they was dug in good. I—"

"Who else?" Webster said.

"They said Myles got his chest shot up, and Sergeant Holder took a couple in the stomach when he was layin' down cover fire. Lot of others wounded. McCutcheon got it."

"What?" Webster cried.

McCutcheon! "No, man. He doesn't even have to fly anymore. Did he get shot down?"

"Hell, no! He went crawlin' up there. You know how hot he was on the glory. He disobeyed three direct orders. He wasn't even supposed to leave the company area, but he got on the first lift ship goin' out there. When it landed they told him not to get out of the ship but he did and then they told him not to move from where the platoon was, but he took all these grenades and crawled up to where Charlie was dug in, and he got one in the ass, then two fifties through the head."

"No! He shouldn't have done it."

"He was supposed to come in tomorrow," Webster said.

"He shouldn't have done it." Morgan couldn't shake the picture of the bullet penetrating McCutcheon's fat ass.

"What about Chambers?" Webster asked.

"Chambers. Where's Chambers?" He was coming in tomorrow too.

"His ship took a round and they went down in a rice paddy. He's okay, but they're gonna work on it tonight and fly in tomorrow. Hart said he had to clean the weapons. I told him to fuck Hart, but he's gonna stay out anyway. I was so damn scared I pissed my pants a little. Sergeant Paley about went crazy. He must've killed twenty of the bastards. Crawled up there after McCutcheon and started flippin' grenades in the holes. One of them came out all blasted to shit and Paley cut his ears off with a bayonet. It was bad shit. Worst in a long time."

"Jesus, McCutcheon. He shouldn't have gone up there, Hancock. Why didn't someone stop him?"

"They couldn't, Morgan. No one never seen McCutcheon like that. He couldn't hear nobody. I thought he was done with that hero shit, but—"

"How many rifles wounded?" Webster asked.

"Fifteen, maybe more."

"Anyone in gunnery?"

"No."

"Jesus!" DeWolf shook his head.

"Yeah," Hancock said, "you don't want to go volunteerin' for no combat like your buddy here."

"No chance."

All four men toyed nervously with their beer cans.

A sudden thought made Morgan's head rise, and he glanced quickly at the others to make sure they hadn't seen. He lit a cigarette and exhaled slowly, making the flame waver on the match for a few seconds before it went out. He set his face in a serious expression, cast his eyes down sadly, but he couldn't stop the thought. He felt envious because he'd been cheated out of today's battle. He wanted to run to the flight line and fly a helicopter back to the field himself. But it was over; the soldiers were back at the field base now, drinking beer and coffee, discussing the day's action. He hated the NVA's for waiting till he'd gone in.

"Well," Hancock said, "I reckon we won't be in no Hueys again, huh? After that shit it sure was nice knowing I was on my last flight in them damn things."

No one said anything.

Hancock took another can and drank. "I reckon there ain't no use in feelin' all shitty. Nothin' we can do but drink up and forget it. Come on, Morgan, we gonna get drunk or sit here and mope all night?"

"Fuck it!" He drained his beer and slammed it on the table.

"You got any booze in your hooch, Cock?" Webster asked.

"Two-fifths of Johnny Walker Red. Let's get out of here. Look at all these new guys, sittin' here acting like they seen some shit."

One of the new men at another table looked up and caught Hancock's eye.

"What's happening there, new fish?" Hancock sneered. "One of my buddies just got killed, so don't look like you're such hot shit sittin' down here tryin' to drink."

The new man looked away.

"Sorry motherfuckers," Hancock said, drawing out each syllable.

"Let's go," Webster said. "You comin', DeWolf?"

"I'm gonna play poker."

Morgan walked over by the bar, afraid his physical closeness would reveal his secret to the others.

Hancock moved behind the new man, reached down, and jerked out his chair, sending him sprawling on the floor. Hancock stepped back as the others at the table pushed out their chairs. "Come on, you cocksuckers. I ain't scared to take on all of you. Man oughta be able to drink in his own club without a bunch of recruits gapin' at him."

"Come on, Cock," Webster said. "Let's split."

"I don't care. I'll fight all these fuckers right now. I'm a man and I ain't gotta take this shit!"

"They just don't know what's happening. Come on."

"Okay, but I ain't scared."

"I know you ain't, man."

Morgan stepped out of Hancock's hooch shortly after

midnight. He slipped to one knee on the wet concrete step. After recovering himself, he stood still for a moment listening to the rain run off the roof onto his cap, then stepped off the concrete, slipped again, and fell face down in the mud. He grabbed the beer can before all the fluid ran out and, after rolling over, put its muddy rim to his lips and turned the can upside down. Gulping furiously, he swallowed most of the mixture of beer and whiskey. The rest ran off his cheeks, down his chin, and around his neck. Some went in his nose, and when he snorted, his nostrils filled with fluid. He turned over again, raised himself to his knees, and alternately pressing the flaps of his nose, blew the snot into the mud. Crawling on all fours toward Headquarters Company, he wiped his nose on his shoulder. After a few yards he moved his baseball cap so the bill stuck out over one ear. He cocked his head, stuck out his tongue, and tasted rain. He barked "Ruff, ruff, ruff," into the night, then rolled on his back and laughed for five minutes.

"'teeeeehn-shun!" he suddenly shouted and rose to a squatting position. He dropped one knee in the mud. "Okay, men. We got a long way to go. The enemy is all around us. Ghoul juice is running low. You gotta be quiet. No smoking. No beating your meat or pickin' boogers. We gotta move all hunched over, so no one'll see the whites of our eyes. No smiling. We'll reconnoiter around the vicinity of the area known as Overhead, which is now enemy territory. From there we'll move directly to that place formerly designated as a staging area for drunkards known as the immederite area. Not the immediate area, but the immederite area, henceforth to be known as the *inter*mederite area. We'll bivouac there, where it's written that ghoul juice'll spout from the mud if you lay there long enough. It's near the ditch where you'll get deuce-and-a-half tread marks on your face if you lay *there* long enough. Ready? Go."

He ran through the mud down the slight incline toward Headquarters Company. The ground dipped sharply a few yards before the barracks, and he suddenly found himself in the air. He tucked his head, somersaulted, and crashed into the wall of the commo billets. A few groans arose from those sleeping inside.

"Shhhh!" he whispered. "Humpty Dumpty's platoon will now advance on the intermederite area. You're doing just fine, men."

He walked quietly along the wall of the barrack until he hit the path. He turned to his left and tiptoed stealthily along, crossing battalion road and sneaking behind the mess hall.

Ten yards from the objective he dropped to his knees and squinted through the darkness. He made out the shaving tables standing near the entrance to his tent, two water cans and three small benches sitting beside them. He lay on his stomach and crawled forward. He stopped two feet from the benches. "Stout, Fisher, Zastrow, Padgett, Slagel, Barry. What's happening, you old motherfuckers? I been out in the shit and just brought my men in. It was a bitch, but it's nice to be back in the old intermederite area drinking ghoul juice with you guys. We all gotta go home soon, but we can write each other and meet at the Olympics in Mexico in sixty-eight."

He folded his arms beneath his chest and shivered his body farther into the mud. "Boy, it makes me feel all warm to be back here again. It was some bad shit out there. Probably not as bad as you guys have seen, but any of that shit's bad. Now I'm back so we can drink like in the old days. Fisher, maybe you can get the jeep and we can go up to Qui Nhon and get a whole pallet of beer like we used to, huh? Here, I got about fifteen bucks to chip in, huh?"

He rolled to one side and pulled a wallet from his back pocket. He opened it and drew out a ten and a five-dollar bill. "Here," he said, rolling on his stomach and extending his arms. "Take it. We'll just buy some beer and talk easy and watch the monkeys fuck like we used to, and we'll meet in Mexico in sixty-eight and talk old times like they won't be able to touch us then."

The bills dropped from his hands and his hands and

forearms dropped from the air and he dropped his face in the mud and rubbed it back and forth. "No, they won't be able to touch us anymore. The cocksuckin' lifers'll still be cocksuckin' lifers and they won't be able to touch us no motherfuckin' more."

"Morgan. Mor*gan!* Come on, man."

"Who's that? Slagel? Stout? Padgett? Who?"

"This here's DeWolf's sorry ass. Those guys've been gone for months. It's rough, man, but you only got a few more days. Don't fuck yourself up. Let's have a beer or go to sleep, one."

"You got any beer, DeWolf?"

"I keep beer."

"Let's have a beer, DeWolf." Inside the tent he sat on his cot, opened the can, and took two sips.

"You guys really put it away tonight, didn't you?"

"It was pretty bad shit." He swung his legs onto the cot and lay down. "Bad shit, DeWolf, but I reckon they can't fuck with me much more, huh?" He watched DeWolf get up, pour the remainder of his beer in the mud, and crawl under his mosquito net and into his sleeping bag.

Morgan stared at the canvas ceiling, moving his lips with a soft smacking sound, trying to taste something.

27

CHAMBERS WAS NOT asleep when Staff Sergeant Hart came to wake him at five, and he lay on his back listening as the platoon fell in at five thirty. Hart came back to get him after he was missed at reveille, and Chambers told him quietly that he had been on the flight line till two and was going to rest until his ship went in. He watched the tent ceiling and smoked.

Knowing he should have known better, knowing now that the final trickery of war was simply that it wasn't over until you were home safely in your bed. Like games again—never finished till the final gun. Knowing now too that the last insult to his sense of humanity was plainly that war did not allow him one.

He had killed again yesterday, not instinctively or willingly. The decision had been rational—like solving a problem in simple math—a hurried weighing of the gunner's limited options a hundred feet above the battle. The three North Vietnamese had departed their foxhole, creeping toward the rifle platoon's right flank. He had no choice but to pour the relentless stream of death from his machine gun on them.

Why him of all people? When most of the gunners had never shot anyone directly, had no idea of whether they'd killed or not, why was he always having to kill soldiers face to face? How many more lay slaughtered beneath the jungle canopy, unseen by their executioners?

So it had seemed logical—even necessary—that his ship would be shot down. When the bullet had smashed up through the floor, tearing the wiring on the ceiling and causing a loss of power, he had said yes out loud. As the ship escaped the line of battle and went down in a rice paddy a mile beyond, he only wondered why the bullet couldn't have been fired a second earlier to hit the box of thermite grenades on the floor. Why not a second later to hit him in the balls?

And for the rest of the day and the night and into the morning, while they sling-loaded the ship to the field base, had chow, told weary tales, while Maddin and the maintenance sergeant replaced the wires and tracked the rotor blades, he kept waiting for McCutcheon to show up offering help and advice. Even through the sleepless hours on his sleeping bag this morning, he expected McCutcheon to stumble through the tent flaps and wearily grab himself a soda.

He should have known that too, knew that he had known but never acknowledged that the line chief had wanted to die. Too bad he couldn't have gone home before his wish was granted. He'd admired McCutcheon, grudgingly, because he alone believed in the war, worked hard, and felt himself an important part of the effort. Stupid reasoning. What was he really playing for but his own death? And he probably didn't even know it.

At six thirty he went to the mess tent. The eggs frying in a sea of grease repelled him, and he moved on to the large bucket of coffee at the end of the serving line. He filled his canteen cup and walked the few yards to the eating tent. Between the spread flaps at one end he paused, then went to a table for a can of Pet milk. The white fluid disappeared beneath the black mass of lazily steaming coffee, then roiled up on the sides, tanning the inky surface. At one table Hart pontificated to four of the new young gunners, who listened with eager faces. In the rear of the tent six riflemen hunched silently over their chow.

"Your gear all ready, Chambers?" Hart asked.

He nodded.

"Take it out to the bird and load it on. As soon as Culpepper finishes breakfast, I'll send him out so you can show him a couple more things before you leave."

He nodded again, took two steps toward the riflemen, and stopped. No one he even cared to say good-bye to. Todd took a bullet in the leg yesterday and could now be anywhere from the base camp to Japan.

Back at his tent, he sat on the sandbags, swallowed some coffee, then threw what was left on the sand. It soaked in, leaving a dark-brown stain covered with tiny bubbles that glistened, winked, and popped as he folded his canteen cup.

At least the morning looked pleasant, was quiet. Bright sun in the east, and to the south only a faint trace of fog hovered over the hill. He crawled back into his tent, unfastened the tops of the sunken canisters, and began to pull out the beers and sodas. For what? Whoever took the tent could have them. He squatted and rolled his sleeping bag. Along with his steel pot, pistol belt, grenade launcher, and shaving kit, he put the bag outside and sat down for a last beer and to savor the silence in the tent. No noise from outside, the whole company still subdued from yesterday. He envisioned everyone walking stealthily about, brooding solemnly on his fears, and carefully waiting for the day to return to normal.

For him it was different. He enjoyed the silent periods as the fatigue overcame the nervous twitch and gnawing doubt. Like the sky after a tornado, when it no longer threatens, seems nearly dead. Only slowly it comes back to life. That licking of the sunlight, just like a voice or laugh or flight without a loss. The sky seems almost misshapen with daylight, as the men are shrunk in wanting to forget and brighten over death.

For him it had to be different. Everyone else always wanted to watch the waterfalls, but he would climb up high to watch the smooth moving stillness of the water before it fell. Even while making love, he liked the pure exhaustion afterward, liked most the still moment when effort ceased before he throbbed out life. In the cathedrals he used to hope that if he stood there long enough, a concrete pillar would absorb him.

Outside the tent he strapped on his pistol belt, dropped his steel pot on his head, and slung his grenade launcher. He tucked the sleeping bag under one arm and trudged toward the flight line.

Culpepper, a new replacement who'd just come out yesterday, was already there, moving around, looking at the side guns on another ship from different angles. "Think you got it figured out?" He threw his sleeping bag on the floor of his ship.

"Looks pretty complicated," Culpepper said. "Take you long to learn it?"

"Little while. That grenade launcher on our ship is kind of hard. If you get a bird with side guns, keep them clean and watch the ammo when you load. Don't be afraid to take the guns apart. It's the only way you'll learn to put them back together again. Even if you aren't sure, take them apart and clean them anyway. Someone'll always be around to help you, and if not, just use your head to figure it out. You don't keep them clean, they'll gum up on you, and first thing you know, you'll be in a shit storm and the things won't work. It's a pain, but it passes time and may help you in the long run."

"Should I oil them every day?"

"Just a little. Too much and they'll stick. Clean them every three days. Landing in this sand blows all kinds of shit into them."

"You think I'll see a lot of action?"

"Who knows? Just stay ready. There hasn't been a lot lately, but you saw what happened yesterday. You never know. Hope you don't see too much."

"But it's pretty boring otherwise, huh?"

"That's better than getting killed. Don't worry, you'll see your share. Now get up in the seat, clear the gun, and hang it on the cord, and I'll show you how to shoot."

Culpepper climbed into the ship, settled himself on the seat, and hung the machine gun from the elastic cord. The new gunner set the stock on his lap, then raised his hand and felt where the elastic cord hung from the ceiling of the ship. He ran his hand slowly down the cord, then braced the stock firmly against his side. He looked up suddenly, grinning.

As Chambers stared at Culpepper's sparkling teeth, an immense wave of fatigue washed over him. Must be from not sleeping last night. No. Culpepper smiled wetly while Orville's mouth was dry.

"Look okay, Chambers?"

Get hold of yourself. It was as though Culpepper looked at

him across a desert, now five feet, now five thousand miles, through an impenetrable wall of shimmering waves of heat. They rose like vertical rivers of water glass reflected in his mouth.

"Chambers! Do I look okay?"

Get hold! "Put your right foot on the edge of the floor and brace your left against the doorjamb." Too many miles to cross; Culpepper's mouth, wet smiling promise, would be dried out by the time he got there.

"How's that supposed to help?"

"Stabilizes you for shooting straighter. You can hold the gun in line and turn your body while the ship's moving." And it will jabber forever in your head.

"What's it like on gun runs?"

"Tracers keep you on target. Just shoot till you can't see it anymore. When the ship's turning and you're shooting out the back, point the gun down so you don't hit the tail boom." And when your mouth dries, out, you'll smell nothing.

"Bipbipbipbipbipbipbipbipbip!" shot out of Culpepper's mouth as he playfully jerked the machine gun on the cord. "I bet that old chopper's talkin' when all six of them babies is goin' at once."

"Put the gun up and I'll show you how to hold your ammo."

Settled on the seat inside the helicopter, he drew the long belt of ammunition out of the box with care, hung it on his knees, and looked across the helipad to where the crew chief worked on top of the colonel's ship.

"Just a second, Chambers, I got to take a leak." Culpepper disappeared under the tail boom.

In a week he'd be lost in the cold, quiet, black and white woods. The air frozen, cracking when the branches could no longer hold the residue of snow. Exquisite sound, like a drop of water falling from the empty cathedral dome to the empty cathedral floor, like a bullet cracking up the empty bore through the vacant sky. He wanted to see a bird leave a branch, the snow falling, rustling the air. The powder follows the chunks and quietly buries them.

"Okay, Chambers, I'm ready!" Culpepper shouted as he bounded up to the door. He rubbed his hands together. "Anyone ever get their nuts shot off sitting up there?"

"Not that I've heard of. You might sit on a flak jacket though, just to protect them."

"Good idea."

"You got this young soldier all squared away, Chambers?"

He whirled and faced Captain Sanders. "Oh. Morning, sir. Are you going to fly us in?"

"I'm going to Bangkok. What do you think, Culpepper? Going to like firing on those little gooks?"

"Looks like fun, sir."

"I remember the first one I got," Sanders said. "A little NVA in a clearing. Hit him dead in the ass with a grenade and split him in half. The little bastard turned over and we flew down real low and seen he was still alive. He looked scared as hell, like he was begging either to be finished off or let alone, I don't know which. I picked the bird up and dumped about twenty more on him. Nothing left but smoke when I finished."

"Damn, sir, you don't play, do you?" Culpepper said.

"Can't afford to. We ought to be going pretty soon. I don't want to miss out on any of that Thai pussy. Where the hell is Maddin? Chambers, where's Maddin at?"

"Huh?"

"Maddin, where the hell is he?"

"I don't know. Might be at Headquarters Company."

"Go get him. I want to get out of here."

He looked at Sanders while he got down from the helicopter. "Me too, sir," he said.

He found Maddin sitting on the skid of the recovery ship, sharing a joint with the two riggers.

"Chambers old buddy," Maddin said. "Sit down for a little puff. We were just going to get Colonel Snider and see if he wanted to get fucked up with us."

Chambers sat in front of the skid and took a deep drag. "Maddin, Sanders is over at our ship, and he wants to go."

"If Sanders can reach his dick around and touch his asshole, he ought to fuck himself. What if I don't feel like flying today? Maybe I just want to sit here and smoke dope and talk shit till the war's over. But, Chambers, I know today is your day, and just as a personal favor, I'm going to crew that ship so you can go home."

"Thanks."

"Sanders is going on R&R, huh? That dude probably won't be able to *buy* pussy. He's so crusty and funky that he don't even change his drawers. He takes them off once a month, rolls them up, and smokes 'em."

"Say, uh, Maddin."

"Oh, yeah, we're going in, right, Chambers? I'm coming."

Chambers said good-bye to the recovery crew and walked with Maddin toward their ship. "Maddin, you got the reddest eyes. I hope Sanders doesn't notice."

"Chambers, you know Sanders don't notice nothing but his sorry-ass self. I could walk out there blind drunk and bare-assed naked, and he'd think I was in full battle dress."

"Where the hell you been, Maddin?" Sanders shouted as they approached the ship.

"I got the diarrhea, sir. I couldn't get off the stool to save my soul."

"That's a lotta shit," Sanders said.

"Whole lot, sir."

"Okay, okay. You best put a cork in your ass, because I'm gonna run this bird up and we're leaving."

"Roger, sir." Maddin walked around to the other side of the ship and strapped on his gear.

"You flying in with us, Culpepper?" Chambers asked.

"Hart wants me to stay out here."

"Good luck, then."

"I'll take care of business for you."

"I bet you will." He slid into his flight helmet, fastened his harness in front, and jumped up on the seat. Culpepper shrank as the helicopter rose from the brown helipad and corkscrewed into the sky.

Chambers had made fair marks in high school. He couldn't remember for sure, but thought he'd had slightly better than a B average. As soon as he got home he'd check. Give the secretaries at the high school a surprise, him walking in and having transcripts sent to the university. As the ship swung over the river and glistening rice paddies, he thought of bridges and the river between the two cities, of the smaller, slower, browner Minnesota River close to his home. It sometimes flooded in the spring.

Visualizing himself in college, he imagined an old man in a tidy, dark, wooden room. He would smoke cigars when he studied. He'd be a freshman, twenty-five years old, but people began older, and he'd have a head start, knowing German and the basics of art history. Maybe he'd take some engineering to learn about stress and prepare to build his own house someday.

He carried no pictures in his wallet, no sad and shabby mementos in his pockets or around his neck. His small tin box of postcards was safely tucked away in his duffel bag. When he allowed himself to think about women—about love—it was from the reproduction of Botticelli's "Pallas and the Centaur" that he constructed an ideal from facial expression and bodily tension. Or perhaps it wasn't love. More of a statement about relating. Of isolation and loneliness. Of strength and vulnerability. He wasn't as vulnerable as the Centaur, but he couldn't resist indulging his fantasy. He pictured himself before a fireplace with a blizzard raging beyond the walls. His Pallas would be there, her face all sympathy and forgiveness and comfort to his weariness. His feelings would be beyond words; they could be conveyed only by gesture. And he wouldn't need words either. The particular expression of her face would be sufficient; her reaching out to touch his hair with the least bit of playfulness would communicate all he wished to know.

Radio static crackled; he winced as Maddin coughed into the mike. "I bet your buddies are whooping it up in Sin City today. Those clowns'll be lucky to catch their plane home."

"Not straight like you and me, huh, Maddin?"

"You'll probably be down there this afternoon."

"I think I'll stay away this trip."

"What?"

"You heard me."

"I can see you staying away from the clappy cunt, but aren't you even gonna get no souvenirs to take home?"

"Who would I take them to?"

"Some of that cheap shit might help you into some pussy."

"If I have to use that crap to get it, I'll go without."

"Suit yourself, cool breeze."

"I got to." He switched the intercom back and tried not to listen to Sanders' expectations for his R&R. Huge green jungle leaves reflected the sun in their dew, sparkling in accompaniment to the regular drone of the engine. He felt exhausted, but peaceful. No longer any need to exert himself.

Thinking about Sin City made him more tired. He couldn't stand the stench. Sperm. Piss and shit and puke. Cheap booze, sweat, and cigarette smoke. Used-up females who smelled like rotting corpses. Mingled, the stink came back to him as the helicopter raced through the morning air. Smells had to be stored in the memory too. Afraid of vomiting, he leaned into the air and inhaled deeply.

Morgan had said that one would have to puke out the experience to be shut of it. Morgan would do it in Mississippi. He'd drive from Georgia until he found a desolate stretch on one of the narrow, lonely, eerie roads in the country. With two-fifths of Old Mr. Boston, he would climb a hill and drink alone until he could drink no more, then he would drink some more. He would drink so much that he'd have the most agonizing vomit ever. A total emptying. He might even have to puke out his entire stomach, but once he did, he could start over again, eating good food and drinking mellow wine. Morgan had laughed all the time he told it, but was in dead earnest and would do what he said if given the opportunity, if only so he could tell about it later.

Poor Morgan. He made Orville tired now too, with his whining and self-degradation. Too bad Morgan couldn't have been in his place yesterday to finally get his wish. Or too bad he couldn't have been in McCutcheon's. He wondered how badly Morgan wanted to die—probably not as much as the line chief. Morgan could never go home until he'd faced death on the most ridiculous terms possible. He'd said he wanted to know what the last strand of the rope was made of; once he found out he'd climb back down or back up (he wasn't quite sure which way), unless that last strand couldn't hold him.

Whether or not Morgan had hung by the final thread, he couldn't tell. The day he'd killed the woman and Barry had died beside him might have been the time, but it was too momentous to even think about in those terms. No one came away from that experience with glib expressions as to how it made him feel. There could be only grief and fatigue and guilt. And yet Orville had felt a certain relaxation in Morgan's body that day, as though the inner warfare might possibly be burning itself out. But then there had been the other night. And there were the dead people too. What right did anyone have . . . ?

He caught himself beating on his flight helmet with the palm of his hand and looked quickly over at Maddin, but the crew chief's head was turned. The pilots hadn't seen him either. He leaned into the rushing air. He had to get some sleep tonight.

His father's face burst through a cloud like a movie monster's arising from the deep. Outrage burned in those angry eyes, outrage at not having even the remains of his first two sons and at his youngest for joining an organization that had brought him nearer to death every day. How did impotent old men withstand the taunts of rowdy children? He felt that he understood his mother, living in continual worry, but resigned and nearly serene. She might die if he did, or she might do nothing. Either way, without flourish. But he had lost sleep trying to understand his father.

Martin Chambers, MD, country doctor, gentleman farmer, saver of life, hater of it too, taker of it for his son's sake. Would he take the life of the entire planet if given the opportunity? Chambers, flying between green and blue, imagined his father with an assassin's eye, leering vengefully from beneath the thick foliage. His father must have hated him at times. By now he might have even grown content in that hatred. And so he'd have to readjust himself again. If he anticipated his third son's death, it would probably cause more pain to accept the fact of his life. It would be a long month ahead at home, getting to know his mother and father again—perhaps for the first time.

Neither of them had said much when he didn't go to college, and he felt that their worry had mainly been about what he would do with his life. In her letters his mother seemed happy about his decision to start school; he'd be close to home and moving toward some goal. She must be suspicious of what he'd chosen to study, but she'd never say so—that wasn't a woman's place. His father would be suspicious if he became a priest.

When Maddin tugged his harness, he noticed the slight bounce of the ship. Vertical vibration—the rotor blades were already out of track. Maddin looked panicked, and the voices of the pilots suddenly grew louder.

"Maddin," Sanders said, "you got this bird in track last night, right?"

"Yes, sir. I don't know what's wrong. Feels like it's slipping out pretty quick."

The bouncing got worse.

"What do you think it is?"

"I don't know, sir." Maddin looked afraid, really afraid.

"Maintenance sergeant said it was okay, sir. Maybe you ought to set it down."

"She's still holding at sixty-seven hundred RPM," Warrant Officer Eastman said. "Damn, Captain," he said as the jerk became more pronounced, "let's set this thing down."

They had been flying down a long valley and had pulled up to a thousand feet to clear the ridge where the valley ended in a box canyon. The northern perimeter of the base camp was four miles beyond the ridge, down a formerly lush ravine that had been napalmed to desolation.

Orville bobbed his head in time with the increasing vibration within the ship.

"There ain't no place to set down right here," Sanders said, glancing hurriedly in every direction. "We have to clear that ridge, then autorotate to the bottom of the valley. This thing's shaking like the rotor head's been split. Maybe we took a round from somewhere. You see any tracers?"

"Jesus Christ! No, sir. You think we'll make that ridge?" Maddin was scared shitless, his face white, as was his hand where it gripped the mike button.

"We're losing RPM," Eastman said. "I don't know if we can clear that ridge. Jesus, sir, I don't think we can!"

"I'll take it," Sanders said.

Maddin looked crazy. Everyone looked crazy. Orville turned his head out the door, nodding in rhythm with the vibration. The ground came up at him slowly and in jerks, then it fell jerkily away.

He didn't want to watch Sanders straining. The vibrating had become so bad that he shook in his seat. A weird, steady racket increased inside his head. He couldn't tell which way the ground was coming, and the voices in his ears were foreign. He turned around, avoided looking at anyone, and unplugged his flight helmet. He looked back out the door, setting his eyes in the sky. Vibrating furiously in his seat, he listened to a purely mechanical clatter.

Suddenly it stopped. He held his breath as something

resembling two boomerangs flashed into the sky to the right front of the ship. He had never experienced such a stillness. His entire body tingled. His lungs relaxed, and an immense volume of air pushed out of his open mouth. The sky fell upward, like light from the floor above when a glass-doored elevator goes down. Then everything rushed furiously, and he remembered Captain Sloane saying, "A helicopter without its rotor blades has as much air dynamics as a grand piano."

Blue went to green, then black, then orange everywhere. Somehow he was out of his harness, in green and black again, moving in a bad smell. He heard a scream echoing as though he were at the bottom of a well, screaming to himself at the top. Then he saw only orange and he evaporated like the last drop of morning dew from the petal of a flower.

28

MORGAN STEPPED out of the New York bar (the first on the left as you entered Sin City) and patted his flabby stomach. The two beers hadn't gone down so badly. He'd had a big breakfast at the base, a hot shower and shave, and he'd even changed his clothes. His feet felt fine. He still couldn't remember what happened last night. He recalled going to Hancock's hooch, but not leaving. One more night to add to the many.

Within its rectangle Sin City had fifty concrete block-houses, each with a bar and eight little fucking rooms. Lengthwise, twenty houses lined each side, with another ten spanning the width at the rear. A block wall stood at the front, with a small shack where MP's checked the passes, dog tags, and ID cards of the entering soldiers. The middle of Sin City was a vacant lot of mud and debris except for three restaurants and a souvenir shop near the back of the compound.

Morgan hiked up his pants and looked to either side like a cowboy coming out of a saloon. He moved up five doors to the Dixie bar. Three soldiers sat around a table with two girls. "Come on and sit down, buddy," one of them said.

"Too much action for me. I'll just have a beer and count the four days I've got left in this place." He sat down and looked out the window, tensing as he thought about home. What would he do? Who would he see? How would he announce his return? The last letter he'd written was to his sister three weeks ago, saying he'd be home before Christmas. Well, he'd be there before that, and he'd probably be drunk a lot. Drunk all the fucking time.

Drunk. What a perfect word. He didn't even have to drink much to get drunk anymore. Maybe that's the way it went: At first you got drunk quickly, then you reached a point where you could hold it for a while, then you'd been drunk so much you could take one beer, think DRUNK, and there you were.

But it wasn't funny anymore, not like in S-1 when he'd down four beers for breakfast. It was funny then, even when he drank a fifth a night, because he never knew where he'd wake up, and someone always told a good story about what he did. It wasn't funny anymore because his guts were a mess and he was weak and fat and smoked fifty cigarettes a day and if he had to run two hundred yards he'd die. Combat was supposed to make you tough. Combat made you shit a lot.

He wondered if Chambers would stay with him in Oakland, wondered if their strained relationship would resolve itself before they left. Orville understood plenty and he accepted too. Morgan wanted him and his sister to get together, even though his sister had a man. She could talk to him about architecture, and they could both take care of him when he was drunk. He knew Chambers was tired of his shit. He disapproved. He understood, he even accepted, but he disapproved. So Chambers didn't respect him anymore. So fuck it.

Maybe it wouldn't be good to have Orville there when he got back. He'd make him feel guilty or constrained. Because Orville didn't find anything funny about people making asses of themselves. Okay, but why be so serious all the time? Lighten up, man. Jesus, if it wasn't grim enough. So you make an ass of yourself. So what? Chambers never made an ass of himself. Gibraltar. Enough, enough, enough. If he made an ass of himself at home, tough shit. The important thing was to make an ass of himself right now. He drank up and left the Dixie.

The sky had clouded over and soon the track that ran in front of the whorehouses would be a river of mud. He walked to the other side of Sin City, stopping about twenty feet in front of the Miami. It had been in the picture from *Time* that his father had sent him shortly after Sin City opened. Old paternal nudge in the ribs about which direction Oriental cunt ran. Sin City. Built to prevent the division from being decimated by the clap. The Army doctors gave shots once a week.

He found Clampitt with a girl in his lap. He and Webster had met Clampitt at finance that morning, and the young gunner had asked to accompany them to Sin City. He was one of Hart's boys who'd made sergeant, but had been breaking away lately and wasn't really that bad. With four days left, who cared anyway?

"You light yet?" Clampitt asked.

"Nope. You?"

"We've just been talking."

"Does she read Spinoza?"

"What?"

"Just to show that there's no hard feelings about you making sergeant, Clampitt, I'm going to buy you a piece of ass. . . . Hey, girl, for how many p. you boom-boom my friend?"

"Boom-boom four hundred p."

"You chop-chop too?"

"No chop-chop. Chop-chop number ten."

"Come on, you chop-chop extra hundred p."

"No chop-chop. Only boom-boom."

He waved five hundred piasters in front of her. "Come on, special chop-chop just for my friend."

"No chop-chop. You number ten thou."

"Six hundred p. chop-chop, boom-boom." He grabbed her shirt and waved the money in her face.

"Let me take my time, Morg," Clampitt said. "You know these Buddhist chicks don't blow. Only the Catholics do."

He started to put the money in his pocket.

"Six hundred p.?" the girl said.

He winked at Clampitt. "That's right, Baby-san. Okay? You take care of my friend. You're not about to reach nirvana anyway." He dangled the bills in front of her again.

"Okay." She took the money, disappeared behind the bar, then quickly reappeared. "Come on, GI," she said to Clampitt.

Ten minutes later Webster bounded through the doorway. "Morg, baby, they got this Pakistani broad at the San Francisco that throws an honest-to-God fuck." He sat down. "You got to try this out. Good, good, gooooood!"

"Later. You want to go to old town, see what's up?" He felt shitty about Clampitt's whore and wanted to get away.

"Let's relax a little first."

"Okay. Maybe I'll knock off a shot." He went to the bar and made arrangements with a girl who had just come out of the back. He took another beer to the room. She pulled off her pink blouse and black pajama bottoms and flopped on the mat. He removed his shirt and slid his pants and drawers below his knees, leaving his boots on. He looked at the girl, raised the can to his lips, then leaned over and spit a mouthful of beer on her stomach.

"You number ten!" She jumped up.

"Here, wipe it off with my shirt."

She took his T-shirt and wiped her belly. "Be nice, now, GI. Let's have nice boom-boom."

"You play awhile first." He leaned back while she rubbed him.

In five minutes she said, "Come on, GI, you boom-boom now."

He settled into the rhythm and rubbed her thighs with his hands. Her head lolled to one side with her eyes shut and mouth open as if she were asleep. He dropped his face and kissed her salty neck. She smelled like shit. He closed his eyes, put himself back in his room at Berkeley with Emily, the soft-thighed teller from the Wells Fargo Bank, and after a few minutes he came. He got two breaths in before she slid out from under him. He swung his feet over the pallet thinking how much better it was just whacking off. "Jesus Christ," he said when she pulled an Army canteen cup half full of water from under the pallet and splashed her crotch. "You got some real good hygiene here."

"You like boom-boom, GI?"

"Terrific." He restrained himself from pushing her over. He wiped the sweat from his chest and stomach with his T-shirt, put it on, hitched up his pants, and walked out.

In the back of the donkey cart, three feet off the ground, Morgan gripped a supporting pole of the canopy, feeling like a monkey on display as they moved down the highway toward old town.

"Come on, mule!" Webster yelled from the front. The reins cracked, but the cart went no faster. "You want to drive, Morg?"

He turned. "Why not?"

"Get in back, Papa-san." Webster pointed his thumb over his shoulder.

"You let me now." The old man next to him grabbed for the reins.

Webster picked up the man and put him in the back. "Now stay put."

Morgan moved past him and grabbed the reins, seating himself on the little bench as a pair of GI's pointed and jeered from the side of the road. "Come on, little giddy-up go." He thrashed the reins up and down, and the donkey broke into a trot.

As they neared the first dirt street into town, he spied Lang's father's laundry off to the side. In the rush of getting ready to leave, he'd forgotten all about it.

"We stop here," the old man said. He ran around in front and tried to slow the donkey.

Webster grabbed the reins and cracked them once again.

"You stop. God damn!" Papa-san said.

"Come on, Web. Let's go up to the laundry before the MP's come." He wanted to get away from the old man and see Lang.

Webster dropped the reins, and they jumped down and walked away.

"Wait. You-you! You owe one hundred fifty p."

"Sorry about that shit, Papa-san," Webster said.

"You pay one-fifty, fucker!"

Webster walked over to the man, picked him up beneath the arms, and shook him in the air. "Little gook talk some big shit." He set him down hard on the driver's seat and threw two hundred piasters into the cart. "Maybe I fuck your daughter this afternoon." They walked away.

"Man, Web, you're getting a little rough."

"Christ, I'll be glad to pull out of here. What are we doing, anyway? That clown's probably made more money in the last year than in his whole sorry life."

"Don't let it get you down today." The nasty depression

started, and he wanted desperately to stop it. "Let's have a beer at the laundry. This cute little girl lives there. She's about eight, but she'll really be fine someday. I used to relax here when I was clerkin'."

Papa-san, hustling and efficient, met them beneath the canopy. He pumped Morgan's hand and sought approval for his entrepreneurial skills. He now had three men ironing for him instead of one, his boys were shining shoes on the highway near Sin City, and a new blue and white sign saying "Yankee Laundry" gleamed on the canopy roof.

Lang peered around the entrance to the mud hut. When Morgan caught her eye, her head disappeared. "Hi, Lang. Papa-san, bring beers."

"Kid looks okay," Webster said. "Does she appear again, or have we had the whole show?"

"'She'll be out. She's real shy. She's never said a word. Just looks at you or maybe sits in your lap."

Papa-san brought the beer, looked around, then leaned over and asked them if they wanted to boom-boom.

"No boom-boom here," Morgan said. "Not good Lang see. Papa-san number ten thou."

"Lang no know," Papa-san said. "Me go do laundry now."

"Shit, Morgan, he'll probably have Lang turnin' tricks by her twelfth birthday."

He didn't reply, knowing it was true. Maybe before she was twelve. "Come out here, Lang!"

After a couple of minutes she came out the door and walked around the men who were ironing.

"How you been, Lang? You miss me?"

She played on one of the ironing tables, staring at them occasionally.

"Come here, Lang." He patted his thighs. "Come sit down."

She looked at him and blinked twice. Her open mouth displayed crooked, pale-yellow teeth. Morgan thought of bringing her to the States for orthodontia. He hunched down and beckoned to her with his right index finger. She smiled quickly and turned her head.

"You give candy," she said.

He pulled some Life Savers from his front pocket. "Here, Lang."

She smiled again, advanced at half steps, reached out, and grabbed the candy. She turned the tube slowly in her hands, then fled into the mud hut.

He called after her twice but she didn't return.

"Let's go," Webster said. "At least you heard her talk."

"I can't figure it. She used to stay out here for hours."

"Maybe she's greasin' Life Savers with a boyfriend."

"Hell with it."

They walked up a block, then turned right onto the main street. "Looks like a fucking ghost town." The street was utterly still, as though it had been cleared for a duel between the sheriff and a hired gun. Thick wire mesh still covered the fronts of the old bar. Paint peeled from the faded pastel signs that had been so bright the first time he'd come to town with Stubbs. The buildings seemed ready to collapse into the mud at any moment.

"Jesus, Web, there's people living in those places." He pointed to the side where two immobile women stared at them from behind the wire. Their gaunt faces reminded him of concentration-camp victims staring through fences at the liberating soldiers. "This gives me the creeps. There could be VC in there."

"No chance," Webster said. "They make too much money off this place to fuck with it during the day."

As the rain began to fall, they went into a laundry. Laundries were the only businesses in old town not off limits now. A woman with a light-brown, passive face served them beer while they made small talk about going home. The ghostliness of the laundry—of the entire town—made Morgan gloomy. He thought of the hamlet where he'd shot the woman, of the hundreds of deserted hamlets and villages he'd seen all over the country. Where did all the people go?

He saw the whole country empty, mud and dust covering bleached bones and the skeletons of ruined aircraft. "Let's go outside, Web. I like the rain."

He walked into the middle of the street, tilted his head back, and let the drops splash on his face.

"Come on," Webster said. "Let's go get laid."

They walked farther up the street, and then he stopped again. "It's all gone away now, huh?" He pointed to the marketplace a hundred feet in front of them. An old man sat beneath the roof on a bench, a pile of withered collard greens in front of him. A woman sat listlessly at the far end with two thin dogs. "Used to be at least fifty people, like an old bazaar. All gone now, though."

"Come on, we're getting soaked." Webster led him to a small walkway off the back street that led out of town. They entered an alcove with a well in the middle, two doors and two windows behind it.

Inside, candles spread a dingy light over the front room. Two GI's sat at a table with three girls and an old woman.

"You look a little wet," one of them said.

"My buddy likes to play in the rain." Webster pointed to the young girls. "Just these three?"

"One more," the woman said, flashing black teeth.

"They chop-chop here," one soldier said. "Whole thing five hundred p."

Mama-san brought out the other girl, who had buck teeth, thin slits of eyes, and a flat nose. Webster picked the free girl at the table, and Morgan went in back with the new arrival. The small room had bunk beds that looked American. He took off his shirt and sat on the lower bed.

"You ain't too pretty, are you, Baby-san?"

"No Englis." She pulled off her top and sat down. Her tits looked as if they'd just sprouted. He reached out and squeezed, then took a big swallow of beer.

"Damn, you are a baby-san." Thirteen or fourteen at the most. "You'll be over the hill at eighteen."

"No Englis. You chop-chop?"

"No, I don't sop-sop," he said, imitating her pronunciation. "You chop-chop, suck my cock."

She nodded. "Me chop-chop now."

He undid his belt, pulled down his pants and drawers, and leaned back. She started to crawl up on him but he stopped her. "You take pants off too." He pointed to her pajamas and gestured that she take them off. She did, then curled up beside him and put her head in his lap while he massaged her buttocks and thighs. She had hardly any pubic hair. He snorted and pushed her on the floor. "You better get up or you'll catch cold or crabs." He fell back against the wall.

"Number ten," she said, "number ten thou."

"Come on up, Baby-san. You still got work to do. I'll behave." She started on him again and this time he closed his eyes and made a quick succession of images of girls he'd been with. Slagel's sister. Christ, was she fine. A contented groan rose involuntarily in his throat.

What a great time they'd had in New York that last weekend before sailing to Germany. He and Padgett and Slagel had adjoining rooms in the Biltmore, had money and women, and while they stayed in bed and drank a lot, they walked along the Hudson and rode the Staten Island ferry too. It had been pure energy without the low points that always came when he drank just to forget. He'd felt alive then, again in Italy, and he hadn't felt much alive since Italy unless someone was shooting at him. Padgett and Slagel were gone and nothing countered that. Though he couldn't imagine Slagel all crippled because he'd only seen him full of life (the face still grinned in his head), he'd kissed Padgett in the hospital, and he kept seeing the dead and alive faces like a flipping coin.

"Boom-boom now," the girl said and lay back on the bed.

She was tight and the only expression on her face was pain whenever he jerked or pushed too hard. He moved his hips in a slow circle, causing her to grimace more.

"Me only baby-san," she said.

It was a job to her like shucking corn or picking rice. Thirteen fucking years old! He thought of Slagel's sister again but Slagel's face grinned at him too and he couldn't think of Emily twice in the same day and everyone else kept flicking through his mind but none of them would settle.

He pulled out and she groaned and he flipped her on her stomach. "You got baby-san asshole too?" He thought she'd put up a fight, but she let him go ahead. Not as tight as he'd expected, but the dryness hurt. "You work nine to six with an hour for lunch?"

"No Englis."

He'd never come. He grabbed her buttocks as though they were two cantaloupes and pushed her flat on her stomach. "You chop-chop again."

"You long time, GI. *Beaucoup* beer."

"Chop-chop!" He pulled her head to his crotch.

After a moment she gasped and lay back. He plunged into her and in ten minutes the muscles in his legs began to tingle and he knew it was nearly over. His arms relaxed. In a monsoon sweat, he couldn't wait to come and stop. He finally released, and after a couple of deep breaths he rolled off and rubbed his stomach as the girl ran out of the room.

They drank for another half hour, refused to pay, then left with the other GI's, each of them straddling the well and pissing into it before staggering back to the highway. They caught rides on Hondas, leaping off at the road to Sin City and running to the whorehouses without paying the drivers. They flashed their passes, stumbled through the entrance, and stood panting in the mud.

"Wild, huh, Web?" It seemed as if every GI in the Army had found his way to Sin City.

"I'd like to have a dollar for every bucket of jizz that's been dropped here today."

Morgan smelled sperm, saw it running in gray rivers out the backs of the whorehouses. "Let's just watch for a minute." This might be the most incredible sight in the war. He hadn't been to Sin City since before his R&R, when three-fourths of division had been in the field. It had been quiet, almost sleepy, like this morning. There were more soldiers now, but something else filled the air too, something that went beyond pandemonium and the innocent fun of soldiers on a spree. It was as if the very spirit of lunacy had been spread over the place like fertilizer, had deserted every nuthouse in the world and come to rest in this concrete rectangle in South Vietnam.

Thunder rumbled lowly behind dirty gray and black clouds. A soldier staggered out of the Far West, barking unintelligible commands. He fell to the ground, then did push-ups while counting cadence aloud. Everyone was drunk or drugged or beaten out of himself. Some men trudged wearily around the track in an endless processional, looking as if they'd forgotten where they were going. Others were more animated, faces filled with desperate frenzy, as though they couldn't get enough of . . . what? Black soldiers clustered around the entrances to the four bars at the far corner, dancing to soul music, while a pair of scrawny, long-haired South Vietnamese twanged electric guitars in an adjacent building.

"Let's go see Clampitt," Webster said. "Then maybe I'll buy you that Pakistan broad's pussy."

"I need some rest before that." Thinking of the sheer effort of fucking brought bile to his mouth.

They got Clampitt and went to a restaurant in the middle of Sin City where they ate hamburgers—dogburgers—and discussed the battle of the day before.

Morgan drifted off. The dead men's gear had been brought in that morning, and he'd seen McCutcheon's steel pot at S-4. Two holes, where one bullet had gone in and out, stared up from the top like empty eye sockets, and a single larger hole yawned on the side. That bullet had stayed inside his head. Visualizing McCutcheon's face brought vague outlines of others to mind, then he heard names read off in a dull repetitive monotone. The names blurred like the faces. He could remember them each one after the other if he wanted to, but it was easier to see one big mass of face and name that grew and grew. Not like a balloon, but like a city dump. You could recognize an old chair or shoe—if you wanted to. But the fact remained that it was a dump.

He got rid of the dead names and faces, feeling warm about the soldiers he knew. Everything they'd been through *was* important, and no one had the right to meddle with it. Surely Webster felt that as he talked of throttling demonstrators if they gave him any trouble. The world saw soldiers as uniforms, but soldiers knew each other like wives or the very best of friends, where everything was shared. Right down to the pimples on your ass and the tiniest bit of fear in your heart.

They left the restaurant at four. As the food had absorbed the booze, he'd begun to feel healthier, more clearheaded. Outside was still crazy with soldiers bent upon their pleasure.

A trooper ran out of the Longhorn and grabbed his arm. "Have you seen Deakin?"

"What?"

"'Deakin. You must have seen him." Desperation flashed across the man's face. "Where's he at? Where's Deakin?"

"I think he's over at the KC."

"Never known him to go there. You positive it was Deakin?"

"Had to be him. You can't miss Deakin."

"Yeah. You can't. KC. Thanks, buddy." He let go and loped around the track.

"What was that all about?" Webster asked.

"Hell if I know."

The plastic-strip door of the San Francisco had been pulled down and trampled in the mud and was half buried. He stepped up onto the concrete floor and looked around the room. Dark gray, like most of the sky. No electricity, and no one had bothered to light candles. Cans and mud and cigarette butts soaked in a thin layer of beer on the floor. One soldier tried to teach a whore how to dance to a Rolling Stones record. Webster stepped up beside him and pointed to the Pakistani leaning against the bar. She was big and fleshy, and her faded olive-drab skin looked like old fatigues.

"Kind of fucked in here, huh, Morg?"

"I'm all right." He refused to let it get to him.

Webster led him up to the whore. "You boom-boom my friend. I pay." He slurred his words drunkenly.

The whore smiled and shook her head. "Too long time. Too much beer. No come."

"Oh, come on," Webster said.

"No long time."

Morgan hadn't cared at first, but the soft contours of her body made him more interested. She might be a nice way to finish. "Okay," he said, "we go fifteen minutes." He pointed to his watch and spread his palm three times. "I don't come then, we quit."

"Sounds fair," Webster said. "How about it?" He shook the whore's arm.

"Okay," she said. "Five hundred p."

He put his arm around her and rubbed his groin against her thigh.

When they got to the room he took off all his clothes. He felt like sticking his bare feet into all that flesh. He rubbed her belly, stroking her arm with his other hand, wanting to dive on her and roll around. He didn't care about the minutes or whether he could come or not. He wanted the feel of all that flesh. He palmed and squeezed and frantically kissed her breasts.

"Relax, baby," she said. She turned him on his back and kissed his chest and stomach, rubbing her hands along his thighs and crotch. She was going to blow him and he hadn't even asked. He let out a loud groan. She went slowly up and down for a minute, then rolled off and lay on her back. He got between her legs, rose on his knees, and looked at her. Then he fell forward, barely breaking the fall with his hands. She put him in and started to move. Exquisite. He didn't do anything with his hips. She did it all. His hands went everywhere. So soft and warm, as though she had no bones and was just an undulating mass of softness beneath him. He burrowed his face between her breasts, on her neck, in her armpits while his hands ran crazily up and down her legs and her ass and her back.

He barely noticed when the tingling started. She had wrapped her legs around him and rocked slowly from side to side while he kneaded the ample flesh on her ass. Then all of a sudden he felt it coming and he stopped and stiffened and a cold blue zone came up behind his eyes where time dissolved. Then everything caved in and he fell into her flesh again, moaning, swinging his head back and forth, back and forth.

She gently stroked his back and rocked a little. He brought his head up and looked at her, but her eyes were still closed. He groaned as though waking and rested his cheek on her shoulder.

"Hey, GI, you still got four minutes left."

"Damn! That was out of sight. You're number one."

She squatted on the floor to douche.

"How long you been here?"

"Two month."

"Make *beaucoup* money, huh?"

"Vietnamese girl no like. GI like. Make money."

"When you go back to Pakistan?"

"Maybe few month. Maybe go Saigon. You go home soon?"

"Four days."

"What do in States?"

"Go back to school."

"For what?"

"Don't know."

"Why go?"

"Don't know. No like work." He shrugged.

She shrugged too. "No understand."

He nodded.

When they got to the Miami, Clampitt was in the back. "Might as well go when he gets out, huh?" Webster said.

"I'm about run down."

They ordered drinks, then sat praising the Pakistani. His fatigues were still damp from the rain, and his cold feet had begun to hurt.

"There you fuckers are!" Hancock stomped over from the entrance and dropped in a chair. "I been lookin' for you since three. I got drunk on shit-burnin' detail this morning, and it took me till two before they'd let me come down. No one told you, did they, Morg?"

"What?"

"Good. I hoped you wouldn't just hear it."

"What are you talking about?" Webster asked.

"About Chambers and them."

"What about them?" He hoped Hart wasn't keeping them in the field. He wanted to talk to Chambers tonight.

"Hey, Hancock," Clampitt bellowed from the hall, "how'd you get off detail?"

"Come here, Clampitt. This is damn serious."

"What, Cock?"

"Wait a minute, Morgan."

Clampitt came over and sat down.

"Well?"

"They got it," Hancock said. "Chambers, Maddin, Captain Sanders, and Mr. Eastman. They crashed this morning on the way in. I hate telling you guys, but I didn't want no one else doing it."

No one said anything. Morgan's stomach suddenly felt emptier than ever before. He shook his head in short jerks. "You're bullshitting."

"I wish I was. They crashed and burned. Someone said the main rotor flew off."

The main rotor flew off and they crashed and burned. That couldn't happen. He finished his beer, walked to the bar, and ordered six more. He had to be calm because that couldn't happen. While the papa-san got the beer, he grabbed a bottle of Old Grand-dad and took four swallows. He threw the bottle into a corner behind the bar, where it smashed on the concrete, splattering glass and whiskey all over the record player. Papa-san started to say something, but Morgan scooped up the beers and walked away. He set five on the table and drank the sixth straight down. He felt absolutely calm, but he couldn't understand what anyone said.

Hancock grabbed a whore and disappeared into the back.

He was the only fucking one left. He sat rigidly on the front of the chair, one hand palm down on his thigh, the other carrying beer and cigarettes alternately to his lips. A polished metal ball sat in his stomach.

He looked over his shoulder and the papa-san stood behind him, palm out, lips moving. He spit beer in the palm, then pushed the old man down. Both Webster's and Clampitt's mouths moved too but he couldn't hear anything but squeaking like a tape recorder being run very fast.

"I think I'm going crazy." He stood up and threw three beer cans behind the bar. He knocked the record player on the floor, knocked down the display of stolen American beers, smashed the shelf of potato chips and cigarettes. He picked up a chair and crashed it through the wooden bars in the window. He shook Clampitt off his back, picked up a table, and hurled it behind the bar. Webster and Clampitt grabbed him, pulled him out the door, and started up the track. He looked over his shoulder as Papa-san and two MP's went into the Miami.

They pulled him into the KC and sat him down. A soldier sat across the room, forehead to forearm, a pile of vomit on the floor beside him.

Morgan tried to get up but they held him. "I know him. I just want to say hello."

"Okay," Webster said. "You sure you're all right?"

He could hear again! "Fine. Fine."

He tapped the other soldier on the arm. He wasn't sure if it was the same guy, but when the tear- and puke-stained face came up, he knew it was. "You find Deakin?"

"Don't play with me, man."

"I'm not. You asked me, remember?"

"No."

"I told you he'd be here."

"Deakin's dead, man. Deakin's been dead for three months."

He picked up another chair, but Webster and Clampitt grabbed him again. He gave up and sat down, feeling drunk and tired.

He really was the last fucking one, and he should have been killed first because he was the rottenest of the whole group. He could never take it seriously in Germany when they'd talk about it and someone would bring up a reservation. "Nothing'll happen to us. We're too lucky." So all the reservations were canceled and off they trotted like the fair-haired boys and now they were all fucked up but him and it was his goddamn fault! He squirmed once in the chair, but they held him down.

He couldn't get loose this way. He'd have to play it cool, act normal, then slip away when they weren't watching. He'd walk in the opposite direction from camp until someone shot him off the road. Maybe he could hide out at Lang's until dark, then head north or west into the jungle until the VC blew his shit away.

Hundreds of soldiers stood at the top of the hill where the road to Sin City met Highway 19. The dump trucks were filling with screaming, jeering troops. He led Webster, Hancock, and Clampitt into the throng, then ducked between some soldiers and moved away.

"Morgan, Morgan, you want ride?"

He whirled. Papa-san from the laundry with a donkey cart. "Papa-san, you take me back to laundry for boom-boom."

"No. MP's."

"I hide. Please, Papa-san. I give you two hundred p., five hundred for boom-boom." He picked up two old ponchos from the back of the cart. "I hide under these."

"Okay. Okay." Papa-san looked around.

"No sweaty-dah, Papa-san." He curled up beneath the ponchos, shivering on the cold damp wood. It didn't matter anymore. He had to get back to the laundry and boom-boom. His excitement grew as the cart started down the highway. Tonight he'd go walking in the jungle.

The cart jerked to a halt in front of the laundry and he peered out from beneath the ponchos. The highway was deserted. It would be dark before long. He hustled off the cart and sat on a bench under the canopy. He gave Papa-san a thousand piasters.

"You go in there." Papa-san pointed to a room across from the one where he worked and where the family lived. "I bring girl."

Lang watched him from the laundry door.

"What's happening, Lang?" He went into the other room to wait. Part-time chicken coop. Bits of feathers and shit carpeted the dirt floor, and what seemed like a solid must hung in the air. He sat down on a pallet against the far wall, wondering who the girl would be. He'd never seen any women here except the old mama-san and Lang. What difference did it make? He didn't want a woman anyway. He lay back and stared at the ceiling.

The room darkened, and he looked up. A woman hung a cloth over the doorway. When she got close to him, he groaned as if he'd bitten into a wormy apple. Hideous. Old, skinny, and wrinkled. She sat down and took off her blouse, and he groaned again, but took off his shirt anyway. Christ, what did it matter? She got all her clothes off and lay on the pallet and didn't say a word.

"Baby, you must have been over the hill before Dien Bien Phu." He scowled as he felt her skinny legs. He threw his shirt on the floor and dropped his pants below his knees. He lay down and put his arms around her. No resistance and no attraction. She wasn't going to do him any favors. All business. She squeezed his prick, moving it up and down. It hurt a little, then the blood began to flow. When he got hard, she pulled him toward her. He put it in and lay there for a moment. Neither moved. He opened his eyes; she looked straight at him. She smiled thinly and moved her hips twice, telling him to get on with it. He wanted to go to sleep.

He lay still for another minute, and after she moved again, he started too. He went for five minutes, just up and down, hardly aware of where he was or what he did. She did nothing. He put his arms beneath her and pulled her close but got no warmth. He moved faster but she didn't have much juice, and it hurt. He moved his hips in a circle, then up and down, then did Morse code. SOS. Shit on shingle. He tried designs. Three times for a triangle, then a square, then he tried six equidistant points on a circle, then he laughed and jerked his entire body and came down hard until he knew he was hurting her. He spread his arms and snapped his fingers. He fell out.

"Whoaaaaah, Nellie!" He grabbed her hand and directed it to his prick. "Put it back in, Grandma-san."

"No more."

"You ain't done yet. Put it in." He jerked her hand.

She put it in and he thought of other games he could play. He remembered the joke about colored guys getting big dicks from putting it in fast and pulling it out slow. He tried that a couple of times, but it hurt when he lunged too quickly, so he made more designs but pretty soon that got boring so he reached underneath her and jammed his right index finger up her asshole. He did it suddenly, and she jerked and gasped and he fell out. He rolled on his back and laughed. He hugged himself and rolled from side to side.

She rose to leave and his left arm shot out and grabbed her. "You ain't goin' nowhere, bitch." He flung her back on the bed.

"No more. No more. You *beaucoup* beer. You no can do."

"Bullshit no can do." He crawled on top of her and pinned her arms back with his hands. "Put it in your cunt. I'll show you no can do."

He burrowed into her neck and thrashed furiously. He tried to think of someone but they all looked old with wrinkled mouths and then there were just too many dead people. He went limp and fell out. He tried to ram it back in but couldn't. He slapped her twice before she pushed him to the side. She slid off the end of the pallet. As she bent for her clothes, he caught her arm. He rose on his knees and grabbed her throat and squeezed.

"You're gonna pay for it, motherfucker!" he bellowed. "You're gonna pay the bill!" He jerked her neck twice, then she brought her arms up and knocked his hands off. She whirled and ran for the entrance. He crawled off the bed and tried to chase her, but his pants were down around his ankles and he had to take short, waddling steps. "Come back, you pig-assed bitch!" He tore the curtain down behind her. On the next step his belt caught beneath his boot and he sprawled in the dirt near one of the ironing tables. "Come back here, motherfucker!" he screamed into the dirt. He looked up and Lang stood in the doorway staring at him through the dingy air.

29

THE COOLNESS of the ground creeping into his buttocks and back woke him. His watch was gone, and a featureless darkness surrounded him. He heard voices from Papa-san's hooch. Why hadn't they slit his throat? Or turned him over to the MP's or VC? Maybe he was dead and would lie on this cold earth forever.

He raised himself on his elbows. His prick was shriveled and bloody and peppered with specks of dirt. Rain thudded on the bamboo canopy above him. He pulled up his pants and went back in the room, where he wiped himself with his T-shirt and threw it under the pallet.

At the edge of the highway he stood still, staring at the monotonous rainy darkness, soaked. Orville had been killed, and Morgan had resolved to go walking in the jungle until an AK-47 blew his shit away. He stared at his watchless wrist, knowing he'd be in big trouble when he got back to base. A jeep rumbled somewhere behind him, and he leaped into a muddy ditch until it passed. He'd have to be careful from here on. He'd tell the MP at the gate that he'd been knocked out and rolled.

Ten feet beyond the road that led down to Sin City he heard something move in the ditch, but before he could turn, someone grabbed him from behind. He froze, knowing he'd be dead in seconds. He went for the knife in his pocket, but the grip was too strong. "Let go!"

"Was you scared, Morgan?"

"Hancock, you son of a bitch. You could've given me heart failure."

"I bet you thought Charlie had your ass. I bet you thought it was all over."

"You shouldn't play around like that!"

"You went back to old town, huh?"

"So what?"

"I figured you did. How come you didn't tell us?"

"I don't know. Come on, we're late."

"Hell no. I got my pass in my pocket and I didn't sign out, so they can't prove nothing."

"Me too, but they might miss us."

"Webster's fixing it up."

"I want to go back. I'm sick of this place."

"Let's stay down all night. Nothing's gonna happen. MP's get us if we go in now."

"I don't know. I don't know what to do. I'm tired." He thought he might faint.

"I can't go back there tonight. I hate that place and I ain't goin' back and I don't want to stay here alone. Come on, buddy. We'll get us some whores and lay up all night."

He stared at Hancock for a moment. "Why not?" The idea was so preposterous that he could only agree to it. He followed Hancock into Sin City, drank whiskey as the fat gunner dickered with the whores and nearly brawled with two South Vietnamese soldiers. The liquor made him immediately drunk, and as they moved around the track from bar to bar, amid the beer cans and broken bottles and bits of dirty paper, he knew he had died and would wander Sin City forever as punishment. The strange sad plunkings of Oriental music floated through the windows on the erratic flickering of candle flames. Singsong staccato voices raised the volume, drove it into his brain like incessant pinpricks. He heard men and women laughing, babies crying, Hancock trying to tell him something as he took his money. Outside four Hondas fired up and sputtered into the night, him on the back of one, hugging the bony torso of a Vietnamese driver.

He entered a room somewhere with Hancock and two women. His eyes fastened on the double bed in the middle of the floor, on the blanket and sheets and big soft pillows. He wallowed beneath the covers, tucking up his legs so he could scratch out the pain and chill in his feet. He buried his head in the pillow, drowning the incoherent voices of Hancock and the women.

His bladder woke him. He pushed up on his arms and peered over his shoulder, remembering. A passive body lay beside him, no doubt his own sweet whore. He put on his boots and stumbled back to the candlelit kitchen where an old mama-san dozed in a wicker chair. She raised her head and flashed obsidian teeth his way.

He started out the back entryway, stopped, then moved to the side. What if they were waiting for him outside, waiting to blow his head off with a bazooka or a fifty caliber? Fighting a temptation to piss on the floor, he stepped into the night. No movement or strange shapes. He cleared the doorway, stiffening in anticipation of the barrage. Maybe they'd wait until he got his dick out. He took a few steps down the dirt path, then stopped and pissed. It sounded like a drum roll. His bowels thundered; people must be listening for miles around. Back in the house, he gestured at his ass to Mama-san. From a box behind her she brought out two rolls of C-ration toilet paper.

In the cultivated area off the dirt path, he wiped forlornly. No reason to be afraid. Webster was right. Things were set up too well for even the VC to rock the boat. The whores and their families made money, the VC and South Vietnamese government too; the GI's got laid, and the generals and colonels didn't have to worry about guys going crazy or turning queer. Even the doctors got to do their humanitarian bit, and the sergeants had another favor to dangle before you. Perfect for everyone. Absolutely.

At the front of the house he sat against a coconut tree three feet from the road. The stiff coco palms clicked against each other in the breeze, and the black sky hung above him like a giant hood. His exhaustion and fatigue had pushed him beyond the need for sleep. The tears came slowly and quietly, causing only the slightest break in his breathing. He dragged at his cigarette, but had to cough out the smoke. After wiping his mouth and eyes, he stared at the ground. He thought of Orville, knowing he couldn't cry over people anymore. Too many of them. A barely audible whining rose from his throat and hung on his palate like a ball of fuzz. He let out a squeal and bit into his forearm to stop it.

What was he crying for but his own sorry ass? Here it was, one or three or five o'clock in the morning, and in five days he'd be home listening to his friends talk about literature and politics, and now he was sitting in a muddy road, and in five days he'd have absolutely nothing to say. He shook his head, trying to hear what was left of his brain sloshing around in a pool of alcohol. He thought of reenlisting, then banged his head against the tree as he saw himself, red-nosed and rheumy-eyed, flying in a pilotless helicopter for life. Why didn't they send everyone to a rehab center to learn to talk again, to dress and eat and sleep soundly.

He couldn't imagine what it would be like with his sister. A year younger than he, she taught elementary school in Oakland and went on protest marches in Berkeley. She was never harsh in her letters, but he feared her condemnation once he was home. Maybe everyone would condemn him. He guessed he deserved it. But he could atone. No drinking or smoking dope. Studying hard and going to art movies to get his mind right again. He could do it. He had to. The war was over, and he had to forget it.

Back inside the house he took off his boots, draped his fatigues over a chair, and crawled into bed. The girl stirred beside him, and he took her in his arms, pressing against her hot body, trying to absorb the warmth. In a few minutes, still shivering with chill, he began to get hard.

The girl woke up when he climbed on top of her. "Sleep now," she said. "Boom-boom later."

"Boom-boom now." He'd paid his money; he should at least get one shot.

Her hand moved lazily down and put him in. He pumped twice, wincing as his sores opened, then he stopped. He was already getting limp. But he'd paid. He moved again, shrinking. In a minute he fell out. He rolled on his back, huffing and wheezing, and rubbed the sweat around on his soft belly.

"You *beaucoup* beer, GI. Boom-boom later. Be better." She patted his cheek, turned her back to him, and seemed to fall asleep instantly.

He felt a sudden pang of guilt as he thought that Orville might be watching him now, had been watching him all day. What right did he have to worry about his life at home, to try for his money's worth fucking, when his best friend hadn't even been dead twenty-four hours? What right did he have to go on living? He should have died too.

How could the rotor blades have come off? They were fastened on in at least six places with locking nuts and cotter pins. The shaft was too strong to split, even if hit by a round. Why had Chambers even stayed out the last night? He rolled on his stomach and turned his face to the wall. Searching for feelings, he found nothing, not even rage at Hart.

He went to the chair, took his knife from his pocket, and brought it back to the bed. He pressed the dull, rusty blade against his leg and pushed, but it wouldn't cut. He stuck the point into the flab on his stomach, but pulled it away when it began to hurt. What was he trying to prove? He smeared the trickle of blood in widening circles on his belly until it dried, then turned on his stomach and sank his head into the pillow.

He still thought he might be dead, might be wandering in the afterlife. The feeling came to him briefly the next morning as he ate the mama-san's rice and drank tea, joking with Hancock and the whores. It came at the moment when his belly finally warmed up, when he began to feel comfortable. Later, when he and Hancock stopped for a beer on the way back to base, he felt it again, heard his name called from within his head. He felt no panic.

He knew it was over one way or the other. That afternoon, as he lay on his cot listening to the rain pop on the canvas above him, he knew that if he wasn't a ghost in the central highlands he was a lifer in the fucking Army. He couldn't possibly get out. He had signed some paper while drunk, giving up six more years. Perhaps he'd committed a crime, and they'd be waiting with the shackles when he stepped off the plane in California.

He stayed sober that night, wandering about the battalion, looking for something to do. He stood in front of the new wooden S-1 office for ten minutes, remembering Stubbs, Greene, and Chase. He walked up to the officers' club and stood in front of it, remembering last Christmas Eve when he'd shined the jeep lights on the door. Behind the club he stared at the dark parade field, wondering when he'd get his medal, wondering if they had award ceremonies in the afterlife.

Time moved chronologically. No matter what happened, time went on. He went to sleep, woke up, ate, processed out at division personnel, got drunk, and woke up the next morning in the mud behind his tent, where he and Fisher used to drink. He cleaned himself, spent the afternoon bullshitting, preparing for his departure the next day. He ran into a soldier who had just returned to battalion after taking eighty hunks of shrapnel in October and who could barely talk. Stuttering and stammering, he tried to gnaw words out of air that must have seemed like concrete in his mouth.

At the short-timers' party that night he felt as if he were sitting in a pile of rundown, broken clocks. All the excitement was false, and he couldn't capture the buoyant feelings of camaraderie that had made him so happy the night he'd left Fulda for the war. Boredom drove him to bed at ten. Time passed. In the morning they left for the airfield, and by one that afternoon a fat sergeant in pressed fatigues and spit-shined jungle boots was telling them how to behave in the outprocessing camp at Pleiku. They ate, were assigned bunks, and as night fell, they clattered into the bleachers to watch a movie.

"Sure was some year," Clampitt said.

"We'll never forget this one." Webster stamped his feet on the rickety bleachers.

It was no good. It had all been said long ago. Between them there must have been two hundred looks at watches before the outdoor lights went off. As the first frames flickered on the screen, everyone shrank into himself. Afterward, bed. No one had to say anything anymore.

Old Crockett said that Vietnam was nothing compared to Korea. "It was so cold there you'd piss your pants before you'd hang your dick out." Morgan's father said that neither was anything compared to the Big War in Europe, where he'd served as a foot soldier for three years. The Marine whom Morgan had met on R&R proclaimed that only the Army had it easy, had two or three hot meals a day, were back in their sleeping bags every night, had beer and pussy. Morgan agreed with them all. He hadn't had it so bad. He didn't know what tough was like.

He woke up with the commander of the relief's hand on his shoulder. He put on his boots and stumbled into the darkness, realizing that he'd risen for the last time in Vietnam. At the barbed-wire entrance to the tent area where the departing soldiers slept, he leaned on his shotgun and shivered in the morning chill.

The sun came up behind the thick sky, making it uniformly gray as on nearly every day in Fulda. A few hundred yards below him, to the south, three rows of fresh concrete barracks were almost finished. Beyond them lay an immense clearing of short, light-brown scrub grass running right up to a hill of dense green jungle. The clearing was peaceful. The weeds drooped beneath the rain and dew from last night, and the sky looked as if it might collapse and bury them. Troops emerged from the tents, walked past him to the mess hall with quiet, sleepy faces. The sergeant of the guard picked up his shotgun at seven and sent him off to breakfast.

As the truck pulled up to the airfield, a C-141 took off. The names were read off for the next flight; the men walked through the gate and formed up in order in front of three Quonset huts and a group of conex boxes. A sergeant told them that their plane would arrive in forty-five minutes and that it wouldn't even shut down. The new troops would file off, they would file on, and the bird would take off.

Webster was his only friend on this flight. Hancock would be on the next one, four hours behind them, so they'd probably meet in Oakland.

While Webster got Cokes, he went into the little latrine. He opened his fly and winced as his prick came unstuck from his drawers. The burning started with the first spurt of urine. He gritted his teeth and stomped the floor with his right foot until he was done. Another service benefit. If you're good enough, I want you. Choice, not chance. He couldn't kick about that. It had all been his choice. The Army. Europe. Vietnam. Combat. The whores, of course. He wouldn't choose to see a doctor now.

They took their cold cans to the edge of the runway, where the soldiers for the flight stood with their eyes glued to the south.

"Here she comes! Here she comes!" someone shouted. Cheers rose from the men as they scrambled back to their duffel bags.

He watched the gleaming speck for a moment, then the sergeant with his clipboard yelled, "Form up, god damn it! Form up! No one moves till I give the word."

Someone shrieked as the jet touched down, bounced a few

feet, and settled on the runway. The flaps went down, and the engines roared like a blast furnace. The noise ceased as the plane coasted slowly toward them. It stopped in front of the formation, a low whine coming from the casing by the wheels.

"First line, get moving!" the sergeant yelled. "Up the back and into the front of the aircraft."

Only three green-clad figures had come off the back ramp when the jeers started from the departing soldiers.

"Welcome, new guys!"

"You'll love it here!"

"Sorry about that, new guys."

"What's your girl's phone number?"

"Does your mama know you're over here?"

"Fuck you, new guys."

"FTA. All the way."

"Fuck the Army."

"Fuck Vietnam."

He was in the third line of the formation. It didn't move until more than fifty new guys had come off the plane. He couldn't take his eyes off them. Their fatigues looked as if they'd never been washed. Their pink faces grinned uncomfortably at the taunts.

"Move out, man," the soldier behind him said.

He picked up his bag and started toward the plane. His eyes riveted on a fat new guy, his face nearly purple, straining under his duffel bag as he moved away from the jet. The bag teetered, and the man nearly fell, then straightened up, looking into Morgan's face with wide moon eyes. His breathing sounded like a small whirlwind.

Morgan stopped dead, staring at the hapless soldier. He felt a speech coming, an explosive vomiting of lessons learned. The new guy looked so afraid, so utterly bewildered. "Turn around, man."

"Huh?"

"Turn around." For a moment he thought he might laugh at the new guy's bafflement.

"I can't."

"Then three tears in the bucket, man. They don't flow, mother fuck it."

"Move out!" The man behind him shoved him forward.

"You there," the sergeant said. "Drop your bag and get your ass on the plane."

He threw his bag on the pile and ran up the tonguelike ramp as the last new guy stepped down.